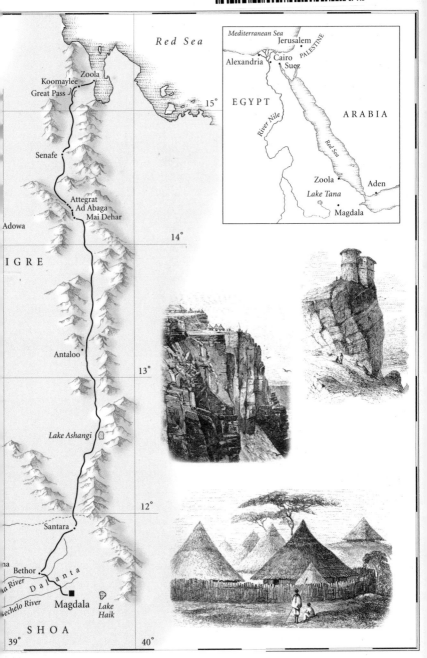

Red Sea

Koomaylee
Zoola
Great Pass

15°

Senafe

Attegrat
Ad Abaga
Mai Dehar

Adowa

TIGRE

14°

Antaloo

13°

Lake Ashangi

12°

Santara

Bethor

Dalanta

ma River

echelo River

Magdala

Lake
Haik

SHOA

39°

40°

Mediterranean Sea
Jerusalem
Alexandria
Cairo
Suez

PALESTINE

EGYPT

ARABIA

River Nile

Red Sea

Zoola
Aden

Lake Tana

Magdala

FLASHMAN
ON THE MARCH

THE FLASHMAN PAPERS
(in chronological order)

FLASHMAN
(Britain, India, and Afghanistan, 1839–42)

ROYAL FLASH
(England 1842–43, Germany 1847–48)

FLASHMAN'S LADY
(England, Borneo, and Madagascar, 1842–45)

FLASHMAN AND THE MOUNTAIN OF LIGHT
(Indian Punjab 1845–46)

FLASH FOR FREEDOM!
(England, West Africa, U.S.A. 1848–49)

FLASHMAN AND THE REDSKINS
(U.S.A. 1849–50 and 1875–76)

FLASHMAN AT THE CHARGE
(England, Crimea, and Central Asia, 1854–55)

FLASHMAN IN THE GREAT GAME
(Scotland, India, 1856–58)

FLASHMAN AND THE ANGEL OF THE LORD
(India, South Africa, U.S.A., 1858–59)

FLASHMAN AND THE DRAGON
(China, 1860)

FLASHMAN AND THE TIGER
(England, Europe, Africa, 1878–94)

Also by George MacDonald Fraser
Mr American
The Pyrates
The Candlemass Road
Black Ajax

SHORT STORIES
The General Danced at Dawn
McAuslan in the Rough
The Sheikh and the Dustbin

HISTORY
The Steel Bonnets:
*The Story of the Anglo-Scottish
Border Reivers*

AUTOBIOGRAPHY
Quartered Safe Out Here
The Light's on at Signpost

The Hollywood History of the World

FLASHMAN
ON THE MARCH

from
The Flashman Papers
1867–8

EDITED AND ARRANGED
by

George MacDonald Fraser

This edition published 2005
by BCA
by arrangement with HarperCollins*Publishers*

Hardback CN 137893
Paperback CN 137789

Text maps by Ken Lewis
Endpaper map by John Gilkes

Set in Postscript Linotype Times Roman
with Garamond 3 display
by Palimpsest Book Production Limited,
Polmont, Stirlingshire

Printed and bound in Germany by
GGP Media GmbH, Poessneck

For Kath,
twelve in a row

FLASHMAN, Harry Paget, brigadier-general, V.C., K.C.B., K.C.I.E.: Chevalier, Legion of Honour; Order of Maria Theresa, Austria; Order of the Elephant, Denmark (temporary); U.S. Medal of Honor; San Serafino Order of Purity and Truth, 4th class; b. May 5, 1822, s. of H. Buckley Flashman, Esq., Ashby, and Hon. Alicia Paget; m. Elspeth Rennie Morrison, d. of Lord Paisley, one s., one d. Educ. Rugby School, 11th Hussars, 17th Lancers. Served Afghanistan 1841–2 (medals, thanks of Parliament); chief of staff to H.M. James Brooke, Rajah of Sarawak, Batang Luper expedn, 1844; milit. adviser with unique rank of sergeant-general to H.M. Queen Ranavalona of Madagascar, 1844–5; Sutlej campaign, 1845–6 (Ferozeshah, Sobraon, envoy extraordinary to Maharani Jeendan, Court of Lahore); polit. adviser to Herr (later Chancellor Prince) von Bismarck, Schleswig-Holstein, 1847–8; Crimea, staff (Alma, Sevastopol, Balaclava), prisoner of war, 1854; artillery adviser to Atalik Ghazi, Syr Daria campaign, 1855; India, Sepoy Mutiny, 1857–8, dip, envoy to H.R.H. the Maharani of Jhansi, trooper 3rd Native Cavalry, Meerut, subseq. att. Rowbotham's Mosstroopers, Cawnpore, (Lucknow, Gwalior, etc., V.C.); adjutant to Captain John Brown, Harper's Ferry, 1859; China campaign 1860, polit. mission to Nanking, Taiping Rebellion, polit. and other services, Imperial Court, Pekin; U.S. Army (major, Union forces, 1862, colonel (staff) Army of the Confederacy, 1863); a.d.c. to H.I.M. Maximilian, Emperor of Mexico, 1867; interpreter and observer Sioux campaign, U.S., 1875–6 (Camp Robinson conference, Little Big Horn, etc.); Zulu War, 1879 (Isandhlwana, Rorke's Drift); Egypt 1882 (Kassassin, Tel-el-Kebir); personal bodyguard to H.I.M. Franz-Josef, Emperor of Austria, 1883; Sudan 1884–5 (Khartoum); Pekin Legations, 1900. Travelled widely in military and civilian capacities, among them supercargo, merchant marine (West Africa), agriculturist (Mississippi valley), wagon captain and hotelier (Santa Fe Trail); buffalo hunter and scout (Oregon Trail); courier (Underground Railroad); majordomo (India), prospector (Australia); trader and missionary (Solomon Islands, Fly River, etc.), lottery supervisor (Manila), diamond broker and horse coper (Punjab), dep. marshal (U.S.), occasional actor and impersonator. Hon. mbr of numerous societies and clubs, including Sons of the Volsungs (Strackenz), Mimbreno Apache Copper Mines band (New Mexico), Khokand Horde (Central Asia), Kit Carson's Boys (Colorado), Brown's Lambs (Maryland), M.C.C., White's and United Service (London, both resigned), Blackjack (Batavia). Chmn, Flashman and Bottomley, Ltd; dir. British Opium Trading Co.; governor, Rugby School; hon. pres. Mission for Reclamation of Reduced Females. Publications: Dawns and Departures of a Soldier's Life; Twixt Cossack and Cannon; The Case Against Army Reform. Recreations: oriental studies, angling, cricket (performed first recorded "hat trick", wickets of Felix, Pilch, Mynn, for 14 runs, Rugby Past and Present v. Kent, Lord's 1842; five for 12, Mynn's Casuals v. All-England XI, 1843). Add: Gandamack Lodge, Ashby, Leics.

Explanatory Note

In the campaigns covered by the first eleven packets of his auto-
biographical Papers – Afghanistan, First Sikh War, Crimea, Indian
Mutiny, Brooke's expedition against the Borneo pirates, the march
to Pekin, Custer's Little Big Horn debacle – Sir Harry Flashman,
V.C., etc., the notorious Victorian hero and poltroon, has always
been at or near the heart of the action, a reluctant and often jaundiced eye-witness of people and events, and uncomfortably aware
of history unfolding about him.

Not so in the Abyssinian War of 1868, surely the strangest of all
imperial campaigns, when a British Indian army invaded one of the
least known and most dangerous countries on earth, and in the face
of apparently insuperable hazards, and predictions of certain failure,
marched and fought their way across a trackless wilderness of rocky
chasm and jagged mountain to their goal, did what they had come
to do, and marched out again with hardly a casualty. There has
never perhaps been a success like it in the history of war. It took
twelve thousand men, a mighty fleet, nine million pounds (a staggering sum at that time), a meticulous if extravagant organisation,
and a remarkable old soldier – and all to rescue a tiny group of
British citizens held captive by a mad monster of an African king.
Those were, to quote Flashman, the days.

But if he bore no share in the campaign proper, Flashman's was
still the vital part on which success or failure hung – the intelligence
mission which was to take him into a series of fearful perils (some
of them new even to him) in a war-torn land of mystery, treachery,
intrigue, lonely castles, ghost cities, the most beautiful (and savage)
women in Africa, and at last into the power of the demented tyrant

vii

in his stronghold at the back of beyond. All of which he records with his customary shameless honesty, and it may be that along with the light he casts on a unique chapter of imperial history, he invites a comparison with a later and less glorious day.

For Flashman's story is about a British army sent out in a good and honest cause by a government who knew what honour meant. It was not sent without initial follies and hesitations in high places, or until every hope of a peaceful issue was gone. It went with the fear of disaster hanging over it, but with the British public in no doubt that it was right. It served no politician's vanity or interest. It went without messianic rhetoric. There were no false excuses, no deceits, no cover-ups or lies, just a decent resolve to do a government's first duty: to protect its people, whatever the cost. To quote Flashman again, those were the days.

As with previous Papers, I have merely corrected his spelling, which in this instance meant introducing consistency into his bizarre renderings of Abyssinian names.

G.M.F.

viii

FLASHMAN
ON THE MARCH

"Half a million in silver, did you say?"

"In Maria Theresa dollars. Worth a hundred thou' in quids." He held up a gleaming coin, broad as a crown, with the old girl double-chinned on one side and the Austrian arms on t'other. "Dam' dis-inheritin' old bitch, what? Mind, they say she was a plum in her youth, blonde and buxom, just your sort, Flashy –"

"Ne'er mind my sort. The cash must reach this place in Africa within four weeks? And the chap who was to have escorted it is laid up in Venice with yellow jack?"

"Or the clap, or the sailor's itch, or heaven knows what." He spun the coin, grinning foxy-like. "You've changed your mind, haven't you? You're game to do it yourself! Good old Flash!"

"Don't rush your fences, Speed, my boy. When's it due to be shipped out?"

"Wednesday. Lloyd packet to Alexandria. But with Sturgess comin' all over yellow in Venice, that won't do, and there ain't another Alex boat for a fortnight – far too late, and the Embassy'll run my guts up the flagpole, as though 'twas my fault, confound 'em –"

"Aye, it's hell in the diplomatic. Well, tell you what, Speed – I'll ride guard on your dollars to Alex for you, but I ain't waiting till Wednesday. I want to be clear of this blasted town by dawn tomorrow, so you'd best drum up a steam-launch and crew, and get your precious treasure aboard tonight – where is it just now?"

"At the station, the Strada Ferrata – but dammit, Flash, a private charter'll cost the moon –"

"You've got Embassy dibs, haven't you? Then use 'em! The station ain't spitting distance from the Klutsch mole, and if you get

1

a move on you can have the gelt loaded by midnight. Heavens, man, steam craft and spaghetti sailors are ten a penny in Trieste! If you're in such a sweat to get the dollars to Africa –"

"You may believe it! Let me see . . . quick run to Alex, then train to Cairo and on to Suez – no camel caravans across the desert these days, but you'll need to hire nigger porters –"

"For which you'll furnish me cash!"

He waved a hand. "Sturgess would've had to hire 'em, anyway. At Suez one of our Navy sloops'll take you down the Red Sea – there are shoals of 'em, chasin' the slavers, and I'll give you an Embassy order. They'll have you at Zoola – that's the port for Abyssinia – by the middle of February, and it can't take above a week to get the silver up-country to this place called Attegrat. That's where General Napier will be."

"Napier? Not Bob the Bughunter? What the blazes is he doing in Abyssinia? We haven't got a station there."

"We have by now, you may be sure!" He was laughing in disbelief. "D'you mean to tell me you haven't heard? Why, he's invadin' the place! With an army from India! The silver is to help fund his campaign, don't you see? Good God, Flashy, where have you been? Oh, I was forgettin' – Mexico. Dash it, don't they have newspapers there?"

"Hold up, can't you? *Why* is he invading?"

"To rescue the captives – our consul, envoys, missionaries! They're held prisoner by this mad cannibal king, and he's chainin' 'em, and floggin' 'em, and kickin' up no end of a row! Theodore, his name is – and you mean to say you've not heard of him? I'll be damned – why, there's been uproar in Parliament, our gracious Queen writin' letters, a penny or more on the income tax – it's true! Now d'you see why this silver must reach Napier double quick – if it don't, he'll be adrift in the middle of nowhere with not a penny to his name, and your old chum Speedicut will be a human sacrifice at the openin' of the new Foreign Office!"

"But why should Napier need Austrian silver? Hasn't he got any sterling?"

"Abyssinian niggers won't touch it, or anythin' except Maria

2

Theresas. Purest silver,[1] you see, and Napier must have it for food and forage when he marches up-country to fight his war."

"So it's a war-chest? You never said a dam' word about war last night."

"You never gave me a chance, did you? Soon as I told you I was in Dickie's meadow,[2] with this damned fortune to be shipped and Sturgess in dock, what sympathy did dear old friend Flashy offer? The horse's laugh, and wished me joy! All for England, home, and the beauteous Elspeth, you were . . . and now," says he, with that old leery Speedicut look, "all of a sudden, you're in the dooce of a hurry to oblige . . . What's up, Flash?"

"Not a dam' thing. I'm sick of Trieste and want away, that's all!"

"And can't wait a day? You and Hookey Walker!"

"Now, see here, Speed, d'ye want me to shift your blasted bullion, or don't you? Well, I go tonight or not at all, and since this cash is so all-fired important to Napier, your Embassy funds can stand the row for my passage home, too, when the thing's done! Well, what d'ye say?"

"That something *is* up, no error!" His eyes widened. "I say, the Austrian traps ain't after you, are they – 'cos if they were I daren't assist your flight, silver or no silver! Dash it, I'm a diplomat –"

"Of course 'tain't the traps! What sort of fellow d'ye think I am? Good God, ha'nt we been chums since boyhood?"

"Yes, and it's 'cos I know what kind of chum you can be that I repeat 'What's up, Flash?'" He filled my glass and pushed it across. "Come *up*, old boy! This is old Speed, remember, and you can't humbug him."

Well, true enough, I couldn't, and since you, dear reader, may be sharing his curiosity, I'll tell you what I told him that night in the Hôtel Victoria – not the smartest pub in Trieste, but as a patriotic little minion of our Vienna Embassy, Speedicut was bound to put up there – and it should explain the somewhat cryptic exchanges with which I've begun this chapter of my memoirs. If they've seemed a mite bewildering you'll see presently that they were the simplest way of setting out the preliminaries to my tale of the strangest campaign in the whole history of British arms – and that

3

takes in some damned odd affairs, a few of which I've borne a reluctant hand in myself. But Abyssinia took the cake, currants and all. Never anything like it, and never will be again.

For me, the business began in the summer of '67, on the day when that almighty idiot, the Emperor Maximilian of Mexico, strode out before a Juarista firing squad, unbuttoned his shirt cool as a trout, and cried "*Viva Mejico! Viva la independencia!* Shoot, soldiers, through the heart!" Which they did, with surprising accuracy for a platoon of dagoes, thereby depriving Mexico of its crowned head and Flashy of his employer and protector. I was an anxious spectator skulking in cover on a rooftop nearby, and when I saw Max take a header into the dust I knew that the time had come for me to slip my cable.

You see, I'd been his fairly loyal aide-de-camp in his recent futile struggle against Juarez's republicans – not a post I'd taken from choice, but I'd been a deserter from the French Foreign Legion at the time.[3] They were polluting Mexico with their presence in those days, supporting Max on behalf of his sponsor, that ghastly louse Louis Napoleon, and I'd been only too glad of the refuge Max had offered me – he'd been under the mistaken impression that I'd saved his life in an ambush at Texatl, poor ass, when in fact I'd been one of Jesus Montero's gang of ambushers, but we needn't go into that at the moment. What mattered was that Max had taken me on the strength, and had given the Legion peelers the rightabout when they'd come clamouring for my unhappy carcase.

Then the Frogs cleared out in March of '67, leaving Max in the lurch with typical Gallic loyalty, but while that removed one menace to my wellbeing, there remained others from which Max could be no protection, quick or dead – like the Juaristas, who'd rather have strung up a royalist a.d.c. than eaten their dinners, or that persevering old bandolero Jesus Montero, who was bound to find out eventually that I didn't know where Montezuma's treasure was. Hell of a place, Mexico, and dam' confused.

But all you need to know for the present is that after Max bought the bullet I'd have joined him in the dead-cart if it hadn't been for the delectable Princess Agnes Salm-Salm, and the still happily ignorant Jesus. They'd been my associates in a botched attempt to rescue Max on the eve of his execution. We'd failed because (you'll hardly credit this) the great clown had refused point-blank to escape because it didn't sort with his imperial dignity, Austro-Hungarian royalty preferring to die rather than go over the wall. Well, hell mend 'em, I say, and if the House of Hapsburg goes to the knackers it won't be my fault; I've done my unwilling best for them, ungrateful bastards.[4]

At all events, darling Aggie and greasy Jesus had seen me safe to Vera Cruz, where she had devised the most capital scheme for getting me out of the country. Max having been brother to the Austrian Emperor Franz Josef, his death had caused a sensation in Vienna; they hadn't done a dam' thing useful to save his life, but they made up for it with his corpse, sending a warship to ferry it home, with a real live admiral and a great retinue of court reptiles. And since Aggie was the wife of a German princeling, a heroine of the royalist campaign, and handsome as Hebe, they were all over her when we went aboard the Novara frigate at Sacraficios. Admiral Tegethoff, a bluff old sport, all beard and belly, munched her knuckles and gave glad welcome even to the begrimed and ragged peon whom she presented as the *hoch und wohlgeboren* Oberst Sir Harry Flashman, former aide, champion, and all-round hero of the campaign and the ill-starred attempt to snatch his imperial majesty from the firing squad.

"The Emperor's English right arm, gentlemen!" says Aggie, who was a great hand at the flashing-eyed flourish. "So his majesty called him. Who more fitting to guard his royal master and friend on his last journey home?"

Blessed if they could think of anyone fitter, and I was received with polite enthusiasm: the reptiles left off sneering at my beastly peasant appearance and clicked their heels, old Tegethoff stopped just short of embracing me, and I was aware of the awestruck admiration in the wide blue eyes of the enchanting blonde poppet whom he presented as his great-niece, Gertrude von und zum something-or-other. My worldly Aggie noticed it too, and observed afterwards, when we made our adieus at the ship's rail, that if I looked

5

like a scarecrow I was at least a most romantic one.

"The poor little idiot will doubtless break her foolish heart over you en voyage," says she. "And afterwards wonder what she saw in the so dashing English rascal."

"Jealous of her, princess?" says I, and she burst out laughing.

"Of her youth, perhaps – not of her infatuation." She gave that slantendicular smile that had been driving me wild for months. "Well, not very much. But if I were sixteen again, like her, who knows? *Adios*, dear Harry." And being royally careless of propriety, she kissed me full on the lips before the startled squareheads – and for a delightful moment it was the kiss of the lover she'd never been, which I still count a real conquest. Pity she was so crazy about her husband, I remember thinking, as she waved an elegant hand from her carriage and was gone.[5]

After that they towed Max's coffin out to the ship in a barge and hoisted it inboard, and as the newly appointed escort to his cadaver I was bound to give Tegethoff and his entourage a squint at the deceased, so that they could be sure they'd got the right chap. It was no end of a business, for his Mexican courtiers had done him proud with no fewer than three coffins, one of rosewood, a second of zinc, and the third of cedar, with Max inside the last like one of those Russian dolls. He'd been embalmed, and I must say he looked in capital fettle, bar being a touch yellow and his hair starting to fall out. We screwed him in again, a chaplain said a prayer, and all that remained was to weigh anchor to thunderous salutes from various attendant warships, and for me to remind Tegethoff that a bath and a change of clobber would be in order.

I've never had any great love for the cabbage-chewers, having been given my bellyful by Bismarck and his gang in the Schleswig-Holstein affair,* and Tegethoff's party included more than one of the crop-headed schlager-swingers whom I find especially detestable, but I'm bound to say that on that voyage, which lasted from late November '67 to the middle of January, they couldn't have been more amiable and hospitable – until the very morning we

* See *Royal Flash*.

6

dropped anchor off Trieste, when Tegethoff discovered that I'd been giving his great-niece a few exercises they don't usually teach in young ladies' seminaries.

Aggie had been right, you see: the silly chit had gone nutty on me at first sight, and who's to blame her? Stalwart Flashy all bronzed and war-weary in sombrero and whiskers might well flutter a maiden heart, and if at forty-five I was old enough to be her father, that never stopped an adoring innocent yet, and you may be sure it don't stop me either. Puppy-fat and golden sausage curls ain't my style as a rule, but combined with a creamy complexion, parted rosebud lips, and great forget-me-not eyes alight with idiotic worship, they have their attraction. For one thing they awoke blissful memories of Elspeth on that balmy evening when I first rattled her in the bushes by the Clyde. The resemblance was more than physical, for both were brainless, although my darling half-wit is not without a certain native cunning, but what made dear little Fraulein Gertrude specially irresistible was her truly unfathomable ignorance of the more interesting facts of life, and her touching faith in me as a guide and mentor.

Her attachment to me on the voyage was treated as something of a joke by Tegethoff's people, who seemed to regard her as a child still, more fool they, and since her duenna was usually too sea-sick to interfere, we were together a good deal. She was the most artless prattler, and was soon confiding her girlish secrets, dreams, and fears; I learned that her doting great-uncle had brought her on the cruise as a betrothal present, and that on her return to Vienna she was to be married to a most aristocratic swell, a graf no less, whom she had never seen and who was on the brink of the grave, being all of thirty years old.

"It is such an honour," sighs she, "and my duty, Mama says, but how am I to be worthy of it? I know nothing of how to be a wife, much less a great lady. I am too young, and foolish, and . . . and *little*! He is a great man, a cousin to the Emperor, and I am only a *lesser* person! How do I know how to please him, or what it is that men like, and who is to tell me?" Yearning, dammit, drowning me in her blue limpid pools, with her fat young juggs heaving like blancmange.

Strip off, lie back, and enjoy it, would have been the soundest advice, but I patted her hand, smiled paternally, and said she mustn't worry her pretty little head, her graf was sure to like her.

"Oh, so easy to say!" cries she. "But if he should not? How to win his affection?" She rounded on me eagerly. "If it were you –" and from her soulful flutter she plainly wished it was, sensible girl "– if it were you, how could I best win your heart? How make you . . . oh, admire me, and honour me, and . . . and love me! What would delight you most that I could do?"

You may talk about sitting birds, but where a lesser man might have taken swift advantage of that guileless purity, I'm proud to say that I did not. She might be the answer to a lecher's prayer, but I knew it would take delicate management and patience before we could have her setting to partners in the Calcutta Quadrille. So I went gently to work, indulgent uncle in the first week, brotherly arm about her shoulders in the second, peck on the cheek in the third, touch on the lips at Christmas to make her think, sudden lustful growl and passionate kiss for New Year, meeting her startled-fawn bewilderment with a nice blend of wistful adoration and unholy desire which melted the little simpleton altogether, and bulled her speechless all the way along the Adriatic. Very discreet, mind; a ship's a small place, and chaste young ladies tend to be excitable the first few times and need to be hushed. Elspeth, and my second wife, Duchess Irma, were like ecstatic banshees, I remember.

Unfortunately, she shared another characteristic with Elspeth – she had no more discretion than the town crier, and just as Elspeth had babbled joyfully of our jolly rogering to her elder sister, who had promptly relayed it to her horrified parents, so sweet imbecile Gertrude had confided in her duenna, who had swooned before passing on the glad news to old Tegethoff.

This must have been on the very morning we dropped anchor off the Molo St Carlo at Trieste and I was supervising the lifting of the coffin from below decks, and in the very act of securing Max's crown and archducal cap to the lid, when Tegethoff damned near fell down the companion, with a couple of aides at his heels trying to restrain him. He was in full fig, cocked hat and ceremonial sword which he was trying to lug out, purple with rage, and bellowing *"Verräter! Vergewaltiger! Pirat!"** which summed up things nicely and explained why he was behaving like Attila with apoplexy.

One of the aides clung to his sword-arm and hauled him back by main force, while the other, a hulking junkerish brute with scars all over his ugly dial, whipped his glove across my face before dashing it at my feet and stamping off. That was all they had time for just then, what with the barge coming alongside to take Max on shore leave, the Duke of Wurtemburg and all the other big guns lined up on the landing stage, the waterfront swathed in black, and muted brass bands playing a cheery Wagnerian air. But I can take a hint, and saw that by the time they'd finished escorting Max to the Vienna train, I had best be in the nearest deep cover, lying doggo.

So I let the pall-bearers get their load on deck, waited until the guns of the assembled shipping had started their salutes and Tegethoff and Co. would be safely away, and slunk ashore with a hastily packed valise. The cortège was proceeding along the boulevard beyond the Grand Canal which runs into the heart of the city; solemn music, mobs of chanting clergy, friars carrying crosses, battalions of infantry, and I thought *"Hasta la vista*, old Max" and hurried up-town to lose myself for a few hours.[6] Tegethoff's gang would be off to Vienna with the corpse presently, nursing their wrath against me, no doubt, but unable to indulge it, and then I could consider how the devil I was to raise the blunt for a passage to England, for bar a few pesos and Yankee dollars my pockets were to let.

Trieste ain't much of a town unless you're in trade or banking or some other shady pursuit; Napoleon's spymaster, Fouché, is buried there, and Richard the Lionheart did time in jail, but the only other excitements are the Tergesteum bazaar and the Corso, which is the main drag between the new and old cities, and you can stare at shop windows and drink coffee to bursting point.

At evening I mooched up to the Exchange plaza and into the

---

* "Traitor! Rapist! Pirate!"

casino club, where the smart set foregathered and I thought I might run across some sporting rich widow eager for carnal amusement, but I'd barely begun to survey the fashionable throng when I found myself face to face with the last man I'd have thought to meet, my old chum of Rugby and the Cider Cellars, Speedicut, whom I'd barely seen since the night the Minor Club in St James's was raided, and we'd fled from the peelers and I'd found refuge in the carriage (and later the bed) of Lola Montez, bless her black heart. That had been all of twenty-five years before, but we knew each other on the instant, and there was great rejoicing, in a wary sort of way, for we'd never been your usual bosom pals, both being leery by nature.

So now I learned that he was in the diplomatic, which didn't surprise me, for he was a born toad-eater with a great gift of genteel sponging and an aversion to work. He was full of woe because, as you'll already have gathered, he'd brought this fortune in silver down from Vienna for shipment to Abyssinia, and lo! the appointed escort had fallen by the way and he was at his wit's end to find another – couldn't go himself, diplomatic duty bound him to Austrian soil, etc., etc.... It was at that point that it dawned on him that here was good old Harry, knight of the realm, hero of Crimea and the Mutiny, darling of Horse Guards, and just the chap who could be trusted with a vital mission in his country's service. Why, I was heaven-sent and no mistake, dear old lad that I was!

There wasn't a hope of touching him for a loan to see me home, for coming of nabob wealth he was as mean as Solomon Levi, but by pretending interest I was able to take a decent dinner off him at the Locanda Granda before telling him, fairly politely, for one hates to offend, what he could do with his cargo of dollars. He howled a bit, but didn't press me, for he hadn't really expected me to agree, and we parted on fair terms, he to visit the station to see that his minions were taking care of the doubloons, I to find a cheap bed for the night. And I hadn't turned the corner before I saw something that had me skipping for the nearest alleyway with my un-digested dinner in sudden turmoil. Not twenty yards away across the street, the Austrian lout who'd slapped my face and hurled his challenge at my feet was conferring with two uniformed constables and a bearded villain in a billycock hat with plain-clothes peeler written all over him. And there were two armed troopers in tow as well.

Even as I watched them disperse, the officer mounting the steps to the Locanda which I'd just left, the fearful truth was dawning – Tegethoff had left this swine behind to track me down and either hale me to justice as a ravisher of youth (squareheads have the most primitive views about this, as I'd discovered in Munich in '47 when Bismarck's bullies interrupted my dalliance with that blubbery slut Baroness Pechmann), or more likely cut me up in a sabre duel. Trieste had suddenly become too hot to hold me – so now you know why a couple of hours later I was in Speedicut's room at the Victoria, clamouring to be allowed to remove his bullion for him, to Abyssinia or Timbuctoo or any damned place away from Austrian vengeance.

In my funk I even conjured up the nightmare thought that if Tegethoff got his hands on me and instituted inquiries, he might easily discover I was a Legion deserter and hand me over to the bloody Frogs, in which case I'd end my days as a slave in their penal battalion in the Sahara. A groundless fear, looking back, but I'm a great one for starting at shadows, as you may know. I didn't mention this particular phantasm to Speed, but I did tell him all about Gertrude, 'cos that sort of thing was nuts to him, and he was lost in admiration of my behaviour both as amorist and fugitive.

"How the blazes you always contrive to slide out o' harm's way beats me – aye, often as not with some charmer languishin' after you! Well, 'twas dam' lucky for you I was here this time!"

"Lucky for both of us. So, now that you know all about my guilty past, d'you still feel like trusting me with your half-million? No fears that I might tool along the coast to Monte Carlo and blue the lot at the wheel?"

Put like that, with a wink and a grin, he didn't care for it above half, but common sense told him I wasn't going to levant,* and he'd no choice, anyway. So a couple of hours after midnight, there I was

---

* To steal away, abscond.

at the Klutsch mole, watching Speed's clerk settle up with the skipper of a neat little smack or yawl or whatever they call 'em, while its crew of Antonios chattered and loafed on the hatches – even in those days Trieste was more Italian than Austrian – and here came Speed in haste across the deserted plaza from the station, with a squad of Royal Marines from his Embassy wheeling the goods on a hand-cart: scores of little strong-boxes with the locks sealed with the royal arms.[7] There were four of the Bootnecks[8] under a sergeant with a jaw like a pike, all very trim with their Sniders slung; Speed's dollars would be safe from sea pirates and land banditti with this lot on hand.

It may have been my jest about Monte or his natural fear at seeing his precious cargo pass out of his ken, but now that the die was cast Speed had a fit of the doubtfuls; earlier he'd been begging me to come to his rescue, but now he was chewing his lip as they swung the boxes down to the deck with the Eyeties jabbering and the sergeant giving 'em Billingsgate, while I took an easy cheroot at the rail, trying my Italian pidgin on the skipper.

"This ain't a joke, Flash!" says Speed. "It's bloody serious! You're carryin' my career along with those dollars – my good name, dammit!" As if he had one. "Jesus, if anything should go wrong! You will take care, old chap, won't you? I mean, you'll do nothin' wild . . . you know, like . . . like . . ." He broke off, not caring to say "like buggering off to Pago Pago with the loot". Instead he concluded glumly: "'Tain't insured, you know – not a penny of it!"

I assured him that his specie would reach Napier safely in less than four weeks, but he still looked blue and none too eager to hand over the Embassy passport requesting and requiring H.M. servants, civil and military, to speed me on my way, and a letter for Napier, asking him to give me a warrant and funds for my passage home. I shook hands briskly before he could change his mind, and as we shoved off and the skipper spun the wheel and his crew dragged the sail aloft, damned if he wasn't here again, running along the mole, waving and hollering:

"I say, Flash, I forgot to ask you for a receipt!"

I told him to forge my signature if it would make him sleep

sounder, and his bleating faded on the warm night air as we stood out from the mole, the little vessel heeling over suddenly as the wind cracked in her sail; the skipper bawled commands as the hands scampered barefoot to tail on to the lines, and I looked back at the great brightly lit crescent of the Trieste waterfront and felt a mighty relief, thinking, well, Flashy my boy, that's another town you're glad to say goodbye to on short acquaintance, and here's to a jolly holiday cruise to a new horizon and an old friend, and then hey! for a swift passage home, and Elspeth waiting. Strange, little Gertrude was fading from memory already, but I found myself reflecting that thanks to my tuition her princeling husband would be either delighted or scandalised on his wedding night – possibly both, the lucky fellow.

You gather from this that I was in a tranquil, optimistic mood as I set off on my Abyssinian odyssey, ass that I was. You'd ha' thought, after all I'd seen and suffered in my time, that I'd have remembered all the occasions when I'd set off carefree and unsuspecting along some seemingly primrose path only to go head first into the pit of damnation at t'other end. But you never can tell.

I couldn't foresee, as I stood content in the bow, watching the green fire foaming up from the forefoot, feeling the soft Adriatic breeze on my face, hearing the oaths and laughter of the Jollies and the strangled wailing of some frenzied tenor in the crew – I couldn't foresee the screaming charge of long-haired warriors swinging their hideous sickle-blades against the Sikh bayonets, or the huge mound of rotting corpses under the precipice at Islamgee, or the ghastly forest of crucifixes at Gondar, or feel the agonising bite of steel bars against my body as I swung caged in the freezing gale above a yawning void, or imagine the ghastly transformation of an urbane, cultivated monarch into a murderous tyrant shrieking with hysterical glee as he slashed and hacked at his bound victims.

No, I foresaw none of those horrors, or that amazing unknown country, Prester John's fabled land of inaccessible mountain barriers and bottomless chasms, and wild, war-loving beautiful folk, into which Napier was to lead such an expedition as had not been seen since Cortes and Pisarro (so Henty says), through impossible hazards and hopeless odds – and somehow lead it out again. A land of mystery and terror and cruelty, and the loveliest women in all Africa . . . a smiling golden nymph in her little leather tunic, teasing me as she sat by a woodland stream plaiting her braids . . . a gaudy barbarian queen lounging on cushions surrounded by her tame lions . . . a tawny young beauty remarking to my captors: "If we feed him into the fire, little by little, he will speak . . ."

Aye, it's an interesting country, Abyssinia.

If you've read my previous memoirs you'll know me better than Speedicut did, and won't share his misgivings about trusting me with a cool half million in silver. Old Flash may be a model of the best vices – lechery, treachery, poltroonery, deceit, and dereliction of duty, all present and correct, as you know, and they're not the half of it – but larceny ain't his style at all. Oh, stern necessity may have led to my lifting this and that on occasion, but nothing on the grand scale – why, you may remember I once had the chance to make away with the great Koh-i-noor diamond,* but wasn't tempted for an instant. If there's one thing your true-bred coward values, it's peace of mind, and you can't have that if you're a hunted outlaw forever far from home. Also, pocketing a diamond's one thing, but stacks of strong-boxes weighing God knows what and guarded by five stout lads are a very different palaver.

Speed had spoken lightly of a quick trip to Alexandria, but with that pack of dilatory dagoes tacking to and fro and putting about between the heel of Italy and Crete, we must have covered all of two thousand miles, and half the time allotted me to reach Napier had gone before we sighted Egypt. It's a sand-blown dunghill at any time, but I was dam' glad to see it after that dead bore of a voyage – and no dreary haul across the desert in prospect either. The camel journey was a penance I'd endured in the past, but now it was rails all the way from Alex to Suez, by way of Cairo, and what had once taken days of arse-burning discomfort was now a

* See *Flashman and the Mountain of Light*.

journey of eight hours, thanks to our engineers who'd won the concession in the teeth of frantic French opposition. They were hellish jealous of their great canal, which was then within a year of completion, with gangs of thousands of the unfortunate fellaheen being mercilessly flogged on the last lap, for it was built with slave labour in all but name.[9]

We didn't linger in Alexandria; Egypt's the last place you want to carry a cargo of valuables, so I made a quick sortie to the Hôtel de l'Europe for a bath and a civilised breakfast while the Marine sergeant drummed up the local donkey drivers to carry the boxes to the station, and then we were rattling away, four hours to Cairo, another four on the express to Suez, and before bed-time I'd presented myself to the port captain and was dining in the Navy mess. Abyssinia was on every lip, and when it was understood that the celebrated Flashy was bringing Napier his war-chest,[10] it was heave and ho with a vengeance. A steam sloop commanded by a cheerful infant named Ballantyne with a sun-peeled nose and a shock of fair hair bleached almost white by the sun was placed at my disposal, his tars hoisted the strong-boxes aboard and stowed them below, the Jollies were crammed into the tiny focsle, and as the sun came up next morning we were thrashing down the Gulf of Suez to the Red Sea proper, having been in and out of Egypt in twenty-four hours, which is a day longer than you'd care to spend there.

The Suez gulf isn't more than ten miles across at its narrowest point, and Ballantyne, who was as full of gas and high spirits as a twenty-year-old with an independent command can be, informed me that this was where the Children of Israel had made their famous crossing in the Exodus, "but it's all balls and Banbury about the sea being parted and Pharaoh's army being drowned, you know. There are places where you can *walk* from Egypt to the Sinai at low tide, and an old Gyppo nigger told me it wasn't Pharaoh who was chasing 'em, either, but a lot of rascally Bedouin Arabs, and after Moses had got over at low water, the tide came in and the buddoos were drowned and serve 'em right. And there wasn't a blessed chariot to be seen when the tide went out, so there!"[11]

His bosun said beggin' his pardon, sir, but that was blasphemy,

16

and they fell to arguing while the tars grinned and chaffed and my Bootneck sergeant scowled disapproval; he wasn't used to the free and easy style of these Navy youngsters who couldn't help bringing their fifth-form ways to sea, and treated their men more like a football team of which they were captain, than a crew. It was natural enough: the young cornet or ensign in the Army, when he joined his regiment for the first time, entered a world of rigid formality and discipline, but here was this lad just out of his 'teens with a little floating kingdom all his own, sent to fight slavers and pirates, chase smugglers, shepherd pilgrims, and escort the precious bullion on which a whole British army would depend – and not a senior to turn to for advice or guidance, but only his own sense and judgment. Young Ballantyne couldn't follow orders, because he hadn't any beyond a roving commission; his crew were all older than he was, but he must live with 'em and mess with 'em, share their hardships and dangers as one of 'em, and make them like and trust him because he was what he was, so that when he said "Go!" they'd obey, even unto death.

I'd never have done for the Navy. You may fool soldiers by holding aloof and looking martial, but Jack would have seen through me before we'd crossed the bar. That's the hellish thing about life aboard ship – there's nowhere to hide either your carcase or your nature.

We had a taste of Ballantyne's the second day out, just after we'd passed the Ras Mohammed point at the foot of Sinai, and the hand in the bows spotted a low, ugly-looking craft with a great lateen sail which sheered away at sight of us, running for a little cluster of islands near the Egyptian shore.

"Slaver, pound to a penny!" yells our young Nelson. "Bosun, clear away the gun. Tomkins, open the arms chest! Sir Harry, I'd be obliged if your fellows would take station two either side, ready to fire if need be. Tally-ho!" And he seized the wheel while his engineer thundered his motor and our little sloop fairly flew over the water. Ballantyne's dozen tars were diving below deck and emerging with pieces and cutlasses, and I directed my sergeant to place his fellows at the rail as requested, and shocked his military soul by countermanding his order to them to put on their hats and coats. You shoot straighter in shirt-sleeves when there's an African sun blazing down on you.

But they didn't get the chance, for the slavers reached a rocky island ahead of us and abandoned ship, taking their human cargo with them. We were still half a mile off and powerless to interfere as a dozen or so white-robed Arabs and upwards of a hundred naked niggers, men, women, and children, were tumbling ashore and up into the rocks; we could hear their squeals and the crack of the courbashes as the slavers lashed them on, the leader of the gang turning to jeer and gesture obscenely as we hove to a pistol-shot off shore. Ballantyne danced with rage and shook his fist.

"You disgusting bastards, I'll larn you!" yells he, his voice fairly cracking. "Bosun, stand by the gun – no, belay that! Marines, take aim at that son-of-a-bitch – no, dammit, belay that too!" For the slavers' leader had snatched up one of the infants as a shield, and his rascals followed suit or mingled with the panic-stricken slaves so that we daren't fire.

"Oh, you cads!" bawls Ballantyne. "Oh, you cowardly rotters! You shan't escape us! Run her in, bosun! Stand by with your cut-lasses, you men! We'll settle your hash, you beastly black villains! They can't outrun us with the slaves! Pistols, Tomkins, and load two for me! And two for Sir Harry – and a cutlass! We'll run 'em to earth in a jiffy, sir, what? Ha-ha!"

He was such a happy little blood-spiller, just bursting to be at the enemy, that I hated to spoil his fun, but I was shot if I was going to be plunged into a cut-and-thrust brawl with those desperate brutes – and I had the perfect excuse for overriding him. I bellowed an order to the engineer to hold on, and cut short Ballantyne's falsetto protest.

"Sorry, my lad, it's no go! We're carrying an army's treasury, and it ain't to be risked for a gaggle of slaves!"

"But we can cut 'em up in no time, and rescue the poor souls!" cries he. "We've done it before, you know! Bosun'll tell you –"

"Well, you ain't doing it today," says I, and he was hitting Top C until the bosun shook his head and said I was right, beggin' your

18

pardon, sir, can't risk the dollars no-how. Ballantyne looked as though he would cry, but made the best of it like a good 'un.

"Quite right, Sir Harry, I wasn't thinkin'! Forgive me – dam' thoughtless! I say, though, we can sink the beggars' boat! That'll spoil their filthy trade for them! Bosun, man the gun!"

"Wot abaht the slaves, sir?" says bosun. "Them black devils is liable to cut their throats aht o' spite if we sink her."

Ballantyne weighed this for a good two seconds, frowning judicially like Buggins Major undecided whether to thrash Juggins Minor or set him a hundred lines of Virgil. Then he snapped: "No. If we don't scupper 'em those poor creatures will be sold like cattle. They cannot be worse off if they and those fiends are left stranded. And by gum there'll be one less hell-ship runnin' black ivory!"

Bosun touched his hat, but pointed out that their six-pounder would take all day to smash the slaver's timbers. "Then burn the bugger!" cries Ballantyne, and two men were sent in the gig to set her ablaze with bundles of tow. She went up like a November bonfire, while the slavers screamed helplessly from the hillside. Then we stood off, Ballantyne scowling and vowing vengeance.

"It's too bad!" says he. "The white-livered ruffians always take to the nearest shore, but we've chased 'em and brought off the slaves two or three times, 'cos they never make a fight of it, the chicken-hearted scoundrels!" He stared back at the shore and the blazing vessel. "Aye, they're well up in the rocks, the beasts – and you must be careful, you know. Chum of mine, Jack Legerwood, chased one gang too far, just a couple of months ago. They caught him, made an awful mess of him, poor old chap. Gad, if I could only lay hands on them!"

You know my opinion of heroics, and I'd not break sweat myself to save a parcel of handless niggers being sold into slavery – which is probably no worse than the lives they've been living in some desert pesthole, and may well be a blessed change for the females who find a billet in some randy bashaw's hareem. I mentioned this to Ballantyne, and he blushed crimson and exclaimed: "I say!" A true-blue Arnoldian paladin, he was, pure of heart and full of

Christian zeal to cherish the weak and have a grand time cutting up the ungodly.

But I ain't mocking him, much, and I've a sight more use for him and his like than for the psalm-smiting Holy Joes who pay lip-service to delivering the heathen from error's chain by preaching and giving their ha'pence to the Anti-Slavery Society, but spare never a thought for young Ballantyne holding the sea-lanes for civilisation and Jack Legerwood dying the kind of death you wouldn't wish for your worst enemy. I've even heard 'em maligned like my old shipmate Brooke* for taking a high hand and shooting first and hammering slavers and pirates and brigands like the wrath of God. Censure's so easy at a distance, but I've seen them on the frontiers, schoolboys with the down still on their cheeks doing a man's work and getting a seedeboy's pay[12] and damn-all thanks and more often than not a bullet for their twenty-first birthday – why, I'd just seen one, too young to vote, weighing a hundred black lives in the balance, and deciding, in a couple of seconds, the kind of fearful question his reverend seniors at home would have shied a mile from.

I think he was right, by the way, and I speak from experience, having shirked responsibility too often to count. But the Ballantynes and Legerwoods didn't, and if the slave trade has been swept off the face of the seas, it hasn't really been the work of reformers and statesmen with lofty ideals in London and Paris and Washington, but because a long-forgotten host of fairly feckless young Britons did it for fun. And you may tell the historians I said so.

It's about a thousand miles from Sinai to the Abyssinian port of Zoola, and I supposed our frisky little steamer would cover it in no time, but it didn't. Halfway the boiler sprang a leak, and it was the grace of God that we were off Jedda at the time, for in those days it was the only place worth a dam on the whole benighted Red Sea coast, being the port where the Muslim pilgrims disembark for Mecca, which lies a couple of days' march inland. Consequently the place is aswarm with them, arriving and departing

* See *Flashman's Lady*.

in every kind of boat from Chinese junks and ancient steamers to feluccas and coracles. We had a consul there, and the Navy were always on hand; they used the place as a rendezvous, with a supply depot and smithy where our engineer was able to get his kettle mended.

There's a place called El Golea in the deep Sahara which they say is the hottest spot on earth, but I'll put my money on Jedda – or anywhere else on the Red Sea for that matter. We sweltered for days, and the bosun won a bet from the marines by frying an egg on the deck. The waterfront was a bedlam of boats, and the town itself was choked with a vast milling horde of pilgrims who turned it into a human ant-heap, with the heat and stench rising from it in choking waves which I'll swear were visible above the famous white walls. I lay gasping under an awning trying to ignore the deafening din of a million niggers shouting and wailing as I leafed through an old copy of *Punch* in which there was a rhyme about Britons in chains in Abyssinia, and a cartoon of Emperor Theodore as a thick-lipped sambo – well wide of the mark, as I was to discover.

Punch didn't think much of our expedition, and had a fine old grouse about War Office muddle, and the cost to the middle classes which they said should be defrayed by nabbing Theodore and exhibiting him in a cage at the Egyptian Hall on Piccadilly at a shilling a time.[13]

If I was impatient of delay, Ballantyne was fit to burst; there were a couple of sloops like ours about to weigh anchor for some place down the Arabian coast where our native spies had word of a great cargo of slaves coming from the African shore, and our young hero was like a baby denied its bottle.

"More than a thousand slaves bound for El Confound-it,* and we're stuck in this beastly hole! Of all the luck! We'll never be fit in time!"

"Oh, I dunno," says our informant, another sprightly juvenile, modishly clad in jellaba, brass-buttoned jacket, and pirate head-scarf.

* Presumably Al Qunfudhah, a port on the Saudi Arabian coast.

"Slavers mayn't show for a week yet, and Confound-it ain't far across from Zoola. Tell your engineer you'll stop his grog if he don't get a move on, why don't you?"

A dam' silly suggestion, since the surest way to make a British workman take his time is to threaten him, especially if you call him a Port Mahon baboon into the bargain, and it was all of another ten days, a week later than Speed had reckoned, before we were steaming down Annesley Bay, the gulf on which Zoola lies. And d'you know, only now, with my first glimpse of the Abyssinian shore, did it come home to me that apart from the sketch I'd been given by Speed, and a few scraps I'd picked up from Ballantyne and the boys at Jedda, I knew nothing about the country or people or why we were going to war with them, really. I'd left Trieste in the deuce of a hurry, quite elated at escaping the consequences of my evil conduct and the novelty of the commission I'd been given, and here I was, with the job almost done, and wondering for the first time what the dickens it was all about.

And since you, honest reader, know no more than I did myself as we threaded our way through the vast fleet assembled in Annesley Bay and were engulfed in Zoola's two most charming attractions, borne by the land breeze – a fine powdery dust that hung over us in a cloud, and the most appalling stench – it seems a proper time to tell you of things which I had yet to learn, about Abyssinia and the *casus belli* that had brought Napier and his army all the way from India to this mysterious coast.

To begin with, you must understand that the Abyssinians are like no other Africans, being some kind of Semitic folk who came from Arabia in the far-off time, handsome, cruel, and bloodthirsty, but civilised beyond any in the continent bar the Egyptians, with whom they shared a fierce mutual hatred, partly because the Gyppoes were forever carrying off their beautiful women and boys as slaves, partly because the Abs (as I call 'em for convenience) are devout and violently militant Christians, and can't abide Muslims – or Roman Catholics. Very orthodox, they are, having been Christian long before we were, and of fairly primitive doctrine – I've seen church paintings (admission one dollar) of a Byzantinish-looking St George

22

slaying the dragon while Pharaoh's daughter and her handmaidens look on in admiration, and a depiction of the Last Supper with places laid for fourteen.

And their Christianity don't run to morality, not far at least. They lie and deceive with a will, drink to excess, slaughter each other for amusement, and the women couple like stoats. The corollary to their adage that "a virtuous woman is a crown to her husband" is that there are dam' few crowned heads in Abyssinia, and hear, hear! say I, for 'twould be a cruel shame to have all that splendid married pulchritude going to waste.

They don't look at all negroid; indeed, the Ab females fit my notion of Cleopatra with their straight noses, chiselled lips, almond eyes, saucy shapes, and in many cases skins no darker than an Italian's. They know how to preen, too, the Shoho women of the north in shell-embroidered black cloaks over tight leather tunics from bosom to thigh, jolly fetching, and the Galla girls of the south, reckoned the handsomest of all, their perfect faces framed by elaborate oiled braids plaited from crown to shoulder. Some go naked to the waist, with little aprons made of thongs, and by gad they can stand the exposure. But if they're fair, they're fierce; one I knew was such a peach that the slavers who'd taken her expected a record price, but were disappointed when she discouraged the buyers by juggling a throwing-knife during the bidding, and they had to *give* her away.

In the men, the Egyptian look is enhanced by their white cotton robes, and their laziness, for they're the idlest folk alive except when fighting, which they are much of the time, for everyone's a warrior and goes armed. They don't seem to know what fear is; the younger nobles have a curious custom of waiting at river fords to challenge travellers to single combat – and how they came by that Arthurian custom must be an interesting story.

Their houses aren't much better than large huts, thatched and simply furnished, although they have occasional castle-like buildings on hill-tops; their towns are large walled villages with what seem to be permanent fairs and markets, and even their cities (if you can call 'em that) are no more than a collection of houses on top of a massive precipitous height called an *amba*. Magdala, the goal of Napier's expedition, was like that; you don't need battlements when you have sheer rock walls below you.[14]

So there you have the Abs, a pretty rum lot, first brought to our notice in the 1770s by a Scotch eccentric whom nobody believed – mind you, he was pretty rum himself, fooling about with the Barbary corsairs, seeking the source of the Nile, and finally breaking his neck while helping a lady downstairs, which shows that even the most seasoned mad adventurers can't be too careful.[15]

Very few Europeans had ventured into Abyssinia before him, for it was a traveller's nightmare, rugged and desolate beyond description, racked by perpetual civil wars in which the tribal leaders fought for the supreme lordship. One of these, Ras Ali, had made himself king of most of the country by 1840, but made the mistake of giving his daughter, Tewabetch the Beautiful, in marriage to an ambitious young mercenary, Lijkassa, the son of a woman who sold tapeworm medicine, which the Abs take in quantity as a result of their partiality to raw beef, 'nuff said. But he was a first-class soldier, clever, brave, and unscrupulous, and in no time he'd usurped the throne.

While still a lad, he'd become convinced that he was the Messiah named in an old prophecy and would become the greatest king on earth, master of all Ethiopia and Egypt; he would scourge the infidels out of Palestine, purge Jerusalem of its defilers (the Muslims), and would be called Theodore. So he changed his name accordingly, and proclaimed himself Emperor and King of Kings. He was young, handsome, muscular, literate (unlike most Abs), and full of reforming notions, like abolishing slavery and generally improving the lot of the commonalty. If he had a tendency to berserk rages, butchering his enemies, holding mass executions, flogging people to death or cutting off their limbs and leaving 'em for the wild beasts, well, savage despots can't afford to behave like Tiny Tim.

His queen was a moderating influence, and so were two Englishmen, Plowden, our consul, and Bell, a soldier of fortune who became Theodore's chamberlain. Unfortunately all three died almost simultaneously, the two Britons cut up by rebels and

24

Tewabetch of natural causes. Theodore massacred the rebels in reprisal, but with the three best influences in his life gone, he began to behave like a real absolute monarch at last, taking to drink and concubines and committing even more atrocities than before. He married again, but since his bride was the daughter of a rival claimant to the throne whom Theodore had humiliated and imprisoned, the marriage was not a success.

We sent out a new consul, Captain Cameron, who presented Theodore with two pistols from Queen Victoria. This so delighted him that he wrote a letter proposing that he send an envoy to London, and remarking that he'd wiped out Plowden's murderers "to win the friendship of her majesty".

You'd have thought he couldn't say fairer than that, but would you believe that those monumental half-wits at the F.O. didn't give his letter to the Queen, or even acknowledge it? Why? Oh, other things, like Bertie the Bounder's wedding to Alexandra of Denmark,[16] were occupying their lordships' attention, and who was this distant African upstart, anyway? Or quite possibly some chinless oaf simply mistook it for his wine bill and tossed it into a pigeonhole. God knows how our foreign affairs haven't been one long catalogue of disaster . . . stay, though, they have, haven't they?

What followed was inevitable, with a short-tempered, arrogant barbarian monarch who thought he was God's anointed. After a year of being ignored he arrested Cameron, who'd visited Egypt, Theodore's mortal enemy, to investigate cotton supplies which we were liable to need with the American Civil War disrupting our business. Then a missionary called Stern (who was trying to convert Abyssinian Jews to Christianity, if you'll believe it) published offensive remarks about Theodore. Result: Cameron chained, flogged, and stretched on the rack; Stern brutally beaten and two of his servants lashed to death with hippo-hide whips; other Europeans arrested and bound with cords soaked so that they cut their limbs; missionaries forced to watch the death by torture of malefactors whose blood the executioners smeared on the horrified spectators . . . and so on, while the letter whose delivery might have prevented these horrors lay unanswered in Whitehall.

Eventually a reply was sent, the messenger being a wily oriental gentleman named Hormuzd Rassam from our Aden office who delayed six months before venturing up-country with conciliatory messages and presents which included a swing for Theodore's children. (Gad, I'm proud to be British!) Much good it did: Rassam and his party were added to the chain gang, and at long last, after four years in which the public had heard little beyond rumours, Parliament awoke, members began to ask where Abyssinia was, and the Russell government, having stifled debate on the remarkable ground that it might irritate Theodore, fell from office, leaving the mess to the Tories who, not without agonised dithering, ordered Napier to take a force from India to Abyssinia, make a final demand for the prisoners' release, and then "take such measures as he thinks expedient", and good luck to him.

You notice that with typical parliamentary poltroonery the Derby–D'Israeli gang left it up to the soldier to make the fatal decision, but for once I could understand if not sympathise, for if ever a government was caught between Scylla and t'other thing, they were. On the one hand, they couldn't leave the prisoners in Theodore's clutches, for our credit's sake – what, have a tinpot nigger king showing us his arse? Abandoning Britons, and telling the world we couldn't defend our own? Letting India, where we'd been given an almighty fright only ten years before, see that we could be defied with impunity? "Never!" cries John Bull, even if it took an army of thousands to free a handful, and cost the three and a half million of Dizzy's estimate, and lasted months or years, still it must be done, and that was flat.

On the other hand, it was odds on that invasion would fail. Abyssinia was tropical territory incognita, our army would be cut off miles from the sea, without reserves, in country without roads or reliable water supply, where every ounce of food, gear, and ammunition would have to be carried – where? There was no certain information of where the captives were exactly, and what if Theodore cut their throats or carried them into the trackless fastnesses hundreds of miles inland? And what of the hundreds of thousands of ferocious tribesmen between the coast and Magdala – if indeed Magdala proved to be the goal? What if, as seemed very likely, Napier's army vanished into the wilds of Prester John and never came out again?

That, I'm told, was the tenor of the warnings and prophecies that filled the press when the government's decision became known: the expedition was doomed, but it would have to go anyway.[17]

But none of that was clear to me as we steamed into the dust and stink of Zoola on that fine February morning. I didn't have the benefit of public opinion from home, and at Jedda they'd been far too taken up with pirates and pilgrims to give thought to the consequences of what was happening in the mysterious south, beyond the far-off peaks dimly seen through the haze that hung over Annesley Bay. But now you know the how and why of Napier's expedition, and enough of the land and people for the moment. And from what I've told you, you may have been struck by a thought which has absolutely occurred to me only now, as I write: for perhaps the first time in her long and turbulent history Britain was going into a war which everyone believed we were going to lose. Everyone, that is, except Bughunter Bob Napier.

The expedition had been ashore for three months, but still supply ships and troopers and men-of-war were arriving daily to swell the fleet of steamships, sailing vessels, and small craft discharging cargo on to the causeway running out into the bay. It had a railway with bogies moving the goods inshore, where they were piled in mountains of bales and boxes among the tent-lines which stretched away into the distance.

It was a quartermaster's nightmare, too much gear coming ashore too quickly and nowhere to put it, with confusion worse confounded by the milling mob of what someone called the "pier-head democracy" – staff men and Madras coolies, generals and drummer-boys, dockside gangs both black and white labouring under despairing civilian overseers, work parties of soldiers ignoring the bawlings of perspiring non-coms, clerks and water-carriers and native women forage-cutters, every sort and colour of African and Asiatic, and a positive Noah's Ark of animals. Next to our berth on the causeway, elephants were being hoisted ashore from a barge, squealing and trumpeting as they swung perilously aloft in their belly-bands, and the crane-tackles groaned and shuddered until the great beasts came to earth with a dangerous thrashing of trunks and limbs; cursing troopers were saddling and loading mules which had one leg strapped up to prevent their lashing out; water-hoys were pumping their streams into huge wheeled tanks on the railway – for every drop of drink in Zoola had to be brought ashore from the condensers of the ships in the bay – and even as I stepped ashore one of the hoses burst asunder, gushing over the pack-mules and swirling round the feet of the

28

elephants which bellowed and reared in panic as their drivers clung to their trunks to quiet them.

Britannia's bridgehead into Abyssinia was, in fact, a godless mess, made infinitely worse by the dust and the stink. Beyond the harbour and camp lay a wide plain with mountains far off, but you could barely see them through the fawn-coloured cloud that hung over the tents and sheds and rooties* and even the waters of the bay, covering everything in a fine powder which you had to be constantly brushing off your clothes and skin, and spitting out.

But it was nothing to the stink, a foul carrion-reek that took you by the throat and made breathing a poisonous misery.

"If you think this is bad you should ha' been here a month ago," says the transport wallah who supervised the loading of my strong-boxes into a railway bogie; he was a languid, amiable young haw-haw named Twentyman, a Hussar, complete with fly-whisk and followed by a *chico*† with a bucket of camphorated water whose duty it was to supply his master with wet clouts to sponge away the dust. "What is it? Thousands o' dead beasts rottin', that's what. Cavalry mounts droppin' like flies, mules too, no one knows why, vets never saw the like." He dropped his wet rag into the bucket with a weary sigh. "Thank God for the vultures or we'd ha' had an epidemic."

I introduced myself, expecting to have to explain my arrival, but no such thing.

"We know all about you, Sir Harry!" says he blithely. "Mail sloop from Jedda brought word of you last week, deputation from H.Q.'s been waitin' for three days, great excitement, what? And these are the long-awaited *spondulikos*, are they? Splendid, chuck 'em aboard, sarn't, and you, dragoman, summon your stout lads to give us a shove, there's a good chap!"

I bade a hasty farewell to Ballantyne, who was itching to get himself and his ship back into fresh air, and climbed into the bogie with Twentyman, followed by the Marines, who seated themselves on the strong-boxes.

* Indian regiments' tents.
† Native child.

29

"Sound move, sarn't, keep their posteriors planted just so," says Twentyman approvingly. "Can't be too careful with the 33rd on hand, thievin' Irish scoundrels to a man, desperate fellows. So keep an eye down on the dollars, or Paddy'll be over the hedge with his pockets jinglin', what? . . . [18] I say, dragoman, *jildi jao, sub admi push karo!*"*

The dragoman bellowed and belaboured the coolies with his staff, and we were propelled towards the head of the causeway. I said it was as well they had a railway, with freight as heavy as mine, and how far did it go.

"Five miles, so far," says Twentyman cheerfully. "It's about a hundred and twenty to Attegrat, so it's mules for you, I'm afraid, sir. They do twelve miles a day, supposin' you can get 'em, for we've fewer than ten thousand pack animals when we're supposed to have *thirty* thousand. Well, I ask you! Bombay *bandobast*,† what?"

I thanked God privately that I wasn't part of the expedition, and asked how quickly I could get word to Napier of my arrival.

"Oh, couple of hours – telegraph's only halfway to Attegrat, but we've flag signallin' by day, magnesium flare lamps for night messages, latest thing, bang-up-to-date, what? Ah, there's one o' the deputation! Hollo, Henty, he's here at last!"

As we jumped down, a burly, beef-faced chap in a dust coat and kepi was striding up, grinning hugely, with his hand out.

"Don't remember me, Sir Harry, I'll be bound!" cries he. "George Henty[19] of the *Standard* – we shared a billet with Billy Russell and Lew Nolan at Sevastopol, and you went down with dysentery. Before poor old Lew got himself killed, and you and Cardigan charged to glory!"‡

He pumped my fin like a long-lost brother, but shot if I could place him.

"D'ye know, you launched my journalistic career?" cries he. "I

* "Hurry up, everybody push!"
† Organisation.
‡ See *Flashman at the Charge*.

was in the hospital commissariat, you know, until I offered a piece to the *Advertiser* describing your part in the Charge, and . . . well, here I am, eh?" I found myself wondering if he was the idiot who'd written that foul purple tosh which George Paget, curse him, had clipped out and framed and hung in the 4th Lights' mess, all about "with what nobility and power the gallant Flashman rode, his eye flashing terribly." And farting like a deflating balloon, had they but known.

My immediate thought was to give this familiar brute a set-down, but it's best to keep in with the press, so I cried, to be sure, I remembered him well, and how had he been all these years? He went rosy with gratitude at being remembered by the famous Flashy.

"But here's another who's been counting the hours to see you!" cries he, and there, emerging from a tent, came Giant Despair dressed for a gypsy wedding, and I could only stand and gape.

Bar Mangas Colorado, he was the biggest man I'd ever seen in my life, closer to seven feet than six and built like an overgrown gorilla. His enormous body was wrapped in a robe made of lions' manes which covered him from the white scarf round his neck to his massive half-boots, he wore a black beard to his chest, horn-rimmed spectacles, and a smoking-cap, and carried a throwing spear in one hand and a straw umbrella in the other. To complete this bespoke costume, he had a sabre on his hip, a revolver in his belt, and a round native shield slung on his back. When he grinned, with a fierce glitter of teeth in the beard, he looked like a Ghazi on hasheesh – and then he spoke, brisk and high-pitched, his huge hand gently enfolding mine, and he might have been a vicar welcoming me to the sale of work.

"Charles Speedy, Sir Harry, used to be adjutant of the Tenth Punjabis, saw you once on the Grand Trunk, near Fatehpur, oh, ever so long ago, but you didn't see me."

Then you must have been lying down in cover and wearing mufti, thinks I. My astonishment showed, for he gave a whimsical shrug and spread his arms in display.

"Sir Robert Napier likes me to dress native, thinks it impresses the local *sidis*, bless 'em! I'm his political adviser, and at present your committee of welcome." He gave another alarming grin, accompanied by even more alarming words. "Can't tell you how glad we all are to have you with us."

Now, that was the very first intimation I had of the possible ghastly sequel to the mission I was carrying out simply to oblige an old school chum. Of course, you could interpret the words two ways, and I lost no time in putting him right.

"I ain't *with* you. Delivering the messages, rather." I nodded at the boxes which the coolies were unloading under the watchful eye of Twentyman and my Bootneck sergeant. "I hear it'll take ten days to get 'em up to Napier by mule. How short o' the ready is he?"

"Tight, but one chestful of dollars should cover his immediate needs, and we'll get those to him inside forty-eight hours. Can't have his pockets to let when he meets the King of Tigre to arrange our passage through his territory. Napier's been waiting beyond Attegrat for days, but his majesty's hanging back, scared to commit himself, likely. Theodore may be a long way off, but these petty rulers go in terror of him still." He gave his great booming laugh. "As political, 'twill fall to me to persuade King Kussai that we'll be the winning side, so the sooner we're south-bound the better. You and I and Henty here can split a chest of silver among our saddle-bags, with a couple of led-beasts. Hear that, George? You can stop scribbling and do something useful for a change!"

"Tain't every day two such lions as Sir Harry Flashman, V.C., and the *Basha Fallaka* shake hands," says Henty, pocketing his notebook. "You're good copy, Charlie, the pair of you. When do we leave, then?"

"After tiffin," says Speedy. "If that suits, Sir Harry?" Henty laughed and said no wonder the Abs called him *Basha Fallaka*, which means Quick Chief, and was their pun on Speedy's name.

I was deciding he was a sight too quick for me. Here I was, hardly ten minutes ashore, and I was being dragooned into the saddle by a crazy Goliath in Hallowe'en rig to go tearing up-country on a forty-eight-hour gallop to Napier's command post. True, I'd sworn to Speedicut* that I'd see his dollars all the way to Attegrat, but that had been back in Trieste with the hosts of Midian prowling round, and now here was Napier's own political on hand to collect the dibs – and after that mention of being "with" them I'd no wish to venture nearer the theatre of operations than I must, in case Napier got a notion to drag me into the stew. I know these bloody generals. I'd been there before.

On t'other hand, I was well retired, hadn't worn the Queen's coat since China in '60, and I'd need Napier's personal *kitab*† for a paid passage home. He'd expect me to call on him, and offhand I couldn't think of a good excuse for not doing so, fool that I was. I should have told Speedy I was sickening for mumps, or pleaded my belly, or done any damned thing to stay at a safe distance from a campaign which, to judge from the gloom at tiffin, promised to be the biggest catastrophe since the Kabul retreat.

I've told you of the pessimism which, unknown to me, was prevailing at home, but now I was hearing it from the men on the spot, grousing in their shirt-sleeves in the stifling heat of the messtent: Native Infantry officers, Punjabi Pioneers, King's Own, cavalrymen from the Scinde Horse irregulars and Native Cavalry regiments, Baluch, Madras Sappers, even a Dragoon Guardee, and altogether as mixed a collection as you could hope to find, all croaking like the never-wearied rook. In short order I gathered that fat-headed Bombay politicals had hampered Napier at every turn and thrown his plans into disarray; that our transport was in chaos because they'd hired drivers who were the scum of the Levant, Greeks and dagoes and the like, who'd mutinied and had to be replaced by Persians and Hindus; that we were far too soft with the Abs, as witness Pottinger's giving way to a crowd of Shohos who'd blocked the road, and the armed attack on a sentry which

* It obviously did not occur to Flashman that the similarity of the names Speedicut and Speedy might be confusing. Had this been pointed out to him he would no doubt have retorted that they were, in fact, the respective surnames of his Rugby schoolfellow and the political officer of Abyssinia, that this was not his fault, and that he had no intention of offending truth by calling one of them Smith or Snodgrass.
† Literally, book (Hind.) but in this sense, official warrant.

had had to be repulsed by the bayonets of Cooper's Irishmen; that we were fools to rely on local intelligence which reported Theodore and the captives in half a dozen different places at once; that with the mercury at 116 (and that on a cool day) we'd have an epidemic if the army wasn't moved up-country to the high ground; that baboons were swinging on the telegraph wires, which would have to be coated in rubber and buried – I'd heard the like from the Khyber to Chattanooga, and if the words were different the tune was the same.

"Oh, for the Army Works Corps that we had in Crimea!"

"As if they'd make a ha'porth o' difference! God Himself couldn't lay more than a mile of road a day over solid rock sky-high with boulders."

"Mile a day should get us to Magdala next year, what?"

"Ah, so we shan't be in and out by April?" General laughter.

"Dam' lucky if we get out at all. See here – twelve thousand men, three-quarters of 'em on support, depots, transport, and so on, two thousand to go for Magdala –"

"Flyin' column, you mean? Napier's good at those."

"Flyin' column be damned! – in country where you'll make ten miles a day with luck? An' it's four hundred miles! So where d'you find mule forage for forty days, to say nothin' of takin' elephants and mountain guns and mortars over ground that'd have Hannibal cryin' for his pension?"

"Talkin' like a book, ye are. An' will the tribes let us be? They say Theodore can put a hundred thousand into the field."

"If the chiefs support him. Merewether reckons they won't."

"Does he, now? D'ye know, I don't reckon Merewether's optimism counts for much against odds of fifty to one."[20]

"Oh, shield-and-spear niggers. Not much firepower."

"That's not the point, confound it!" This from a grizzled major of Baluch. "Time and distance are our enemy – not the tribes! We're not here for conquest or victory, even! Eating, not fighting, is going to be what matters! Aye, survival!" This was greeted by a brief silence, followed by a drawl from a Scinde Horse subaltern.

"Ah, well . . . any volunteers for the relief expedition in two years' time?" Some laughter, by no means hearty.

The usual grumble-and-grin of men in the field, if you like, but with a decided note of uncertainty in it – and these weren't just any soldiers, but the best India could show. Still, I might have dismissed them as croakers if Speedy's silence during the meal hadn't convinced me that he shared their misgivings.

You see, we poltroons have a talent for spotting heroes – we have to, in order to steer well clear of them – and from what I learned from Henty, who sat by me at tiffin, Speedy was a prime specimen, and an expert to boot. A gentle giant who looked like the wrath of God but had no side at all, had served in four armies, and probably killed more men than the dysentery. He knew Abyssinia inside out, spoke Amharic, which is the principal lingo of the country, and had been drill instructor in the service of Emperor Theodore, who had particularly admired his party trick of cleaving a sheep in two (lengthwise, God help us) with a single sword-stroke. But they'd fallen out, and Speedy had been farming and fighting Maoris in New Zealand when the present crisis arose; Napier had insisted on having him as his political, and Speedy had rolled up for service with nothing but the clothes he stood in and a couple of blankets.

That tells you the sort of chap he was,[21] another of the crazy gentleman-adventurers who infested the frontiers in the earlies, and when a fellow with his authority don't contradict croaking, you draw your own conclusions – mine being that I must lose no time in tapping Napier for my ticket home.

Just for interest I asked Speedy, when we were making ready for our departure up-country, how he thought Napier might set about the campaign, and was shocked when he said coolly that his only hope was to go hell-for-leather for Magdala with a small force, trust to luck he'd find the prisoners there, and high-tail it back to civilisation double-quick.

"You went with Grant to Pekin, didn't you, and Gough to the Sutlej – aye, and Sherman to the sea?" He shook his shaggy head. "'Tain't that kind of trip. They knew where they were going, with proper transport, commissariat, lines of communication, knowing who and where their enemy was, and with force enough to do the trick. Napier's got none o' that. As that old Baluch said, it's time and the country he's up against, and all he can do is raid and run."

"Man to man, what are the odds?"

He thought a moment, tugging his beard. "Even chance. Six to four against if 'twas anyone else, but Napier's the best since old Colin Campbell. Yes, I'd risk a monkey* on him – if I had one!"

He was all action now, breaking the seals on one of the strong-boxes and having the glittering mass of Maria Theresas transferred to saddle-bags by the Marines, with the sergeant watching like a hawk to see that no coins stuck to crafty fingers – he made 'em strip to their drawers and bare feet to make sure no one slipped cash into his clothing, and Twentyman again gave thanks that the 33rd weren't on hand.

"Aye, a parcel of Fenian thieves," says Speedy, "but well worth their salt when they form square. Did you hear that they went on an almighty drunk, and when Cooper swore they'd be left down-country their spokesmen asked for fifty lashes a man if only they could join the advance? What could Cooper do but pardon them, the impudent rascals?"

The Provost-Marshal was called to take charge of the remaining boxes, and I commended my Bootnecks to him as the best guard for the dollars he could hope to find. Their sergeant smiled for the first time in our acquaintance, and I supplied a little touch of Flashy by thanking him and his file for their good and trusty work, shaking hands with each man by name, which I knew must go well. Popularity Jack, that's me.

The weight of the specie was such that we needed half a dozen beasts apart from our own,[22] and Speedy decided that so many led-horses must slow us down, so a half-section of the Scinde Horse were whistled up, stalwart frontier riders in the long green coats and trowsers, with red sash and puggaree, that I hadn't seen since the Mutiny, each man with a twin-barrelled rifle and sword

* £500.

– not the chaps I'd have picked myself, since half of them were Pathans who'd sooner steal than sleep. But Speedy swore by them, and to my gratification their havildar was a leathery veteran from the Mogala country who claimed to remember "Bloody Lance", as he addressed me, pouring out the old tale of how Ifflass-mann slaughtered the four Gilzais – so much lying tommy-rot, you understand, but I dare say I could still dine out on it in the caravanserais along the Jugdulluk road.[*]

We saddled up, Speedy inspecting the saddle-bags on every "Scindee", and then we set ahead through the bedlam of the camp; five miles it stretched from the Zoola causeway, on either side of the railway tracks, with the two locomotives puffing and squealing up and down. They weren't used on the causeway itself, for fear of their weight causing a landslip. What with piled gear, work gangs, Ab vendors who'd set up their stalls as a bazaar in the tent-lines, and no attempt to bring order to the camp, it took us the best part of an hour to reach open country, and Speedy cursed the delay. I didn't mind, for there was plenty to take the eye, chiefly the Shoho girls with their saucy smiles and hair frizzed into great turbans, bare to their loincloths and well pleased with the catcalls they drew as they sashayed along with their pots balanced on their heads.

"Fine crop of half-caste babes there'll be by Christmas," says Speedy. "Can't blame our fellows either; 'tain't often they run into beauties like these beyond the borders."

There was an elephant train loading up on the edge of the camp, half a dozen of the enormous brutes kneeling, each beside a sloping ramp up which the great mortars and Armstrong guns were being hauled to be secured on platforms on the elephants' backs. Speedy explained that there was no other way the heavy artillery could be carried through the ravines and along the narrow winding paths cut into the cliff-sides in the high country; the lighter mountain guns could be taken apart and carried by led-mules.

"That old Baluch major was right, you see. We stand or fall

---

[*] For the story of how Flashman earned the nickname "Bloody Lance" in Afghanistan, see the first volume of his memoirs, *Flashman*.

on animal transport; without it we're dead in our tracks in the middle of nowhere. And transport depends on forage, and forage depends on money." He slapped his saddle-bag of coin. "That's Napier's life-blood you've brought us. This'll keep him going for a day or so, and God willing the mules'll bring up the rest within the fortnight."

"Can we count on the tribes for supplies? Some of the fellows at tiffin seemed to think they might fight."

He shook his head. "Not at the moment. They're too glad to see us – and our dollars. Fact is, the common folk would like nothing better than to have us conquer the country and rule it. We pay, we'd give 'em peace from their endless civil wars, protect 'em from rebels and bandits and locusts and slavers, maybe even relieve their poverty – d'you know that many are so poor they'll sell their wives and daughters, even? They're priest-ridden, too; their kangaroo Christian church gets two-thirds of the peasantry's produce – aye, two-thirds! The king and their chiefs get a cut of what's left, so there ain't too much over for the brigands to pinch, is there?"

I wondered if we'd add Abyssinia to our savage possessions, but he said there was no chance of that. "We're here to free the prisoners – *bus*!"* says he. "Oh, the chiefs are all for our removing Theodore and installing one of them in his place, but Napier won't play politics, or take sides, and so he's told 'em. They can't believe we ain't bent on conquest – and I dare say our European pals and the Yankees share their view – but they're dead wrong. Even the Tories think Britannia's got quite enough empire, thank'ee very much, and stands in no need of the most advanced barbarians in Africa, whose idea of politics is civil war and massacre. Anyway," he added, "what profit is there in a country that's mostly rock and desert? Why, no colonists would look at it!"

I asked what had brought him here, into Theodore's service, too, and why he'd left it. He rode for a moment in thought, chin down on his chest, and then laughed almost as though he was embarrassed.

"Blowed if I can think of one good reason! They're a murderous

* That's all, finished, stop (Hind.).

lot of pirates, cruel, untrustworthy, immoral, and bone idle – and I like 'em! Why? 'Cos they're brave, and clever, and love to laugh, and they're so dam' contradictory!" He pointed to a herd of bullocks that were being driven into a corral by Ab cow-whackers. "Those fellows are so sharp they'll get the better of our commissaries at a bargain, bamboozle 'em with figures – and yet they can't write, and believe that we're buying the bullocks as food for the elephants! And that's the God's truth." He paused, and laughed again. "But I guess my best reason for liking Habesh – that's Arabic for Abyssinia – is that they like us. We treat 'em fair, and unlike the rest of Africa they're smart enough to admire us, and know they can learn from us, from our engineers and scientists, aye, and our military. You know what they call us? The Sons of Shaitan – and it's a compliment!"

"And Theodore? You must know him better than anyone else."

"I don't know him at all. No one does." He took off his specs and polished them carefully. "He's not just one man, he's many – and they're all dam' dangerous. You're going to ask me what he's liable to do, will he fight, will he run, will he hold the captives to ransom, will he murder them – and I haven't the foggiest notion. So I'll not try to answer. Better to let Napier tell you."

And that, I may tell you, sent a shiver down my spine for it prompted the question why Napier should want to tell me anything at all. I was pondering this when Speedy added:

"As to why I left Theodore, 'twas because he'd been listening to lies about me, and I'd no wish to wake up some morning face down on a bed of spear-points. So I asked for my back pay and a clear road. 'Suppose I'll not let you leave?' says he.

"'Then I'll fight,' says I, 'and you know I'm not an infant.'

"'I can have you killed,' says he.

"'Ah, but how quickly?' says I, and laid my hand on my hilt. He had no fear, but he paused, and then smiled and embraced me and said I should have my money, a horse, and a spear, and God be with me." He chucked his reins. "Let's raise the pace, shall we?"

From Zoola the barren scrub-land rises slowly to the base of the hills, and it took us five hours' uncomfortable riding across stone-choked dry river beds and little slithering screes before we came to the plateau from which you could look back at the huge panorama of the distant camp like a sand-table model, and Annesley Bay with its forest of shipping, and the Red Sea beyond. Ahead of us lay the way station of Koomaylee, in a broad basin with sheer cliffs towering on either hand and a massive rampart of stone before us, crimson in the sunset save for the gloomy mouth of the Great Pass which splits it in two as though some god had gashed it with a cleaver. That's the real gateway to Abyssinia, and at dusk it looks like the road to the Underworld. Beyond it lay range upon range of mighty peaks, rising ever higher as far as you could see.

The Himalays and the Rockies, magnificent as they are, never made me feel as small and helpless as those hellish Abyssinian highlands; they had a power to overwhelm, to make you feel you were in an alien, dreadful world, a desert of peaks that someone likened to the legs of an overturned table, thrusting into a sky of burnished steel. I was seeing them for the first time that night at Koomaylee, and I remember thinking that while the Hindu Kush and the Sangre de Cristo may convince you that they're the roof of the world, they don't frighten. Abyssinia did.

My only other memory of Koomaylee, where we bedded down with the Madras Sappers, is of the Norton pumps, like a row of gigantic hallstands, spouting a never-ending stream of wonderful ice-cold water, utterly unlike the stale condensed sludge of Zoola, into the hundred-foot wooden reservoirs. We sank it by the quart. "God bless America," says Henty, "for if they can work as well up-country we shan't go thirsty at any rate."

Next day we traversed the Great Pass, mile after mile through that astonishing defile which narrows to as little as five yards in places, with eight hundred feet of solid granite either side and only a strip of sky far overhead to remind you that with luck you won't meet Charon this trip. We rode single file, the Scindees full of oaths and wonder as we passed through pretty groves of mimosa and laurel, with brilliantly coloured birds fluttering overhead, and when the pass widened at last there were little meadows of wild flowers, splendid woodland of pine and fir on the lower slopes, stands of the magnificent candelabra cactus, pink and white and crimson, and the surrounding peaks changed in the sunlight from orange to silver that looked like snow but was in fact white lichen – and all this in a country which would presently turn from fairyland into a burning desert of barren mountain and bottomless ravine where your way might lie through boulder-filled gullies or along winding cliff paths, or across a plateau as level as a billiard table with a drop of a thousand feet to left and right, and similar flat-topped bluffs rising like islands all the way to the horizon.

But I don't purpose to write a tourist guide, and if you want a vade mecum from Zoola to Magdala you must turn to Henty or that Yankee blowhard Henry Stanley. They'll tell you all about the scenery, and describe the army's labours in making their slow way from the coast up-country, building every yard of their road as they went, blasting away rocks and pounding 'em flat to make a highway for the columns of bullock-carts and mule trains and elephants and camels who hindered us as we pushed on through Senafe, a great supply station which had been Napier's head-quarters before he'd advanced to Attegrat a couple of weeks before our arrival – Speedicut's judgment of his whereabouts had not been far out. There were troops on the move all the way: I recognised the blue and silver of the 3rd Native Cavalry, the brown puggarees and cotton robes of the Punjabi Pioneers with their picks and shovels at the slope, and the celebrated coats of many colours of the motley crowd of border ruffians, Sikhs, Pathans, Punjabis, and the like, who composed the famous 10th Native Infantry. They looked as always like revellers at a fancy-dress ball, in red puggarees, green puggarees, violet caps, jackets and pantaloons of every shape and hue. A detachment of King's Own, swinging along in sober khaki, showed altogether drab by comparison, and as Speedy observed, the Baluch in their green coats and black pants, with their band playing "Highland Laddie", looked a sight more like British soldiers than our fellows did.

Well, God help you, Theodore, if this lot catches up with you, thinks I, reflecting that Napier must have had the time of his life choosing such a fine variety. There were Dragoon Guards swapping rum and baccy for chapattis with Bengal Lancers, pigtailed

Chinese railway gangers in plate hats giggling and waving to black-avised Cameronian sharpshooters who glowered in response as they filed grimly by, pieces at the trail, long lines of mules bearing the wheels and barrels of the 2000-yard mountain artillery and the tubes and rockets of the Naval Brigade, escorted by bluejackets with their cutlasses slung – twelve thousand horse, foot, and guns bound for the heart of darkness at a cost of £333 a man (each of whom had recently received a rise in pay of tuppence per diem). And all to rescue a handful of Britons from a savage prison at the back of beyond. Aye, those were the days.

We'd been three nights on the road and two days in the saddle when we reached Attegrat and learned that Napier was still up ahead awaiting the King of Tigre, who was said to have overcome his fears and was expected any day. This news had Speedy and Henty off at the gallop, one to do his diplomatic duty, t'other athirst for "copy". I was left to see the silver delivered to the paymaster, and to follow at my leisure. Another day a-horseback in the heat, but since no one knew if or when Napier would return to Attegrat, there was nothing else for it.

Attegrat's a shallow valley two miles across, and the tents of our main force, four to five thousand British and Indian troops, were strung out along the valley side, all mighty *klim-blim* and orderly compared to the Frog's knapsack of Zoola. Trust Napier; he'd always had an eye like a gimlet and a knack of being into everything. Not that he was a martinet, but it all had to be just so for him.

Being off station, he could hardly be blamed for the piece of disciplinary folly I saw on my way to the paymaster's tent. A native driver, bare to the waist and tied to a gun-wheel, was being flogged in a half-hearted way, and for once the off-duty loafers who'd assembled to watch the sport were encouraging the flogger to go easy and voicing sympathy for the floggee. It transpired that the unfortunate nigger had dared to shoot and wound an Ab robber who'd been trying to despoil him at pistol-point – and for this he'd been awarded a dozen lashes! Well, I'm all for a hearty flogging myself, but this seemed to be a poor excuse, and I learned from a disgusted paymaster that it had been ordered only because Krapf,

42

an idiot clergyman who'd attached himself to the expedition as an expert,[23] had convinced the Provost-Marshal, another idiot, that there would be a native uprising if the Abs weren't placated by having the driver whipped.

"Wait until the chief hears about this!" fumes my informant. "We're far too soft with these blasted savages, givin' in to the bastards every time, and a wretched *sidi* is thrashed for nothing! Well, I just hope that next time he *lets* himself be robbed, and bills that clown Krapf for the loss! Depend upon it, these damned people despise us as weaklings, and they'll become insolent to the point of fightin' us if we don't show who's master!"

I was glad to be shot of the silver, an uncomfortable responsibility when it was being carried by that troop of thieving blackguards; their reluctance to part with their saddle-bags was pitiful to see. In all modesty, I believe that their respect for "Bloody Lance" was what had stopped the villains from trying to filch the odd dollar. It was all tallied out on the paymaster's table, and since he'd been informed by signal that the rest was coming up, he made out a receipt to be handed over on its arrival. I haven't had it yet.

Napier was to meet his princely savage at a place called Mai Dehar, a short day's ride ahead, so with the Scindees as escort I set off after tiffin across the valley and past the collection of huts that makes up Attegrat village. There's a church and a ruined palace, but what takes the eye is the veritable Bluebeard's castle perched on an eminence high above the valley, a massive keep with four great turrets at each corner. A sinister sight even in broad day, grim and forbidding behind its curtain wall.

Our way wound through the hills into a desolation where we began to see all the signs of civil war and spoiling, with villages ruined and abandoned, burned huts, fallow fields, and hardly a living creature except at a distance. The villages still inhabited were all on rising ground, stoutly walled, and on every peak there was a stark adobe tower after the style of the one at Attegrat; some were a good fifty feet high and of five or six storey, built on the lips of precipices, crouched like vultures over the valleys below. A proper simile, for my havildar explained that these were the holds of robber barons who preyed on the countryside, and between them and the slave-raiding Gallas from the south the peasantry had a deuced thin time – it reminded him, he said cheerfully, of home, that blessed frontier where honest chaps lived by pillage and extortion, with only the interfering British Sirkar to mar the idyll. I pointed out that the Sirkar also paid the wages of him and his fellow-thieves when they took a holiday from crime, and he admitted that we had our uses.

We covered about twenty miles through that waste land, and lay overnight by the well serving the nearby village of Ad Abaga; the wells, being low-lying, are necessarily outside the walls of all the hill communities. I was thankful for my escort of bearded evil faces as we sat round our fire listening to the jackals and the occasional horrid heh-heh of a hyena while we watched the moon rise to silhouette another of those nightmare cliff-castles. I remarked on its ghastly look, and the Scindee havildar chuckled.

"The husoor has heard the story of that castle? No? Of the strange Lady of the Fortress who is seen by no one? The tale runs that she is the wife of a robber chief who is a prisoner of the King of Lasta –" he pointed to the distant mountains "– and that she has vowed that the sun shall not shine or the rain fall on her head until he is home again. Others believe she is under a spell, an enchantress bound by some great magician to dwell forever confined and solitary."

"A regular Lady of Shalott, eh? And what do the Scindees think?"

"Why, that she bribed the King of Lasta to kidnap her man so that she might beguile herself with lusty servitors!" cries he, and his ruffians chortled approval. I quoted Ilderim Khan's adage: "A Gilzai and a grandmother for scandal!" and they fairly hooted.

Our way next day lay through more broken country and tumbledown remains of raided villages, across a plateau so rough that it was late afternoon before we came up with Napier's pickets on the crest that overlooks Mai Dehar, a shallow valley cut across by a stream, where John Bull first came face to face with Prester John.

A momentous meeting and a splendid spectacle, by all accounts, with our stalwart ranks of King's Own, native cavalry and infantry, and artillery firing salutes from the near side of the stream, while

44

the Tigre army, four thousand strong, suddenly came into view on the far crest, drums thundering as they formed a vast half-moon formation with their monarch in its midst. I say "by all accounts" because I arrived too late to see it, and if you want the colourful details you must refer again to Henty and Stanley or any of the great rabble of correspondents who were on hand.[*]

They'll tell you how Napier rode to the meeting on an elephant, but had to get off because it scared the Tigre horses, and finally arrived in the royal presence on a charger, which he presented as a gift to King Kussai, along with a rifle, receiving in return a shield, spear, lion tippet, and a white mule. They spent the day in the King's tent confabbing, and when Kussai remarked that he didn't care for invaders, much, but would stretch a point if they were Christians, Napier replied diplomatically that he liked all Abs except those who imprisoned our people. Ah, says Kussai, you mean Theodore, an evil son-of-a-bitch who'll stand deposing, and I'm just the lad to replace him. Alas, says Napier, we ain't concerned with Ab politics, just our captives, which of course means we shan't help your competitors either. Can't say fairer than that, concedes Kussai, carry on through my dominions, give Theodore his gruel and leave the rival claimants to me.

That was the gist of it, but Henty and Co. will also hold you spellbound with descriptions of the barbaric splendour of the Tigre warriors in their velvet mantles, lion-mane robes, shirts all colours of the rainbow, bearing sickle-bladed swords, shields, lances, and a few muskets, their officers in flowing silk head-dresses, Bedouin style, with silver fillets round the forehead, and braided hair and beards. They'll comment on the noble bearing of young King Kussai in his red-fringed toga and gold gauntlets, mild in speech and manner and not the smartest despot between Cairo and the Cape, perhaps, but amiable to a degree, being in no doubt which side his bread was buttered.

The proceedings concluded with ceremonial inspections, Napier running the rule over the Tigre army, strapping fellows if primitively

[*] This meeting took place on February 25.

45

armed, and Kussai being treated to a display of foot drill and manoeuvres by our gallant lads; there were those who thought we'd have done better to show the Abs our Armstrong guns and rockets in action, by way of warning, for they seem to have come away from that first encounter convinced that while we'd be invincible on the plain, we'd be no match for their irregulars in the high country.

All this was over by the time we breasted the slope to the crest where the pickets were stationed, with the sun setting behind them, and here came a young subaltern of the 3rd Native Cavalry, mighty trim in his blue and silver, cantering downhill to meet us. He greeted me by name, explaining that he'd been on the q.v. all day, with instructions to bring me to Napier's tent as soon as I was sighted – which would have been flattering if I hadn't, as you know, been leery of generals who can't wait to see me. With good cause, for . . .

"I wonder, Sir Harry, if you'd be good enough to wear this?" says he, holding out a long hooded cloak of the kind the Heavies wore in those days. "And my *rissaldar* will look after your Scindees."

I looked from the cloak to him and his *rissaldar*, who was throwing me a salaam and calling my escort to attention, and the tiny doubt that had been stirring at the back of my mind since Speedy had rejoiced at my being "with" the expedition grew suddenly into a dreadful foreboding as he put the cloak into my reluctant hand.

"What the devil's this?" I demanded.

"If you would please keep it close about you," says he. "Sir Robert wishes your presence to be known to as few people as possible, especially the enem— that is, our Abyssinian friends. There are a number of them moving about our lines, you see . . . oh, perfectly cordial, merely curious –"

"And why the hell shouldn't they see me? I ain't in purdah!"

"Sir Robert thinks it best, sir." He was pink but firm, all of twenty but not to be over-awed even by the famous Flashy. "Indeed, he insists. So, if you wouldn't mind, sir . . . the hood will conceal your features, you see."

It was ridiculous – alarmingly so, but there was no use to protest. I threw the cloak round my shoulders, drew the hood forward, and followed over the crest and down the slope to our lines already lit by storm lanterns against the gathering dusk. Sure enough, there were tall Ab warriors, and womenfolk and children, moving among the tents, staring at our fellows and the *jawans** who'd plainly been put on their best behaviour, for they were calling greetings to the Abs, offering them seats by their fires, glad-eyeing the Shoho girls, and letting the *chicos* play with their equipment. My conductor led the way to a big marquee set apart, with a couple of Dragoons with drawn sabres at the fly, and the gigantic figure of Speedy between them, handing me down and ushering me inside.

"None o' the press gang saw him?" My escort assured him they hadn't. This was too much, and I said so.

"Of all the dam' nonsense! Henty's seen me, hasn't he? Why shouldn't the rest of 'em?"

"Henty's safe," says Speedy. "The rest ain't, least of all the confounded nosey-parker Stanley – you know him, the Chicago wallah.[24] He'd trumpet your arrival to the four winds!"

"And who'd give a mad clergyman's fart if he did? Why shouldn't he? Oh, the blazes with this! Where's Bob Napier, then? Or has he gone off the deep end too?" I flung off the cloak, and was about to give my disquiet full flow when I realised that my auditors – the escort, Speedy, and a bookish-looking Sapper captain – were glancing apprehensively at the far end of the tent – and there he was, the Bughunter in person, and even in my agitation my first thought was that if ever a played-out veteran needed a long furlough, he did. He'd always looked middling tired, with his down-turned brows and pouchy eyes and drowsy moustache, but now he was old, too, regarding me with a tolerant but weary smile as he rose from behind his table and came forward under the lamp.

"You must not mind Sir Harry's John Company manners, gentlemen," says he. "The first time I heard his voice he was

* Indian soldiers.

addressing a governor-general of India in the most cavalier terms. You remember the great diamond, twenty years ago, at Kussoor?"* And blessed if he wasn't bright-eyed with memory. "Give me your hand, old comrade, and welcome indeed, for I never was so pleased to see anyone, I can tell you!"

That was the moment when I knew, beyond all doubt, that the doom had come upon me yet again.

* See *Flashman and the Mountain of Light*.

If you've read *Tom Brown* you may remember a worthy called Crab Jones, of whom Hughes said that he was the coolest fish in Rugby, and if he were tumbled into the moon this minute he'd pick himself up without taking his hands out of his pockets. Bob Napier had always reminded me of Crab, in the Sikh War, the Mutiny, China, and along the frontier: the same sure, unhurried style, the quiet voice, the methodical calm that drove his more excitable subordinates wild. He was also the best engineer in the army, and the most successful commander of troops I ever knew.

He was nearing sixty in Abyssinia, and if he looked worn it was no wonder. We'd shared several campaigns, but he'd had the rougher passage every time, thanks to his talent for getting in harm's way – and out again, usually leaking blood. God knows how many wounds he'd taken; once, I recall, he'd had his field-glasses shot out of his hand, three bullet-holes in his coat, and a slug through his foot – he probably clicked his tongue and frowned that time. Not surprisingly, he was as often sick as well; he'd been in a shocking state, they say, when he licked Tantia Topi in the Mutiny, and according to Colin Campbell there had been "no twa pun o' him hingin' straight" when he'd planned the capture of Lucknow. (That means he wasn't at all well, by the way.) When he wasn't being all heroic, chasing Sikhs with elephant guns and hammering Pathans on the border, he'd laid half the canals and most of the roads in northern India, from Lahore to the Khyber, and built Darjeeling. Now, on the brink of retirement and pension, they'd handed him the poisoned chalice of Abyssinia . . . and here he was, welcoming me with that famous smile which everyone remembered, perhaps because it was so out of keeping with the stern, old-fashioned figurehead, asking about my doings, remarking how well I looked, inquiring after Elspeth (whom he'd never met), drumming up sandwiches and beer for my refreshment, observing again what luck it was my turning up like this, and how glad they were of the Maria Theresas.

Dashed unnerving, so much cordiality from a man who'd never been one of your hearties. In a generation of great captains like Campbell and Rose and Outram, such giants as the Lawrences and Nicholson and Havelock and Harry Smith, to say nothing of fighting madmen like Hope Grant and Rake Hodson, Napier had always been the modest, quiet man on the edge of the party, only occasionally showing a flash of sardonic humour, but always happy to escape to his work and his studies, music and painting and peering at rocks.*

Since he'd mentioned the dollars, I reminded him tactfully that I'd been homeward bound when I'd allowed Speedicut to press me into the service, and hinted politely that I'd be obliged for a warrant and a trifle of journey money to see me on my way again.

"See to that, Moore, if you please," says he to the Sapper, whom he introduced as his secretary and interpreter. "By the way, how many languages do you have, Moore? A dozen? How does that compare with your store . . . Sir Harry?" He'd been on the brink of calling me "Flashman", being my senior by ten years, and now a general; mere "Harry" would have been beyond him altogether these days, and I made a note not to address him by the old familiar "Bob".

I said I might scratch by in a dozen, but wasn't fluent in more than six.

"One of them being Arabic, I seem to remember," says Napier, which set me worrying. Why Arabic? He didn't enlarge, but dismissed Moore and my escort and settled back in his chair, motioning Speedy to take a seat by the table. "Well, this is quite splendid, Sir

* See Appendix II.

Harry. I gather from Vienna's message that you've been in Mexico lately. Political *indaba*,* was it?"

"Not exactly, sir. Foreign enlistment, you might say."

"I see. So you have no official position just now? On the retired list?" He nodded. "Well, Moore will have your warrant ready in the morning . . . if you want to use it immediately, that is." He glanced at Speedy, and Speedy, sitting there in his barbarous finery like the King of the Cannibal Islands, smiled ever so roguish, as though he were in on some jolly secret.

"I don't follow, sir . . . why shouldn't I use it?"

"No reason at all," says Napier, "except that, knowing your . . . your knack for adventurous service, shall I call it? . . . it had occurred to me that you might care to postpone your departure . . . in a good cause after your own heart?" He ended on a question, and Speedy chuckled, damn him, watching me with the idiot grin of one waiting to see a glad surprise sprung.

"It is an altogether unofficial thing, and indeed must be strictly secret." Napier sat forward, instinctively lowering his voice. "You are entirely strange in the country, Sir Harry, and care has been taken that no highland Abyssinian should lay eyes on you, and that your presence here is unknown to all but a few of our own people who can be relied upon. You see, there is a part to be played – a secret and, it may well be, a perilous part, and one that no other man in the Army could even attempt to play." He paused, his hooded eyes on mine. "A part on which the success or failure of the expedition may well depend." He paused again. "Shall I continue?"

At this point, when it was plain that some beastly folly was about to be unveiled, Inner Flashman would gladly have cried: "Not unless you wish to risk seeing a grown man burst into tears and run wailing into the Abyssinian night!" Outer Flashman, poor devil, could only sit sweating nonchalantly, going red in the face with funk and hoping that Napier might construe it as apoplectic rage at the prospect of having my travel arrangements upset. He took stricken silence for assent, and rose, beckoning me to an easel on which was a map of

* Affair, business (Swahili).

the country – a most odd map in that it had length but little breadth, like the one which I attach to this memoir, and was made up of several photographs glued together, something I had never seen before.

"You know what's to do – find Theodore and secure the release of the captives by whatever means. Here are we at Attegrat, and there is Theodore, with his army, on the road from Debra Tabor to Magdala. Between us lie three hundred miles of country which, as I've no doubt our croakers will have told you –" he gave an amused snort "– is an impassable wilderness of unclimbable peaks and bottomless chasms in which certain disaster awaits if our supply should fail, or hostile tribes bar our way or lay waste the country, or Theodore himself engages us with overwhelming force, or any one of a hundred difficulties arises to bring us to a standstill."

He paused to see how I was taking this, and gave one of his little tired sighs.

"Well, Sir Harry, I can tell you that with your silver to pay our way, we'll not fail of supply, if we move swiftly. The tribes . . ." he shrugged "are unpredictable and untrustworthy. Kussai of Tigre has thirty thousand warriors, and Menelek of Shoa and Gobayzy of Lasta each as many, but they will not trouble us unless we show signs of faltering or failure. Kussai offers us passage and assistance, and all three hope we shall depose Theodore. Then they will scramble for his throne."

"They're mortal scared of him," put in Speedy. "Menelek besieged Magdala last year, but thought better of it. He and Gobayzy are still in the field with their armies, willing to wound but afraid to strike." He scratched his beard thoughtfully. "Can't say I blame Gobayzy. He sent a message of defiance to Theodore last month, and Theodore gave his messenger the slow death – that's halfcutting off the limbs at knees and elbows, twisting 'em to seal the arteries, and leaving the victim for the wild beasts. I've seen it done," he added, no doubt seeking to cheer me up.

"Quite so," says Napier briskly. "It is of a piece with the atrocities he has been inflicting for years past on his southern provinces." He touched a spot on the map west of Magdala. "Gondar, where he has been repressing rebellion by wholesale slaughter, torturing tens of thousands to death, laying waste the countryside. Debra Tabor, which he has burned and whose inhabitants have suffered indescribable cruelties, crucifixions, mass burnings alive, and the like. He seems to have gone completely mad, for all Abyssinia is in a ferment against him, except for his army, and that is dwindling, we're told, through constant desertions. At the moment he is leading it back to Magdala, but slowly, because he is carrying his heavy guns and like us is having to build his road as he goes, no doubt with the labour of rebels enslaved in Gondar."

"He always likes to have a few political enemies to slaughter from time to time," says Speedy. "He'll execute 'em in hundreds along the way. Thank God our folk are in Magdala and spared that march! When I think of the torture and abuse they've suffered . . ." His huge hands clenched on the spear lying across his knees, and he growled deep in his throat. "One o' these days I'll have a word with his majesty on the treatment of white prisoners!"

Napier received this with polite interest before resuming. "In any event, he will reach Magdala before we do. He may make his stand there. I hope and believe he will. But if he doubts his ability to withstand a siege, he may retire into the southern wilderness, taking the captives with him –"

"Unless he's chopped 'em first!" grunts Speedy.

"That, too, is a possibility," says Napier quietly. "Or he may march to meet us, and we must be prepared to fight him in the passes, perhaps even without our artillery if our transport should prove too slow. That would be a hard thing, but if we must we shall abandon guns, baggage, tents, porters, auxiliaries, and all the rest, and meet him with rifle and bayonet and sixty rounds a man, as we did against the Hassemezeia in the Black Mountain. God willing, we shall have done with him before the June rains, but if not we shall march and fight through them. And at need we shall follow him to the Congo or the Cape."

They were the kind of words you'd expect to hear from a Brooke or a Custer, spoken with a heroic flourish and a fist on the table. Napier said them with all the fervour of a man reading a railway time-table . . . but I thought, farewell and adieu, Brother Theodore, your goose is cooked; this quiet old buffer with the dreary whiskers may not shout the odds, but what he says he will surely do. It remained to be seen what ghastly part he expected me to play in the doing. He touched the map again, drawing his finger in an arc south of Magdala.

"Whether he flees, or is driven southward after we defeat him, that is where his line of retreat must be cut off. And that can be done only with native help – no, not Gobayzy or Menelek, who are not only untrustworthy but would certainly regard a request for assistance as weakness on our part, and might even turn on us. We must enlist a people who are implacable enemies of Theodore but have no political interest in his fate or, for that matter, in Abyssinia, which they regard simply as a source of plunder and slaves. They are the Gallas, of whom you may have heard. Speedy, you have the floor."

"Thank'ee, Sir Robert," says Speedy, and stood up, possibly to assist thought, for he stood frowning a moment, scratching his beard with his spear. "The Gallas," says he. "Aye. You remember the Ghazis in Afghanistan, Sir Harry? Well, the Gallas are cut from the same cloth – ferocious, cruel, mad as bloody hatters!" He snapped his fingers. "No, I can give you a better comparison than the Ghazis – some fellows you know from the American West. Aye, the Gallas are the Apaches of Abyssinia! They seem to live only for raid and murder and abduction – the Lord alone knows how many youths and maidens they carry off each year and sell into Egypt and Arabia. You saw those burned villages and wasted fields on the way here? Those were Galla work. They are a monstrous crew, and as wicked and dangerous as any tribe in Africa. They loathe Theodore because they're Mohammedans – so far as they're anything – and he tried to Christianise 'em, mostly by fire and sword and massacre. He didn't succeed, but he captured their great *amba* at Magdala, and made it his capital just so that he could keep an eye on 'em. And they're waiting and praying for the day when they can tear him down!"

"And with our arrival they believe that day may be coming," says Napier, and Speedy, who'd been going like a camp-meeting preacher, took the hint and sat down. "And we must convince them that it is at hand. They fear Theodore, with good cause, and they will not move against him unless they are certain that we are determined on his overthrow and will not rest until he is dead or our prisoner."

So that was it. Flashy, ambassador extraordinary to a nation of bloodthirsty slave-traders, charged with the task of talking them into a war against a barbarian tyrant who was probably a good deal more civilised than they were themselves – that was what was about to be proposed, plain as print. Fortunately, it was impossible; there was something that Napier, in his eagerness to plunge me into the soup, had overlooked. Perhaps my relief showed in glad surprise which he misunderstood, for he nodded, with a glance at Speedy, who was gleaming in anticipation.

"I see you read my mind, Sir Harry," says Napier. "Yes, it is a task for you, and you alone. I said no other man in the Army could play the part required – for it is a part, and one that you have played before, when you entered Lahore disguised as an Afridi horse-coper, when you smuggled Kavanagh out of Lucknow, when you spent months as a *sowar* of native cavalry at Meerut before the Mutiny." He was smiling again, no doubt at my ruptured expression. "But your unique fitness for the work aside, I know it is the kind of service that you have always sought, and excelled at, which is why, I am not ashamed to say, I thanked Almighty God in my prayers when the telegraph told me it was you who was bringing the silver from Trieste."

It was no consolation to me that Speedy was regarding me with something like worship at this recital of my supposed heroics. Of all the godless suggestions! I tried to compose my features into the right expression of bewildered amused regret as I kicked his appalling proposal into touch.

"But, sir, you're forgetting something! Of course I'd do it like a shot, or any other useful work . . ." Safe enough, thinks I, fool that I was. ". . . but I don't speak Amharic, or any other local dialect, for that matter –"

"But you do speak Arabic!" cries Speedy. "That'll serve your turn. There's no lack of Arabic speakers up-country, especially among the Mohammedan Gallas, and Queen Masteeat is one of 'em."

"Queen who?"

"Masteeat, Queen o' the Wollo Gallas, the strongest – aye, and the most savage – tribe in the Galla confederacy. She's the lass who'll decide whether they march against Theodore or not. Win her over and we've won the Gallas, by the thousand!" He gave another of his booming laughs that set his barbaric ornaments shaking. "Mind you, it may be easier said than done. She's a remarkable lady, and I doubt if there's been a shrewder or more ruthless crowned female in this neck of the world since Cleopatra!"

"Yes, you did say she was formidable," murmurs Napier. "Indeed, she must be to hold sway over such people. And she is young, and a widow, is she not?" he went on, his eyes on the big moths fluttering round the lamp. "Personable?"

"What Galla girl isn't?" grins Speedy. "Masteeat means 'looking glass', so there you are. Not that she's a girl in years – fair, fat, and forty rather, a real stately Juno, but with a fine bright eye and a whale of an appetite . . . for her vittles, I mean, regular glutton –"

"To be sure," nods Napier. "What more?"

"Well, tell you the truth, Sir Robert, I was less interested in her looks than in getting out of her presence *ek dum* – when a playful tyrant with power of life and death starts to wonder whether a chap my size could tackle a full-grown lion with a knife . . . well, I'm glad to bid her good day!"

"Dear me. Why should she wonder any such thing?"

"Well, sir, she was three parts drunk at the time, but I reckon the real reason was feminine pique 'cos I'd declined a post in her service." He said it straight-faced, the great idiot; some fellows don't know a gift mare when she kicks 'em in the trinkets. "She'd ha' pitted me against one of her pet monsters if her chamberlain hadn't dissuaded her. Oh, she's a rum 'un, Queen Masteeat. Jolly enough foxed, but wilful and sharp as a sabre when sober, for all her languid airs. Why, for two years she's ruled the confederacy in despite of her elder sister Warkite, Queen of the Ambo Gallas, and there's a third claimant –"

"Thank you, Speedy," interrupted Napier. "Well . . . however wilful her majesty, she will hardly fail to respect a senior officer of a British army advancing on Magdala. What do you think, Sir Harry?"

Since Speedy had thrown my Arabic in my face I'd been listening to their exchanges with mounting alarm, and now I made for the only bolthole I could see, while playing up like an eager Dick Champion.

"Why, of course I'll go, sir, if you wish it – nothing I'd like better!" A ringing laugh followed by a rueful smile. "But . . . I hate to say it . . . surely Captain Speedy is far fitter for this work than I? He knows this queen, and speaks her first language, and knows the country and customs –"

"That is precisely what disqualifies him – every Abyssinian knows him, and secrecy is essential. Theodore's spies inform him of every move we make – but he must not know that I have sent an envoy to the Gallas." Napier spoke with solemn emphasis, tapping a finger. "He would surely set his agents to work to prevent their lending us aid. He might even encompass the death of Queen Masteeat – and your life would not be worth two *pice* if he knew of your mission. You will be deep in enemy country, remember. That is why you must put on native garb again, a harmless Asian traveller going about his affairs unsuspected."

You'll notice that what had begun as an invitation had become a cut-and-dried certainty in the mind of this abominable dotard. I'd be skulking behind enemy lines, figged out like Ali Baba, risking capture by a maniac who twisted his victims' limbs off, and playing travelling salesman to a demented bitch who thought it ever so jolly to throw visitors to the lions – and not a thing to be done about it except feign eagerness with a churning stomach and a grin of glad hurrah, as I sat sweating in that stifling tent with Napier regarding me like a prize pupil and the benighted buffoon Speedy clapping me on the shoulder.

Once again I was hoist with my undeserved reputation for derring-do, my fraudulent record of desperate service, and once again I couldn't refuse – not and keep my good name. Time was

I'd have wriggled and lied and gone to any length to escape from the coils of duty, but experience had taught me to recognise a hopeless case, and this was a beauty – for Napier was right: on the face of it, I *was* the only man. And I was too great a poltroon to face the disgrace and disgust and social and professional ruin if I shirked and slunk home . . . no, I hadn't the game for that.

So I did my damnedest to look like a greyhound in the slips, stiffening the sinews and imitating tigers – and damme if Napier wasn't regarding me with decidedly wry amusement.

"I see that I was right in supposing the mission to be one after your own heart. I wonder," he sounded almost jocular, "if it is perhaps rendered doubly attractive by the fact that it concerns a royal lady of . . . striking personality. You may not be aware, Speedy, that Sir Harry has great experience in that line. When he was employed as envoy extraordinary to the court of the Maharani of the Punjab he so far succeeded that her majesty proposed marriage. Or so Sir Henry Lawrence assured me. And I recall that on the Pekin expedition the army was consumed with jealousy of the favour shown to him by the Empress of China." He made a curious noise which I could only interpret as a roguish chuckle. "Really, my dear Sir Harry, you should consider giving a course of lectures at Sandhurst or Addiscombe on the subject of courtly address."

My, wasn't this free and easy chat, though? Could he be hinting at the unspoken thought, which had certainly been in the pious minds of Broadfoot and Elgin,[25] that I'd best secure royal co-operation by galloping her into what a Frenchman of my acquaintance called a condition of swoon? Surely not? They'd been worldly, wily politicals, but this was a grave, straight-laced senior of the old school who'd never dream . . . and then I remembered that this same Napier, with his antique whiskers and one foot in the grave, had recently married a spanking little filly of eighteen, which had plainly influenced his outlook on commerce with the fair sex; no wonder he looked as though he'd been fed through the mangle.[26] Yes, I knew what he was thinking, the randy old rake; well, I was in no mood to appreciate his lewd levity, if that's what it was. I said the reports of my diplomatic success had been greatly exaggerated, and that the Army had a deuce of an imagination.

"But, seriously, sir, are you sure I'm the best man for this?" Bursting with eagerness to go, you see, but voicing honest doubt. "I mean, it's too big a thing to risk failure, I can see that, and while I'd do my level best, well . . . It wouldn't do," I burst out, "if I let you down through ignorance or inexperience of the country –"

"My dear Sir Harry," says he, so moved by my manly modesty that he put a hand on my shoulder, "I know of no man less likely to fail, and none in whom I repose such trust," and that, with him looking noble and Speedy muttering "Hear, hear!" was my fate signed, sealed, and shoved down the drain, and I could only await my marching orders looking resolute and wondering how I might still slide out, God only knew how, along the way to the lair of this royal Medusa.

Napier lost no time, calling in Moore to make notes and taking me flat aback by saying I must set out that same night. "It is essential you be beyond the possibility of detection before dawn. You need not go far. The guide who is to escort you to Queen Masteeat lives only a few miles hence, and will afford you a roof to rest and prepare for your journey. And to let your beard start to grow," he added, "so that Khasim Tamwar may present a rather less European appearance."

"That's my nom de guerre, is it? Who am I?"

"An Indian subject of the Nizam of Hyderabad, whom you served as a diplomat in Syria and Arabia, now travelling to Galla to buy their famous horses for the Nizam's cavalry – the Gallas ride like centaurs, by the way. You will naturally present the Nizam's compliments to her majesty, and . . ." he raised a finger for emphasis ". . . *to her alone* will you reveal that you are a British officer and my envoy." He took a doubtful tug at his moustache. "For your own safety I wish you could remain Indian, but if she is to be persuaded to go to war your true identity may be essential. You agree, Speedy?"

"Let him be Sir Harry Flashman," grins Speedy. "Clean-shaven, if possible. I dare say that's what fetched the Empress of China."

Napier chose not to be amused. "It is no light thing he will be asking her to do. Her life and her people's lives depend upon it." He returned to the map. "I spoke of cutting off Theodore's retreat, and we may have to settle for that, but I am hoping for something more – a steel ring of Galla warriors round Magdala to prevent his even leaving it, to hold him there until we have forced our way through the passes. Then, if he refuses to surrender, we shall take the place by storm." He gave me his steady look. "That steel ring is what I want of Queen Masteeat. It will be for you to persuade her."

My innards set to partners at the prospect, but there was a question to be asked.

"If she's like any queen of my acquaintance, she'll have to be bought. Since you tell me Magdala was a Galla place, I guess she'll want it back. But what more?"

"The possession of Magdala is a political question, and no concern of ours. You may offer her fifty thousand dollars to invest the city. If she is unwilling to do more than harass Theodore's retreat, you will lower the payment at your discretion."

And if she threatens to feed my essentials to her lions, how discreet should I be then, eh? But I kept the thought to myself.

Napier sat silent a moment, then spoke slowly. "I'm sorry, Sir Harry, but that is all the brief I can give you. Speedy has shown us her character: shrewd, formidable, but capricious, by turns amiable and ruthless, and no doubt as cruel as such despots usually are. But her present situation and ambitions are hidden from us. That she is Theodore's mortal enemy is all we can tell with certainty. Yours is a task," says he, shaking his grizzled head, "which might tax a seasoned ambassador, but I know you will succeed as you have done in the past, and then," the old lined face lit up again with that brilliant smile, "you can do what no mere diplomat could do, by offering Queen Masteeat a soldierly skill far beyond her own commanders', to direct the investment of Magdala and, if she wills it, lead her troops into battle!"

She ain't going to get the chance to will it, you dear old optimist, thinks I, 'cos supposing I get the length of seeing and persuading her, the last thing I'll ask for is command of her rabble of bloodthirsty niggers. But of course I slapped my knee and stiffened the sinews some more, and Speedy swore that he envied me the trip. God help him, I've no doubt he meant it.

"With Theodore on the road from Debra Tabor to Magdala," says he, moving to the map, "it's my guess that Masteeat will be on the move herself, court, council, army and all, keeping an eye on his line of march. Her country lies south of Magdala, but unless I'm mistaken she'll have come west, somewhere along the Nile[27] – see, there – between the Bechelo and Lake Tana."

"How far are we from the Nile?" asks Napier.

"About three hundred miles, sir, but Sir Harry may have to skirt about. Still, riding steady and with not too many troubles en route, he should be there in a fortnight or thereabouts."

"This is February the twenty-fifth," muses Napier, "and God willing I shall have the army before Magdala by the end of March. You have four weeks, Sir Harry, in which to find Queen Masteeat, exercise your persuasive arts . . ." he said it with a dead straight face " . . . and bring her army to encircle Theodore." He pulled out a battered half-hunter. "It will be full dark soon, and the less time you lose, the better. We took the liberty," he went on calmly, "of counting on your help, and behind the screen yonder you will find the dress and accoutrements appropriate to Khasim Tamwar, diplomat and horse-coper of Hyderabad. You have every confidence in the guide, Speedy?"

"Absolute, sir. Uliba-Wark knows the Amhara country like a book, and just how to seek out Queen Masteeat. You couldn't wish for a better *jancada*,* Sir Harry, believe me."

"Excellent," says Napier. "I suggest we make them known to each other without delay." And as Speedy went out: "Meanwhile, Sir Harry, perhaps while you change you can reflect on any questions or observations you wish to put to me. Now, Moore, tomorrow's orders . . ."

The suddenness of it struck me dumb. I'd been slapped in the face before with commissions there was no avoiding, but always there had been a breathing space, of hours at least, in which to digest the thing, gather my scattered wits, fight down my dinner, and wonder how best to shirk my duty. But here, after the barest

---

* A guide and escort of unusual reliability (Hind.).

instruction, this cool old bastard was launching me to damnation with barely time to change my shirt – which was what I found myself doing a moment later in the screened corner of the tent, like a man in a nightmare, automatically donning the native clobber because there was nothing else for it, the *pyjamys* and tunic and doeskin boots (which fitted, for a wonder), winding the waist-sash and slinging the cloak, vowing I'd be damned if I'd wear a puggaree, they could find me a hood or Arabi *kafilyeh* . . . and now there was bustle beyond the screen, Napier had given over dictating and was demanding of Speedy if they'd been seen, and Speedy was reassuring him and turning to me with a triumphant grin as I emerged in my fancy dress . . . and stopped dead in my tracks.

"Your *jancada*, Sir Harry!" cries he. "Guide, philosopher, and friend, what? Uliba-Wark – Sir Harry Flashman!"

After the shocks of the past hour I should have been ready for anything, but this was the sharpest yet, and I realised from Speedy's eager look, and Napier's watchful eye, that they'd known it would be, and were on edge to see how I'd take it. Behind Speedy stood two tall Ab warriors, wrapped in their dark *shamas*,* but by his side was a woman such as I'd not seen yet in my brief stay in the country. The word that came into my mind was "gazelle", for she was tall and slender and carried herself with a grace that promised speed and sudden energy; her face was strong and handsome rather than beautiful, almond-shaped after the style of the Malagassy belles I remembered, with heavy chiselled lips and pale amber skin that shone with a cosmetic oil of some kind. Her blue-black hair was cut in a fringe low on the brow, with thick braids to her shoulders. She wore a long black cloak embroidered with shells, but when she turned towards me it fell open, and Moore the Sapper, who'd been staring at her like a boy in a toyshop, dam' near bit his pencil in two, for beneath she wore only a leather tunic which covered her like a second skin from bosom to thigh, exposing bare arms and shoulders and long splendid legs. Light buskins, sundry necklaces and bangles, and ladder-shaped gold earrings completed her

---

* Robe, not unlike a toga.

costume, and she carried a light spear, slim as a wand and needle-tipped.

She was appraising me in a quite unfeminine way, amiable enough but with a decided damn-you-me-lad air, and taking in that striking shape in its close-fitting leather I could have wished the pair of us far away in Arcady. You know me; every new one is the ideal woman, especially when there's that light in the eye that tells me we're two of a mind. What lay ahead might be as grim as ever, but there should be jolly compensations.

"*Salaam*, Uliba-Wark," says I, giving her my Flashy smile, open and comradely, and from her raised chin and lazy glance I knew I'd read her aright, and our fancy was mutual.

"*Salaam aleikum, farangi effendi*," says she, cool and formal, and Speedy added promptly, in English: "You may depend upon her for your life, Sir Harry. I have."

"And so shall I," says I, likewise in English. Speedy spoke to her in what I took to be Amharic, and Napier motioned me aside.

"There was so much for you to digest in so little time that we thought it best to keep the introduction of your escort to the last," says he. "Do I take it that you have no . . . reservations?"

"Because she's a woman? Lord, no! When I think of some of the ladies I've had to depend on, Sir Robert . . ." I could have smiled, thinking of Cassy the killing slave, or the Silk One sabre in hand, or Lakshmibai at the head of her riders, or black Aphrodite bashing Redskins with her brolly, or my own daft, dauntless Elspeth. "Well, I'd not have swapped 'em for any man – and this one will know her business, or I'm no judge. You don't hesitate to let her know my name, I notice."

"A measure of the trust Speedy reposes in her. And it would have been difficult – and indeed dangerous – to try to deceive her. She is," says he, frowning, "an unusual woman. Her husband, a petty chieftain, is at present a prisoner in the hands of King Gobayzy of Lasta, and the . . . lady, Madam Uliba-Wark, has let it be known that she will not set foot outside her citadel until he is restored to her –"

"So this is the Lady of Shalott?" I had to explain that I'd heard of her. "Well, she's outside it now, with a vengeance!"[28]

"Her husband's subjects are unaware of that. While she is away with you, they will suppose her secluded by her vow, which makes a convenient excuse for her absence from public view."

"You mean it was cooked up just for this? Phew! Speedy knows her of old, I gather . . . is she a political of ours?"

"Not quite that. She will be paid for this service, of course. Which reminds me, Moore has a purse of two hundred dollars for your expenses . . . Yes," says he, taking another tug at his face-furniture, hesitant-like, "another thing you should know is that, ah, Madam . . . Uliba is peculiarly qualified for this mission by being herself a Galla – indeed, she is the younger half-sister of the rival queens, Masteeat and Warkite, the child of a concubine, and so excluded from the throne. A position," he sounded almost apologetic, "which Speedy tells me she very much resents."

Well, he'd kept the best for the last, hadn't he? I began to see why I'd been instructed by careful stages, and why he'd interrupted Speedy a while ago, so that only now, at the eleventh hour, had the full mischief become plain – I was to be escorted, on my embassy to a queenly barbarian, by a jealous sibling who was no doubt itching to cut her big sister's throat and seize her throne . . . and didn't she look the part, too, a real Abyssinian Goneril with that handsome figurehead and arrogant tilt to her chin, toying with her little spear and knowing dam' well that everyone in the tent was eyeing her shape – by gad, it was all there, though. You can see I was distracted, what with the prospect of deadly danger, diplomatic complications, a possible attempted coup d'etat, a siege to arrange . . . and two weeks in the intimate company of as splendid a piece of bounce as I'd seen since . . . since that fat little bundle on the voyage to Trieste – not that Fraulein von Thingamabob could compare with this superb Amazon. I won't deny I'd rather have been squiring Elspeth to a Belgravia bunfight in safe, humdrum old England, but what the devil, when your fate's fixed, you make the best of it, and now that Napier was asking if there was anything more he could do for me, I did what I'd done so often, and put on a Flashy brag, the bravado of despair, I guess it is, the fraudster's instinct to play out the charade.

"I'd be obliged for a revolver and fifty rounds, sir. Oh, and a box of cheroots, if you have one to spare."

D'you know, he clapped his hands, and when I think back to that strange, fateful evening at Mai Dehar, my most vivid memory isn't of the bizarre commission they laid on me, or the pantomime figure of Speedy in his outlandish toggery, or even of those sleek polished limbs a-glow in the lamplight . . . no, what I remember is a tired, lined old face lit by a sudden brilliant smile.

"Come closer, into the firelight where I can see you," says Uliba-Wark. "If you are to be a horse-trader out of Hindustan you'd best look like one."

I shifted my seat before the fire until our faces were no more than a foot apart, and was pleasantly aware of smooth shoulders and well-filled tunic bodice, and the faint musky perfume of oiled skin as she leaned forward, black eyes intent. She put out a hand to feel my hair, which fortunately I was wearing long, and flicked at my whiskers with disdain.

"Those must go, and you'll let your hair grow and oil it with *ghi* in the Indian fashion." She ran a finger-tip through my moustache, cool as you please. "Less hair on your upper lip and no beard." So much for your notions, Napier. "You can speak the tongue of India, at need?"

"More than one of them, sultana," says I. "And better than my Arabic, for which you must forgive me. It is a long time since I was among the *badawi*."

"You speak it well enough," says she. "Why do you call me sultana? I am no queen."

"You look like one." It's a compliment I've found useful with barbarian ladies, and it made this one laugh with a curl of those enchanting lips that looked as though they'd been carved from purple marble.

"That has been said to me before," says she, "and surely you have said it to others." She sat back, folding her long legs beneath her, mocking me. "Well, Khasim Tamwar, for so I must think of you now, you are a very handsome rogue of a horse-trader with a tongue to match, and now that we've exchanged our compliments we can leave flirting for the moment and be serious."

Napier was right; she was unusual. Talking to her in my halting Arabic, and accustoming my ears to hers, so musically different in accent from the guttural desert speech, I found her a bewildering contradiction: she looked like a noble savage, a primitive from out yonder, but with a thoroughly worldly mind, unless I was much mistaken, and while she bore herself with the freedom and authority of a man, she was as conscious of her sex and how to use it as any coquette on the boulevards.

She'd charmed Napier, no question, which I'd have thought nigh impossible for a half-naked female savage toting a spear, but he'd referred to her, hesitantly, as "Madam" and inclined his head gallantly over her hand on parting. And he'd been ready to consign me, and the fate of my mission, to her without a qualm, apparently; you know how bare had been his instructions to me, and it was only at the last minute that he'd touched on the vital matter of how I should communicate with him after I'd reached Queen Masteeat. If all went well with her, no doubt she'd provide a messenger; if things went wrong . . . well, we'd just have to wait and see, what?

I doubt if I've ever been sent into the deep field with a more definite object and less instruction on how to attain it, but now that we were under way, sitting round a camp-fire a mile or so from Mai Dehar, I felt encouraged by the way Uliba-Wark had taken things in her stride: one moment I'd been wrapping the money-belt of two hundred dollars under my sash, being bidden God speed by Napier and having my hand mangled by Speedy – and the next we were out in the chill dark, her two Ab escorts hasting ahead up the hill, dim shadows disappearing over the crest behind the camp. She hadn't even motioned me to follow, just a glance to make sure I was keeping pace with her. In a moment we'd passed beyond the glow of the camp, and I'd lost her in the gloom until a slim hand closed on mine, leading me at a swift walk – and that guidance, steady and sure, had confirmed what I'd said to Napier: she knew her business.

She'd picked her way over the broken ground without a check, to this little hollow in the lee of a cliff where a fire burned, and the escorts were waiting with four picketed horses. They had food and drink ready on a wooden platter, and with only Napier's sandwiches inside me I was sharp set. There was a curried pasty which Uliba-Wark divided among the four of us, and some delicious little balls like the *bittebolle* they serve in Holland, only these weren't meat but, as I discovered on inquiry, powdered locusts bound with fat. It was too late by then, so I calmed my stomach with some of the liquor they call *tej*, which is a fermentation of honey and barley, guaranteed to put you under the table if you ain't careful, but capital in moderation.

As we ate I studied the escorts, and a formidable pair they were, tall, splendidly built, black as night but not negroid with their long heads and chins and straight noses. They bore the curved swords and spears common to all Ab warriors, and one had a short bow and quiver of darts, but their *shamas* carried the red border which marked them as of the better class, and one wore the silver gauntlets which I later discovered were emblems of knighthood. Even so, he spoke only when Uliba-Wark addressed him, in Amharic, replying with respect, and saluting her gravely when the meal was done and she sent them out of earshot so that she could make her appraisal of my appearance, as I've told you, and then discuss our next move.

"Presently we shall ride to my husband's citadel, which we must reach before dawn. We rest here only because there are things I should tell you without delay. First, if harm should befall, or we should be separated on our journey, you must ride straight for Lake Tana. It is two hundred miles from here, due south-west – you have a compass? Good. There you will follow the east bank of the lake as far as Baheerdar where the Abai* river leaves the lake. Wait there until I come or send word."

"Hold on – what should separate us? How many of us will there be?"

"The four of us . . . then only you and I. We are to be secret, remember?"

---

* The Blue Nile.

"Yes, I know, but . . . you spoke of harm. Is it likely . . . before we reach wherever Queen Masteeat is, I mean?"

If I sounded anxious, well, I was. It seemed to amuse her.

"Habesh is a perilous place at any time, and more so for me. They must have told you that Gobayzy of Lasta holds my husband prisoner – and he would gladly hold me also. His armed bands are in our way south, and I have other enemies . . . and some who would be friends, aye, closer friends than I would wish, eager to replace my absent lord." She was laughing, bigod. "Oh, I am not a safe companion, *farangi*! But I know the way to Queen Masteeat, and the *Basha Fallaka* could trust no one else. So . . . do you fear to travel with me?"

I do like saucy bitches, and they didn't come saucier than this one, lounging in the firelight which turned her naked limbs to gold, knowing precisely the effect she was having on me. And a moment ago she'd been telling me not to flirt. So I gave her my Flashiest leer.

"I might ask you the same question, sultana. I can be a danger-ous companion, too – especially for a defenceless female without a man to protect her. D'you miss your husband, by the way?"

The black eyes widened – and so did the lazy smile. "I do not miss him at all," murmurs she, with a little chuckle. "But do you truly think I am defenceless?"

One of the things that has always enchanted me about African women with an appetite is that they don't waste time before indulging it. Where their European sisters have to be jollied into the supine position, often over weeks like my fat fraulein, ladies of colour tend to make straight for the mutton – I think of Ranavalona of Madagascar who had me fornicating under water within a few minutes of our meeting, Black Aphrodite in the buffalo wallow, and dear Mrs Popplewell who couldn't wait to get the door shut, hardly. And here was this elegant barbarian giving an invitation if ever I heard one – and she'd even got her escorts out of the way.

"It depends who's attacking you," says I, and leaning close to her I took that voluptuous lower lip between both of mine, very gently at first, and then, as her mouth stirred, interested-like, my better nature asserted itself and I was about to apply the Flashman half-nelson (buttock in one hand, tit in t'other) when she drew her head back from mine, without undue haste, surveyed me calmly for a moment, then took my face between her hands, and kissed me lightly, with a touch of her tongue along my lips.

"What is the name of the place on Lake Tana where you are to wait for me?" she asked. "You have forgotten. A little dalliance, a wanton kiss, and it has gone from your mind like chaff in the wind –"

"Baheerdar," says I, "where the Abai river leaves the east bank of Lake Tana," and would have gone for her in earnest, but she burst out laughing and slid from my grasp, catching my wrists in hands surprisingly strong. "No, enough! This is not the place, or the occasion, and we have long miles to travel before dawn." To my astonishment she held out a hand, inviting me to shake it. "I should have known better than to doubt one who has the trust of the *Basha Fallaka* and the wise old soldier who smiles."

She was smiling herself now without mockery, and it's how I think of her still, the proud Ethiopian head with its laughing eyes, and the lovely oiled limbs shining in the firelight. "Perhaps we shall be dangerous for each other," says she. "But I think we shall travel well together."

I know when to let it be, so I accepted her handshake and asked if she had any further instructions for me. She thought for a moment, and the laughter went out of her eyes. "One thing more. I know you have been at war since before I was born, and are a seasoned soldier accustomed to command. But you do not know Habesh. I do, and on our journey my word must be law. If there is danger of a sudden, and I command, you obey at once, without question. Is it so?"

I knew from her look that she was half expecting an argument, so I didn't give her one, but nodded grave-faced and touched my brow in acknowledgment. "In your own words, Uliba-Wark . . . I think we shall travel well together." She liked that, as I meant she should.

It was close on midnight, and the chill of the late evening was turning to bitter cold as we made ready for the road. The two escorts had materialised from the dark without being summoned so far as I could see, and they saddled the horses and doused the fire. The knightly one spoke to Uliba in Amharic, pointing off into the dark, evidently suggesting a line of march. They conversed for a minute, she shook her head, and he gave a little shrug as though to say "Well, please yourself, but . . ." and signed to his mate to take the lead. So we left the little hollow, Uliba riding second, myself third, and the knight in the rear. It was slow going at first, in pitch darkness over uneven stony ground, but after an hour the moon rose, and Uliba had us moving at a steady canter.

It was the first time since arriving in Napier's camp that I'd had a decent spell for reflection, and by rights I should have had two foods for thought: one, how on earth I was going to keep a whole skin in the trials ahead, and two, a pleasant daydream in which I showed the imperious Madam Uliba that while she might command in emergencies, she'd take orders from Flashy when it came to thrashing the mattress. But I couldn't give proper attention to either, because as we rode through the still dark, frozen by the biting wind despite our cloaks, I felt a growing unease that I couldn't place. You might say my predicament was cause enough, but 'twasn't that; unknown danger ahead is one thing, but this was close and imminent, instinct telling me that out there, beyond the shadowy rocks outlined in the moonlight, there was an unseen menace keeping pace with us.

The knight riding rearguard felt it too. Twice he spurred out on the flank, and once approached Uliba-Wark, but got no change, seemingly, for he rode back past me shaking his head. Soon after I heard his hoof-beats cease, and saw he was sitting motionless, head turning as he listened for . . . what?

When a good scout shows wary, I have conniptions. I couldn't ask him what was up, so I galloped forward to Uliba and demanded what ailed him.

"He fears for my safety," says she, "and it makes an old woman of him."

71

"He don't look like a grandmama to me," says I. "And I ain't one either – but I know when I'm being dogged!"

"If there were enemies abroad they would have fallen on us before now, not when we are within two miles of the citadel!" scoffs she. "Besides, there is nothing to be seen or heard."

I might have quoted Kit Carson's wisdom that it's when you *don't* see or hear the bastards that they're waiting to drygulch you, but I didn't need to. At that very moment came the bark of a baboon out in the dark to our left, another bark sounded ahead, Uliba's head came up in alarm, the Ab who was riding point gave a blood-curdling scream, and the knight came tearing up from the rear, yelling in Amharic. Something told me he wasn't suggesting that this would be a capital spot for a picnic, and I didn't need Uliba's command to put my head down and my heels in and go like billy-be-damned. The leading Ab was toppling from his horse, and as I thundered past him he was floundering on the rocks, howling, with an arrow between his shoulders.

I slid down my screw's flank, hand on bridle, foot cocked over the saddle, Cheyenne fashion, and not before time, for above me shafts were buzzing like angry hornets, one smacked quivering into the saddle beside my leg, and here was Uliba alongside, crouched low and pointing ahead, and on my other side the knight was galloping full tilt, yelling at her, possibly "I told you so!" in Amharic. It occurred to me briefly that I was in the company of like minds, for neither of them had so much as checked to ask after the arrow-smitten Ab, who was still bawling the odds behind us. Ahead was a narrow gully, and as we swept into it the knight reined his horse back on its haunches and leaped down, sword in hand. He slipped his shield on to his left arm and yelled to Uliba, his teeth bared in a savage grin, shaking his sword in salute.

"On!" cries Uliba fiercely, and she must have been gratified by my prompt obedience. We raced up the gully knee to knee, and then it was down a rocky scree, with our beasts slithering and stumbling, and on to level ground, while faintly behind us the clash of steel mingled with yelling voices, one of them raised in what sounded like a war-cry.

She didn't check until we'd covered a good half-mile, and then turned to look back. The first dawn light was coming over the ground, but there was no sign of movement at the distant gully.

"Who are they?" I cried. "Not Theodore's people?"

She gave a little grimace of disgust, drawing the shell-embroidered cloak close about her. "No. One of my suitors and his jackals. They must have been lying in wait while another tracked us and signalled our approach. Sarafa was right, after all."

"Your escort . . . who stayed behind?"

She nodded. "He will hold them for a while. He is a very expert swordsman." Suddenly her voice was weary. "He will be glad to die for my sake."

Well, there's one born every minute, but old Colonel Tact muttered something about devotion and greater love and similar tarradiddle, only to be shocked by the most brutal valedictory I've ever heard in my life, and damned if she didn't brush away a tear as she snapped it out.

"He loved my body. And I loved his. And he is dying not for any love of me, but because he made oath to my husband to guard me with his life." She jerked her reins, wheeling her mount. "Come! Even Sarafa cannot hold them forever."

Her domestic arrangements were no concern of mine, but I confess I found it singular that her lover should give his life for an oath sworn to a husband for whom she'd said she didn't care two straws. Deep waters here, evidently, but of less immediate moment than the halloo which was breaking out behind us as a little cavalcade of riders came scrambling down the distant scree. Sarafa had plainly handed in his dixie, and we were off like the wind towards a rocky crest a mile away.

When we'd covered about half the distance I stole a look back and was relieved to see we were holding our own, and I was just demanding of Uliba how far it was to her citadel when I felt my horse stumble, and knew that she'd gone lame. Uliba let out a cry of dismay as the screw staggered, and even as I swung clear, landing on all fours, the thought was in my mind: will she ride on and leave me as she left Sarafa and the unfortunate arrow-fancier?

She didn't, wheeling and calling to me to mount behind her, which was dam' sporting and completely useless, since they'd have run us down in a couple of furlongs – they were coming on like the Heavy Brigade, yelling in triumph, half a dozen robed figures brandishing their lances, sure now of a capture and kill.

"Down, sultana!" cries I, drawing the pistol Napier had given me, and seeing what I was at she slipped from the saddle and down beside me as I took cover in a clump of rocks. I was hoping to God our pursuers had no firearms, but even if they had we'd no choice but to make a stand. It was a piece I'd never handled before, an American Joslyn .44 with five shots in the cylinder, any one guaranteed to stop a rhino in its tracks. My immediate aim was to stop a horse, for I'm no Hickok and knew that if I let them come near enough to shoot a rider, and missed him, they'd be all over us.

So I rested the long barrel on a rock, waited with my heart thumping, sighted on the foremost horse, took the pressure, and let fly at thirty yards. The beast went down like a stone, screaming, her rider flew head-first into a boulder and with any luck cracked his skull, and his mates hauled their wind with cries of alarm and sheered off out of range.

"Kill them!" Uliba was blazing with rage. "Shoot the swine! See there – the one with the lion scarf! That is Yando, Gobayzy's toad! Kill the bastard, I say! Kill him!"

"Not at this range," says I. "Keep a grip of that bridle, will you? We're going to need that screw!"

They didn't have firearms, fortunately, and seemed to be at a loss until their leader, Yando, sent forward a reluctant scout to see how their fallen companion had fared. The fellow came on in little runs from boulder to boulder, while I lay doggo, calming Uliba's demands that I blow him to damnation. When he reached the fallen body I tried a snap-shot which missed but struck splinters from a rock beside him; he scuttled off in panic, and they made no further sortie, but started shouting at us, and Uliba got to her feet and called back. From the spirited exchanges which ensued, in Amharic, between her and Yando, a burly brute with a hectoring manner, I gathered he was making an informal proposal which she was declining in grossly insulting terms, for from cajoling he passed to threatening and concluded in a veritable passion, jumping up and down, stamping, and hurling his fine lion robe to the ground. I decided to try a long shot at him, and missed again but winged one of his companions, to Uliba's delight.

That discouraged them, and presently they rode off, Yando shouting what sounded like a mixture of pleas and menaces.

"They will return," says Uliba. "Yando dare not go back to Gobayzy with a tale of failure. We shall have them round my citadel before night, so the sooner we are within the walls the better."

She rode her horse and I led my lame screw, and as we went I demanded and got an explanation of our recent stirring encounter. She gave it straight-faced matter-of-fact, as though it were an account of everyday social activities among the smart set – which I guess it was, Abyssinian style.

Her husband, she reminded me, was held prisoner by King Gobayzy of Lasta, who had lustful designs on her and had threatened to have hubby dismembered at length unless she placed herself at his majesty's disposal. This she had declined to do, so Gobayzy had ordered Yando, a local petty chief, to abduct her. But Yando too had designs on her, and these being troubled times, with Gobayzy at sporadic war with Theodore, had decided to take her for himself, possibly passing her on to Gobayzy later or fobbing him off with some fiction. Hence Yando's ambush, foiled by resourceful Flashy. Whether her husband remained whole and intact or not, she forgot to mention.

I could see now what she had meant by referring to her "suitors", and how right she'd been to describe herself as an unsafe travelling companion. Half Abyssinia seemed to be nuts on her, eager to abduct her, and happy to butcher her chance associates, such as myself – and this was the woman who was to guide me through hostile country and present me to her barmy half-sister whom she might well try to depose. By Gad, Speedy could pick 'em, couldn't he just?

In addition to which, she was the sort who abandoned lovers to their fate, and didn't seem to care if someone dissected the man she'd sworn to love, honour and obey . . . but then again, she had a lovely figure, and such legs as the faithful imagine on the houris of paradise.

And she was not without womanly sentiment. "God send that Sarafa died quickly in the fight," says she. "If he was taken alive Yando will give him a thousand deaths because he was my lover."

I said Yando might not be aware of that, and she looked at me in astonishment. "Why, Sarafa will taunt him with it!" cries she. "He will throw it in Yando's face!" She didn't add "Wouldn't you?" possibly because she thought the question superfluous.

Once over the ridge we came in sight of the citadel, and it didn't look any less sinister on second viewing, perched high on a rocky outcrop with a drop of hundreds of feet to the valley below. We reached it in half an hour, and I became aware that it was two towers joined together, six storeys high judging from the window spaces, the farther tower actually projecting out over the void beneath. It was a steep climb to the main door, and before we reached it the womenfolk of the tower were hurrying down to us, full of chatter and alarm, clamouring their questions at Uliba, but sparing a glance for the handsome stranger with the interesting whiskers. I'm not unused to female attention, as you know, but I don't recall more brazen preening and ogling than I got from Uliba-Wark's domestics. Plainly they were no strangers to the hayloft and the long grass.

One reason for their shameless glad-eyeing soon became apparent: Uliba-Wark's stronghold proved to be almost entirely devoid of men, the few there were being either grey-bearded dotards or small boys. Presumably the young ones were away at the civil wars, as conscripts or mercenaries, but I never found out, on account of not speaking the lingo. It's a damned bore, as you know, for you stand like a tailor's dummy while the world prattles about you, and worse for me, I think, because I'm used to slinging the bat* wherever I am.

They're mighty strange places, these Abyssinian castles, not

---

* Speak the language (Army slang, from Hind.).

unlike our Border peels, with rooms piled on each other like so many boxes connected by stairs that are no better than ladders. Since from what Uliba had said we might have to withstand a siege, I was relieved to find that the main door was a massive affair which it would have taken artillery to breach, and the adobe walls were feet thick, with narrow windows well above ground level, offering a good field of fire. With my Joslyn and fifty rounds I could give a warm reception to anyone toiling up the path to our eyrie.

If I'd had any doubts about Uliba-Wark's importance, they would have been dispelled by the respect amounting to reverence with which she was treated. They fairly grovelled to her, not only the slaves, who made up half the citadel's residents, but the free women and the two elderly men who seemed to act as stewards or chamberlains. She delivered a brisk speech to the assembled staff in the great ground-floor hall which seemed to be used as a common room, but what she said was Amharic to me, except at the point where she indicated me, and the whole gang turned in my direction and bowed. When she'd dismissed them I was conducted to an airy chamber on the third floor, bone clean and well if sparsely furnished with a good *charpoy*,* leather chair, table, wash-stand, rug on the floor and leather curtain on the arrow-slit window – I've stayed in country inns at home that were less decent and comfortable.

To my disappointment I was attended by the village idiot supervised by a stout dragon with a moustache who must have been the only Plain Jane in the place, for the dollymops who'd been on hand at our arrival had been typical Ab, which is to say they'd ranged from comely to ravishing. I wondered if Uliba had decided I'd be safer with a fat crone; if so, it wasn't a bad omen.

Not having had a wink of sleep since our bivouac at Ad Abaga the night before last, I slept the day through, and it was evening when I was summoned to a spacious apartment on the second floor and had my first taste of formal Ab dining. What is the norm, I can't say, because on later occasions I've lounged on cushions on

---

* Native frame-and-cord bedstead.

the floor, and sat up at a table like a Christian, but Chez Uliba we reclined on *charpoys*, Roman orgy fashion, with a low table apiece. But what lent the meal a delightful charm was that the girls waiting on us wore nothing but little aprons of leather laces – I think they had brass collars and a bracelet or two as well, but I can't say I took much note. You don't, when your *maise** is being poured by a lovely little Hebe who rests her bare poont on your shoulder as she stoops to your cup; how I resisted the temptation to turn my head and go munch, I cannot imagine.

If you suppose, by the way, that I am unduly susceptible, you should read the recollections of J. A. St John, Esq., who travelled in Abyssinia in the 1840s and appears to have spent most of his time goggling at boobies, on which he was obviously an authority. He has drooling descriptions of slave-girls, and a most scholarly passage in which he compares Ethiopian juggs to Egyptian ones, and finds the former "more finely shaped and better placed"; the negro bosom he discounts as having a tendency to droop, which suggests to me that he never got the length of Zululand or Dahomey where the ladies give glorious meaning to the term double-breasted. That by the way. I admire the female form myself, but J. A. St John needed a course of cold baths if you ask me.[29]

To resume. The meal consisted of two kinds of beef, the cooked variety which was roasted black with peppers, and the raw stuff which they call *brundo* – it's not bad at all when served with chutney, but I didn't try it at the time. There was fruit for dessert, and the inevitable *tej* dispensed from long-necked flasks by the bouncing boobies brigade, and all the sweeter for that.

The two chamberlain chaps shared our nuncheon, as did two of the females, tawny languid ladies who weren't domestics but more like companions to the mistress of the house, for they talked to her on equal terms, were well dressed and decked with costume jewellery, and plainly thought no small beer of themselves. But then all Ab women do, with cause; the waitresses, whom I spent the time admiring because Uliba didn't bother to translate the table talk

---

* Mead.

for my benefit, showed no embarrassment at being looked at, the saucy little dears. Uliba, by the way, had discarded her tunic in favour of an exquisite saffron robe which looked like silk, worn toga-fashion with one bare shoulder and two huge hooped golden earrings under her braids.

Just as the meal was ending there was a commotion in the room below, with female voices raised in anger, and presently one of the maids brought up the ladder-stair a girl who was the peachiest thing I'd seen so far, even in that company. She was tawnier than most, but with a long lovely Egyptian face and huge eyes which at the moment were disfigured by weeping. In fact, she seemed torn between grief and rage, sobbing into her cupped hands one moment, shaking her fists and raging the next, to the scandal of the women attendants and the wrath of the elders, all of whom contributed to the row, so that it was bedlam until Uliba snapped them into silence.

She spoke sharply to the weeping girl, who answered sullenly at first, then furiously, stamping and giving Uliba what sounded like dog's abuse, to which she responded with an icy anger which changed the beauty's tune altogether, for she flung herself down by Uliba's *charpoy*, wailing and smothering her feet with kisses. Uliba spoke to her quietly, and the wench rose, drying her eyes, but then suddenly rounded on *me* of all people, letting fly another stormy volley, at which Uliba lost her temper altogether, boxed her ears, and sent her squalling down the stair again. The ladies and elders withdrew, leaving the two of us alone while the pap-flashers cleared away the dishes.

I was all agog to know what had ailed the girl. Uliba was still snarling in Amharic as she disposed herself on her *charpoy* again, but then she began to laugh while her *tej* cup was refilled, and informed me that the hysteric had been Sarafa's woman, now presumably a widow, and consequently madder than a cut snake.

"I told her he had stayed to front Yando's fighters of his own free choice, and the insolent bitch swore that you should have stayed also, but she supposed that you had supplanted Sarafa in my bed, and so were precious to me!" She banged her cup down, angry and merry together. "Ha! And then, because it is not known whether

Sarafa is dead or taken, she falls to pleading with me to bargain with Yando for his life. *Bemouti*!* Well she knows what price I'd have to pay, and when I refuse her she calls me a heartless whore that stole her man and left him to die because I had found a new lover! And this from a slave-girl, to me!"

I agreed that discipline below stairs had gone to the devil these days. "So she wasn't Sarafa's wife, then, just his bit o' black velvet?"

"His concubine, once – as though that gave her the right to rail at me!" She soothed herself with a sip of *tej*. "I should have the little slut whipped! Or sold to the Egyptians!"

What struck me, of course, was that the grieving tart had assumed that I was Uliba's latest mount. Natural enough, perhaps, but it prompted a disquieting thought. What with all the to-do of ambush and flight, I'd given no thought to the part I was meant to be playing, and hadn't even had the chance to remove my whiskers or take the first steps in transforming myself into Khasim Tamwar.

"Does she know who I am – what I am? Do the rest of them, those two old files, or the women?"

"To them you are an Indian traveller. So I have told them, and why should they not believe it? They have never seen an Englishman before. It is when we go south, among the knowing folk, that your disguise must be complete."

"And when will we go?"

"Perhaps the day after tomorrow, if there is no sign of Yando. That will give time to change the hair on your face while we rest and prepare for the journey."

"Very good, sultana . . . Now, tell me, what precisely did you say to that noisy young woman when she accused me of being your lover?"

She regarded me with open amusement as she reclined on her *charpoy*, a very picture of sexual impudence in her silken robe with one shapely thigh and bare shoulder displayed, and if it hadn't been for the maids chirruping among the dishes at the end of the room I'd have made a plunge at her. To no avail, judging by her reply.

* By my death!

80

"Why, I told her the truth – that you were no lover of mine. The brazen wretch swore that I lied, and when I said I had known you but a few hours, and on horseback, too, she cried, 'Aye, but what of the future?' I said that was in God's hands, and she might sleep at my chamber door tonight if she wished, to be sure that no lover came creeping in to me."

"That was dam' considerate of you! But I tell you what, sultana, I've a notion worth two o' that – why don't she sleep at *my* chamber door, eh? Now, that would really convince her!"

She considered me for a long moment, the strong disdainful face impassive, and then a little imp began to play at the corner of the carved mouth and she swung her legs off the *charpoy* in one graceful movement and stood looking down at me.

"I told her the future was in God's hands," says she coolly. "It is also in mine." And with that she stooped, brushed her lips on mine, and walked swiftly away, leaving me to the shrill giggles of the maids and the reflection that she was a teasing, provoking, wanton baggage adept at stoking what old Arnold called the flames of lust . . . and giving me a gentle hint that the fire brigade would be along shortly.

And it was, as I'd expected. I know women, you see, and long experience had taught me that when they start playing Delilah it's a sure sign that they're coming to the boil themselves. So it came as no surprise, after I'd said my prayers (you may guess their content) and was drowsing in happy anticipation on the *charpoy* in my peaceful chamber, listening to the distant creaks and murmurs of the sleeping castle, and the occasional cry of some night beast out yonder, that a soft footfall should approach my room, and a gentle draught stir the air as the door opened and softly closed again.

But I'm a wary bird, and my hand was on the Joslyn beneath my pillow, only to let go as a tall figure advanced silently into the shaft of moonlight from the high narrow window – a figure in a robe of saffron silk which slid to the floor without a sound, revealing a splendid golden body swaying slowly towards me, slim hands clasped over her breasts and then falling away to caress her hips as she passed from the moonbeam into the shadow, kneeling on the *charpoy* and leaning down over me, her expert fingers and those wonderful lips questing across my body.

Ordinarily I'd have said "Good evening", or "Come in, my dear, it's your birthday", but she had insisted, you remember, that in moments of crisis she and she alone should take the lead, so what could a dutiful soldier do but lie to attention as she made a meal of me, teasing and fondling until I was fit to burst, at which point fortunately she began to conduct herself like some randy Roman empress in a rogering competition, bestriding me furiously with ecstatic cries, those unseen lips finding mine at last as she plunged and writhed in a perfect frenzy, grunting and gasping with an abandon which I shouldn't have thought her style at all, but you never can tell how they'll behave in the happy throes, and when she concluded her performance by throwing up her arms and screaming, I confess I entered into the spirit of the thing uninvited, going "brrr!" between her boobies as she collapsed whimpering on my ruined carcase.

"Uliba-Wark," says I, when I'd got my breath back, "from the moment we met I knew our love was fated, and I'm here to tell you you're the best ride I've had since I left home." For I like to give credit where it's due, you know.

I spoke in Arabic, and she replied in a distracted way in what sounded like Amharic, heaving herself up to full stretch above me, and for the first time her head was in the moonlight – the beautiful Egyptian head and shining black eyes of Sarafa's woman. She, too, was breathing with difficulty, smiling at me in a most ingratiating way and murmuring a question which I could only suppose was a plea for a high mark from the examiner.

Well, she'd earned it, eighty per cent at least, even if my immediate instinct had been to cry "Sold! Impostor!" But that would have been downright discourteous, after the little darling had exerted herself so splendidly, and I was too blissfully sated to tax myself with wondering why Uliba-Wark had put her up to it, or why, so soon after her hysterics of grief for Sarafa, his bint had been ready, nay eager, to pleasure herself groggy with your correspondent – on whom, I may say, she worked her wicked will twice more before daybreak, the naughty little glutton. Seeking consolation?

Obeying mistress's orders? Beglamoured by Flashy's whiskers? Who could tell?

A moment ago I said that I knew women . . . and I should have added that what I know is that there's no explaining 'em, or understanding 'em, or telling what they'll do next. If you're lucky enough to be bedded unexpected with a beauty like Sarafa's wench, you must just follow the wisdom imparted to me by an Oriental lady of my acquaintance, after she'd filled me with hasheesh and ridden me ruined: "Lick up the honey, stranger, and ask no questions."

So I didn't, rising late and greeting Uliba-Wark and her household with cheerful composure and not a word or sign to suggest that I'd spent half the night trollop-wrestling. That Sarafa's lass had been less discreet was plain from the reluctance of Uliba's ladies and elder statesmen to meet not only my eye but my presence, and the shameless giggling and whispering of the Bosom Brigade when they served me breakfast. I confess I'd hoped that Uliba herself might have her curiosity piqued by my nonchalance, but if it was, she didn't show it. Her first words to me were that Yando and his gang hadn't put in an appearance, so we should be able to set off south next day.

"But he may be about still, on the watch, so we shall ride out before dawn. There will only be the two of us, remember, without Sarafa and his man to scout, so we must go warily and quickly. Come, I'll show you the way we must follow in the dark."

The vantage point was the top of the far tower overhanging the valley, which we reached up various ladder-stairs, and a pretty picture she made climbing nimbly in her little leather tunic, with Flashy panting wearily in her wake. I was breathless by the time we reached the roof, despite a brief rest while I studied a peculiar contraption in the top chamber: a massive hook dangling in the middle of the room from a rope which ran over a great wheel in the ceiling to a windlass near the wall. Most sinister it looked, but when I asked Uliba about it she said simply, "That is the dungeon," and directed my attention to the astonishing panorama before us.

South in the misty distance towered the huge silver peaks of the Ab highlands, beyond a vast rocky plateau criss-crossed by forested strips and ravines. Immediately below us, at a depth so dizzy that I automatically kept a hold on the parapet, lay the valley floor, a boulder-strewn river-bottom along which a thin thread of silver indicated the stream which flowed out of a jungly cleft ten miles away.

"That is our road, along the river to the woods," says Uliba. "Once under cover of the trees we shall be safe from pursuit. If we should be parted in the dark, we shall rendezvous by the white rocks yonder, where the river emerges. If I don't arrive in twelve hours . . ." she pointed to the mountains ". . . Lake Tana lies beyond the ranges. You remember the names of the river and village? And the compass bearing? You are sure? Good . . . Well, since I see that you are more intent on staring foolishly at me than in studying the road on which your life depends, I suggest that we go down, and you can use the rest of the day changing yourself from a moon-struck *farangi* soldier into an Indian traveller with his wits about him. Come."

She said it with a smile, ever so pleasantly, and she looked so delectable in that shiny leather corset of which I had been mentally stripping her, that I thought, oh, what the devil, the blazes with pretences, let's have the cards on the table.

"Hold on," says I, and took her gently by the arm as she moved past me. She turned in mild surprise, and I'll swear she expected lustful assault then and there, so I stared into those proud fearless eyes for a long moment, and then said: "You have the damnedest way of punishing insolent slave-girls, haven't you?"

A split second's bewilderment, and then delight that I'd been first to mention it. "Punishment? You think that was why I sent Malee to you?" She started to laugh. "I do not believe it! You have far too brave an opinion of yourself to think you could be a penance to any woman! Punishment, indeed!"

"Well, thank'ee ma'am, but you did speak of whipping or selling her, you know."

"Oh, fool's talk! What, whip or sell Malee, who was my play-mate? Who prepared my bridal bed? Who would give her life for me, even as Sarafa did? I owe her too much kindness and friendship for that!"

"So much kindness that you stole her lover?"

"What has that to do with anything? I took him because he pleased me – and since my own husband dallied with Malee when he'd tired of me, why should I not enjoy Sarafa?"

A fair question, which had me stumped. It was being borne in on me that the moral climate of Abyssinia was not quite that of our own polite society – not that Uliba's Belgravian sisters are averse to a cut off the joint from time to time, but they know enough to keep quiet about it. But I was still well in the dark.

"You say she's your old playmate, bosom pal, God knows what – yet she harangues you like a fishwife in public, calls you a heartless whore, and you box her ears –"

"We have been calling each other that and worse since we were ten years old and rivals for the same schoolboy!" cries she, laughing. "Not that I could ever rival Malee! Is she not lovely? You seem to have found her so, from what she tells me," she added, with a sniff in her voice. "The little slut could hardly keep her eyes open."

"Well, now you know what you missed," says I. "Sending me a proxy-doxy in your own dress to fool me in the dark! Is that some kind of Abyssinian insult?"

"First a punishment, now an insult!" cries she gleefully. "No, *effendi*, merely a whim, a little trick, a jest to remind the great *farangi* soldier that the wild barbarian woman will do what she will do in her own good time . . . not his." The carved lips were pouting impudently, and suddenly laughing before I could deal with 'em. "But if it will soothe your manly pride, know that I sent Malee to you at her own request . . . no, truly, when she had cried out her tantrum, and implored my forgiveness, as she always does, she begged me. Why? Because she believes that you are my new fancy, and whatever I have, why, Malee must have, too. And she's a lecherous strumpet, as you've no doubt discovered, with the appetite of a rutting baboon. So I indulge her." She arched her brows, playful-like. "Am I not a kind mistress to my bondwomen?"

"Perhaps too kind, sultana. Oh, I ain't complaining . . . but I'll tell you something about slaves: however devoted and loving and like bloody spaniels they seem, they never forgive their owners for owning 'em." They don't, either, though what prompted me to say it just then, I don't know, unless I was just mentally marking time while debating whether to kiss her before I wrenched off that scanty tunic, or after. But I debated too long, and she was off with a laughing dismissal of my caution, and down the ladder-stair before I could get to work.

I spent the day imagining Khasim Tamwar, which is the key to disguise. You must "catch the man" if you're to impersonate him faithfully, as I'd learned to do in the past with Crown Prince Carl Gustaf (dignified royal duffer) and Makarram Khan (truculent Pathan ruffian) and my military self (bluff mutton-headed hero), to name but a few. I decided Khasim would be a bit of a languid exquisite, and carefully shaved my splendid moustache to a mere line along the upper lip, got rid of my whiskers, and spent time oiling and curling myself a lovelock with a hot iron – frontier style rather than Hyderabadi, but no one in Abyssinia would know the difference. I'd grow a little imperial, too, and remember to point my toes as I walked, which ain't difficult for a cavalryman.

Finally I boned a length of silk off my room dragon to improvise a tight turban, and having spruced up my boots, *pyjamys* and sash, stood forth for Uliba's inspection. "Oho!" says she, mighty droll, "is it the Indian horse-trader or the Prince of the Seventh Sea-Coast? My ladies must see this wonder – and Malee, too!"

"Half a tick," says I. "They know me as Khasim Tamwar, but what tale are you telling 'em to explain our going south together?"

"What is to explain if I make a pleasure journey to the Sea of Tana with a handsome stranger? Let their imaginations work!" Which they did, judging by their slantendicular looks and the smirks of the booby-sporters, but Malee wasn't to be seen. Fagged out, no doubt.

In the evening Uliba took me to a little room off the stables where we packed our bags for the trip – spare clobber of *shamas* and boots and waterproof cloaks, blankets and utensils, biltong and bread and *teff**-cakes, flasks of *maise* and *tej*, cheese and dried fruit

* Millet.

87

and locust-balls, God help me. We split my two hundred dollars between us, at my suggestion since she'd have to do the buying of necessities along the way, and in addition to my Joslyn and cartridge-belt I had a dagger and sword from the citadel's armoury – not one of their sickle-blades but a straight cross-hilted weapon with *Deus vult* engraved on the blade – a Crusader sword, bigod, and why not, for if it was seven hundred years out of date it was still in Christian land.

It took us until supper-time to complete our packages, and to see that all was well in the stables, where she had picked out two fine Arab mares and a led-animal. Afterwards we retired early, since we were to be up by three and away by four, bidding each other a decorous good night in which I kept my hands to myself with difficulty, for while Malee had taken some of the edge off my carnal appetite, Uliba's leather-clad bounties were a quivering temptation. Still, I knew it wouldn't be long before the mistress decided she'd like a share of the jollification of which the maid had apparently spoken so highly, and on that consoling thought I fell asleep.

When I woke it took a moment to identify the noise that had disturbed me. Judging by the moonlight it must be past midnight; there was nothing out of the way in the sounds of the sleeping castle – and then I heard it, a faint whisper beyond my door, low and urgent. For an instant I wondered if it could be Uliba, but the language was recognisably Amharic, and I caught one of the few words I knew – "*tenisu*", which means "get up". It was a woman's voice; could it be Malee after another nightcap, but if so why hadn't she just breezed in as before? There it came again; with a soft chuckle, I called to enter, without result, so I hopped out and opened the door, and sure enough, Malee it was, eyes wild in the light of the lamp she carried, and as she stepped back swiftly from the threshold I turned and hurled myself towards my *charpoy*, grabbing for the Joslyn under the pillow.

Another split second and I'd have had it, but the men who'd been waiting with her were too quick. Even as my hand touched the butt, one of them landed on my back, wiry hands seizing my neck, while the other grabbed my wrist and snatched up the pistol with a yell of triumph. He covered me, his mate rolled off me, and as I came off the *charpoy* there was a shouted order from the doorway, and here was a hulking brute with a breastplate over his *shama* whom I recognised in horror as Yando, and Malee beside him squealing with excitement.

I know when I'm cornered, and I put up my hands. Yando let out a bellow of laughter, and the chap with my Joslyn shoved it into my ribs, shouting words which needed no translation as he urged me towards the door and down the ladder-stairs to the hall on the lower floor. His pal went first, menacing me with a spear as I came down while the pistoleer followed; Yando and Malee came last, she chattering like a parakeet and he roaring to his minions, no doubt to keep a tight grip on me.

The place was in uproar, women having hysterics, bare tits bouncing in alarm, elders dithering, and Uliba, teeth bared in fury, a stalwart Ab spearman at her side, two more with sickle-swords menacing the wailing crowd.

What had happened, if not why, was clear: my instinct about mistrusting slaves had been sound, and Malee had admitted Yando and his gang. This was confirmed by the demeanour of all parties. I couldn't understand a word, but there was no mistaking the gleeful triumph of Malee's tirade at Uliba, or Uliba's snarling rage as she made for Malee, who took refuge behind Yando. The Ab guarding Uliba wrestled her back, Yando addressed her at the top of his voice in gloating amusement, she blazed back at him, the women's hysterics increased with bosoms heaving to admiration, and I decided to put in my ha'porth with my best parade-ground roar.

"*Chubbarao!*" They stopped yelling. "Uliba-Wark, tell them who I am!"

It was common sense: whatever Yando might have done to an anonymous stranger within Uliba's gates, he'd not dare misuse an envoy from the British army now invading his country. And if the revelation jeopardised my ridiculous mission to the Galla queen, so much the better.

"Tell him!" I repeated, in Arabic, and from the look he turned on Uliba I knew he didn't understand a word. "He won't dare harm us if he knows who I am! You'll be safe, too!"

She looked at me without a word and then let fly a volley at Yando – and God alone knows what she said, but it drove him into a violent fury: he absolutely grabbed her by the shoulders, bawling into her face. They raged at each other until he thrust her away and turned to my captors, an outflung hand pointing at me, his pug face contorted with bestial anger, and before I knew it I was being thrust aloft again, the pistol wallah jabbing me with my own barrel, and the spearman offering assistance.

I went, but not quietly, you may be sure, damning their eyes for villains and swearing vows of revenge, in English, Arabic, and Hindi, to no avail whatever. They forced me up into the room which Uliba had described as "the dungeon", and here came Yando and another of his thugs bringing up the rear. He snapped an order, grinning malevolently, and I was flung down and bound wrist and ankle by two of the brutes while the third began to drag something from the shadows in a corner of the room.

Light was beginning to filter through the high windows, glinting on the hook dangling by a stout rope from its pulley, and terror gripped me as Yando, shouting with laughter, took hold of it, and I saw that what the third man was dragging forward was a frame shaped like an iron maiden, but made of metal strips, not unlike the irons in which they used to enclose hanged felons. It was hinged at one side, and as Yando threw it open my captors hoisted me up and thrust me into it. Yando snapped it closed, bolting it with a large pin attached to an immensely long fine steel chain which he held coiled in his hand. They lifted me parallel to the floor, hanging me on the hook by a loop on the back of the frame, so that I swung face down.

That was when I began to scream in earnest, struggling helpless in that ghastly cage, staring through its slender bars at the floor boards three feet below. Then Yando tugged on the coiled chain, withdrawing the pin so that the frame fell suddenly open, and I came crashing to the floor and lay half stunned.

D'ye know, in that moment I was a miserable Rugby fag again, being tossed in a blanket by the evil swine Bully Dawson, whose delight it was to heave us aloft and then pull the blanket aside so that we came down smash. I'd squealed for mercy then, but my pleas were nothing to the howls I put up now as they lifted me, thrusting me back into the dangling contraption, snapping it shut about me. Yando replaced the pin which held it closed, and they set me swinging again.

I still couldn't see what they intended, except that it must be something hellish, but now Yando was leering at me through the bars, jabbering in Amharic as I wailed to be let alone, please, oh please, I'd done nothing, and I was a British officer, oh Jesus help me – and then they flung back a great trapdoor in the floor directly under me, and I shrieked myself hoarse as I writhed vainly in that hideous steel coffin, staring at the unbelievable horror revealed beneath the floor of the chamber, which overhung the cliff-top on which the tower was perched.

A blast of icy air smote me as the trap crashed open. Mist was wreathing below, partly concealing the gaping void and the cliff-face which I knew dropped sheer for thousands of feet – and Yando was flourishing the steel chain, displaying its great length and taunting me in Amharic as he showed in mime how he could draw the pin free at a distance, dropping me to hideous death. In my panic even my voice failed me; I could only mouth silently at that dreadful face, so close that I could catch the foulness of his breath – and to this day I can still see the pores in his disgusting black snout.

He shouted an order, and two of his minions were at the wheel controlling the hook. There was a sudden clank, and as I fell abruptly a few inches with a sickening jolt, I found my voice again, screaming my head off as I was lowered with the steady clanking of that vile machine to the level of the trap, and then through it into the biting wind and swirling mist, knowing that the fine chain which could jerk free the pin was paying out above, its end in the hand of that fiend gloating down at me. The lowering stopped with a jar and a last distant clank, and I was hanging in my imprisoning cage, ten feet beneath the floor, staring down into eternity.

Or so it seemed. In my catalogue of terrors, heights come second only to physical torture, and I have nightmares still in which I'm toppling after de Gautet into the boiling depths of the Jotunschlucht, or being hurled down to the death-pits of Ambohipotsey, or dangling ballock-naked beneath that balcony in Lahore. But nothing can compare to the crotch-tightening horror of seeing, through the blowing mist, the limitless depth beneath me, down that cliff-face now clearly visible dwindling away to the jagged pinnacles of rock rising from its base, and beyond them the valley floor to which that bastard Yando could send me hurtling with one twitch of his hand, down and down and down, falling, falling, falling for an eternity through half a mile of freezing nothing with the shrill wind drowning my dying scream until life ended in shattering bloody impact far below.

I wonder I didn't go mad, waiting for the moment when I'd be launched into emptiness. What devilish cruelty had devised this lingering horror, and what subterranean "dungeon" offered less hope of escape or could provide a more awful tomb? I daren't even struggle, for fear of jolting loose the pin, sobbing feebly as I swung slowly to and fro, a helpless human pendulum . . . oh merciful God, was it possible the ghastly moment of release would never come, and I'd be left to hang until I starved or perished of freezing cold or did go mad at the last?

D'you know what saved me from gibbering lunacy? The anguish of cold and the bite of steel bars into my flesh may have helped, but I believe it was pure funk that made me lose consciousness, sinking into an oblivion in which pain and fear and misery and hopelessness merged into a kind of trance in which they ceased to have meaning. Or perhaps, as confounded Dick Burton suggested when I described my ordeal to him, I simply fell asleep. That, he opined, would have been the thing to do. Damned idiot had no imagination whatever.

Trance, coma, sleep, or delirium, it lasted for hours, for when I came to, in agony from the constriction of my bonds and the bite of the bars into my almost paralysed limbs, the wind had dropped and the cold somewhat abated; if it hadn't I'd ha' been dead. There was sunlight bathing the cliff, I remember, and then I must have swooned again, for when I regained consciousness for the second time the sun had gone, and it was early evening, although I'd no notion of this at the time.

Now, I've described as best I can what it's like to be hung over the edge of the world, spider-fashion at the end of a thread (except that he can climb up and you can't), but when all's said and done, even the most hellish ordeal ends, in death or survival. Mine finished with a distant clank which meant nothing to me; I heard it, but didn't understand it, or what was happening as I was drawn slowly upward through the trap and into the "dungeon" again.

Other things I remember: the crash of the trap closing; the steel frame being opened and strong hands lowering me on to a soft bed; my limbs being chafed and rubbed with warm oil; the sting of *tej* in my mouth and throat; voices in Amharic . . . and then, through a lamplit haze, Uliba-Wark looking down at me, the handsome face tense with concern, the fine eyes troubled – and that, I can tell you, was a happy sight to waken to. She was kneeling by the mattress on which I lay, still in that beastly "dungeon", but with the trap safely closed. Above her stood a tall, fine-looking fellow of about my age, dressed in princely fashion with not only a red-fringed *shama* and knight's gauntlets, but a silver coronet in his braided hair, with little horns, and metal tails trailing to his shoulders.

I must have been still fairly lost, for all I remember after that is being covered with a blanket, and soft heavy lips kissing my brow, and then drifting into sleep undisturbed by visions of bottomless chasms. It's a great advantage of cowardice that escape from peril elates you beyond terrified reaction; that comes later, when you think back, and is best treated by liberal applications of booze.

I didn't stir for above twelve hours, and woke to find myself in the same spot, aching damnably in every joint, with weals on my torso from the pressure of those damned steel strips, but in my right mind, full of beans, ready for grub and for Uliba-Wark.

She came as I was contemplating a loving squeeze at either of the barely clad damsels who were massaging my tired limbs, or the third who was removing the remnants of my breakfast; fortunately, perhaps, contemplation was as far as I got, for she came briskly in, sent the wenches scampering with a sharp word, looked at me carefully, took my face in her hands and kissed me in excellent style, but withdrew when I became familiar, and seated herself at the foot of my mattress. My breakfast lass had left a flask of *tej*, and Uliba filled two cups. "Listen," says she, so I did, and was treated to a tale fit for the wildest of penny dreadfuls – but true, as the wildest tales often are, in my experience.

As I'd guessed, Malee (whose eccentric behaviour we'll discuss presently) had been the traitress within the gates, somehow getting word out to Yando, who'd been on the lurk nearby, and unbarring the gate for him and his gang in the small hours. They'd overrun the garrison of bints and dodderers without difficulty, and Yando, whose style I couldn't but admire, had offered Uliba a stark choice: give Yando his jollies or it would be the long drop for Flashy.

"That godless bitch Malee, that deceitful snake, had told him you were dear to me!" She spat out the words as though they were red-hot. "Oh, let her come within reach of my hand, and I'll make the lying harlot pray for death! As for Yando . . ." I waited agog for sensational details, for since I was here safe and sound I must suppose that she'd submitted to his beastly passion for my sake, the plucky little woman. But she was vague, hinting that she'd managed to temporise while some of her folk, who'd fled after Yando's invasion, had run for help to an *amba* a few miles away.

Its owner was yet another of her admirers (of whom I must say there seemed to be an inexhaustible supply), a civilised and genteel one for a change, named Daoud. He had lost no time in bringing a troop of riders to the rescue, capturing Yando and slaughtering most of his followers. Malee had wisely made herself scarce, and Flashy had been wound up and revived.

Whether Daoud and Co. had arrived in time to save Uliba from a fate which most ladies of my acquaintance regard as infinitely preferable to death, I still ain't sure, but from her subsequent behaviour I rather think they didn't, and he had his wicked will of her. But you'll judge for yourselves.

Another mystery which I still can't fathom is Malee. Her rage at Uliba's desertion of Sarafa I can understand, and her later pretended

94

repentance and reconciliation with her mistress while preparing to betray her. But deciding along the way to pass the night romping with the lodger don't quite fit, somehow. I'm as immodest as the next man, but it seemed odd, and still does. Not to Uliba.

"I told you, anything I have, she must have also. She believed you were my lover; that was enough." She shrugged. "Besides, she needs men as a drunkard needs *tej*. But she is no matter. Yando is." She stood up, pacing across the chamber while I took happy stock of the proud Ethiopian profile with its heavy braids, and the elegant shape in the ridiculously scanty tunic. She turned to regard me gravely.

"He knows who you are. I was a fool not to realise that he has been watching this *amba* for a week past, hoping to surprise me. He saw me leave three nights ago to visit Napier *effendi*'s camp, where you and I met. He saw me leave again with you, and knew you must be a British soldier – what else could you be?" She gritted her teeth in self-reproach. "And I am reputed shrewd! I, the woman of excellent head, forgot that there are no spies like the spies of Habesh!"

"What of it? It don't matter two straws to Yando that I'm British! He chased us here to get *you*, not me, and however sharp he and his spies are, he can have no notion why I'm here, or what for . . . why, Malee told him I was your lover! Well, there you are! Why should he suspect that I'm an envoy, going south to –"

"What he may suspect matters nothing!" cries she. "What matters is that he *knew* three days ago you were British, so did his men, and two of them escaped us! So how long, think you, will it be before the news reaches Theodore, who has an eye at every window and an ear at every door?" She came to kneel by the mattress, face and voice urgent.

"What says Theodore, then? He says, 'Here is a British army advancing against me. Here is a British officer riding by night with Uliba-Wark, half-sister of Queen Masteeat of Wollo Galla. What can this mean? Can it be that the English general is sending an envoy to enlist the aid of my enemies against me?'" She broke off impatiently. "That much a child could guess, and Theodore is no child!"

My first thought was, well, there's an end to my mission, thank God. My second was that Napier wouldn't think so. He'd never stand my crying off; Galla was too vital for that, whatever the risk. And giving up didn't even cross Uliba's mind.

"So now our journey will be doubly dangerous," says she. "Theodore will have his watchers out for us from Gondar to the Ashangi lake. God willing, they will be seeking an Englishman, not an Indian horse-pedlar."

"They'll be looking for you, too –"

"Which is why I must teach you enough Amharic to act as our purchaser and bid good day to passers-by." She looked me over. "Are you strong enough to start tomorrow, before dawn?"

"I'm strong enough for more than that," says I, and caught her arm before she could stand up, drawing her down beside me. She didn't resist as I clasped her to me, revelling in the suppleness of her body, and when I clamped my mouth on her lips they remained closed only for a long teasing moment, suddenly opening avidly, her tongue thrusting against mine, her hands clasping fiercely behind my head. Trumpeter, sound! thinks I, digging my claws into her buttocks and doing my level best to eat her, at which she suddenly writhed free with surprising strength and scrambled up, gasping, her mouth quivering and her eyes wide and wild. I was lunging up in pursuit, but she stayed me with a hand.

"Wait!" says she. "First, there is something to be done – something you should see!"

She went to the ladder-stair and shouted down. A female voice replied, and after a moment a man's. She barked out a command, and presently there were disputatious voices raised below, sounds of ascension, and here came the princely chap who I realised must be the timely rescuer Daoud, followed by a couple of strapping lads who, to my amazement, were bringing with them a damned disgruntled Yando.

He let out a tirade of screaming abuse at the sight of Uliba, one of his escorts hit him a smashing blow across the mouth, and the pair of them gripped him while another two sturdy minions appeared, and, at Daoud's instructions, brought out that hellish cage in which I'd been given the fresh air treatment, and which had been tactfully hidden away in the shadows since I'd vacated it.

Yando squealed like a steam whistle at the sight of it, bloodshot eyes bugging and ape face contorted in panic, and I've seldom seen a sight more gratifying. As you know, I'm a cruel bastard, and if there's one thing I enjoy it's seeing another cruel bastard get his cocoa. In this case it was so dam' poetic, too; my heart went out to Uliba as she stood there sneering, arms akimbo, and my one regret was that I couldn't understand the taunts with which she was encouraging Yando as they encased him.

They had the devil of a job, for he was as strong as a bull, and for a reason which I didn't understand until later, they hadn't bound his hands. It took all four of them, and they had to beat him half-senseless before they had him caged and the pin in place. Then they hung the cage on the hook and threw back the trap and we all stood round appreciating his screams for mercy – I knew that's what they were because they sounded so like my own. On Uliba's instructions he had been placed in the cage face up, so we were treated to his interesting expressions as he was lowered slowly into the void, the men on the windlass stopping the process when he was only a bare yard below the floor level, not nearly as far down as I had been, but convenient for the spectators.

The long chain to the securing pin was coiled on the floor, and Uliba picked it up, holding it out for Yando to see and smiling down at him. She gave it a gentle tug, moving the pin just a little, and addressed what sounded like a question to him, which had Daoud's followers in whoops. Daoud himself gave the ghost of a smile, and I had a feeling that he regarded the adored object's conduct as not at all the thing (as Elspeth would say). He said something to her, and she shrugged and replied offhand, at which Daoud, after a long look at me, bowed to her and retired, followed by his gang mighty glum; they'd been looking forward to watching Yando take flight.

Uliba was in no hurry to put him out of his misery. She stood on the brink of the trap mocking him in a voice husky with excitement while he woke the echoes with his pleas and curses, writhing so that the cage jerked and swung like a cork on a string. A diverting sight, but I was more intent on studying her face, lips parted, laughing in delight as she toyed with the chain, drawing the long pin ever so slowly and then, with a last taunt, suddenly whipping it free.

The cage flew open, spilling him out – and now I saw that leaving his hands free had been the exquisite refinement of cruelty, for he was able to grab the edge of the cage even as he fell, and there he was, clinging for dear life as he swung over the giddy mist-streaked abyss, shrieking his ugly head off.

Talk about the female o' the species if you like – Uliba cried in glee, clapping her hands, fairly revelling in the brute's anguish, and now she sweetened his last moments with a gesture which I doubt even Ranavalona or the Empress Tsu-hsi or my little Apache charmer Sonsee-array would have thought of – and they knew how to tickle their male victims, I can tell you. She leaned over, jeering down into that glaring agonised face, and with slow deliberation undid the laces of her leather tunic and let it fall, leaving her naked but for a loincloth. She puckered her lips at him in a mockery of kissing, and told me to replace the trapdoor.

"Slowly, to give him time to think," murmurs she, so I did as I was told, lowering the door gently; it couldn't close entirely flush because of the suspending rope, but enough to cut off the horrid sight and sound of that wailing wretch, clinging in terror until pain and cold should loosen his hold. Uliba turned to me, her mouth shaking as if with an ague, and there was a light in her eyes which a lady novelist would certainly have called unholy. She flung her arms round my neck, pulling my face down to hers, gasping what I could only assume were indelicate suggestions, for in her agitation the poor thing was babbling in Amharic. Let's make hay while she's hot, thinks I, and swung her up in my arms, unbreeching myself skilfully with one hand while clasping that lovely trembling flesh with the other, planted her firmly in the saddle to the accompaniment of gratifying squeals, and was making her the happiest of women as we subsided on to the mattress.

You never can tell, I've found, what different women will prefer as a stimulating accompaniment to *la galop*. I think of dear Lola with her hairbrush, Jeendan and her canes, Mandeville booted and spurred, Cleonie humming French nursery rhymes, and my own dear wife gossiping relentlessly to the last blissful moment and beyond. Each to her taste and God bless her, say I, but going at it like a Simla widow while a former admirer is dying by inches under the bed is not, I think, in the best of taste. Not that I gave a dam; Flashy *in ecstatio* has no thought to spare for tottering thrones or collapsing empires, let alone beastly rivals collecting their well-deserved rations.

Speaking of whom, when we'd exhausted our rapture and recovered sufficiently to raise the trap for a look-see, Yando had gone.

If you take a look at my map you'll see how our road lay, from Ad Abaga south-west to Lake Tana, easy riding for the most part, while over the mountains to eastward Napier's army was grinding its way through those impossible highlands of huge peaks and deep chasms, carving a road along precipices, round mountain tops, and across rock-strewn plateaux. Horse, foot, guns, mules, and elephants, growing lighter and hungrier by the mile as they abandoned gear and clothing and camp-followers, pressing on desperately beyond hope of return in the race for Magdala, while far to the south Theodore's dwindling army and motley rabble of prisoners were closing on the capital from Debra Tabor, with fewer miles to travel but hampered by the ponderous artillery dragged in his train, including his mighty mortar "Sevastopol".

I don't know which of them, the British general or the mad monarch, deserves the higher marks for leadership and determination and sheer ability in taking an army through and over hellish country, but you could say they were a matched pair and not be far wrong. They reached their goals against all the odds, and Hannibal and Marlborough couldn't have done better.

Our immediate concern was to keep well clear of the various forces converging on Magdala, and somehow make our way to Queen Masteeat undetected. "We must ride wide to westward to avoid Gobayzy's scouts," says Uliba-Wark. "They will be along the Takazy river from Micara as far south as the Kerissa fork, so we shall go by way of Idaga, and then south over the river past Sokar and Gondar to the lake." She traced a slim finger through the sand on which she had made a rough map with grass stems and pebbles. "It is a long way about, but there is no other safe path."

"This one is safe, is it?" says I, and she laughed.

"In Habesh, where is safety? Who knows what raiding bands are abroad in Lasta these days, scavenging after the armies? Rebels, outlaws, brigands, slavers – perhaps even the main powers of Menelek and Gobayzy, although I think they will be farther south, in Begemder, watching Theodore and waiting. Somewhere thereabouts we should find Masteeat also, but only when we reach the lake will we have sure word of them. Meanwhile we ride carefully, by secret ways, approaching villages and *ambas* only when we must." She swept a hand across the sand, obliterating her map, smiling lazily as she dusted her fingers and sat closer, stroking her cheek against mine. "It will be slow, but we have time . . . and we know how to beguile it, do we not?"

Having had her first taste of Flashy only the day before, she was still in honeymoon mood, so we beguiled away there and then, on the riverbank just within the edge of the woodland which she had pointed out to me from the top of her tower. We had slipped out of the citadel in the cold small hours, as she had planned, and she had picked her unerring way down to the valley floor and along the river in the dark to the shelter of the trees. Somewhere along the way we must have passed the remains of Yando spread over the rocks, but she didn't pause to pay respects, and before daylight we were snug in cover, having breakfast and a flask of *tej*, considering our route, and enjoying the aforesaid bout of hareem gymnastics, in the course of which we rolled down the bank into the water, not that Uliba seemed to notice, the dear enamoured girl, for she thrashed about in the shallows like a landed trout.

A happy prelude to our journey, and a prudent one, I always think, for while the old Duke said one should never miss the opportunity of a run-off or a sleep, I say never miss the chance of a rattle, especially when going into mortal danger, for it may be your last, and you don't want to die a prey to vain regret. Also, it puts you in fettle, and I was in prime trim when we set forward that morning through countryside as fresh and fair as an English spring, along wooded valleys where clear streams bubbled under the sycamores and wild flowers grew by the water's edge – and by afternoon we were pushing our way through fields of waving grass as high as our horses' heads, and by evening ascending a rocky desert slope towards mountains of fantastic shapes, twisted peaks and ugly cliffs looming over us as night came down. That's Habesh, elysium followed by Valley of the Shadow, and not improved by the savagery of its inhabitants.

I'd seen the havoc wreaked by war and foray on the road up from Zoola to Attegrat, and what we encountered on our ride west to Idaga was of a piece: the occasional burned-out village and deserted farm, the carcases of beasts lying in neglected fields, the distant smoke-clouds where raiders had been at work, the peasants still going doggedly about their business but keeping their distance. There were armed guards on the *ambas* and hill-top communities, and escorts for the water porters carrying their cargoes up from the wells.

We kept well clear of them all at first, for Uliba was known in the countryside and in the towns of Adowa and Axum not far to our north, and we daren't risk her being recognised. So the task of buying food and drink along the way fell on Khasim Tamwar, who needs must learn enough elementary Amharic to enable him to ask for *woha* (water), *halib* (milk), *engard* (bread) and *quantah* (dried meat), while putting on his most charming Hyderabadi smile and proffering the little sticks of salt which are the local small change and the only currency in the country apart from the Maria Theresa dollar – known as the *gourshi*, and worth five salt sticks. I've a gift for languages, as you know, and got a smattering of Amharic in no time.[30] It's gone now, but I must have become reasonably fluent, because by the end of my Abyssinian odyssey I was conversing with Abs who had no Arabic; even in the first week, with Uliba's tuition, I had enough to haggle with, for I remember at one farm I got two guinea fowls and a mess of kidmeat for two "salts", which she assured me was well below the going rate.

She stayed far out of sight with the led-beast whenever I went shopping, and since my foreign garb and eccentric vocabulary seemed to excite no interest, let alone suspicion, I began to think her fear of Yando's rascals spreading word of our coming might be groundless. She shook her head, and said it would be different beyond the Takazy river. "Theodore will be on the watch for us down yonder, you may be sure. Hereabouts the folk care nothing for him and his policies, and they are used to foreigners far stranger than an Indian horse-coper."

She told me that only a couple of years before a Neapolitan lunatic named de Bisson had invaded this region, hoping to found a kingdom; he'd had a rabble of mercenaries, uniformed, bemedalled, and armed to the teeth, and his beauteous wife in the full fig of a Zouave cavalryman, red britches, kepi and all, but the local tribes had given them the rightabout, and he and his gang had been lucky to get out alive, much the worse for wear. He'd tried to sue the Egyptian Government for not supporting him, without success, and retired to the Riviera in disgust.

"After such a portent, who is going to think twice about a mere wanderer from Hindustan?" says Uliba. "Whatever befalls later, all is well now, so let us be thankful, and travel well together."

So we did, but if that ride to the Takazy passed without disaster it was thanks to her woodcraft; she was an even better *jancada* than Speedy had said, with that strange gift that you get in the half-wild (like Bridger and Carson) of being able to sense a living presence long before she'd seen or heard it. Time and again she turned us aside into cover of rocks or undergrowth where we waited until, sure enough, a few minutes later a camel train or a party of peasants would heave in view and pass by. And once she saved our hides altogether, detecting the approach of a gang of slave-traders, armed and mounted, lashing along a wretched coffle of women and boys.

As we lay watching, one of the boys collapsed, and when flogging didn't revive him, the gang rode on another thirty yards or so, when two of them, laughing and plainly challenging each other, turned in their saddles and used the feebly stirring form for target practice, hurling their lances – and hitting him, too, at that distance. They retrieved their lances from the dying boy's body, yelling with delight, and galloped after their companions. I was as shocked by their accuracy as by their callousness, but Uliba merely remarked that a Galla warrior could hit any target up to fifty yards with a spear or a knife or even a stone snatched up at random.

"Those bastards were Gallas?" cries I, astonished. "But they're your people, ain't they? Why, they may know where Masteeat's to be found! Why did you not –"

"Bid them good day? I thought of it," says she, "when I recognised their leader – one of those who speared the boy – as my cousin. But he is an Ambo Galla, a subject of Queen Warkite, and while he and some other of my relatives might well prefer me, or even Masteeat, as monarch of all Galla – for no one loves Warkite, a sour old bitch – still, he is a slave-trader, after all, and I would fetch a splendid price at El Khartoum . . . and even more," she added complacently, "at Jibout' or Zanzibar; the coast buyers have finer discernment than the Soudanis."

"Holy smoke! D'you mean he'd sell *you* – his kinswoman? And a chief's wife?"

"He would sell his own mother . . . and quite probably has. And if I am kin, and half-royal, still, I had the poor taste to wed a Christian. No, he would surely have sold me – and you. A white eunuch would be a novelty in Arabia."

I almost fell over. "A white . . . I ain't a bloody eunuch!"

"You would have been if they had seen us. Did you not mark the baubles which decorated their lances? Those were the genitals of prisoners and enemies."

A discouraging tidbit of information, you'll allow, and if I'd seen the remotest chance of a flight to safety, or even known where the hell I was, I might well have turned tail on the spot, Napier or no Napier. But being entirely out of reckoning, I'd no choice but to follow on, trusting to luck and consoling myself that there are worse travelling companions than a long-legged expert savage who's taken a passionate fancy to you. That's the best of memory, when terrors and hardships no longer matter, and I can look back and still see her reclining by the stream, dabbling her toes as she anoints those sleek limbs with her cosmetic oil until they gleam like bronze in the firelight, humming softly as she plaits her braids, and lying back smiling with her head on her little wooden pillow, holding out a hand to me.

104

But if that first week had its idyllic moments, they ended when we crossed the Takazy and rode south into a new and horrible world. I've seen more war-scarred country than I care to remember, from the shattered ruin of the Summer Palace and the corpse-choked waters of the Sutlej to the putrid mud of the Crimea and the scorched highway blazed by Sherman from Atlanta to the sea, but what lay before us now was beyond description. Even the war of the Taipings, the bloodiest in human history, which seemed to carpet China with dead in heaps of countless thousands, was no more frightful than the charnelhouse that Theodore had made in Lasta and Gondar and Begemder.

From the river down to Lake Tana is more than a hundred and twenty miles, and I doubt if we saw more than a score of living things in all that distance, bar vultures, hyenas, scorpions, and white ants, or a building whole and standing except for some of the flat-roofed stone houses which the better-off inhabit. Of the normal round thatched homes of the populace, there wasn't one; every village and farm was a cold charred ruin in a vast graveyard where skeletons human and animal lay in the rubble. The fields and plain had been swept clean of people and their beasts; in the wooded valleys of the high country even the birds seemed to have gone, and we rode in an eerie silence. I dare say there were folk living in Micara and Sokar, small towns to which we gave a wide berth, as we did to the few *ambas* and adobe forts which showed signs of being occupied. I couldn't fathom it, for plainly this had been a well-inhabited, prosperous land; where the devil had everyone gone?

"Most of them are dead," says Uliba. "This was rebel country, remember, and it is not Theodore's way to spare any who resist him, man, woman or child. If we have seen none of Gobayzy's troops it can mean only that they have gone south after Theodore – and doubtless the banditti have gone also, for what is left to steal in Lasta?" We had reined in on the outskirts of yet another ruined village, beside a little walled enclosure filled with a great pile of bones, many of them plainly belonging to infants. I ain't over-queasy, as you know, but the thought of how they'd come to be there turned my stomach. Uliba viewed them dispassionately.

"Thus Theodore wins the love of his people. You see now why

Habesh rejoices in your British invasion; whether it delivers your captives or not, it will surely destroy him."

Amen to that, thinks I. Until that moment I'd given little enough thought to this monster of an emperor and the atrocities he'd committed on his own people. You hear folk like Napier and Speedy talk of them, but it means nothing – and then you see 'em at point-blank, and can't conceive of such wickedness. Until you come to Gondar, that is, and find yourself contemplating Hell on earth.

It lay about a hundred miles below the Takazy, and was once the capital of Abyssinia, a metropolis of forty-four churches and a great royal palace, standing on a hill from which there was a magnificent prospect of Lake Tana, forty miles away. For generations it had housed wealthy Muslim merchants and a revered priesthood, a magnet for traders from Egypt and the Soudan and the southern lakes, a city peaceful, flourishing, and rich – which was its undoing. Theodore had taxed it exorbitantly, virtually holding it to ransom, and not unnaturally the city fathers had tended to sympathise with the rebels fleeing the Emperor's vengeance, and give them shelter.

This much Uliba told me as we came down towards it on the fifth day after crossing the river; I wondered if it would be safe to venture close to such a busy centre, and she laughed on a bitter note.

"Over the ridge yonder we shall see great Gondar on its hill," says she, "and you can see how busy are its folk."

We topped the ridge, and sure enough there was a distant rise crowned with buildings, some of 'em imposing adobe and stone structures, so far as I could tell from far off, but the lower slopes were covered in the burned ruins of thousands of the thatched houses of the common folk. There was an odd smell in the air, not the foulness of corruption, but more like an aftermath of decay, musty and stale. There was no sign of life on the hill, or on the plain below it, which was empty save for rows of upright objects that I took at first to be leafless trees, until we rode down to them, and I saw they were great crosses, hundreds of them to the edge of the city. And at the foot of each cross was a little pile of whitened bones, except for a few crosses on which were twisted blackened shapes that had once been human, preserved by some freak of the weather like so many withered mummies.

I could only sit and stare in disbelief, aware that Uliba was watching me with an expression of amused curiosity, resting easy in her saddle with one foot cocked up on the crupper. I dare say I was a sight to see, open-mouthed and appalled, asking myself such futile questions as what kind of creature could have done such a thing, and when, and above all, in God's name, why?

Don't misunderstand me. As I've said, I was inured to mass slaughter, and barbarous cruelty: when you've seen the mounds of Taiping dead, or the ghastly harvest of an Apache raid, you don't gag or faint. But you can be stricken speechless at the sight of a mass carnage that has been conceived and designed and executed with meticulous care – no wild hot-blooded massacre, but a planned methodical operation, with hundreds of timber baulks cut and gathered and fashioned into crosses, hundreds of victims condemned and marshalled and nailed or bound, hundreds of crucifixes reared and planted by hundreds of executioners, hundreds of tortured voices screaming – and whoever had ordered this must have nodded approval and commended it with a "Well done, men, a good day's work", as he turned away from the ghastly sight and sounds and rode off to see what cook was preparing for supper.

Or perhaps he had given orders to crucify the population, and been miles away when his troops did the business.

"Oh, no," says Uliba. "You may be sure that Theodore directed this in person. He would inspect every cross, every hanging body; he may even have driven home nails himself. That is his way, when the devil fit is on him."

"He's mad, then. Stark raving bloody insane!" I was thinking of other charming monarchs I had known, like Ranavalona with her death-pits, and that noble savage Gezo of Dahomey bouncing about on his throne fairly slobbering with glee as his Amazons sliced up his victims with cleavers. Plainly Theodore was from the same stable. It's enough to make you turn republican.

Uliba shrugged. "Mad, perhaps. Or merely Abyssinian. Oh, you think of us as a fierce warlike people who love to fight – and we are, and you understand and admire that because it is in your nature also. But do you understand the joy of killing for its own sake? The delight in blood and the agony of the dying?" She shook her head. "From all I have heard, that is not in the British nature."

You should see a Newgate scragging, you poor ignorant aborigine, thinks I. Or Flashy breaking de Gautet's toes and pitching him into the Jotunschlucht with a merry jest, capital fun, and a deed after your own heart, sultana, you who gloated so joyfully over Yando's performance on the flying trapeze. But sadistic spite in paying off a personal score is one thing; torturing to death an entire population whom you don't even know, and whose only offence is that their civic rulers gave shelter to a parcel of rebels, is rather different.

It hadn't properly sunk in, when Uliba had spoken of Theodore's sparing no man, woman, or child, but it did now, as we rode through that ghastly forest of the dead which even the vultures had abandoned, and mounted the slope through the blackened ruins of Gondar city. Eerie silence hung over it like a shroud, and the stench of burned timber was overpowering, even though the fire had been dead for months. I'd have passed the infernal place by, not only for its foulness but because there might be enemies lurking, but Uliba, who seemed indifferent to the horrors we'd seen, brushed my fears aside.

"Only ghosts live in Gondar since Theodore destroyed it, more than a year ago. The peasants call it accursed, and even the outlaw bands avoid it." She turned in her saddle to look back over the charred rubble to the rows of crosses below. "But it is well that you should see. If your general doubts the kind of enemy he has to deal with, you can tell him."

I wondered if Napier would credit it, that a Christian king could spit in the eye of Christianity by turning crucifixion into a kind of blasphemy – for that's how it would seem to my pious countrymen. And yet that wasn't the worst of it, as I learned when we'd led our screws through the rubble-strewn streets and past the shattered walls of what had once been shops and churches and stone houses, and came to the broad plaza before the burned-out shell of the huge palace (once the largest building, they say, between Egypt and the Cape) where long-dead kings of Abyssinia had kept their courts amidst the wealth and splendour of a continent. If Prester John existed, this was where he'd sat his throne, where the scorpions and lizards now scuttled among the broken masonry. Once it must have been the wonder of Africa, a great city of fabulous wealth and ten thousand inhabitants; now it reminded me of those age-old ruins of North Africa and Middle Asia, and I must have asked aloud for the twentieth time what in God's name had possessed Theodore to destroy such grandeur.

"Because he hated it," says Uliba contemptuously. "Not only for its comfort given to rebels, but for its splendour and treasure and traditions that seemed to mock his stolen royalty. Gondar the Great, the glory of Habesh, a noble city of nobles, was a living reproach to the purge-seller's brat."

It came on to rain at sunset, one of those crashing tropical downpours with sheet lightning crackling on the western horizon and thunder booming overhead, so we bivouacked in the porch of one of the four churches which were the only buildings Theodore had left standing. It was dry and snug with the outer door pulled to, cutting us off from the city's desolation, and when I'd lit a fire with one of my vesuvians[31] (Uliba, such a worldly-wise and cultivated little savage in so many ways, had cried out in alarm the first time I'd used one) she set to work preparing a stew of game and kid. I led our beasts through the arch into the empty nave, where I spread their fodder and rubbed them down, and took a quick dekko around in the last of the light from the high unglazed windows.

Theodore might have spared the building, but he'd stripped it bare. There was nothing but a broken font and a bare altar, behind which was another of those crazy frescoes which I've already told you of: this one depicted the Children of Israel crossing the Red Sea, pursued by Pharaoh's army who were holding their muskets over their heads, presumably to keep their Ancient Egyptian powder dry.

For the rest, there was nothing but a heavy trapdoor in the wooden floor which covered the area before the altar; elsewhere the floor was bare earth to the walls, in one of which there was a closed side door. I heaved up the trap, whose slats were warped and shrunk with age, and there beneath was a small cellar, about twelve feet by twelve and eight deep, empty but for a few ancient pots and no doubt interesting assorted insect life.

I replaced the trap and joined Uliba in the porch, where we ate our supper by the shadowy firelight with the storm bellowing outside. And now she told me the full unspeakable tale of what Theodore had done to the old city in the autumn of '66.

"He had wrested tribute from it in the past, so the people expected no more than another shearing of their golden fleece, and came out to greet their emperor, protesting loyalty and hoping to win his favour. They might as well have tried to charm a crocodile. Although the rebels had fled away at his approach, their recent presence was all the excuse Theodore needed to loot the city to its final ruin. The wealth of Selassie, the gold of Kooksuam, the silver of Bata, the gems from the mines of Solomon beyond the Mountains of the Moon, the silks and paintings and even the precious manuscripts were all plundered to the uttermost scrap and coin. Never was such a pillaging . . . aye, they lived richly in the Gondar that was."

She poured us cups of *tej* and sat back against the wall, golden in the firelight, sipping her cup and telling her dreadful tale as lightly as a fairy story.

"But to strip the city to its ruin was not enough, Gondar itself must cease to be. Its citizens, all ten thousand, were herded out like cattle, and the whole town given to the flames: the palace, the treasury, the forty churches, the fine homes of the rich and the hovels of the poor. Gondar burned from end to end, and the glow was seen in the sky from Lake Ashangi to the frontiers of Tigre and Soudan. And when the priests cried out, calling down curses on his head, he had them bound, hundreds of aged men, and thrown into the fire, so that they burned alive, to the last man. But did that satisfy him, d'you think?"

She leaned forward to pick up the *tej* flask, the black almond eyes watching to see the effect of her story, even smiling a little in anticipation.

"Let me fill your cup, you who love fair women, so that you can steady your spirit while you hear the rest. For now Theodore remembered that when the folk had come out to greet him, they had been led by the girls of the city, dancing and singing. 'Their song was the signal for the rebels to flee!' cries he. 'Traitresses, bring them to me!' And they too, every girl, from child to young woman, were thrown alive into the flames." She paused to sip her drink. "The rest of the people he crucified or cut to pieces. What do you think of that, *effendi*? It is true, you know, every soul in a great city exterminated by the fire, the cross, and the sword, thousand upon thousand. All Habesh knows it.[32] What will your general say?"

"Breathe a sigh of relief, most likely, since 'twill solve a problem that's bound to be exercising him . . . what to do with Theodore, I mean. This makes it simple; the bastard'll have to go."

"You will try him, in a court, and put him to death?"

"Oh, I doubt that. What would we charge him with? We've nothing against him but kidnapping a few of our people, mistreating 'em and so forth. Can't hang him for that. What he does in his own country, to his own folk, ain't our *indaba*. Can't quote you the law, but I'm pretty clear that's how it stands. Why, I can think of two campaigns that I've been in, in India and China, where ghastly things were done by native rulers – women, in fact, dreadful bitches – but we didn't lay a finger on 'em."[33]

"But you said of Theodore, 'he will have to go'!"

"So he will, one way or t'other. Bullet in the back o' the head, shot trying to escape, dead of a surfeit of lampreys, who knows?" I gave her a précis of my Harper's Ferry adventure, where for reasons of state I was supposed to shoot mad John Brown so that the Yankee authorities wouldn't have the embarrassment of trying and topping the daft old bugger – which I didn't, as you probably know. "But that was a different case. Theodore'll have to die, somehow; can't execute him, but can't have him hanging around Aldershot on a pension, either. Public wouldn't stand it. He'll just have to be done in on the quiet, accidental-looking."

"What hypocrites you are!"

111

"No such thing. It's just the civilised way of doing it, that's all. What would you do with him, then?"

She leaned back against the wall in a way which stretched her tunic most distractingly, put her hands behind her head, and gazed pensively up at the flickering fire-shadows on the opposite wall.

"Given to me, he would take a year to die. Perhaps two. First of all I would have the bones of his hands and feet removed one at a time, then the larger bones of his arms and legs. This would be done by our most skilful surgeons, who would sew up the wounds, taking care to keep him alive and conscious . . ." She sighed contentedly, settling down to put her imagination to work. "Next . . ." But I shan't tell you what she said next, because like me you may just have had dinner. I'll say only that I hadn't heard the like since my fourth wife, Sonsee-array, described what she'd done to captured scalp-hunters in the winter of '49.

"You'd not give him the option of a fine, then?" says I. "Just so. Well, my dear, I hope you get the chance, because the evil swine deserves it. But I don't suppose you will, what?"

"If I am Queen of Galla, who knows?" says she softly. "If your general wishes to avoid the responsibility of . . . punishing Theodore . . . might he not leave the task to the ally who had helped him to take Magdala?"

Fortunately I'm an old hand at keeping my countenance when mines are sprung under me, so I took a long pull at my *tej* and thought in haste. For this was her hole card faced with a vengeance, and I must take care.

"That ally, as I understand it, is Queen Masteeat," says I. "She's the one I've been ordered to approach, leastways."

Uliba sat upright, very erect in the firelight, and pushed her hands beneath her braids, raising them from her head, letting them fall, and raising them again, then turning her head to regard me steadily from those slanting black eyes, the heavy lips parting as she took a deep breath. It was calculated and most striking, a gesture that said "Look at me, voluptuous romp that I am, female tigress and woman of destiny, for I'm turning my batteries on you, and by gad you'd best make your mind up." She posed for a long moment, to make sure I noticed, no doubt, and then said:

"If Masteeat were no longer Queen of the Wollos –"

"Then I suppose I'd have to approach Warkite of the Ambos, wouldn't I?"

"Bah!" She spat it out in contempt, swirling her braids. "To what end? Who would follow that dried-up crone against Magdala? You think because she presumes to the throne of all Galla that she can command loyalty even from her own tribe? She is nothing, a name only! She is no rival to Masteeat!"

"Is anyone?" says I, and she fluffed out her braids again, tossing her handsome head, and then burst out laughing.

"So we come to it! Yes, there is one – and you know her!" She leaned towards me, proud and confident. "The *Basha Fallaka* Speedy will have told you all about the third pretender, the concubine's bastard who has twice rebelled – you did not know? – and for her treason was sent from the court of her royal ancestors and forced to marry a commoner, a mere petty chief, a chief so feeble that Gobayzy holds him captive – so who is she to challenge Masteeat, her sister? Masteeat who is strong and crafty and has held her throne against Warkite and such warlords as Gobayzy and Menelek these two years? Masteeat who commands ten thousand swords, oh, aye," she added, sniffing, "and has a way with men, soft-fleshed and indolent as she is. Well, she is not alone in her way with men. Is she?" And she gave her braids another lift and flaunt.

No, she was not, but the diplomatic problem facing me was a nice one. In effect I was being asked: if Queen Masteeat was somehow (and God alone knew how) replaced by Queen Uliba, would I, as Britannia's envoy, recognise and do business with her? That, plainly, would depend on whether she could fill Masteeat's shoes, which at the moment, given her situation, seemed unlikely. Then again, she was plainly intent on a coup d'etat, so she must have reason to believe she could pull it off, no doubt by kicking Masteeat's bucket for her. Ergo, she must be counting on mighty support from within the Wollo Galla community, and since, as she'd remarked, she did have a way of enlisting masculine sympathy, no doubt that support would be forthcoming. Sufficient to do the trick?

That I couldn't tell. But the immediate question was, if she did succeed in mounting a palace revolution, what help, if any, would she expect from old Flashy?

You see my dilemma. She was my only hope of reaching Queen Masteeat, and must not be antagonised. And however unlikely it seemed, if by some freak of chance and design she managed to supplant Masteeat in the next two weeks, she would be the key to Galla support against Theodore – but if she tried a coup and it failed, I daren't be any part of it. Not only would Napier be left without a Galla to bless himself with, my essentials would be used to decorate somebody's spear. The whole thing was wild and imponderable and downright impossible to predict or plan for, so all I could do for the moment was keep this mad hoyden sweet and see how the sparks fell.

All this in a matter of seconds while she watched me as though I were an opposing duellist, the firelight glinting in her eyes intent on mine, lips parted and expectant. And since there's only one absolutely safe response to that hopeful feminine regard, I gave her my sentimental gentle leer, took her shoulders tenderly in my hands, brought my lips towards hers . . . and stopped dead, the hairs bristling up on my neck.

The storm had blown itself out, and the only sounds about us were the soft crackle of the dying fire, the stirring of our horses in the nave, the faint splash and trickle of water across the ground outside the porch door . . . and now, of a sudden, not far distant, the clatter of a stone disturbed somewhere out in the darkness, the ring of shod hooves, and a voice raised in a harsh shout.

114

If there was a man in those days who could move faster in a crisis than H. P. Flashman, I never met him – but there was a woman who could have given me a head start, Uliba-Wark of Tigre, the nearest thing I ever saw to chain lightning with a link snapped. Before I'd even taken in the meaning of that noise without, she was past me like a whippet, kicking the water *chatti* on to the fire as she sped to the door. A second later I was beside her, peering through a crack in the ramshackle timbers, and there at the other end of the plaza, a bare fifty yards off, torches were flaring in the dark and shadowy figures of men and horses were moving through the ruins.

Had they caught a glimpse of our fire through the rickety timbers? It seemed not; Uliba's quick action had doused it in a hissing cloud of steam, and there was no cry of alarm from the torch-bearers, whoever they might be – a question I put to her in a hysterical squeak as we crouched in the darkness.

"Brigands!" she gasped. "Soudanis, surely – no troops of Habesh or honest travellers would be abroad in this weather at night, least of all in Gondar the accursed!" She didn't need to add that discovery would mean rape and enslavement for her and unspeakable death for me; that's what she'd expected from her own Galla kinsfolk, and Soudanis were notoriously monsters of cruelty. My instinct was that we should bolt from the side door with a couple of horses, but she cut off my breathless suggestion by retorting that they would run us down in no time, and if we lay low the odds were they'd pass us by. Ignoring the only decent shelter in this bloody town? says I, but before she could reply there was a sudden shout from the darkness, followed by a commotion in Arabic which I couldn't make out, and then Uliba's fierce whisper in my ear: "They've smelt our fire!" And as if that wasn't enough, one of the bandits' horses decided to neigh its confounded head off, which brought an answering high-pitched whinny from the nave behind us.

All things considered, I think Uliba and I showed uncommon presence of mind. Through the crack in the door we could see the bandit gang starting towards us in full cry, but before they'd gone a yard I had her by the wrist and was making tracks for the nave; flight from the church on foot was out of the question, there wasn't time to mount up before they'd be on us, but there was that heaven-sent cellar in front of the altar, and with the nave barely lit by the moonshine through the high windows they'd never see the trap. I had it flung back in a twinkling, but to my consternation Uliba pulled free from my grasp and raced to the side door, thrusting it open before running back to me, the clever lass – the bandits would see it and think we'd gone that way; I'd used the same dodge myself when pursued by peelers at home. I swung her down into the cellar, she dropped like an acrobat, and a second later I was slipping over the edge, closing the trap above me as I jumped the last few feet to the cellar floor.

We heard the church door crash open, and pounding feet, but they wasted no time in exclamation, and the first words I heard were a sharp command in Arabic, directing pursuit through the side door. They were in the nave, taking quick stock like the professional chaps they were, and presently their voices filtered down to us through the ill-fitting trap, while we clung together instinctively in the dank little cellar, like children at hide-and-seek.

"Three of them, Sadat?"

"Nay, one of those beasts is a pack-animal. And only two have eaten and drunk by the dead fire, one of them a woman."

"How can you tell?"

"Use your nose, fool! Musk-oil."

"Ha, she should be young, then!" Coarse laughter. "Hey, Yusuf, look well out yonder! She can't have gone far!"

Suddenly light was shining down through the cracks in the trap;

116

they'd brought their torches into the nave, and must have fixed them, for the light shone steady. Oh, God, would they see the trap? We huddled as far back as we could go to the side of the cellar, in the hope that if the trap were opened we'd be out of eyeshot of anyone looking down – unless they dropped in, so to speak . . . Quite so.

We could only wait, Uliba's cheek running sweat against mine, while heavy feet thumped the wooden flooring just above our heads, and Sadat the musk-oil expert was saying that this place would do as well as any other, so let Yakub and Gamal bring the stuff inside, and have a care how they handled it, careless dogs that they were.

Now there was great bustle, with more of the gang arriving, sounds of heaving and exertion and commands, a ponderous weight dropped on the floorboards, and through all the clamour a voice gentling our horses which had been alarmed by the uproar, while another was roaring to Yusuf for news of the fugitives supposedly being pursued through the night. Someone close above us was demanding what should be done with the stuff – and my blood froze at the reply:

"There must be a cellar under the trap yonder! What better place for the goods?" Uliba couldn't repress a gasping sob. Then:

"Why has God ordained that I should ride with fools?" wonders Sadat. "What *worse* place could there be than one where folk are sure to look?"

"Eh? Oh, aye . . . well, then, where shall we put it?"

"Underground, camel-spawn! Yonder, by the wall, you dig a hole, and bury it, and cover all with rubble so that only one lynx-eyed and enlightened by God, like Mahmud here, could hope to find it!"

"Did he call me lynx-eyed and enlightened by God?"

"Aye, but he didn't mean it. Get a spade, clown!"

"Why must I be the one to dig? Oh, lend a hand, then!"

Uliba was limp against me, gasping with relief, and I was shuddering weakly as I heard them hauling some heavy article across the trap, and then came the crunch and scrape and foul language of labourers delving in the packed earth. Above that we heard our horses being appraised and their burdens examined, men coming and going, a disgruntled Yusuf reporting that whoever the bastards were who had fled into the night, they were nowhere to be found, demands for rest and food, to which Sadat (who was evidently their captain) retorted that they were riding out as soon as the goods had been safely concealed, and other conversation of the kind you'd expect to hear from marauders discussing the affairs of the day. I wish now that I'd paid closer attention, for there was interesting stuff about the possibility of enlisting gang members as guards for the Metema caravan, or taking a slap at one of the supply depots being established by the godless *farangi* invaders, but I was in too fine a funk to concern myself with anything but keeping tight hold of Uliba as two interminable hours crawled past, and my heart stopped whenever a footstep came near the trap. Please, dear God, I kept muttering, don't let any of 'em get curious about the cellar . . . and I was just beginning to believe they'd do their business and leave us undisturbed when . . .

"Aye, that's deep enough. Lift it over."

"Will it be safe? When do we return for it?"

"When we've scouted this *farangi* army and seen what's to be had from them . . . perhaps from Theodore, too. He carries his treasury with him, like enough."

"What, despoil Theodore? Go rob a lioness of her cubs!"

"Aye, we'd do better to carry *our* treasury safe to Kassala instead of burying it in this grave of serpents!"

"I hate to leave it here! God knows it cost enough in blood and sweat to get it!"

"Eh, Sadat, let's have another look before we cover it! Just a look . . ."

Cries of agreement, and Sadat, the indulgent ass, let them go ahead, there was a crash as of a lid being thrown back, delighted gloating, a warning snarl to Mahmud to take care, and then an almighty clatter of coin being dropped, ringing and rolling across the boards – and, dear Jesus, dropping through the cracks in the trap to the floor of the cellar! Uliba sobbed, my innards did a cartwheel, and recrimination raged overhead, Mahmud being cursed for an idiot, coins being scraped up, some mean son-of-a-bitch crying that a few had fallen through the trap, Sadat shouting to let 'em alone and get the chest closed and interred, and the mean bastard crying that he was shot if he'd lose them . . . and throwing back the trapdoor.

Torch-glare suddenly lit up the centre of the cellar, but we were in deep shadow against the side wall, and all that we could see through the open trap was two pairs of boots and robed legs up to the thigh; we must be out of their owners' line of vision, but if they stooped to look under the floor, would they see us in the gloom? If they descended . . .

"There they are! By Shaitan, Sadat, if you don't want 'em, I do!" There must have been a dozen or more dollars glinting on the stony rubble of the floor, and as a booted leg swung over the edge of the trap I caught the glint of steel in Uliba's hand in the shadows and my hand was on the butt of my Joslyn – for all the good that would do. The second boot swung down . . .

"Wait, you fool!" roars Sadat, laughing. "Look before you leap, man!"

There was a sudden howl of alarm from the man about to jump, the booted legs shot upwards as he fairly threw himself out of the trap, his mates crowing with mirth, and I stood paralysed between relief and revulsion.

It is the practice of the female scorpion, after giving birth, to carry her young on her back, and even with six of the loathsome little transparent monsters in residence there was still no lack of room on the scaly top of the enormous yellow horror scuttling among the fallen coins. She must have been six disgusting inches long, not counting the great sting curved up and over her ghastly brood – and she wasn't alone in her nest, either; Papa and a couple of uncles were on hand, and a joyous sight they all were, bless their horny little hides, for they'd saved us from detection and death, no error. Not that they'd have done our intruder any harm through his stout half-boots, but they were a grand discouragement to coin collecting.

The trap was slammed shut to a chorus of jeers and taunts, and we were left in darkness and, in my case, imminent danger of heart failure. I was drenched in sweat, and Uliba was shaking as though

119

with an ague. The danger might have passed, but it hadn't gone; the force with which the trap had been closed had broken one of its slats, and through the gap I had a view beside which Mama Scorpion would have looked quite charming: the head and shoulders of a Soudani brigand listening to the orders which Sadat was giving for their departure. The odds are you'll never meet one of the Soudani criminal classes, so I'll tell you that this representative looked like an indescribably evil cathedral gargoyle, hook-nosed and vulpine, with a tuft of beard, a steel cap with chain-mail earguards over black hair falling to his shoulders, and a grinning mouthful of jagged yellow tusks. Happy the bride who wakes up to see that on the pillow, thinks I, and was dam' glad when he moved out of sight.

Presently they left the nave, and we heard them mounting up, but by mutual consent (and not a word said) we stayed put until dawn, by which time we reckoned they'd be well away. It was not comfortable, for with those fine specimens of Buthus Arachnidae rustling about on the floor we daren't sit or lie down, and while like the Soudani we were well shod against their stings, I found myself wondering if the horrid little buggers could climb or jump.[34] My legs were painfully cramped by the time daylight began to filter through the broken trap, but after chafing some life into them and satisfying myself that all seemed quiet Chez Scorpio, I took three hasty strides, hurled back the trap, and swung myself out. Uliba followed quickly – and there we were, chilled to the bone at dawn in an empty church in a ghost city and not a thing to bless ourselves with except the clobber we stood in, my Joslyn and cartridgebelt, and Uliba's knife. Our horses were gone with the saddle-bags containing all our food, gear, spare kit, and dollars, and we were a day's march from Lake Tana and heaven knew how far from Queen Masteeat's camp.

"Well, at least we can put our finances in order," says I. "Like old Ali Baba, we've lain doggo while the Forty Thieves cached their loot; now all we have to do is find it and fill our pockets." She hadn't heard the old tale, so I told it to her while we fossicked about – she was much taken with Morgiana's boiling the robbers

120

in oil, I remember. The cache was easy to find under a layer of rubble by the wall of the nave, and at the cost of skinned fingers and broken nails we clawed up the loose earth to reveal a stout iron-shod chest. It wasn't locked, and when I heaved up the lid we were looking at a sizeable fortune in Maria Theresas, jewellery, wrought precious metal, gold pieces of a currency unknown to me, and carved ivory. We filled my pockets and her wallets with the *gourshis,* a hundred dollars apiece or thereabouts, and reluctantly abandoned the rest except for a fine ebony-hafted Damascus scimitar which I took, and various jewelled bangles, necklaces, and a gold fillet and veil which Uliba fell on with cries of delight – she was a very feminine Amazon, really, preening herself in a polished silver hand mirror and gloating as she threw it and other choice pieces into the cellar so that the Soudanis would have to brave the scorpions to retrieve them, and lamenting that we couldn't capture the female and her young and enclose them in the chest before we reburied it, thus ensuring a jolly surprise for the returning robbers. Quite splendid in her malice, she was; I'd not have been surprised if her braids had stood on end and hissed at me.

Being famished, and not knowing how soon the Soudanis might come back, we made speedy tracks out of Gondar. From a vantage point on the south wall of the ruined palace we could survey the country as far as Lake Tana some forty miles away, a distant gleam of silver in the morning sun, its forested shore stretching away into the haze. The sooner we were under cover in those woods, the better, so we travelled at the Highlander's pace, a mile at the trot and a mile at the stride followed by a moment's rest standing, and then away again. Uliba ran like a Diana and I like a labouring bullock, but not too bad for forty-five, and within the hour we were in sight of a village of the plain called Azez, which I supposed we should avoid, but Uliba said the time for concealment was past now that we were afoot, and besides we'd get no news of Masteeat if we continued to skulk in rocks and bushes.

"We must seek it out, in a safe place where there are safe people to question. No, not in the village." We had stopped in a grove some way short of the little cluster of thatched huts, and she was shading her eyes to scan the low hills beyond. "There should be a monastery over yonder, of monks of St Antonius the Hermit . . . if the wars have passed them by. Monks know everything . . ."

"And if they recognise you? They could pass word to this fellow Gobayzy who's after you, or even to Theodore –"

"We've seen no trace of Gobayzy, no one will recognise me this far south, and Theodore has no more bitter enemy than the Church since he plundered and murdered at Metraha last summer. Anyway, we have no choice, so come, and keep your ears open for the monastery bell."

We set off across the plain, and as we went, skirting well wide of the village, she told me of Theodore's crowning infamy at Metraha, an island in Lake Tana which had been a holy place of sanctuary from time immemorial, and consequently a haven much used by merchants to deposit their treasures – St Paul's crossed with the Bank of England, if you like. Theodore had gained access to it by treachery, looted its vast store of gold, silver, grains, and precious stuff – and then herded the inhabitants, priests, merchants, women, and children into the principal buildings and burned them to death.

"So we run no risk of betrayal to Theodore. Rather," says Uliba complacently, "will the holy fathers show all kindness and respect to a noble lady of Tigre bound for the court of the Queen of the Gallas, who had the misfortune to be robbed of her caravan by Soudani bandits who murdered her servants and would assuredly have slain her (or worse) had she not escaped by night with her faithful Hindee attendant. Hence her destitute condition –"

"Lucky for her she was able to deck her destitution with a few choice trinkets – oh, and a purse of dollars –"

"– which she was fortunate to be able to carry away with her, and from which she will make a generous gift to the monastery's alms chest. If that does not move their pity," says she, "I know nothing of Christian priests. Besides, these will be provincial simpletons, properly awe-stricken in the presence of rank."

I didn't doubt that, but one snag occurred to me. "They're Coptic Christians, ain't they . . . suppose they spot you for a Galla? After all, you're on your way to Masteeat – can you pass as a Christian?"

She gave me her superior smile, and drew from the bosom of her tunic one of the necklaces she'd pinched from the Soudanis' hoard: a fine cord of pale blue silk skilfully intertwined with gold and silver threads. "This is called *matab*; is it not beautiful? All Christians of Habesh wear them from their baptism; it is the first thing these Christos look for in each other. And this one, as you see, is of the most precious kind, such as only the high-born and wealthy would wear . . . ah, but listen! The bell!"

It was tolling faintly, but stopped as we entered the little valley in which stood a plain adobe building of no great size, walled, with an arched gateway, and surrounded by plots too small to be called fields in which white-robed Abs were digging and hoeing without enthusiasm. They stopped to stare as the high-born lady of Tigre, a striking figure in her scanty tunic, boots, and veiled fillet, sashayed towards the gate with her faithful Hindee attendant throwing a chest as he followed dutifully in her wake.

Chanting greeted us as we passed through the archway into a courtyard where a crowd of robed and turbaned jossers were waking the echoes with what I learned later was a Coptic psalm, and plainly we were intruding on a service – or, as it proved, a rehearsal for one, Palm Sunday no less, which fell a week hence. The turbaned lads were priests, bearing strange long wands with heads like crutches, while the commonalty and sundry infants carried palm fronds. To the fore was a dignified old file called the Abba (which I suppose is abbot); he wore a very stylish yellow leather coat and carried a curious article like a catapult with abacus beads between its arms, which he waved from time to time. In attendance were a priest bearing a fancy sort of decorated cross, a tiny *chico* with a bell as big as himself, and two deacons holding up an enormous Bible.[*]

Even as we appeared the singing stopped and the Abba began to read from the Bible, but left off in some confusion when one of the deacons drew his attention to Uliba-Wark, who was listening attentively, hand on hip, nodding approval. Everyone goggled at

---

[*] For a description and illustration of the Palm Sunday ceremony, see Simpson, *Diary*.

her, as well they might, for she was posed like the Queen of Sheba, waving a graceful hand to them to continue, and then turning aside to seat herself on a bench by the gateway. The Abba, who'd been taken flat aback (it dawned on me that there wasn't another female in the courtyard), steadied up and began reading again in a shaky falsetto, but shooting little disturbed glances in Uliba's direction as she crossed her legs and sat back, finger on cheek, gently smiling as though she were watching a show performed for her benefit. The reading finished (cut short, I suspect), the Abba and his gang retired through an inner doorway, shooting more little glances, and presently a bald chap with a staff of office approached Uliba and invited her within. She rose with dignity, made a little gesture to me which I interpreted as an order to scatter a few dollars to the hoi-polloi, and swanned away. I distributed, smirking, bowed tactfully to the cross-bearer who was leading the peasantry in another psalm, and hastened after my mistress like a good little minion.

Even with my limited Amharic I could follow much that was said at the audience which followed in the monastery chapel. Uliba was conducted with great deference to a chair hurriedly placed between the front pews, while the Abba enthroned himself nervously on a stool before the altar, his attendants standing by with palms, crutches, and open mouths. I don't know if Coptic priests are celibate, but these gaped at her like hayseeds at a burlesque show in the Chicago Loop; I don't suppose their modest little Godhutch had ever seen her like, and she played it like the grandest of *dames*, surveying them coolly and turning that elegant profile as she swept off her fillet and veil and handed them carelessly to me, looking stern beside her chair. She charmed them with a gracious apology for interrupting their rehearsal, and the Abba near fell off his stool assuring her that it didn't matter tuppence, honestly, and please how could they serve her excellency?

This before she'd said a word about being a great swell on her way to a queen's court, or being despoiled; she did it simply by style and looks and those remarkable legs, and had them eating out of her dainty palm. Awe-stricken, she'd said they'd be, and awe-struck they were.

124

The account of our adventures which she gave them was succinct and fairly offhand, but it had them agog, knuckles to teeth and gasping concern. The Abba didn't know what Habesh was coming to, what with evil emperors and foreign invaders and plundering rebels and noble ladies molested and robbed by heathen brigands, God forgive them, but what protection and comfort the Church could offer, she should have, and her servant too, infidel though he was. This consisted of food, drink, attention, prayers, the best chamber in the monastery placed at her ladyship's disposal (with a mattress in the passage for Vilkins the butler), and the promise of such clothing, equipment, and transport as could be drummed up overnight.

I was given my vittles in the monks' refectory, watched by curious and none too friendly eyes, for they've no use for non-Christians, and as a "Hindee" I was right beyond the pale. Uliba dined in some state in the Abba's private apartments, and if the news she got was confused and disturbing, it was definite at least on the main point.

"Masteeat has her camp on the Abai river, below the falls which the people of Metcha call the Great Silver Smoke." She was jubilant. "Five days' journey by horse or camel, even by the western shore of Tana – see!" The Abba had given her a map, a pretty coloured thing with Lake Tana all little blue waves with boats afloat, and an Ark at anchor with hippos and pythons and monkeys clambering aboard under the eye of a distinctly Ethiopian Noah, the whole lot being blessed by a dusky Jesus. "Here at Azez we are forty miles from Gorgora, at the head of the lake; another fifty at most to Zage, and perhaps fifty down the Abai –"

"Why not the straight way, by the east shore?" I could see it would cut the journey by as much as a third.

"Because Theodore had his camp at Kourata last year –" she tapped a finger on it "– and he will have troops there still, and who knows how many between the lake and his army which marches on Magdala? He has wasted all Begemder, and these churchmen say he is already at the Jedda ravine, but their news will be a week old; he may be close on Magdala by now."

"And Masteeat's army, by your reckoning, is about ninety miles from Magdala . . . where's Napier, do they know?"

125

"They heard of him last at Antaloo, but that too will be old news. At best, he can hardly be more than a day's march south of the Ashangi lake." She traced a finger up from Magdala; Napier had a good hundred miles to go, by the look of it.

"Well, Theodore can win the race on a tight rein," says I. "If he gets his guns into Magdala . . ." I didn't care to think of that. The place was said to be impregnable, which was doubtless an exaggeration; British troops can take anywhere, given a commander who knows his business, but the Bughunter didn't have time for a siege, not with his striking force at full stretch, with food and forage running low. If he came to a dead stop before Theodore's defences . . . well, it would be a dead stop indeed, far from home and no way back. His army would starve where it stood, and Theodore's highlanders could cut up the remains at leisure . . . no doubt with the rebel warlords joining in. My consolation was that I'd be better placed as a free agent with Uliba, rather than as a hapless lump of cannon-fodder in Napier's Last Stand . . . I had a sudden horrid recollection of Gandamack, with the 44th trapped on the icy slope, Soutar with the colours round his middle, and the Ghazis closing in . . .

I asked about the rebels, and she spat. "Cattle! Cowards! They run in circles, frightened of Theodore, fearful of each other! That much is plain from this old fool of an Abba's tale, but he knows little more to any purpose. That drunken fat sow Masteeat," sneers she with satisfaction, "had the game won, had she used the wits she wastes in guzzling and coupling! Two months ago she stood before Magdala with her army, while its garrison of weaklings and traitors wrung their hands, willing to surrender but in dread of Theodore's vengeance when he returned from plundering in Begemder. Oh, had I stood in her place they'd have surrendered fast enough!" She clenched her fists and shook them, and I believed her. "But she puts off, and idles away her opportunity, and is forced to retreat at last because the hyena Gobayzy and the jackal Menelek come prowling into Galla country, afraid to attack Magdala, but still outnumbering her, so she withdraws to the Abai. It is very well," says she, pleased as Punch. "Things could not stand better!"

Blessed if I could see that, and I said so. "If she has cut and run, what's the use in our going on? She and her army'll be no help to Napier if they're ninety miles away!"

She waved that aside. "Galla armies can move at speed. Besides, she'll have left more warriors in the hills about Magdala, ready for action, than she'll have taken to the Abai. Let the Queen of Wollo Galla but say the word and there will be a steel ring – was not that what your general called it? – round the *amba* of Magdala, with Theodore held fast within."

The Queen of Wollo Galla . . . but which queen? We had been discussing her ambitions, and what part I might be called on to play in realising them, when the Soudanis had interrupted us, and the topic had not been resumed; well, it could be let lie for the moment. That she'd make a bid for her sister's throne, I knew, if not when, where or how. In the meantime it was enough that we knew Masteeat's whereabouts, and that these jovial monks would speed us on our way.

They didn't stint us, either, with the loan of two camels, their saddle-bags filled with grub and flasks of *tej*, cloaks and blankets, and a couple of *chicos* to race ahead to make sure our coast was clear. Uliba made no offer of payment, simply fluttering a queenly hand at me, and I presented the chief deacon with a purse of fifty dollars, to which she added one of her bracelets which she presented in fine Lady Bountiful style to a small girl in the crowd – for every soul in the place, priests, lay brethren, labourers and menials, was on hand to see us off. We mounted the camels, they lurched to their feet, the Abba blessed us, and off we went with a camel groom trotting in our wake; he would bring the beasts back from Lake Tana, where we would seek other transport. A chorus of farewells followed us, and before we were out of earshot they were making a joyful noise to the Lord, either in rehearsal for Palm Sunday or rejoicing for the dollars.

I'm no old Africa hand, and what I'd seen of Abyssinia so far had jaundiced rather than impressed, but I'm bound to say that the Lake Tana country is as close to earthly paradise as I've ever struck, for scenery at least. From Azez to Gorgora on the northern shore is nothing out of the ordinary, but the lake itself beats anything in Switzerland or Italy, a great blue shimmering inland sea fringed by tropical forest, hills, and meadows, for all the world like a glorious garden of exotic flowers and shrubs in groves of splendid trees and ferns. The woods are alive with birds of every colour and size, from tiny feathered mites hardly bigger than butterflies to the mighty hornbill, a black-and-white monster as big as a man, braying as it rushes overhead like some flying dragon. There's an abundance of game, deer and antelopes and monkeys everywhere, buffalo ranging on the slopes, huge hippos surging and bellowing in the lake itself, and the biggest snakes in Africa, twenty-foot pythons in shining coats of many colours, gliding through the shallows.

Good camels can cover the ground as quickly as horses, and we made our first-night camp in a little palm grove only a few miles from the lake. Uliba said it would be safer to steer clear of Gorgora, so next morning we made a bee-line for the western shore and the cover of the jungly forest. It had not been determined precisely *where* on Tana the groom should turn back with the camels, and when Uliba said we'd like to take them as far as the Abai source he had severe conniptions; he was one of your tough, lean Abs who run like stags, and had kept up easily with his long loping stride, but he was shot if he was going to venture any nearer the dreaded

"Negus Toowodros"* than he had to; everyone knew of the carnage that had been wreaked south of the lake, of the burning and blinding and hacking off of ears and noses; why, all Metcha was a smoking desert.

Uliba came the headmistress with him, but he wasn't to be moved, and it was only when she'd offered him twenty dollars and he'd beaten her up to thirty that he reluctantly agreed to come as far as Adeena, near the foot of the lake.

"We could have killed him and kept the camels," says Uliba as we rode on our way with the groom trotting moodily after, "but he might have fought, and what is thirty dollars?" I wondered if she'd have expected me to do the dirty deed; knowing her style, probably not.

It took us the best part of the day to reach Adeena, a little fishing village in a pretty clearing by the shore. They were almost the first folk we'd seen since leaving Azez, friendly enough peasants but, like our groom, apprehensive of what lay farther south, and thankful that Theodore's campaign of terror had not touched them so far. Zage and Baheerdar had been razed to the ground and all the people killed or driven away; yes, Theodore's soldiers were still at Kourata across the lake; but no, nothing would induce them to ferry us anywhere near the city – or indeed, even down the coast. Having seen their boats, crazy coracles of woven bulrushes that were permanently waterlogged, I was happy to continue our journey on foot.

To Uliba's fury, our groom, gossiping at the evening meal which we shared with the village headman, mentioned that we were on our way to find Queen Masteeat. It seemed harmless to me, but she was spitting blood later when she explained that the nearer we got to our goal, the greater our danger, with Theodore's lances on hand. "I knew we should have slit the chattering bastard's throat! Well, he has our dollars, but we'll not bid him goodbye. When all are asleep, do you take the saddle-bags from the camels, and we'll be away before dawn!"

It seemed to me she was starting at shadows. "These folk hate

* "Theodore, King of Kings".

129

Theodore more than you do! They ain't going to give us away."

"And is their hate greater than their fear? Will they be silent if Theodore's riders chance this way? We are not safe this side of the Silver Smoke. The camels could carry us there in a day, but to steal away with them by night might bring a hue and cry down on us."

So we took French leave of Adeena in the small hours, slipping through the shadows with such stealth that I doubt if more than half the population heard us go, but they paid us no mind, presumably turning over and thanking God to be rid of a pair of unwelcome guests. There was a good moon, and with Uliba surefooted as ever it was a pleasant promenade through the shadowy groves until the light went and the chilly mist came in off the water. Then we built a fire, had a welcome snack of the monastery's bread and ham washed down with *tej*, and rolled up together in one blanket, keeping warm in the jolliest way I know.

Next morning we rounded the bay which is the south-western limit of Tana, both in high spirits in the sunshine, swinging along like Phyllis and Corydon in Arcady, with not the least foreboding of the horror ahead. There were a few fishers abroad on the lake, staying afloat for a wonder, and we passed a couple of villages where the peasantry seemed to be taking no harm as they loafed about in their plots. We nooned in a secluded cove where a few water-fowl were disporting themselves out beyond the shallows, and Uliba asked me if I fancied duck for tiffin. I said by all means, if she'd catch them, and she laughed and asked, if she killed 'em, would I fetch 'em ashore? Kill away, says I, wondering, and she picked up a handful of pebbles from the beach, juggled them from hand to hand, and all of a sudden whipped them away like a fast bowler, side-arm, one-two-three! And blessed if she didn't crack the heads of two ducks and lay a third squawking and thrashing in the water!

She'd told me of the Gallas' skill with missiles, but I'd not have believed it if I hadn't seen it. I plunged in and retrieved the poultry, full of congratulation, but she made light of it, saying they had been real sitting birds, and next time she would bring one down on the wing. Again, I believed her. An odd thing: none of the other ducks had so much as stirred, and she told me that the birds and beasts of Lake Tana were so tame that they never minded hunters, not stirring even when the critter beside them was hit.

It was such a glorious day that we swam in the lake, icy cold as it was, and I have a happy memory of Uliba sitting on a smooth black rock like the little mermaid, naked, wet and shining.

We made good time in the afternoon, leaving the forest for a more broken and rocky shoreline, and I noticed that we saw fewer folk along the way, and at last none at all. That was the moment when I caught a drift on the air of that same flat stale stench there had been at Gondar, and Uliba stopped, head raised, and said: "Zage."

We had crossed a few streams running through the rocks into the lake, and now we came to another, a small river really, with steep banks, and as we prepared to descend the weather changed with that speed so typical of Abyssinia, and a storm of hail came down like grapeshot, great lumps the size of schoolboys' marbles that drove us under cover and churned the river mouth and lake surface into foam. You could barely hear yourself speak above the rattle of the downpour, but Uliba was laughing as she pointed to the stream and shouted: "Little Abai! Only a few miles farther now!"

I couldn't make this out: the stream was flowing *into* the lake, and I knew the Abai, which is the Blue Nile, should run *out* of Tana – and thereby hangs a tale, which I heard first from Uliba as we crouched under the broad leaves of a baobab to shelter from the hailstorm, and again years later from the Great Bore of the Nile himself, Daft Dick Burton, at the Travellers' Club. He had a most tremendous bee in his bonnet about it, with which I'll not weary you beyond saying that the *Little* Abai runs *into* Lake Tana *west* of the town of Zage, and *out* again *east* of the town, when it becomes the *Great* Abai and eventually joins the White Nile which rises 'way up yonder in Lake Victoria – or so I gathered from Burton, who was full of bile against the chaps who'd discovered it. God knows why: he'd ha' fought with his own shadow, that one.[35]

At all events, when the hail stopped we crossed and came to the promontory of Zage, the site of a once-populous town now ruined

131

and deserted, thanks to Theodore, who had looted and burned it months before – hence that stale stink of charred wood and desolation. It was half-hidden by trees at the base of the promontory, through which we passed to open ground where there were signs of a disused camp-site, and so came to a swampy tangle of roots on the verge of the lake. Out on the water we could see a couple of fishing craft heading up in the direction of Adeena, and Uliba surveyed them frowning for a long moment before turning to follow the edge of the swamp away from the lake.

She paused again to point eastward to where, beyond the swampy ground, there was a small cluster of huts on the shore. "Baheerdar," says she, smiling. "Remember? D'you think you could have found it?" I said I was glad I hadn't had to try, and she led on again by the swamp, which was now flowing south, quite distinctly, and presently, when we'd pushed our way through marshy thickets buzzing with mosquitoes, and mounted a grassy rise, the swampy flow had become a stream between jungly banks. A mile or so farther on it was broadening into a river proper, shining ruddy in the sunset, and Uliba gave a great heaving sigh and stretched her arms high above her head.

"There it runs – the Great Abai! A few miles to the Silver Smoke, and not far beyond, the camp of my people." She came to my side and put an arm about me, inviting an embrace. "Have we not travelled well together, *effendi*?"

I cried by gad hadn't we just, and gave her a loving squeeze and a hearty kiss, telling her she was the queen of guides – while noting to myself that she was now talking of the camp of *her* people, not Queen Masteeat's. Very soon now I must discover what was at work behind that triumphant smile, and whatever it was, prepare myself for some nimble footwork – oh, and if possible carry out the task Napier had given me, and ensure that the Wollo Gallas closed the trap about Magdala . . . whoever was occupying their tribal throne. I half expected Uliba to advert to it, but she volunteered nothing, so I must wait and see, composing myself to sleep on the banks of the Great Abai, and reflecting unprofitably on the irony that given a small boat and enough grub (and if the Napiers and Ulibas and

132

assorted Abs and Bedouin let me alone) I could have floated a few thousand miles downstream in peace and tranquillity to Shepherd's or the Hôtel du Nil in Cairo.

I awoke suddenly with a hand gripping my arm and another over my mouth, and was about to lash out in panic when I realised they were Uliba's hands, it was just on half-dawn, and she was hissing a warning in my ear.

"Still! Keep down!" She was out of her blanket, snaking away across the turf damp with dew, and I followed her with my innards turning over at this sudden alarm. "See – yonder, across the river!"

I followed her pointing finger, and froze where I lay. On the far side of the water, which was barely fifty yards broad at this point, a line of horsemen was emerging from the jungle, pricking down to the bank. They were lancers, forty or fifty of them, trim in white robes and turbans and breastplates, one or two with chain-mail shoulder guards, their leader wearing a steel casque and knight's gauntlets and carrying a silver shield. They ranged along the bank, dismounting at his word of command to water their horses, their voices drifting across the misty surface.

More in desperation than hope I wondered if they might be Masteeat's people, but Uliba shook her head impatiently and wormed her way backwards into the shelter of the bushes, dragging blanket and saddle-bag with her, and signing to me to do likewise.

"They are Theodore's guardsmen, his household cavalry. That silver shield is carried only by nobles high in his service." Her whisper was fierce but steady. "Those boats we saw last night, making towards Adeena – they must have been at Kourata, bearing word of us and where we were going!" She screwed her eyes shut in fury, clenching her fist. "God of gods, why did I not kill that loose-tongued fool!?"

"Hold on – how d'ye know they're looking for us? You can't be sure –"

"A silver shield abroad before dawn with picked troops of the Emperor? I can be sure they are not on manoeuvres! He would never leave such an elite to garrison Kourata when he is marching on Magdala! No, he will have sent them west the moment he learned (doubtless from Yando's vermin!) that a British officer was coming south, plainly to enlist aid from Masteeat and the Wollo Gallas! They will have been scouring Begemder for us, and now those peasant scum at Adeena have given them our scent. And they are following it."

Talking like a book, as usual, and keeping her head. She signed me to silence and crawled forward again, to a solitary bush, the braided head cocked to listen. After a moment she was back, her lips at my ear.

"They are looking for a place to cross, then they will sweep both banks downstream. And we must be the quarry; no ordinary fugitive would be worth such a hunt."

"Oh, God! What can we do?"

She smiled grimly. "Run! – away from the river, before they can cross. We can circle wide and come back to it, for we'll be swifter afoot in jungle than they can be on horseback. If we can reach the Silver Smoke ahead of them we shall be safe, for they'll venture no closer to Masteeat's army than that." A word of command sounded across the water; they were mounting up again. "But we've no time to lose. It is twenty miles through jungle to the falls."

If you've never travelled in jungle you may be under a false impression, thanks to the tales of blowhards who'll tell you how they've hacked their way through impenetrable undergrowth and been lucky to make two miles a day battling snakes and great hairy spiders. Well, such jungle does exist, and sufficiently hellish it is, as I should know who have gone my mile in Borneo and the Fly River country, but as a rule it ain't so thick, and what you have to look out for is where you're putting your feet. Even such good rain forest as the headwaters of the Blue Nile has its hazards, like sudden swamp and potholes and solid fallen trunks which crumble rottenly and drop you unexpected into the slime; by and large, though, it's fair going, with more trees than thickets, and space to move in. I reckon Uliba and I made a good four miles an hour, which is faster than marching, and if it was hot work it wasn't unbearable in the shade. I doubted if Theodore's cavalry could do as well; with luck, when we circled back to the river, we'd be comfortably ahead of them, provided we kept up our pace.

Moving away from the river must have added two or three miles to our trek, but by sunset Uliba reckoned we had covered enough ground for the day; you don't move in jungle after dark if you have any sense, so we camped among the banyans and acacias, not risking a fire but enjoying the rays of sundown gleaming through the groves, and the last chirping and calling of the millions of coloured birds in the branches overhead. It reminded me of the Madagascar forest, and you mayn't believe it but I felt my eyes stinging at the memory of Elspeth blue-eyed and beautiful, smiling up at me with her golden hair tumbled about her head on the grass, her arms reaching up to me and those lovely lips parting . . . "My jo, my ain dear jo!"

Dear God, that had been more than twenty years ago, that strange idyll of joy and terror mingled, when we'd fled from Antan' with Ranavalona's Hovas on our trail . . . Theodore's riders might be a fearsome crowd, and most professional by the look of them, but at least they were part-civilised, unlike those black monsters . . . Strange, though, how history repeated itself: here I was again, fleeing the forces of darkness through tropic forest in the company of beauteous tumble – not that Uliba could begin to compare in looks, style, deportment, vivacity, elegance, complexion, allure, voluptuousness, abandoned performance, erotic invention, or indeed in any way at all to my glorious Elspeth, at the thought of whom I was beginning to dribble . . . and whom I loved dearly and truly, I may say, and had seen only at brief ecstatic intervals in the past four weary years – no, five, dammit! It was too bad, and I missed her so, and God alone knew what she'd been up to while I was shirking shot and shell at Chancellorsville, Gettysburg, Yellow Tavern, Ford's Theatre, and Queretaro, and look at me now, lachrymose in Ethiopia with the little grey monkeys sneering at me from the trees. Then the rain came on.[36]

It dawned gloriously sunny, however, and we were up and making for the river before first light. The closer we got to it, the thicker grew the jungle, which meant worse going for Theodore's cavalry. At last we sighted the gleam through the undergrowth, and presently came out on a long stretch of sward running along the water's edge. The river was about quarter of a mile across, I dare say, and a landscape painter's dream, grey-green and shining as it slid smoothly by through the little forested islands. The far bank was luxurious foliage backed by green foothills rising to mountains, and to our right, a mile or two downstream, a faint mist hung over the river, with a perfect rainbow above it. Uliba clapped her hands and pointed.

"The Silver Smoke! Am I not the queen of guides, as you said?"

For the first time since we had left Tana there were folk to be seen, fishermen pottering about their ramshackle boats a few hundred yards downstream where the sward margin ended and the jungle overgrew the river's surface. Closer at hand two girls were busy *dhobying* clothing and hanging it to dry on a line by the water's edge, their little coracle drawn up on the bank. They stood up to stare at us, and when one of them waved, Uliba raised a hand. My spirits were rising as we set off down the bank, the birds were carolling, there was a perfumed breeze blowing from the water, we were within a few miles of journey's end, I was absolutely humming "Drink, Puppy, Drink", the larks and snails were no doubt on their respective wings and thorns, God was in his heaven, and on the verge of the jungle, not twenty yards away, a white-robed helmeted lancer was sitting his horse, watching us.

For three heartbeats we simply stared at each other, while I told myself this couldn't be one of the troop we'd seen yesterday, they'd not had time – and then his eyes were wide, a hunter sighting the game, I was snatching out my Joslyn, Uliba was shouting "No!", dashing my hand aside and racing past me, drawing her knife as she ran. Without breaking stride she threw it, straight as an arrow, for his breast, but this fellow knew his business, whipping his shield across to deflect the flying blade, shouting with triumph as he wheeled his mount for the forest.

She'd known that a shot would bring the rest of his gang down on us, but I was bound to risk it now, and was drawing a bead on his back when she stooped, grabbed up a stone, stood poised for an instant, and hurled it after him. It took him just below his helmet

136

rim with a thunk! like an axe hitting wood, his horse reared as he hauled on the reins, and then he was toppling from the saddle, helmet going one way, lance t'other, and hitting the ground with an almighty crash of his back and breast. I bit back a yell of delight, but it was precaution wasted, for before we could stir another step half a dozen lancers were bursting out of the green, taking in the scene in a second, and sweeping down on us.

It was blind instinct that made me blaze away at the leader, for an instant's thought was enough to convince me that I couldn't hope to down them all, and it was folly to waste time firing when I could be flying for dear life. Anyway, I'd missed the bastard, and he was dropping his lance-point and charging me. Uliba was flinging stones, the mad bitch, and yelling defiance; she caught the leader full in the clock and he swerved his horse into the path of a comrade, both coming down in a splendid tangle of lashing hooves. She screamed with delight, and I thought, good luck, lass, you give 'em what for, for I ain't stopping. The river was a bare fifty yards away, and I made for it like a stung whippet; from the tail of my eye I saw Uliba hurl a last missile and then come racing after me.

My goal was the two *dhobi* wenches who had a boat beached; I'd barely have time to thrust it afloat and leap aboard before the hosts of Midian arrived, but it was the only hope – and even as I high-tailed it with Uliba a few paces behind, I found myself thinking, my stars, I've done this before, on the banks of the Ohio, with Cassy the runaway legging it after me and the slave-catchers roaring behind, and they shot me in the arse on the ice-floes, and she'd dragged me to safety – aye, but this time there'd be no Abe Lincoln on the far shore to face down our pursuers . . .

Hooves were thundering horrid close, and I stole a glance which showed a lancer coming full career, point down, not twenty yards behind me; the *dhobi* girls were screaming and scattering, I knew I'd never reach their boat in time, and as I tripped and went down on the shingle, Uliba swerved aside in her flight and leaped like a panther into the path of my pursuer, somehow catching his lance just behind the point with its ghastly burden of somebody's goolies. The glittering steel was diverted, driving into the ground a foot from my hip as I sprawled helpless, the lancer was flung from the saddle, and Uliba, keeping her grip on the weapon, rolled away, came to her feet like an acrobat, wrenched the point free, and drove it into the fallen man's body, screaming like a banshee.

It was no time for thanks or congratulation: I scrambled up and fairly flung myself at the boat, knocking one of the *dhobi* lasses flying, seized its prow and thrust it down the bank into the water. It was more like a canoe than their usual woven tubs, and almost capsized as I heaved myself inboard, grabbing wildly for one of the flat sticks which these benighted clowns use as paddles. Still on shore, Uliba was hurling rocks and howling abuse; at her feet the fallen lancer was kicking like a landed fish with his own weapon pinning him to the earth, there were half a dozen of his fellows within ten yards, but keeping a wary distance, one of them nursing an arm to testify to Uliba's accuracy.

"Noseless pigs! Bullies of the bazaar! Cowardly bastards got by lepers on street-corner whores! Can one unarmed woman make you turn tail, dunghill disturbers that you are!" She was in rare voice, but now two of them couched their lances and charged, and with a last shrieked insult she turned and did a racing dive which brought her within reach of the stern even as I lashed the water with my clumsy oar and the current carried us swiftly downstream and out of their reach. She scrambled in, shouting with laughter and blood-lust, taunting them with obscene curses and gestures as they stood helpless on the shore.

"Procurers of perverts! Offspring of diseased apes! Tell Theodore how Uliba-Wark, Queen of the Gallas, whipped you single-handed!" She stood up to rail at them, and the canoe rocked alarmingly.

"You'll have us over, rot you – sit down and paddle!" The current was strong, and we would have our work cut out to reach the far bank before it took us down to the little jungly islands where I could see the surface breaking into white water which must mean rocks and rapids. But even as I weighed the distance I saw that it was impossible; the green shore was at least four hundred yards off, and with these near-useless paddles we could hardly make headway across the river.

The nearest islands were perhaps a mile distant; with luck we might adjust our course to find the smoothest water between them. I shouted to Uliba to paddle in harmony, but it was all we could do to keep the crazy little boat steady as the speed of the river increased. I turned my head to see how our pursuers were faring; the stretch of open shore from which we'd escaped was enclosed at its downstream end by jungle, so they would make only slow progress that way, but there were the fisher-folk's boats, and I thought they might take to the water after us. But no; they were mounting up, in no haste that I could see, apparently giving up the chase.

We were bearing down at speed on the islands now, and the current was so swift that I could see the water absolutely sloping as it rushed between them. I shouted to Uliba, but there was little we could do to steer the boat; it slipped smoothly down the grey foamy slope which broke either side in white flurries as it dashed over the rocks, but immediately ahead the surface was unruffled, and if the canoe could pass through the great eddy at the foot of the watery slope without foundering, there was smooth water beyond. The islands were slipping past – and once again memory took hold, as I recalled the brown flood of the Ganges below Cawnpore, when we had to scramble in panic on to the mudflats with the muggers snapping at our heels.

There were no crocs this far up the Nile, but I didn't know that as I clung to the gunwale of that rickety craft, absolutely bellowing in dismay as we struck the eddy, wallowed half-submerged for a frightening moment, and then surged through on to the calmer surface. We were sitting in a foot of water, but stayed afloat by a miracle – surface tension, I believe, although I did not define it as such just then. The river was carrying us on at a gentler pace now, but we were in midstream with the banks as far away as ever; we must wait for a bend, when we might be able to guide ourselves to one shore or the other, no matter which, for pursuit must be far behind by now.

I cried this over my shoulder to Uliba, and she called a reply, but I couldn't catch it above the sound of the river, which seemed to be growing louder. I thought that strange, since we'd left the noisy rapids behind, but then I realised it was coming from ahead, a distant rumbling from beyond another crop of little jungly islands strung across the stream. In the distance there was a mist drifting up, stretching from bank to bank, the rumble was growing to a roar, the speed of the current was increasing, rocking us from side to side, and suddenly Uliba was clutching my shoulder, pointing ahead and yelling:

"The Silver Smoke! The Great Silver Smoke!"

I distinctly remember shouting: "The *what*?" – and then it struck me like a blow: it was the Ab name of the Blue Nile falls beyond which Queen Masteeat had her camp. Uliba had said nothing of their size, but from the increasing noise and the appearance of white water ahead among the islands, I guessed that they must be more hazardous than the rapids we'd already passed through, and that it would be a sound move to seek terra firma without delay. Had I known that they were the height of Niagara, I dare say I might have joined Uliba's frenzied paddling with even greater enthusiasm; as it was I flailed the water, blaspheming vigorously at the futility of our efforts to guide the canoe to one of the islands towards which we were rushing. She was shouting something, but the roar of the river had risen to a thunder that blotted out every other noise, even my own anguished bellowing.

It was the damnedest thing: the din was deafening, we were racing along at the very deuce of a clip, and yet the water around us was as smooth as oil. Right in our path was a line of black rocks, great rounded masses gleaming like polished marble, for all the world like the backs of whales, and as our boat collided with the nearest I was sure it must be shattered to pieces. I seized the gunwale, screaming, but the rock must have been slick with river slime, for we shot along its surface for a sickening second before being flung into the eddies beyond; the current whirled the canoe clean round, branches were lashing across my head and shoulders, and I grabbed at them in desperation, tearing my hands on the thorny twigs but holding on, feeling the canoe slew round beneath me.

I'm strong, but how I kept my grip, God knows. We were at the downstream end of a little overgrown islet, a few yards ahead the

140

smooth water was being smashed into foam by the jagged teeth of a rocky ridge, and beyond that a mass of raging white water was vanishing into a mist as thick as London fog. We must be almost on the lip of the fall, and my arms were being dragged from their sockets by the appalling strength of the current tugging the dead weight of the canoe and our two bodies.

I was half-in-half-out of the canoe, and it was slipping slowly away from beneath me. Another second and it would have been gone, leaving me behind, but Uliba, floundering in the water that was swamping it, made a frantic lunge towards me, seized my leg, and clung on with the strength of despair. I shrieked with pain as my palms slipped along the whiplash withies; they were cutting like fire and I was losing my hold, the intolerable weight was dragging me loose, and in another moment both of us would be swept away into that thunderous white death in the mist.

There was only one thing to be done, so I did it, drawing up my free leg and driving my foot down with all my force at Uliba's face staring up at me open-mouthed, half-submerged as she clung to my other knee. I missed, but caught her full on the shoulder, jarring her grip free, and away she went, canoe and all, the gunwale rasping against my legs as it was whirled downstream. One glimpse I had of the white water foaming over those long beautiful legs, and then she was gone. Damnable altogether, cruel waste of good woman-hood, but what would you? Better one should go than two, and greater love hath no man than this, that he lay down someone else's life for his own.

With that dead weight gone I could just keep my grip, and with a mighty heave hauled myself into the thicket, catching a stouter branch and getting a leg over it – and suddenly there was an appalling crack, the branch gave way, and down I went, entangled in a mesh of leaves and withies, under the surface, helpless in the grip of the current which swept me away. I came up, half-drowned, into the fury of the rapids, buffeted against rocks and snags, tossed like a cork this way and that and clutching blindly for a hold that wasn't there, unable even to holler with my mouth and throat full of choking water. A massive black shape surged up before me, one of the great boulders worn smooth by the centuries, and even as I was flung against it with shattering force, hanging spreadeagled half out of the water, I saw beyond it a sight which has since provided me with much food for thought.

Not two yards away the canoe was caught fast beneath the overhanging foliage of another of those islands, and climbing clear of the wreck was Uliba-Wark. She had hold of a stout vine, swinging herself like a gymnast to a clear patch of solid ground, and given a moment for quiet reflection I might have concluded that if I had not been an unutterable swine and selfish hound in kicking her loose, I'd like as not have been safe beside her gasping, "Will you have nuts or a cigar, ma'am?"

As it was, I was slowly slipping from the boulder. Its surface was like a frozen pond, my hands could get no grip as I flailed them on the stone, squealing like billy-be-damned, and while Uliba could not have heard me, she absolutely saw me for a split second before I slid from her view into the torrent, inhaling a bellyful of the Blue Nile as I continued my progress downstream, presently descending one hundred and fifty feet without benefit of canal locks.

Falling down one of the highest waterfalls on earth (so far as I know only the Victoria Falls are appreciably higher) is not like toppling from the lofty side of a ship (which I've done) or from any other dry height. I say "dry" because being engulfed in water which is undoubtedly drowning you quite takes away the sensation of falling, and there is no shock of entering the water at the end of your enforced dive; you arrive cocooned in the stuff and are borne into the depths in a state of complete confusion: you can see nothing but blinding light and hear nothing but continuous thunder, you can't tell which is up and which is down, and only at the uttermost limit of your plunge does some inkling of your situation enter your consciousness, as you begin to rise again.

Even then you're entirely helpless, for your limbs are paralysed by the sheer battering shock, as is your will. I've known what it is to drown, on several occasions, most memorably in the Skrang river with a blowpipe dart in my ribs, and upside down in that infernal drain beneath Jotunberg Castle, and at the bottom of a bath in the amorous clutches of the demented Queen of Madagascar, but only in the maelstrom under the Blue Nile falls was I unable even to struggle feebly as I drifted upwards through that silvery radiance, the agony of suffocation gradually changing to a dreamy languor – and then my head must have broken surface, for I was gasping great painful gulps of air, retching and trying to scream as I felt the undertow drag at my legs, sucking me under again, and reason returned to tell me that to give up now, or faint away, or allow that torpor to enfold me again, was to die.

Whether my pathetic attempt to swim, or some freak of the current, or just a plain miracle took me clear, I can't tell, for all I remember is an engulfing white mist, and after a while gravel under my knees and body, and crawling on to wet rock and lying exhausted in pouring rain – in fact it was the spray thrown up by millions of tons of water pouring over that colossal natural weir into the enormous lagoon at its foot. I managed to roll over on my back and stare up through a glittering rainbow haze at that gigantic white curtain of water falling with the roar of a thousand thunderstorms; I was lying on a flat stone bank apparently at one side of the river and about two furlongs from the fall itself; as I say, how I came there, God alone knows.

If I'd been a half-decent Christian I dare say I'd have sent up a prayer of thanksgiving for my deliverance. Or I might have marvelled at the devil's own luck that preserves rotters where good men get their cocoa. But neither of these things occurred to me, and my last thought before slipping into unconsciousness as I gazed up at that towering cataract, was: "I wonder if anyone's ever done that before?"

I know now that I must have come over the middle of the falls, where the force of the river drives the torrent well out from the cliff, so that I'd been thrown clear of the rocky base and landed in deep water; if I'd taken the plunge from the eastern lip, where the current is slacker and the water pours directly down the cliff-face, I'd have been mangled on the rocks or drowned in the eddy for certain. Even so, I'd fallen from the height of Nelson's Column, and you need nine lives to survive that.

No one believes it,[37] of course, including the small boy and his sister who found me dead to the wide on the rocky shore, and their fisher-folk parents who nursed me through a bout of fever – malaria, by the feel of it – that left me weak as a baby. As for the junior officer commanding the file of Galla soldiers who arrived when word of my presence had spread beyond the little village, he laughed to scorn the notion that anyone could live through the Silver Smoke, even if he was a Hindu heretic and therefore doubtless a sorcerer in league with Shaitan.

"For you are Khasim Tamwar, are you not?" says this handsome young savage, smiling courteously as he squatted down beside my pallet in that peasant's hut. "Horse-trader out of India, seeking audience with our most illustrious queen, Masteeat the Looking Glass?"

And how the devil should he know that? Had I babbled in my fever – or could word have preceded us from the monastery at Azez? He smiled at my astonishment, the cocky subaltern to the life, for all that his classic features were as black as my boot and his braided hair was smeared with butter dripping on to his bare shoulders.

"It is our business to know who comes and goes along the Abai, and when a foreigner speaking Arabic comes from the north, who should it be but the expected traveller from . . . Hyderabad, or some such name?"

"Expected, you say? But how –?"

"No doubt her majesty will tell you," says he coolly. "And you would be wise not to insult her with talk of leaping over waterfalls. She is a kind and loving ruler, but she has a short way with liars . . . Are you fit to travel?"

I was, more or less, so after I'd thanked the peasants and dashed them a few of the dollars which, with my Joslyn, had been bestowed in my sash and so survived the fall, we set off through the jungly forest which encloses the Abai beneath the Tisisat. From an eminence about a mile south I was able to get a full view of that extraordinary wonder of the natural world, all six hundred yards of it from the broken cataracts at its western end to the splendid horseshoe on the east. Aye, the devil certainly looks after his own, thinks I, while my Galla escorts sneered and nudged each other and muttered "Walker!" in Amharic.

They were a formidable crew, the very sort of men I'd have expected from my acquaintance with the female of the species, Uliba-Wark: big, likely youngsters, not one under six feet, active as cats, muscled like wrestlers, and African only in colour. Speedy had said that of all the countless Galla tribes, the Wollos were the pick, and I could believe him and thank God they were Theodore's sworn enemies, for if they'd opposed us I doubt if one of Napier's army would ever have got back to the coast. They're warriors from their cradles, expert fighters, splendid horsemen, and would rather cut throats than eat dinner. Fortunately for their neighbours, the fifty or sixty families of the nation are never done feuding among themselves, for if ever they united they could sweep north Africa from the Red Sea to the Sahara. They must be the most independent folk on earth; those of their tribes who are republican acknowledge no law and pay taxes to no one, and even the Wollos, who recognised Masteeat as their queen, served in her army as volunteers without obligation.

There were a dozen in my escort, all well mounted and dressed accordingly with trowsers not unlike Pathan *pyjamys* under their robes, but barefoot and without head-dresses. They were armed with sickle-swords and those disgusting ballock-festooned lances, but no muskets or pistols. Their subaltern, whose name was Wedaju, explained that while Abs generally were familiar with firearms brought in centuries ago by the Portuguese, the Gallas, being crusty traditionalists who enjoyed slaughter at close quarters, were only now beginning to adopt them. Our conversation arose from the envious interest he showed in my Joslyn, asking if he might examine it; the fact that he didn't simply take it suggested that he regarded me as a guest rather than a prisoner, which set me wondering again how he'd known who I was. But I didn't ask: I'd find out eventually, and it was enough for the moment that I was being civilly treated.

My first concern was plainly Queen Masteeat, and how to present Napier's proposal. One complication at least had been removed: whether Uliba-Wark was still in flight from Theodore's cavalry or had been collared by them, she was no longer in a position to embarrass my mission by trying to usurp her sister's throne, thank God. Fine woman in her way, good *jancada* and capital primitive ride, but she could have been an almighty nuisance, and I was well shot of her. I'd make my pitch to Masteeat in my own way, deploying the Flashy charm and the promise of fifty thou' in Maria Theresas, and see how her majesty played the bowling. And if and when the Wollo Gallas marched forth to besiege Magdala, I'd contrive to keep my safe strategic distance from the action.

Our way lay through forest which thinned out after a few miles into pleasant wooded plain, with low hills on our flank, each with a sentry on its summit. Presently we came on pickets camped out in the groves, passing us through most professional, watchword and all, every man on his feet and jumping to their guard commanders' orders. So we came into their camp proper, a great spread of tents and huts not unlike a Red Indian village, but clean and orderly, and although there were women and children by the hundred, there was no confusion or stink. Everywhere there were Galla warriors, mounted and infantry, plainly at ease but not loafing or lolling; this was a disciplined host, thousands strong and in no way encumbered by their families. No one would ever take this crew by surprise, and I knew just by their look that they'd be able to break camp and be off at an hour's notice. My opinion of Queen Masteeat and her followers was rising swiftly; the most formidable African queen since Cleopatra, Speedy had said, and if her travelling cantonment were anything to judge by, he was right.[38]

Our arrival caused a stir, scores of white-robed armed men closing in on us and a couple of seniors in red-fringed *shamas* calling out to Wedaju in a language I didn't understand. He'd spoken Arabic to me, none too fluently, but what I was hearing now was the Gallas' own tongue, which isn't Amharic or anything like it. Fortunately the Galla aristocracy speak Arabic well; one of the seniors, having cross-examined Wedaju, called out to me:

"Where are your horses, trader?"

I said I was here to buy not to sell, and he cocked his grizzled head and grinned, with his hand on his hilt.

"And you carry purchase money with you through Habesh in time of war? Truly, you are bold travellers who come from Hindustan!"

Those who understood shouted with laughter, watching to see what I made of this jest with just a hint of threat behind it. Wedaju was about to intervene, but I got in first.

"I carry money enough. I carry this also –" And I conjured the Joslyn out of my sash, spun it on my finger, did the border shift, presented it to the senior butt first, and as he reached for it wide-eyed I spun it again to cover him. The watching crowd gave a huge yell of surprise, and then fairly roared. My senior clapped his hands with delight, and in a moment I was surrounded by grinning black faces – if there's one thing the Wollo Gallas like, it's ready wit and impudence, and that silly little incident won me an admiring public before I'd been in their camp five minutes. Style, you see . . . and I tipped my metaphorical hat in memory of dear old Lou Maxwell who'd taught me how to spin a gun in Las Vegas all those years ago.[39]

In the centre of the camp, within a stockade, was a group of permanent buildings: typical Ab dwellings of various sizes, dominated by a great two-storey structure with a conical thatched roof and upper and lower verandahs, which I guessed was the royal residence. Wedaju conducted me to one of the lesser buildings where a dignified old file in red-bordered *shama* and turban, sporting a fine white beard and bearing a red-shafted spear of office, ran a cold eye over me; they conversed in Galla, and at last the chamberlain, as I took him to be, made a stately departure, and Wedaju held out his hand and demanded my Joslyn.

"You are to go into the Queen's presence," says he. "Have no fear, I shall keep it for you, and doubtless it will be returned when her majesty has spoken with you." He paused, weighing the piece in his hand. "That feint you used out yonder – would you show it to me? Some day I shall have such a weapon as this, and it would be good to know . . ."

I showed him, and he practised, chortling, and was expert in no time. "Thank you, friend!" cries he, and I decided that one of my calculated good deeds wouldn't hurt.

"If all speeds well with the Queen, you shall have such a pistol," I told him, and he was still exclaiming his gratitude when the chamberlain returned with two turbaned guardsmen and led the way out, Flashy being ushered in his wake. The guardsmen thrashed aside the crowd who'd been craning their necks at the doorway to see the funny foreigner, and with Wedaju at my elbow we crossed to the big two-storey building, passed in between more turbaned sentries, and waited in a large dim hall while the chamberlain went ahead through a great bead curtain which was presently held aside by two of the loveliest handmaidens you could ever hope to see, true Galla girls with cool damn-you-me-lad expressions and figures to match. The chamberlain's voice called out from within, Wedaju prodded me forward, and I strode into the presence of Masteeat the Looking Glass, Queen of Wollo Galla, and with luck guardian angel of Her Britannic Majesty's army in Abyssinia.

You never know what to expect on encountering royalty. I've seen 'em stark naked except for wings of peacock feathers (Empress

148

of China), giggling drunk in the embrace of a wrestler (Maharani of the Punjab), voluptuously wrapped in wet silk (Queen of Madagascar), wafting to and fro on a swing (Rani of Jhansi), and tramping along looking like an out-of-work charwoman (our own gracious monarch). But I've never seen the like of the court of the Queen of Galla.

Her majesty was at luncheon, which she ate surrounded by lions, four huge maned brutes grouped about the great couch where she lounged on cushions, an arm over the neck of one of the beasts while with her free hand she helped herself to dainties from trays presented by two more fair attendants. Another lion was nuzzling her shoulder from behind, and the remaining two crouched at her feet, one with its head against her knee – for all the world like four great tabbies toadying for scraps, which she fed them from time to time, dainty fingers popping tidbits into jaws I'd not have approached for a pension.

And if that were not enough to bring me to a dead stop, there was something else: seated on a low stool a little way from the couch, regarding me with venomous dislike, was Uliba-Wark.

A split second, and then she was off the stool like a striking snake, whipping the knife from her boot as she launched herself at me, screaming vengeance, and it would have been Flashy R.I.P., Abyssinia 1868, if Wedaju hadn't thrust me aside, caught her wrist as the knife descended, thrown her on her back, and pinned her, all in one lightning movement. She was hollering blue murder as he disarmed her, the old chamberlain was collapsing in an apparent fit, my escorting guardsmen were hastening to put themselves between the commotion and the throne, the apartment seemed to be full of squealing handmaidens . . . and Queen Masteeat gently slapped the muzzle of a lion which had arisen, growling, at the disturbance. Beyond that she didn't blink an eyelid, waiting until Uliba's shrieks had subsided, and applying herself to a chicken leg in the meantime.

"Fair, fat, and forty" was how Speedy had described her. She must have been a stunner as a girl, but sloth and gluttony had plumped out the comely face, and if "fat" was a trifle unkind she still looked as though it might take two strong men to raise her commanding form from its cushioned bed. It was clad in a splendid robe of shimmering blue silk, with one fleshy polished shoulder and arm bare, and if there was plenty of her it all appeared to be complete and in working order. Elspeth would have called her sonsy, signifying bonny and buxom. As a commoner she'd have been a fine figure of a woman; being royalty, she was stately, regal, imposing, statuesque, or any other courtly grovel you please, and a perfectly acceptable piece of mattress-fodder – supposing she had the energy.

For a more lethargic lady I'd seldom seen. The full, good-natured face, as light as creamy coffee between the long oiled braids, was placid, and the large, slightly protruding eyes were almost sleepy as she considered me, toying with the mane of her blasted man-eater. Seeing her so at ease among her cushions, pondering which dish to tackle next, it struck me that if she was as shrewd and ruthless as I'd been told, she knew how to conceal it. Even her voice, when she addressed Uliba, was gentle and bored.

"Is this the man? The horse-trader of India? Tell me in a word, but do not name him."

Uliba said it was, at the top of her voice, with unprintable additions, as she writhed in Wedaju's grasp. "And I shall kill the bastard! The filthy villain would have cast me to death, I who had guided and guarded him! He shall die! As I am a woman, I swear it!"

"And as I am a queen, I shall have you whipped till you weep if you raise your voice in my presence again," says Masteeat mildly. "It would not be the first time . . . remember?"

"I remember!" snaps Uliba, and glared at me. "As I shall remember you also, dog! And I shall have my way in the end, dear sister! When the time comes this jackal shall be paid a traitor's wages!"

"That shall be as God wills." Masteeat indicated the stool. "Sit, child, and be still. You who aspire to a throne should try to behave like a queen. What he did or did not do is for another day. We have greater matters before us now."

Like what goody to guzzle next, apparently, for she was busy at the dishes even as she chided Uliba, sounding like a patient teacher with a naughty pupil, and I guessed this was a scene they'd played many times in Uliba's childhood, and that it drove her wild. She wrenched free of Wedaju, stood blazing silently for a moment, and then stalked back to her stool. Masteeat selected what looked like a large underdone steak, took a hearty bite, chewed reflectively, and directed her handmaiden to take a tray to me, indicating that I should help myself.

I didn't know, then, that this was a considerable honour in Ab court circles. I made a quick survey of the raw beef and roasts, surrounded by cakes and desserts, chose some skewered meat, and bowed civilly in majesty's direction, but she was busy engulfing the last of her steak. Having belched delicately, she wiped her lips with the hem of that beautiful dress, began to spoon a pudding into herself, and signed to the handmaiden, who clapped sharply to call the room to attention. The old chamberlain, having clambered to his feet, bowed and tottered out, followed by the guards and Wedaju, who I was glad to see was taking Uliba's knife with him.

And then, before my wondering eyes, Masteeat laid aside her empty bowl, and clicked her tongue. At this three of the lions rose with a reluctant lethargy to match their mistress's, and padded out, followed by the bowing handmaidens, leaving the fourth lion, evidently a royal favourite, blinking at the Queen's feet and purring like a motor engine.

So there we were, Flashy and the sister-queens, and I'll not waste time rehearsing my bewildered thoughts. All that seemed certain was that if Uliba had attempted a coup, it had misfired, but her elder didn't seem much put out, and was giving courteous attention at last to her visitor.

"You have earned a welcome by your patience," says she, "but first I must know your true name."

"Sir Harry Flashman, ma'am," says I, shoulders back, chin up. "Colonel, British Army, with messages from Sir Robert Napier, general officer commanding Her Britannic Majesty's forces in Abyssinia."

She nodded acknowledgment and glanced at Uliba. "So you were telling the truth. You did well to whisper it in my ear alone."

"Pah!" snaps Uliba. "At last you believe me! The Queen is gracious!"

"Be thankful for that," says Mastéeat. "And for the Queen's mercy."

"I ask no mercy from you!" Uliba was on her feet again. "I never have, and I never will!"

"You have never had to," says Masteeat, stroking her lion's mane. "The baby of the family must always be indulged and excused and forgiven, whatever her fault. Because she is the baby, and knows well how to trade on it."

Uliba let out a squeal like a steam whistle, fists clenched, stamping. "You lie! I never made excuse, or pleaded kinship! I have shown a bare face and fought for what should be mine! I am no hypocrite, like you who talk of the Queen's mercy! What mercy have you shown to my friends, my faithful ones? To Zaneh, and Adilu, and Abite, you cruel heartless woman?" And I'd not have believed it if I hadn't seen it: she burst into tears and stood there, knuckling her eyes.

"What you would have done if they had plotted against *your* throne. But I was less cruel than you would have been. They died quickly – even Zaneh, who betrayed your plot to me weeks ago, hoping for favour. He should have suffered as a double traitor – and you should have known better than to trust a discarded lover . . . oh, stare, girl, do you think I know nothing?" She sounded weary. "I may not punish you for treason, but I could slap you for stupidity."

Uliba went on sobbing, and Masteeat frowned at me as though becoming aware that the family squabble was being earwigged by this foreigner. I was spellbound: Uliba racked by sobs of penitence or rage, you couldn't tell which, looking all forlorn and fetching in her scanty tunic, and the languid matron reclining on her cushions, a study in fatigued perplexity. At last she sighed, pushed the lion aside, and extended a hand towards Uliba.

"Oh, come here, little one! Stop this foolish weeping; you have nothing to weep for!" Uliba gave a mighty gulp, scowled, and tossed her head. "Come, I say!" And damme if Uliba didn't dash the tears from her eyes and move with halting steps to the couch. Masteeat took her hand and pulled her gently to her knees, putting an arm about her shoulders.

"What am I to do with you, daughter of tribulation, sister of strife? You are too big to put across my knee these days . . . and if I did, you would rage and break things . . . and later hang your head and beg forgiveness. Perhaps even make me another gift in amends . . . ?"

She twitched the blue silk robe aside, revealing a massive but beautifully turned leg (ran in the family, no doubt) shod with a golden sandal and bearing two ankle-chains, one of the silver bells popular with Galla ladies, the other of cheap little coloured beads.

Uliba stared and sniffed. "You kept it! All these years . . ."

"Since your sixth birthday, when you flew into a passion because you were not given a pony, and father had you beaten, and you broke my crystal cup in your tantrum," says Masteeat. "And howled with remorse, and presently brought me this anklet as a peace offering."

"I made it with beads stolen from Warkite's gown of state . . . the bitch!" sniffs Uliba, adding sulkily: "I wonder your majesty wears such a tawdry thing!"

Masteeat leaned forward to finger the anklet, and said in that tired, gentle voice: "I have no jewel so precious as that brought to me by a sad, sorry little girl long ago. And if she tries to take my throne, still she is that little girl . . . and so I must love her always."

Uliba gave a wail that combined frustrated rage with that howl of remorse Masteeat had mentioned, and buried her face, while her sister went on in the same gentle, chiding tone.

"But what's to be done with her? Our father Abushir raised her as though she were a true daughter, and she repays his dead spirit by trying to overthrow me, her own sister and rightful Queen, not once but twice, and is forgiven. Then we find her a husband, whom she shames with lovers, and Gobayzy of Lasta takes him prisoner and hopes to compel her to surrender her sweet self as ransom, the pretty antelope . . . more fool Gobayzy!" She stroked Uliba's braids.

"Meanwhile she rebels for a third time . . . and fails . . . and weeps. Oh, a sad tangle . . ."

During these sisterly exchanges I'd been ignored except by the lion, which had ambled up to rub his great head against my ribs – that's how tall he stood – until Masteeat clicked her tongue, at which he trotted out obediently. Meanwhile she continued to pet her "pretty antelope", the murderous virago who'd tried to dethrone her and was being coddled like a prodigal daughter . . . no, I can't fathom women.

"Yet Gobayzy might suit you," murmurs Masteeat. "He's a blockhead, and goes in fear of me, and would rejoice to have my baby sister as his queen –"

"As one of his hareem whores, you mean!" sniffs Uliba. "Kings don't take a concubine's brat as their consort!"

Masteeat slapped her wrist. "Your mother was a gracious and lovely lady whom our father would have made his queen if he could. You should be proud to be her daughter."

"I am proud!" flares Uliba, and started to blub again.

"Good. Then dry your tears, and if Gobayzy is not to your taste we'll say no more of him. There are other panthers in the wood, as who knows better than you." She glanced at me, and whispered to Uliba with a sly smile that suggested she wasn't asking my size in collars. Uliba glared at me and snapped a reply in the Galla tongue, to Masteeat's amusement.

"And still you seek revenge on him? Perverse wretch!"

It seemed a good moment to make my peace with Uliba, but I'd barely assumed an ingratiating grin and started to explain that I'd been trying to save her, truly, when she was on her feet again, spitting hate.

"He lies, the misbegotten bastard! He would have spurned me to my death to save his dirty skin! As I'm a woman, it's true!"

"As I'm a woman, you make my head ache," sighs Masteeat. "Enough! Your tale may be true or not . . . hold your tongue, child! And hear my royal command. You will seek vengeance no further. Great matters are not to be risked for the spite of a reckless girl – and a rebel. You will submit, and show the Colonel Flashman *effendi*

154

the honour and respect due to the Queen's guest. Now, give him the kiss of good faith before you go."

I'd not have credited it that the Uliba I'd known, the savage who'd gloated over Yando's death, the cool hand who'd kept her head in the Gondar pit, the fighting fury who'd downed Theodore's riders, could have been turned into a weeping, fretful, penitent child by the firm authority of an elder sister. But I'd seen it, *mirabile dictu*, anything was possible, and now she hesitated only a raging second before bowing curtly to Masteeat, marching up to me, and planting icy lips for an instant on my cheek. It was like being kissed by a cobra, with an accompanying hiss.

"I know what I know!" Then she was past me through the curtained archway, and Masteeat chuckled.

"Not the most passionate embrace she has given you, I dare say . . . Look beyond the curtain, *effendi* . . . she is one who loves to eavesdrop. No? God be thanked, peace at last! Come, give me your hand."

I helped her to rise, which she did with surprising ease and grace, considering her proportions. Face to face she was a bare half-head below my height, and I was aware of a bodily strength at odds with her indolence; the bare shoulder and arm were smoothly muscled and her grip was strong. For a moment the fine black eyes surveyed me and the plump jolly face was smiling – expectantly, I'll swear, and I thought, here goes, and bowed over her hand, kissing it warmly and at length up towards the elbow – and she burst out laughing, a regular barmaid's guffaw, so I said, "By your majesty's leave", stepped inside her guard, and put my mouth gently on hers.

Risky diplomacy, you'll say, but that knowing smile had told me she'd be all for it. The full lips were wide and welcoming, and for a delightful moment she treated me as though I were her underdone steak. Then she stepped back, giving me a playful push and another slantendicular smile, and without a word poured us two goblets of *tej* from a well-laden buffet at the wall. We drank, and she piled into the snacks and sweetmeats, urging me with her mouth full to keep her company, so I picked a bit, marvelling, for she'd shifted a hearty helping but a few moments ago, and here she was cleaning up a plate of raw beef and a large bowl of mixed fruit, wiping the juice from her chin with her sleeve, heaving a contented sigh, and recharging our goblets. Then without preamble, she asked:

"Did you truly kick the little fool over the Great Silver Smoke? I'd not blame you, for she's a torment and a pest of hell, as well as a great liar. So one can never be sure. No matter." She leaned her ample rump on the buffet. "Why did your general choose her to guide you to me?"

I said I believed Speedy had suggested her, and she clapped her hands in delight. "The *Basha Fallaka*! Oh, what a beautiful man is that! I would have made his fortune, but he would not fight my lion." She sighed and giggled. "Oh, but I was young and wanton then . . . and very drunk! How is he, the rogue? Did he guess, I wonder, that Uliba would attempt my throne again?"

I said cautiously that Napier had mentioned her ambitions, but neither he nor Speedy had taken them too seriously.

"Unlike some besotted clowns in Galla who admire her body and fine airs," scoffs Masteeat. "She has a way with men, as you know, and she is strong and brave and reckless – oh, a heroine, my little sister! If only her judgment of men looked higher than their loins. She thinks that a few lovers in high places can conjure a revolution out of the air, and all Galla will enthrone her by acclaim!" She shook her head and drank. "I knew a month ago that when your general sent her south she would use the occasion to seek out Zaneh and Abite, who had pledged her their regiments. So when she came to the rendezvous she found not them but Wedaju waiting. And now I am plagued with a thrice-rebellious sister, and Zaneh and Abite and a score of others pay with their lives."

For a moment she was solemn as she refilled her goblet, then she brightened.

"Still, the *Basha Fallaka* chose well. She guarded and guided you, and when her silly plot came to nothing she kept faith with you and your people – aye, even though she believed you had betrayed her." She was smiling with real admiration. "Do you know,

156

when Wedaju brought her prisoner to me, and she had stamped and raged and gloried in her treason and cursed her conspirators for fools and cowards . . . why, then she demanded private audience, and told me of your mission. Aye, she is a heroine indeed, when she is not playing the idiot. She keeps her word – which is why I believe her when she vows to take my throne." She tossed her head, swirling her braids, and eyed me. "You wonder why I tolerate her, do you not?"

I said tactfully that her majesty was a marvel of patience, and loved her sister dearly. Masteeat shrugged and refilled our goblets.

"So she thinks. Oh, I have a sisterly affection for her – but not enough to stop me sending her to the stranglers if there was no other way. That startles you? You supposed my endearments sincere?" She smiled coolly over the rim of her cup. "A little, perhaps . . . but their true purpose was to play on her girlish emotions, for she's a romantic, our Uliba-Wark, with a tender heart for kittens and little birds and the fond sister who told her bed-time stories. The same Uliba who can gloat over the torture of an enemy . . ." I thought of Yando hanging terrified ". . . weeps great tears over this –" She drew her robe aside to display the bead anklet. "Lord God, the time my women spent searching for the wretched thing! It served my purpose, as did my embraces. While her shame and remorse last, she will not attempt my throne again, believe me." Seeing my expression, she burst out laughing, refilled her goblet, crammed a handful of sweets into her mouth, washed them down with one great gulp, hiccoughed, picked up the *tej* flask and a dish of dainties and made her stately way, swaying slightly, back to her couch, apologising with an elegant flutter of her fingers for keeping me standing, and begging me to take Uliba's stool.

I wondered had I ever seen her like. Every inch a queen, with the table manners of a starving navvy; tyrant of the toughest savages in Africa and indulgent to the point of lunacy of her wildcat sister; using lions as lapdogs and plainly ready to enjoy amorous jollity with a chap she'd known a bare five minutes; uninhibited, merry, gluttonous, imperious, sentimental and cynical by turns – and unless I was badly in error, as astute and formidable as any crowned female I'd ever met, and they're nobody's fools, these royal ladies. As she proceeded to prove, lolling in cushioned comfort with enough lush inside her to float a frigate.

"But enough of Uliba-Wark. She tells me your *Dedjaz** Napier seeks an alliance against Theodore, but she knew nothing of any price. Now, I am sure that he will have named a sum; and equally sure that he will have urged you to make as cheap a bargain as the silly woman will accept." She took a long swig, mocking me with an eye like a velvet fish-hook. "But I am surest of all that you are too gallant a gentleman to take advantage of a poor African lady."

What could I do but smile in turn, and resolve then and there to pay her the whole kitboodle, as she was sure I would, the crafty trollop. She knew my style, and I knew hers, and 'twasn't my money anyway.

"Since your majesty is graciously pleased to signify your assent to Sir Robert's proposal," says I, all ambassador-like, "I am empowered to promise fifty thousand dollars in Austrian silver of 1780 minting . . ." It was a pleasure to see the light of pure greed mantle that jolly face ". . . provided that your majesty's forces invest Magdala and prevent the Emperor's escape." I bowed, sitting down. "I have the honour to await your majesty's reply."

"And when will the money be paid?"

"When Sir Robert has the honour of paying his respects to your majesty in person."

She gave me her old-fashioned look. "Which means when Theodore is dead or captured, but not before."

"That, ma'am," says I, "is exactly what it means. But you need have no fear. Sir Robert's a man of his word. And so am I."

"Oh, I am very sure of that. Very well; it is promised, it is done." She extended an imperious hand, and again I hastened to help her rise, but this time I drew her plumpness smoothly to me, and was

* General, an abbreviation of *Dedjazmach*.

about to clamp her buttocks and make a meal of her, but she held her face away, looking mischievous. "And until the silver is in my treasury, I hold a hostage, do I not?" She flirted her lips across mine. "Now, you must take counsel with my commanders."

Any doubts I might have had about the military *bandobast* of the Wollo Gallas were banished entirely in the next few hours when I conferred with their commanders. They were as expert and brisk in planning as their queen had been in negotiation, grasped Napier's requirements at once, and knew exactly how to satisfy them. By the time we were done I was confident that whatever the hazards of taking Magdala, the Gallas would do their part to the letter.

There were four of them in the great airy apartment where Fasil, their general in chief, had his head-quarters. He was a mercenary, of the Amoro Galla tribe, notorious for their bravery, ferocity, and hatred of Christians, and didn't he look it? He was a tall grizzled veteran whose hawk profile was marred by a dreadful sword-cut which had cleft both cheeks and the bridge of his nose; his style was all Guardee, sharp with authority and sparing with words. His two immediate subordinates were surprisingly young, hard-case stalwarts commanding infantry and cavalry respectively, full of bounce and confidence of which Fasil was sourly tolerant – not a bad sign. I don't remember their names. Fourth man in was Masteeat's son, Ahmed, a lively, handsome stripling who had inherited his mother's lazy smile without her indolence, for he was restless with energy. He seemed to be Fasil's a.d.c. In attendance there were half a dozen scribes taking notes.

What impressed me at first sight even more than the men was the great scale model, six feet by three, which occupied the centre of the room. It was an exact representation of Magdala and the country round, and beat any sand-table I'd ever seen. I doubt if any military academy of Europe or America could have shown better

– and these were the primitive aborigines whom *Punch* depicted as nigger minstrels.

I made a sketch of it, and if you study it along with my description you'll understand why I examined it with mounting alarm, for it was clear to me that if Theodore defended his *amba* like the professional soldier he was reputed to be, Napier's command was looking disaster in the face.

Until now, you see, all I knew of Magdala was what the croakers said: that it was impregnable if resolutely defended – but that's been an old soldier's tale since Joshua's day, and I'd been ready to believe that the shave* was exaggerated. I wasn't prepared for that sand-table, if it was accurate. Fasil swore it was, to the inch, having been made by their best engineers and artists months earlier, when Masteeat had contemplated an attack on the place.

"And would have taken it, garrisoned by sheep as it is!" cries young Ahmed. "But Menelek and Gobayzy came snapping at our ankles like the dogs they are!"

"I could take it now, prince, if her majesty wishes," brags the infantry wallah, with a cocky grin at me. "Why leave it for the British, who may not restore it to her majesty afterwards?"

"Since when are you a politician?" growls Fasil. "Keep to your trade and let your queen mind hers."

"Oh, give him his way, lord general!" cries the cavalry chap. "Let's see him pit his skill against Theodore's!" He turned to me. "Given leave, my horsemen would have cut the Emperor's rabble to pieces before they'd crossed the Bechelo!"

"Silence, fools!" growls Fasil. "Who are you to dare to reproach her majesty?" The lads protested that they'd meant no such thing, while I sought confirmation of the bad news.

"Theodore is in Magdala already?"

"He reached the *amba* three days ago, and camps his army on Islamgee, under the Magdala cliff," says Fasil. "But his guns are not yet emplaced. When they and his great mortar have been sited, our scouts will bring us instant word, which we shall pass to your

* Rumour.

Dedjaz Napier; thus he will know which height Theodore will defend." He leaned forward and tapped three features in the model with his pointer. "Fala . . . Selassie . . . Magdala . . ."

Look at my map and you'll see them: three flat-topped peaks like the legs of an upturned stool, surrounded by mountains, a wilderness of rock and ravine worthy of Afghanistan. A saddle of land almost two miles long connects Fala and Selassie, and beyond lay the plain of Islamgee and Theodore's army. I walked round the table, weighing it all, and saw that there was only one way for Napier to advance after he'd crossed the Bechelo. I ain't being clever; any fool could ha' seen it.

The road that Theodore had made to transport his artillery wound in a great loop from the Bechelo river through the Arogee plateau, and on to Magdala itself. But that wouldn't do for Napier; it was too perilously close to the broken country bordering the Warki river, where the Abs would have all the advantage of ambush and surprise; the mere sight on the model of the beetling rocky sides of the Warki valley gave me the horrors; let 'em draw you in there and you'd never come out.

The only safe way was to take a long slant to the right and come to Arogee by the spurs running up through Afichu plateau; it might mean some stiff climbing for our troops, but they'd be in fairly open ground all the way, which would suit our infantry and gunners if Theodore were daft enough to offer pitched battle.

The key to the whole puzzle was plainly Fala. If Theodore put guns there he'd be able to bombard our advance over Arogee, but our gunners could give him shot for shot, and once Fala was taken the way to the Islamgee plain and Magdala would be open. And then . . . it would be a question of "so far so good" and put up a prayer.

You may remember pictures of Theodore's great *amba*; the illustrated papers were full of them in '68. It's what they call a volcanic plug, a sheer cylinder of rock over three hundred feet high, with only one precipitous way up guarded by gates and ramparts. If Theodore was ready to fight to a finish and his gunners stood to it, Napier might never take that ghastly height. And his army, cut

162

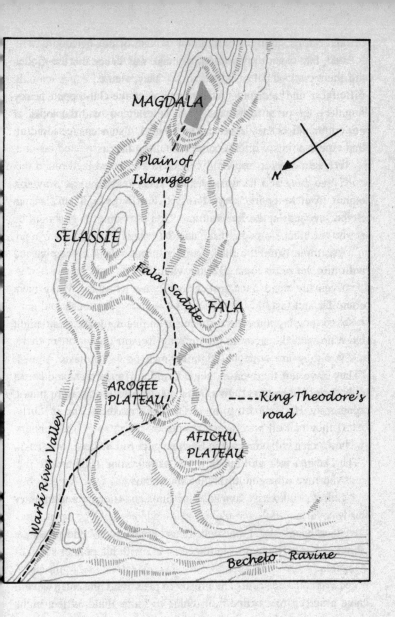

MAGDALA

Plain of
Islamgee

N

SELASSIE

Fala Saddle

FALA

AROGEE
PLATEAU

- - - King Theodore's
road

AFICHU
PLATEAU

Warki River Valley

Bechelo Ravine

off and out of supply, would die at the end of nowhere.

Well, that wasn't my *indaba*. My task was to see that the Gallas did their stuff, and I'm bound to say they seemed eager enough. Fifty thou' and undisputed sovereignty over the Galla confederacy might be the prize to Masteeat, but unless I misread the looks of her commanders they asked nothing better than a chance to adorn their spear-points with Theodore's courting tackle.

"Where's *Dedjaz* Napier, d'you know?" I asked.

"Three days ago he was over the Takazy, at Santara, a week's march from Magdala," says Fasil. "By now he will be close to Bethor, perhaps at the Jedda ravine. God providing, they should be across the Bechelo in . . . three days? Perhaps four."

"Oh, three, surely!" cries young Ahmed. "If he knows we are with him, he must come like the wind!"

"Even the wind must rest, prince," says Cavalry. "They have come far and fast."

"And they lay three days at Santara so that the main force might close up with the advance guard," says Infantry.

"But they are none but fighting men now!" protests Ahmed. "They have left their slaves behind, and will march at speed with only their guns to carry!" To a Galla, all camp-followers were slaves, apparently. He appealed to me. "They will make all haste?"

"If they're well provisioned," says I.

"Your men will come to the Bechelo with full bellies," says Fasil. "The Dalanta folk will see to it, out of hatred of Theodore."

"And love of my mother!" insists Ahmed.

"Indeed, highness," says Fasil tactfully, and Cavalry and Infantry made loyal noises.

"Hear, hear," says I, and asked Fasil precisely how he would set about bottling Theodore. He traced an arc with his pointer south of Magdala.

"Two thousand scouts are already in place, and presently we will have a screen of cavalry from Guna to Lake Haik. Wherever he goes, it will not be southward."

It looked a hell of a long arc, more than a hundred miles. "Your cavalry'll be spread mighty thin, then."

"Not so thin," says he. "There will be twenty thousand riders."

If I stared, d'you wonder? That was three times the force that Theodore could muster, ten times as many as Napier would use to storm Magdala. No wonder Cavalry had said he could have cut Theodore to ribbons, and Infantry had boasted of taking the *amba* with his foot-soldiers. He spoke up now, nodding confidently to me.

"The cavalry will be a reserve, of course; they will not be needed. I shall have three regiments of spearmen deployed between them and the *amba*, should Theodore attempt to break out."

"Then you *will* have the chance to match tactics with Theodore!" cries Cavalry, winking at me. "A battle of the giants . . . but have no fear, foot-soldier, we shall be there."

"So you will," grins Infantry. "Behind us, out of harm's way."

"But close enough to hear cries for help . . ."

Not the way generals in civilised armies talk to each other as a rule, especially before their chief, but among experts outer forms of discipline don't matter too much; the Gallas didn't need to stand on ceremony. There was no bitterness in the young men's rivalry; they were laughing at each other, Ahmed was grinning, and Fasil had the kind of authority that doesn't depend on military etiquette. Listening to them, I knew that they'd do their part; it remained for Napier to attend to his, and he'd need all the prime intelligence I could give him. I questioned Fasil and his lieutenants on every particular: where exactly the infantry would be placed, their precise numbers (eight thousand all told), how long they'd be able to stay in the field, how they'd communicate, what were the lines of retreat from Magdala – all the small change, in fact, and as I noted it I was musing on how best to present it with a view to gaining the most credit.

There was no question of taking my news to Napier in person: he expected me to command the Galla encirclement of Magdala, bless him, and with Theodore's ruffians infesting the northern approaches I'd not have ventured forth for a pension anyway. So I wrote a brief and suitably modest report to say that I'd arrived at Masteeat's court, that she was an eager ally, the Wollos were fallen in and numbered off and could be counted on to stop Theodore's southern bolthole, that he was camped on Islamgee with about seven thousand troops, but until his guns were placed we couldn't tell whether he'd defend Magdala, offer battle, or cut and run. To be continued in our next, the weather remains fine, and please reply by the bearer of this despatch – and make him a present of a revolver.

I asked Fasil for Wedaju as my messenger because he could be trusted to reply intelligently to the sort of questions Napier would ask, and he was the kind of young hero who'd get there, through Hell and high water. He was summoned, and in the presence of Fasil and Co. I added the verbal messages that couldn't be written in case they fell into Theodore's hands: the number and rough disposition of the Galla force, the escape routes which Fasil thought Theodore would most likely take, and most importantly, the lie of the land – this I did by having Wedaju study the sand-table, and satisfy me that he could make a sketch of it from memory for Napier's benefit. I demonstrated what I thought the best route from the Bechelo to Arogee, to which Fasil and his lads gave their approval. Some commanders don't care for suggestions from below, but I knew Bob Napier would weigh mine and follow them unless he saw good reason not to.

Finally, and principally for young Ahmed's benefit, I told Wedaju to assure Napier that the Queen of Wollo Galla had pledged her alliance in the most cordial terms, and shown me every courtesy and consideration, and we could congratulate ourselves on having the support of such an illustrious and enlightened ruler and her fine soldiery. Diplomatic butter, no more, but Ahmed took it large, clasping my hand and vowing that I must repeat it to Mama instanter, so that she could respond with similar compliments and greetings to the British *dedjaz*. And it was right, says he, that we should take the opportunity to inform her majesty that all was in train for the bottling of Theodore, so let us seek her approval as a loyal council should.

I could see that Fasil felt that the less opportunity royalty got to interfere, the better, but you don't argue with a prince of the blood, even if he is your galloper, so off the five of us trooped to her majesty's private apartments, with Wedaju in tow. There we were informed by her doddering chamberlain that her majesty was unable to grant us audience at present, as she had been resting and was now being attired by her ladies for the evening's entertainment (from which I deduced that the *tej* had finally caught up with her and she was being revived and rendered fit for public view). What entertainment, demands Ahmed, and was told, with an obsequious smirk at me, that there was to be a grand reception and feast in honour of the British *baldaraba*.* Capital, says Ahmed, now get out of my way, and such is the politeness of princes that a moment later we were making our bows in the presence, while her handmaidens, caught unawares, tried gamely to disguise her majesty's condition. As I'd suspected, she'd plainly had to be roused from the arms of Bacchus, and was visibly glazed of eye and unsteady on the seat before her dressing-table, with a wench either side to lend unobtrusive support, and her handmaiden-in-chief trying to impart a little dignity by slipping a silver wand into the royal grasp. But she played up well; her head was regally erect, and she greeted us with careful courtesy.

Ahmed wanted me to repeat the flowery part of my message to Napier, but I wasn't having that, and insisted Wedaju should do it to make sure he had it pat. The lad was shocking nervous before his sovereign, but got it out slow and halting after a few false starts. Masteeat listened with solemn attention, stifling an occasional yawn, and once her silver wand slipped from her drowsy hand and was retrieved by Infantry a split second ahead of Cavalry. I only hoped Wedaju would get done while she could still see and sit upright, but when he'd finished she astonished me by extending an imperious hand to him and saying, slowly but clearly:

"And tell the English *dedjaz* also that the Queen of Galla calls the blessing of God on him and his brave soldiers, and bids them have a care, so that they come safely to their journey's end and into the presence of their loving friend, Masteeat, who has them in her heart." Along with their fifty thousand jemmy o' goblins, thinks

* Agent, representative.

cynical Flashy, but when she added, smiling all fondly maternal on Wedaju, "And you, gallant warrior, fare well through all dangers, and know that you take with you the prayers of a grateful and loving queen," I wasn't a bit surprised to see him drop to his knees and press her hand to his forehead and lips, while Infantry and Cavalry fell over each other to join him, Ahmed almost shed a tear of filial devotion, and even grizzled old Fasil looked moist and noble.

If she'd been a beauty in the mould of Yehonala or Lakshmibai, or even as handsome as Uliba-Wark, their adoration (for that's what it was, no error) would have been in order, but she was a hearty piece of middle-aged Eve's flesh of no remarkable allure – that she appealed to me was by the way; I'm a connoisseur of feminine beauty but no discrimination worth a dam, and anyway I'm perversely partial to royal rattle. And yet, she had that quality which I can't describe but which attracts where mere perfection of form and feature are no more exciting than a marble statue.

I guess it's charm, and she spread it over her soldiers like Circe's spell. I suppose she charmed me – and I don't mean only randy-like, but happy captivation. Aye, that must have been it, for I find myself smiling still whenever I think back on her, while Uliba has faded into the shadows.

I came away from that audience a relieved and thankful man, glad to have a moment at last for rest and reflection. Things could hardly have come out better, however hellish they had been since I'd left Napier's camp weeks ago. My worst fears had been realised along the way: the skirmish with Yando's gang, that appalling dangle in the steel cage, the palpitating escape from the Soudani bandits at Gondar, the clash with Theodore's riders, my plunge over Abyssinia's Niagara, the shock of Uliba's reappearance and most uncalled-for assault . . . but here I was again, none the worse bar a bruise or two, duty done in securing the Galla alliance and despatching the glad news to Napier, and no great anxieties ahead that I could see.

True, I'd have to arrange matters so that I could appear to be commanding the Galla operations while keeping clear of the action, but that ain't difficult when you've had years of practice. I'm a prime hand at playing Lionheart without doing a blessed thing (what dear old Tom Hughes called "shouts and great action"), and I could occupy myself splendidly at Galla H.Q., keeping the threads of administration together, don't you know, taking an overall view until I deemed it safe to join the last rally.

Meanwhile I could think of worse billets than the court of good Queen Masteeat. Safe, well stocked and furnished, friendly . . . of course it went without saying that I'd have to do my extra-diplomatic duty by her majesty, but that would be no hardship – and if you wonder how I was so sure of her, I can only say that I had felt her mouth under mine and read the message in her lazy smile. Besides, in Ab society, which as I've told you is probably the most immoral on earth (Cheltenham ain't in it), rogering the hostess is almost obligatory, part of the etiquette, like leaving cards, and not at all out of the way in a country where it's considered a mortal insult to praise a woman's chastity, since it implies that she's not attractive enough to be galloped. Say no more.

But while I knew 'twould be only a matter of time before Masteeat and I had our wicked way with each other, I could never have foreseen the circumstances; indeed, had I been forewarned, I'd not have believed it. I'm neither inexperienced nor a prude; I have known, and been party to, abandoned behaviour, and have even joined in the occasional orgy, but I can take oath that I have never known the like of the reception and feast that the old chamberlain had described as "an entertainment".

It was he who led me all unsuspecting to the dining chamber of the royal residence in which the other guests, about a dozen, were already assembled. The long low dining table was surrounded by cushioned stools set in pairs, one for each couple, and at the head was a spread of cushions for the Queen, who had not yet arrived, and her guest of honour. Fasil, Cavalry, and Infantry were on hand, each with a beauty in tow, the two lads being accompanied by a pair of Masteeat's handmaidens, and Fasil by a quite breathtaking creature of about his own age who may well have been his wife; she had those delicately perfect features you see on some Scandinavian women – and was jet black. The other three couples

I don't remember, except that the women were typically Ab, which is to say peaches. There were no servants at all; we helped ourselves to the *tej* from flagons on the sideboard, and stood about gossiping for all the world like a Belgravia bunfight. Fasil and his juniors talked shop, as soldiers always do, and showed a surprising knowledge of such diverse matters as the Sepoy Mutiny and the war in America, but presently they were set aside by Fasil's black Venus and the handmaidens, and blowed if I wasn't cross-examined about London fashions, hairstyles, and the like. Some of their inquiries would ha' made me blush if I hadn't been revelling in the attentions of three such ravishing inquisitors, bright-eyed, flirtatious, breathing perfume with each gentle laugh.

It struck me that Masteeat must be uncommon tolerant to allow herself to be so outshone, and then I remembered reading somewhere that our old Queen Bess had surrounded herself with the prettiest of pippins, no doubt knowing that there was only one woman who'd be looked at. That was certainly the case when the Queen of Galla made her entrance, stately and smiling sleepily, and somehow contriving to put all the bowing beauties in the shade.

And, dammit, she wasn't even sober yet, to judge from her swaying gait, careless gestures, and ringing laugh. They'd put her in very fair trim, though, with a gold circlet as a sort of coronet, and gold thread cunningly worked into her braids; she had gold chain earrings depending to her broad bare shoulders, and a gold collar clasped about her throat. Her dress was white and of some clinging gauzy stuff cleverly cut to disguise a waist and hips which were undoubtedly overblown and to display a bosom whose development matched her shoulders admirably. She carried a gold wand this time, and the effect of her carriage and manner was overpowering, no other word for it.

When the company had finished its obeisance, she held her arm for me to take, and led the way to the head of the table, where she took her seat among the cushions, indicating that I should join her. She reclined on one elbow, but I decided to sit, as being less awkward and more in keeping with the company, who had their little stools. More *tej* was poured, Masteeat led the company in

170

pledging me, Queen Victoria, Napier, and the British Army, in that order, each toast requiring a full goblet, no heel-taps. We ain't going to eat a great deal, thinks I; they'll be too tight to pick up the grub. But I was dead wrong.

You know what dining out I'd done thus far; rough browsing mostly and not too formal even at Uliba's citadel and the monastery. But I'd never been to a Lord Mayor's Banquet, if you know what I mean, and that was what I was treated to, Habesh style. It's quite alarming.

You sit there, drinking toasts, wondering when the soup's going to arrive, when suddenly the most appalling din breaks out just beyond the door, a full-throated bellowing, peal after peal of some huge body in mortal pain thrashing about to the accompaniment of yelling voices, shrieks of command and cries of desperation, furniture crashing, the bellowing rising to a crescendo – and the guests applauding and your hostess imbibing another pint of *tej*, smacking her lips in anticipation.

And then servants scurry in, and there is planked down in front of you a plate containing a twelve-pound beefsteak, raw, red, and bleeding, and as I live and breathe, it has steam rising from it, which perhaps ain't surprising since thirty seconds before it was part of the living animal which is bawling in agony outside. I'd had raw beef before, in transparently thin slices, cold, and not too bad, but as I gazed at this smoking horror I thought, no, the devil with etiquette, protocol, and diplomatic niceties, I ain't touching it, whatever offence I give. Down the table they were buffing in like mad cannibals, even those elegant beauties, with gore trickling down their lovely chins and being wiped with dainty fingers. I daren't look at Masteeat for fear of what I'd see; the mere sound of her champing made me come all over faint.

"You do not care for the *brundo*?" She laughed, took a hearty draught of *tej*, and called a servant to remove my bloody lump of carcase and replace it with a whole roast chicken. "Our friend Speedy, the great *Basha Fallaka*, shuddered like a girl when the beast was tethered and carved. That is why it was done outside today, so that your delicate senses might not be disturbed!" She struck me lightly on the arm, joshing, so I had to look at her, but either she'd wiped herself or swallowed the steak whole, for the chubby laughing face was clean and shining. "So, eat with good appetite!"

I can't say I did, for the beast was still bellowing piteously outside, and some of the guests were calling for second helpings of the poor brute. And after that, when the roast meats and fowls and fish and stews and curries were served, the voracity with which the company punished each succeeding course quite put me off. God knows my generation were good trenchermen, but they weren't fit to guzzle in Ethiopian company; it was wolf, wolf, wolf with an unrestrained vengeance, and those exquisite females, like so many tawny goddesses in their fine silks and gauzes, laid in as hard as the men. Talk about having hollow legs – and they drank pint for pint, too, taking their cue from her majesty, who bade fair to outstrip her potations of the afternoon.

It was, as you can imagine, a noisy business all round, and by the time the desserts and fruits were reached it was like being in a farmyard at feeding time. It didn't stop them talking, mind; the din of conversation rose as the drink went down, and Masteeat found time between her gargantuan mouthfuls of food and gulps of liquor to call down amiable curses on the head of Uliba-Wark, who had defied a royal command to attend the feast and flounced off in dudgeon when rebuked.

"She becomes tiresome," says Masteeat, and heaved a mighty yawn; the *tej* was coming home to roost at last, and her speech was thick and slow. "I begin to think that what I said half in jest I should decree in earnest . . . send her to Gobayzy." She lowered another gobletful. "A penance for both of them."

Fasil, who was sitting first down the table, shook his head. "Would your majesty know a moment's peace if your half-sister were Gobayzy's queen, with his army at her command?"

"To make another attempt against me?" laughs Masteeat. "Not so, old soldier, Gobayzy would have none of it. He fears the Galla too much . . . most of all the Galla Queen." At which Cavalry and Infantry roared applause, and drank to her, with the others joining in.

172

"And yet," says Fasil, when the shouting had died, "Gobayzy's uncle visited the *Dedjaz* Napier at Santara. What for, if not to stand first with the British . . . in your majesty's room?"

"By God, it is the truth!" cries Infantry. "Did I not say there is no knowing how the British might dispose of Magdala when it is taken!" He scowled half-drunkenly at me. "If Gobayzy worms his way into their confidence, might it not be given to him?" At this there was an uproar of opinion, stilled when Masteeat spoke with tipsy deliberation.

"No." She set down her goblet carefully, and refilled it, more or less, with an unsteady hand. "No. Gobayzy's a . . . a worm, you say . . . Well, what can he give the British? His army of . . . of worms?" She chuckled. "Worms who crawl away at the sight of our spears! No. The British *dedjaz* has chosen already . . ." She threw out an arm across my shoulders. "Chosen already, I say! Has he not?" She leaned towards me, and I prepared to catch her, but she kept her balance. "Has he not?" she repeated, and giggled, enveloping me in *tej* fumes. The great black eyes were half-closed, the smiling lips were moist and parted, and her braids were brushing my face. "Has he not?" she said a third time, her voice a drowsy murmur, and I glanced at Fasil, but he had turned away to his black charmer, and no one else was paying us any heed.

"Has he not?" for the fourth time, drunk as David's sow, but not too far gone to kiss me gently, playing her tongue along my lips, whispering. "Oh . . . beautiful! More beautiful than *Basha Fallaka* . . . Are you all so beautiful, you English . . . ?"

"Just a few of us, ma'am," says I, and she gave a whoop of laughter and heaved her bulk away, knocking over her goblet, which I gallantly rescued and refilled, after a fashion, for I was feeling the worse for wear myself, what with too much booze and the rising clamour and laughter . . . for now the party was becoming lively, and if you don't believe what I'm about to tell you, I can't help it.

Young Cavalry and his bint had evidently had their fill of meat and drink, and were starting to satisfy another appetite, pawing and fondling with increasing passion, and slipping off their stools on to a mattress which some obliging menial must have laid behind their

173

places. Gad's me life, thinks I, not before the savoury, surely, but there was no doubt about it, they were setting to partners in earnest, and Fasil, seated next to them, had unwound a fold of his *shama* and was holding it up to shield the performers from the public gaze, the damned spoilsport – and blow me if Cavalry's other neighbour wasn't doing likewise, providing a complete screen!

But if they'd cut off the sight, they couldn't shut out the sound. Even above the drunken babble of talk, gasps and grunts and rhythmic pounding were audible, followed at last by a prolonged ecstatic wailing that reminded me of little Fraulein Thingamajig on the voyage to Trieste. Well done, Cavalry, that's your sort, thinks I, and looked to see the company, and Masteeat if she still had her senses, express their indignation at such unseemly behaviour – but no one was paying the least attention until Fasil and t'other chap resumed their *shamas* and the happy couple emerged, the bint in some disorder and Cavalry looking as though he'd just been ridden down by the Heavy Brigade. Then, as God's my witness, the whole company raised their glasses in salutation as the lovers resumed their stools.

And then the other diners followed suit, in turn. Whether they observed some order of precedence, like Bishops going into dinner before Rear Admirals, I can't say, but I think not, since Fasil and his consort were next to bat, and he must have been senior to Cavalry, surely. I was caught out, because Cavalry undid his *shama* to give 'em privacy, and nodded and frowned in my direction – and of course I was the nearest chap, and since I didn't wear a *shama* I could only hold up a cushion, which wasn't really adequate. Being fairly foxed, I started to apologise to Fasil, but quickly averted my gaze, thinking that's a position I haven't seen before, but *ex Africa semper aliquid novi*,* as Charity Spring would have said.

Then Infantry and his charmer were at it, and of course the inevitable happened: the others got impatient, and started out of turn, and all order was abandoned. Only the most perfunctory attempts were made to shield the jolly amorists, and the place shook

---

* "Out of Africa there is always something new" – Pliny the Elder.

like a New Orleans brothel in Holy Week. The Abs have two claims to distinction: they're the noisiest eaters and fornicators on earth, and their queen is up there with the leaders. I'd been too intent on the scandalous scene to pay her much heed, and now when I looked she was reclining on one elbow, regarding me glassily over the rim of her *tej* goblet; whether she could see me or not I wasn't sure until she reached out a hand to stroke my cheek, and (of all things) chucked me under the chin, gurgling with laughter and lurching closer.

"Has . . . he . . . not . . . ?" she mumbled drowsily – by jove, she'd lapped the gutter, but d'you know, it was a rum thing, the drunker she got the more I fancied her. I've said she was no great beauty, but there was something damned fetching about the plump polished cheeks between the shining braids, the moist lips trembling in a vacuous smile, the satin skin of her arms and shoulders, the hard juggs thrusting themselves into my grasp, and the wild abandon with which she suddenly revived, clamping her mouth on mine, clawing at my rump, howling and writhing fit to wreck the furniture . . . and I think some considerate chaps must have noticed, for I've a recollection of being secluded by their *shamas*.

I hope we were, anyway . . . not that I imagine anyone would have paid us the slightest heed in the surrounding happy pandemonium, but one has to think of propriety and the good name of the service, especially among native peoples, however trying conditions may sometimes be. As I said to Speedicut, it's hell in the diplomatic.

*   *   *

Elspeth maintains that one of the jolliest things about what she calls houghmagandie is the sweet exchanges of conversation afterwards. What they would have been like with Queen Masteeat of Galla, I cannot say, for she fell asleep at the end of our little frolic, and had to be carried insensible to bed by the more sober of her handmaidens, snoring like a volcano. My stars, but she was a glutton for mutton, and I was a well-ruined ambassador as I picked my way clear of the wreckage of that dining-chamber – would you credit it, Infantry and Cavalry were still going strong, with Fasil's woman, too, while *he* was tucking into a helping of *brundo*, fed to him by his subordinates' laughing lovebirds. No one's ever going to believe this, thinks I; hang it all, Nero himself would have taken one look and cried "Oh, chuck it!" But that's Ab society for you; other folk have dinner parties, but in Habesh they're dinner orgies.[40]

I've no very clear recollection of making my way to the apartment in the palace set aside for me, but I know I suffered a most ghastly bout of "spinning pillow" and had to hang over the side of the bed with the floor racing up to me and receding, time and again, before I finally settled, lying there in the dark wondering how much of Queen Masteeat I could take. She was no refined amorist, that one, strong as a bullock, randy as a stoat, and the roughest ride I could remember since Ranavalona of Madagascar – another Black Pearl of Africa, but before I could make philosophic review of this coincidence, my attention was distracted by a gentle pricking of some sharp point under my right ear, and a soft voice whispering:

"Lie still, friend, and prosper . . . for the moment. Speak . . . and you'll be talking to Shaitan."

I've written elsewhere of the terror of being shocked awake by deadly danger, and of the freezing paralysis that follows. It's happened to me more than once – why, in China I was dragged out of bed into a midnight skirmish, and then into the presence of the lunatic leader of the Taiping Rebellion, but at least in that case my panic was shortlived, since my kidnappers proved to be friends. No such luck in Habesh; half-drunk as I was, there was no mistaking the threat of the knife-point, the lamplit nightmare of the gleaming eyes and teeth in the black faces staring down at me, the gag thrust brutally into my mouth, and the grip of the hands which wrenched me to my feet and ran me from the room, down a rickety staircase, and into the pouring rain of a chill night. Robed figures with swords and spears were about me, and then a blindfold was whipped over my face and I was being half carried, half thrust along, trying to yell for help through my gag and almost swallowing the thing out of sheer funk.

What made it doubly terrifying was the complete silence of my captors: not an order, not a word or a threat after that gloating voice that had woken me; these were professional kidnappers, probably expert assassins, who knew exactly what they were doing, where they were taking me, and why – although the wherefore didn't occur to me, fuddled with fright and liquor as I was, until I was flung down on to a stretcher, swiftly bound to it, and borne off at a run. Only then, when I realised that I was not being hauled out to instant execution, did I ask myself who could be behind this abduction.

The answer seemed horribly clear: Uliba-Wark, thirsting for vengeance – and remembering how she'd dealt with Yando was enough to bring me out in a lather of fear. Oh Lord, and she'd had some ghastly notion of removing a victim's bones one at a time and keeping him in agony for months! Being unable to scream or spew, I could only lie terrified while they jolted me along at speed – heaven knew how far we went, or how long it took; you ain't at your calculating best with a mind a-shudder and a bellyful of drink, but I don't believe they could have kept up that pace more than an hour, over five miles, perhaps, before they halted for a breather and set me down.

The blindfold was stripped away, leaving me blinking in the glare of a torch in the hand of one of the men surrounding me; seven or eight of them, Gallas in white *pyjamy* trowsers and belted robes, strapping fellows fully armed with spears and sickle-swords, one or two with muskets and their leader with a couple of horse pistols in his belt. He was one of your typical Wollos, handsome as Lucifer and every bit as kindly to judge from his sneering grin, but when I rolled my eyes in dumb appeal he pulled out the gag.

I was too parched to speak at first, but probably because he wanted to hear what I had to say, he signed one of the band who held a chaggle to my lips, and the first words I croaked out, to confirm my suspicions, were: "Where is she?"

"The Queen Uliba-Wark?" says he. "Be patient, you will see her presently . . . and she will reward you for your services." It was the same soft mocking voice that had threatened me with a chat to Old Nick, chuckling pleasantly as his gang grinned like a pack of wolves over a peasant, and I gibbered at him.

"What the devil d'you mean? D'you know who I am? A British officer, the envoy of *Dedjaz* Napier, and by God if you don't set me loose this instant, you'll swing higher than Haman, you black son-of-a-bitch! Queen Masteeat will see to it, and that slut Uliba won't be able to shield you –"

He struck me back-handed across the mouth. "Speak foully once more of Queen Uliba-Wark and you'll be unable to speak to Shaitan! For before you die I'll tear your tongue out!" He slapped me again, and resumed his mockery. "No one will know what has become of you, *farangi* fool! Your *dedjaz* may ask what has happened to you, and Queen Uliba-Wark will lament your strange disappearance – oh, aye, by then she will have replaced the Fat Bitch! We shall not fail a second time. She may even order me, Goram, to make a search . . . but by then not enough will remain of your filthy carcase to make a meal for a jackal pup!"

So he wasn't a mercenary, as for a second I'd dared to hope, but a genuine Uliba-worshipper, one of the crazy conspirators who'd survived the botched coup to put her on the throne. And thanks to Masteeat's idiotic indulgence, she was free to make a second attempt – and to butcher me.

"Don't be a fool, Goram," said I, calm and quiet, for I saw yelling wouldn't serve with this one. "*Dedjaz* Napier and the *Basha Fallaka* are cunning men who know Uliba and her plots, and they'll trace you and hunt you down, aye, even if you run to the Mountains of the Moon. But release me and you'll be rewarded – more money than you've ever seen! Why, they're giving fifty thousand dollars to Masteeat just as a gift –"

He clapped a hand over my mouth, and now he was stuffing the gag back between my teeth – he might be loyal to Uliba, but he daren't risk his gang being tempted by a fortune in silver. I tried to spit it out, but he had it bound in a trice, and I could do nothing but heave and roll my eyes. Then he spat in my face.

"If you were tortured for a year, it would be too light a punishment! You would have slain our royal lady – she who had loved you and stood your friend! And you think you can buy me, her sworn warrior who lives only to see her on her rightful throne!" He spat again, and shouted to the others to bear me up. So we set off once more through the night; the rain had stopped, but thunder was rumbling in the distance, with an occasional crackle of lightning in the night sky.

Then the pace was slackening as we went up a steep ascent, and now there was a glow ahead, and a challenge to which Goram replied, and I was carried between great boulders into a rock-girt clearing where a great fire burned, and a half-score of Gallas were resting on their weapons. I was dropped without ceremony in front of a seated figure, cloaked and hooded, and my fearful gaze took in long and beautiful legs elegantly crossed, and above them the lithe figure and handsome face, cold as a basilisk's, of Uliba-Wark.

There was no trace of the fury she'd shown at our last encounter. For a long moment she looked down at me, with a lack of expression that made my skin crawl, and then she rose, shrugging off her cloak, and came to stand beside Goram, one hand on her hip, the other toying with her braids. But not a word did she say, and paid no heed when Goram, having called a question to some sentry out in the darkness, frowned and shrugged and muttered in her ear. Without taking her eyes from mine, she held out her hand, and Goram drew his knife and handed it to her, grinning. She stropped it once, slowly, on her palm, and nodded, and at a word from Goram three of his ruffians seized me, two at the shoulders, one at the ankles, to prevent my struggling.

She signed to Goram to hold out his spear, and to my horror cut the ghastly trophies from its head, slowly and deliberately, to a delighted murmur from the onlookers; she watched me intently, and must have seen the terror in my eyes, for the chiselled lips smiled for the first time, as Goram dropped to one knee beside me and wrenched at my waistband, trying to tear it open.

The horror of that moment is with me still, and always will be: the ring of grinning black faces crowding closer to watch, Goram's foul breath in my nostrils, the bestial leer of the scoundrel gripping my ankles, the knowledge of the agonising, unspeakable abomination Uliba-Wark was about to inflict on me as she placed her feet one either side of my legs and prepared to stoop, knife in hand . . .

. . . and beyond her, on the very edge of the firelight, there appeared a figure which could only be a guardian angel come down from heaven to save poor Flashy from his tormentors, for it was female and beautiful with flowing hair beneath its little white head-dress like a halo, naked to the waist as an avenging fury should be, with a spear raised to hurl – and it wasn't a hallucination or vision conjured by superstitious funk, for she was letting fly with the spear, and the man at my ankles was rearing up with a shriek of mortal anguish, eyes bulging and hands clutching at the bloody point emerging from his chest, flopping forward and spewing gore as he fell over me . . . which effectively cut off my view of the battle royal which was breaking out all around.

The hands at my shoulders were gone, Goram was no longer tearing at my britches, oaths and screams were in my ears and shots were ringing out and steel clashing as I strove to throw off the body of the dying man sprawled over me; he slid sideways, choking on his own blood, and I lay bound and helpless, staring at my incredible salvation.

For a wild moment I wondered if my brief delusion of divine aid hadn't been true after all, for now there was a good score of ministering angels racing into the firelight, half-naked women who howled like Harpies and slashed right and left at the Gallas. But only for a moment: angels don't shout war cries or squeal with pain when they're wounded, nor do they yell with delight while two of 'em hold an enemy down and a third rips him open. And they don't peel like Big Side chargers, either; my spear-thrower had looked like a statue of Diana, but some of her companions were as broad as they were long and could have thrown chests with King Gezo's Dahomey Amazons. They fought with appalling savagery, and the Gallas were hard put to it to hold them; for a few minutes the fight surged to and fro, and then more attackers came leaping out of the dark, the Gallas fell back as the little darlings swept into them in a final charge, hair flying and juggs bouncing, and as two more of my captors went down, hideously slashed, I knew there could be only one end to it.

Goram knew it too, the swine, but where I would have turned and run, the spiteful brute was faithful unto death to his damned Uliba. He cut down one woman, parried a thrust from another, sprang back, shot a look of pure venom in my direction, barked an order, and leaped back into the fight. And to my horror, two of his ruffians broke away from the mêlée and snatched up my stretcher . . . but not to carry me out of harm's way. No, not a bit of it. They threw me on the fire.

As you may know, during my service in the Punjab I had the

misfortune to be basted on a gridiron over a slow fire, and bloody disagreeable it was, leaving me singed and smoking but mercifully underdone. An open blaze is different; two or three seconds and I imagine you burst into flames unless your stretcher happens to be made of stout bullock hide, but even then it's only a matter of time before you come all over of a heat, and your one hope is the arrival of the fire brigade, at speed.

By God, I was lucky. I crashed into the heart of the blaze with a tremendous shower of sparks, and for a heartbeat there was no sensation before the flames began to lick at my feet, which overhung the stretcher, and I'd ha' been horribly maimed at least if one of the angels ('cos that's what she was even if she looked like a female gorilla) hadn't thrust her spear beneath my stretcher and tipped me clear of the blaze with a tremendous heave which deposited me face down with a seared arse and back but no lasting damage.

She and her mates turned me over, and one of 'em had the wit to pour the contents of a chaggle over me, for I was smouldering painfully, and when they pulled the gag out I woke the echoes with complaint and gratitude, mostly complaint, but they very civilly cut me loose from the stretcher, which was uncomfortably hot still, Gorilla Jane helped me to a drink, and they set me with my back to a boulder, where I could take stock of the astonishing scene.

There wasn't a Galla left standing. The onslaught of these amazing females had overwhelmed them in minutes, and by the excited yells and ghastly chopping sounds their wounded were being despatched, with my spear-hurling Diana supervising the slaughter. Her followers were a mixed bag, mostly young and as handsome as Ab women are, but one or two were older and pretty puggish; they were in various states of undress, despite the night chill, some in tunics of Uliba's cut, others in skirts or trowsers, and a few of the younger vain misses flaunted themselves like Diana in flimsy head-dresses, cloaks, and loincloths, a most fetching rig. Every woman-jill of them was fully armed.

Amazons, but very different from the Dahomey variety, who were under discipline and drilled like guardsmen. These were irregulars and, unlike Gezo's Gorgons, they behaved like women; half of them were chattering round their own wounded with squeals of concern and comfort; one very young member of the bare-chest brigade was weeping buckets and pouring dust on her head while they covered the face of her dead comrade – and suddenly she was up and raving shrilly, plunging her spear again and again into a Galla corpse until she noticed a live target hard by: Uliba-Wark! She was bleeding from a dozen wounds, held spreadeagled with Diana apparently interrogating her, when the hysterical stabber ran in and planted her spear in Uliba's body. In an instant the rest were hacking at her like things demented, while the stabber lay wailing and Diana shrugged and turned away, bored like.

I was physically sick on the spot. The Lord knows I had cause to loathe and fear her for the ghastly revenge she had been about to take on me, and I'll not pretend I was sorry to have her cancelled out . . . but to see her slashed to pieces, that beautiful body that I'd held in my arms and loved to ecstasy, butchered by these creatures from the Pit, was more than I could bear. Just for an instant I had the vision of her, gleaming wet and naked, laughing on the black rock in Lake Tana, and I absolutely wept and moaned. Oh, I'm vile all right; we'd travelled well together until her death had become necessary to my survival, and I'd tried to murder her without compunction. Foul work indeed. But would I rather she was still living and doing what she'd been about to do? On the whole, no; but I still stopped my ears against the awful chopping sounds and eldritch laughter of the executioners.

Having known Uliba, I dare say I shouldn't have been astonished to encounter Ab fighting women, but no advance warning could have prepared me for these terrifying bitches. Who the blazes could they be, whose side were they on, and what had I to hope from them? They'd rescued me, no doubt on the ground that anyone whom their enemies wanted to castrate and roast alive must have something to be said for him, but that didn't make 'em bosom pals.

Speaking of which, I couldn't help admiring Diana's as she strode across in my direction. She knew it, too, sweeping back the tails of her cloak and striking a pose, a hand on her pistol butt. Blue eyes, bigod, piercing bright in a lovely face that was no darker than tawny, peacock proud and sassy with it . . . and now came an even greater shock, for she was standing aside to make way for two who were following her, and they were *men*. I hadn't seen either in the fight or its aftermath, but from the deference Diana showed, one of them at least must be a big gun indeed.

He was small and portly and black as your boot, rolling along on stubby legs and standing arms akimbo to survey me. He was bald, with a fringe of woolly white hair, and wore the red-fringed *shama* of consequence. His companion looked like a bodyguard, for he wore a steel back and breast and carried spear and sword, a tall, likely Adonis, middling dark and moved like a dancer, taking station at Portly's shoulder. All three regarded me in silence for a moment, and then Portly opened the bowling, most disconcertingly.

"I know what you are, but not who you are!" He spoke in Amharic, with authority. "So tell me your name, and what you have done that these Galla savages should wish to slay you."

I answered in Arabic, taken aback but head up. "I'm English. My name is Flashman. I'm a colonel . . . a *ras*, a chief in the British Army advancing on Magdala. May I ask who you are?"

There was a gasp from Diana and some of the women who presumably understood Arabic. They'd suspended the agreeable task of polishing off the enemy wounded at Portly's arrival, and crowded in to listen. Diana dropped to one knee to study me more closely – gad, she was a little satin stunner, and I bestowed my most courtly smile on her, which she received with a startled look followed by a disdainful toss of the head and tits. Portly was equally unimpressed.

"I know what a colonel is, and who I am can wait!" snaps he. "So how came a British officer in the hands of the Galla?" He stamped impatiently. "And why should they seek your death?"

This was dangerous ground, and I must hedge until I'd found out who Portly and these dreadful women were. But for his presence I'd have taken them for bandits, like the female dacoits of India; he was obviously someone of official importance – could he be an agent of some petty ruler like Menelek or Gobayzy of whom I'd heard so much – or even of Masteeat's rival, the despised Warkite? All I knew for certain was that the women enjoyed killing Gallas, and weren't likely to be well disposed to anyone whose task it was to enlist them as allies. So I assumed my gallant-pathetic expression and asked Diana if I might have a reviving sip of *tej* and some food, just a morsel would do, to revive me after my ordeal.

Portly made an Ab noise which would translate as "Bah!" but Diana, dear girl, snapped her fingers and Gorilla Jane hastened to offer a flask and wallet of toasted beef. I thought quickly as I imbibed and chewed, decided I'd best not try Portly's patience by asking a second time who he was, and resolved, since the truth wouldn't do, to follow the golden rule by sticking as close to it as possible.

I'd been scouting ahead of Napier's advance, I said, and had been ambushed by these people – Gallas, had he called them? But thank heaven he and his splendid ladies had turned up, and if he would be so obliging as to return me to my army, the British *dedjaz*, who was noted for his generosity, would reward them with dollars and all kinds of good things: food, drink, weapons . . . and of course clothes, silks and satins and ornaments . . .

The women showed eager interest, but Portly gave another furious stamp. "Do I look like a fool? You dare talk to me of dollars and silks as though I were a *fellaheen* beggar or a *bedawi*, and evade my question!" He drew breath, and Diana surprised me by putting in her oar unexpected, with a curl-of-the-lip smile.

"Would your *dedjaz*'s generosity give us the spoiling of Magdala?" Her women gasped eagerly, the bodyguard burst out laughing, and before Portly could explode I said that I couldn't answer for the *dedjaz*, but whatever the spoil of Magdala might be, she could count on getting equivalent value, and meanwhile, the sooner I was restored to my army . . .

"Perhaps he will not be able to take Magdala." The bodyguard spoke for the first time. "It is the strongest *amba* in Habesh."

"He'll take it, soldier," says I. "Have no doubt of that."

"With the help of the Galla warriors of Queen Masteeat?" bawls Portly, taking me flat aback, although I tried desperately to cover it.

"Galla warriors – these people?" I gestured at the bodies. "I don't understand . . . why should the British seek anyone's help? We have no need of it . . . and I know nothing of this queen –"

"You lie!" cries Portly. "All Habesh knows by now that the British seek alliance with the Wollo Galla, and who are you to be ignorant?" He shot out a fat finger. "You have been sent by your *dedjaz* to win the Gallas with silver and a crown for Masteeat! So why, then . . . should they wish you dead?"

When in doubt, play the bewildered loony. That I was blown upon to the far end of Kingdom Come was plain . . . Uliba had been right, Yando's gang had guessed who I was and spread the word. But I daren't admit anything, to unknown accusers, in a country where everybody knew the far end of a fart before it had even erupted. So I babbled.

"I don't know what you mean! My dear sir, how should I know why these foul villains wanted to kill me? As to winning anyone with silver . . ." I threw up my hands. "Please, if you'll only escort me to my army, you'll receive a mighty reward for my return, I assure you." I continued in this vein while he stood glaring, and then Diana, who'd been eyeing me like an Arcadian nymph mistrustful of a satyr of doubtful repute, put in her confounded oar again.

"If we feed him into the fire, little by little, he will speak," says she, but Portly seemed undecided, for he turned away, and after a word with his bodyguard, told Diana curtly to muster the women and prepare to march. She gave a disappointed grunt and issued brisk orders for them to fall in as soon as they'd finished despoiling and mutilating the dead – you can guess what that meant, and I was happy to avert my eyes from that bloodied ground and desecrated bodies – and Uliba's among them! – and those barbarian sluts, some of 'em mere slips of girls, chattering and laughing as they went about their grisly work.

"Are you sick, *farangi*? Why do you look away? Does the sight of blood distress you?" I looked up to find the bodyguard leaning on his spear; Portly was off on a frolic of his own, seemingly. "Nay, surely not; you have seen your own blood run from a wound." He pointed to the star-shaped scar on my hand. "A bullet did that."

"A clean wound is one thing, soldier," says I, and nodded towards the Ladies' De-ballocking Circle. "That is another."

"Aye, true," says he. "Yet it is what the Gallas would have done to you . . . while you still lived. Do the British not believe in retribution, then, eye for eye, burning for burning?"

Diana crowed with laughter. "We do not take their eyes!" She added nauseating particulars, and I wondered if I'd ever found a beauty so detestable.

"We believe in it," I told the bodyguard. "That don't mean I have to watch your disgusting bitches!" It came out as a high-pitched snarl; reaction was overtaking me after the horrors I'd seen and near experienced, and I was on the brink of spewing again.

"Perhaps he is cold with fear at the sight of fighting women!" jeers Diana. "We can unman men before the fight as well as after!" She seated herself on a rock, stretching her legs and folding her arms across her presents for a good boy. "So they fear us, which is why our Lord Toowodros has made special choice of us, and sends us forth to raid and ambush and strike terror in the hearts of his enemies. Is your heart stricken, *ras* of the British?"

The jibe was wasted; only one word mattered. "Your Lord Toowodros? Who the hell is he, then?" Even as I spoke, I knew the answer, and the bodyguard confirmed it, shaking his head at my ignorance.

"Why, the Emperor! The King of Kings, monarch of Habesh, and by the power of God the conqueror that will be of Egypt and Jerusalem! You know him as Theodore."

I could only stare at them in utter consternation. Theodore's people – the last folk on God's earth I wanted to see. I ain't often at a dead nonplus, but I was then, for this was the fear that had been in my mind for weeks – of falling into the hands of the mad tyrant who inflicted unspeakable tortures on his victims, who'd beaten missionaries and lashed their servants to death, who'd stretched Consul Cameron on the rack . . . and, my God, who *knew*, from what Portly had said, of my mission to Masteeat to enlist the Gallas against him . . . Portly? Could he be Theodore in person? For all I knew he might – but surely not, in a night skirmish away from Magdala, where he was supposed to be preparing to fight or run? No, impossible, but I was bound to ask . . .

Diana clapped a hand over her mouth at the question, and the bodyguard laughed outright.

"Do the soldiers of the English queen know so little of their quarry that they think such a fat little hippo as Damash could be the great Emperor – the Lion of Judah? Did he look like a warrior king, a veteran of thirty years in arms?" He glanced at Diana. "Ya, Miriam, what would Gobayzy or Menelek say to Damash as Emperor?"

"Ask rather what Theodore would say to a fool who mistook Damash for the King of Kings," says she. "How would he punish such an insult?"

"Who knows the mind of kings? They are beyond the ken of common folk." He put his head on one side, regarding me. "But I should not account this one a fool, as you do. Did you not hear him answer Damash, saying much, but telling nothing?" He leaned towards me, nursing his spear, his eyes intent on mine. "Perhaps Damash is right, and he is the kind of man the *Dedjaz* Napier would have sent to Masteeat – a man of a long head, skilled in dissimulation and never aiming where he looks." He smiled. "You are that man, are you not, *Ras* Flashman?" Then he was solemn again. "When you come to stand before Toowodros, do not try to deceive him. He loves truth, above all things, and rewards those who deal fairly with him."

"And takes the hands and feet of those who lie, and feeds the rest alive to the birds and beasts," taunts Miriam-Diana.

"Peace, you hyena in woman's shape!" He nodded to me. "I advise as a friend, Englishman. Remember my words." He was turning away.

My mouth was dry with alarm, but I forced my voice to be steady.

"I'd be a fool if I forgot them . . . your majesty."

Miriam-Diana threw back her head with a yell and gave her thigh a ringing slap. "He knew you! By the power of God, he knew you!" She was grinning with delight. "They are not such blind fools, the English!"

The bodyguard who ruled Abyssinia had turned back abruptly, but the solemn look was gone, and his voice was suddenly harsh.

"How did you know me? What did he see?" He looked from me to her, and struck his breast in anger. "What is there here that denotes a king? This is a common soldier!" He shook his spear and slapped himself again, taking two abrupt steps towards me. I gave back, for in a mere moment his earnest, almost friendly manner had given way to shouting rage; it was as though another man had got into his skin, and Miriam was on her feet as though to intervene.

"How did you know me?" he demanded, and jabbed a finger at me. "Have a care! Do not pretend that you saw royalty in my looks and speech, that you could not mistake the descendant of Solomon and Sheba, of Constantine and Alexander! I despise that kind of lie, that courtly flattery! Do not offend me with it!"

Since that was precisely what I'd been about to do, I was briefly at a loss. I'd twigged early enough that he was no common spear-carrier; there's no lack of Abs with handsome figureheads, with fine aquiline noses for looking down, but he had spoken with that calm assurance that you don't find in the private soldier, and I'd marked him down as an Abyssinian gentleman-ranker, so to speak. But there had been something else.

"You spoke of your companion . . . Damash? . . . as a fat little hippo. Common men do not talk so of superiors who wear the red-fringed *shama*. That made me wonder." I climbed to my feet. "But when you cry 'Peace, hyena!' to one who commands the Emperor's fighting women and wears a silver shield on her arm[41] . . . then I do more than wonder. And whether you despise courtly flattery or no, I have stood before the face of many kings and queens in my time, and know the look . . . not at once, perhaps, but at last."

There's no doubt about it, I'm good at dealing with barmy savages. They scare the bile out of me, and perhaps terror lends wings to my wits, for when I think of the monsters I've conversed with and come away with a whole skin, more or less . . . Mangas Colorado, Ranavalona, General Sang-kol-in-sen, Crazy Horse, Dr Arnold, God knows who else . . . well, it took more than luck, I can tell you. You must know when to grovel and scream for mercy, but also when to take 'em aback with impudence or argument or pure bamboozle. To find myself in the presence of Mad King Theodore was enough to turn my bowels to buttermilk, but having seen him quiet and crazy in quick time, and realised that he was intelligent well above par, like many madmen, I knew that straight talk and a firm front to cover my quaking guts were my best bet . . . oh God, I hoped so, and tried not to quiver as I waited, watching him.

You never can tell what they'll do when you answer 'em cool and apparently steady: some laugh, some ponder, some snarl, some set about you (I'm thinking of Arnold), and some, like Theodore, study you in disquieting silence. Then:

"You were quite wrong, you see, Miriam. He is no fool."

"Your majesty was wrong also," says she pertly. "He knew you."

"Not until I had studied him, and seen what manner of man he was. Damash served his turn." To me he said: "What success had you with Queen Masteeat? Oh, we can be plain now: I have known for weeks that a British envoy was on his way to seek her help, and since you reached her yesterday we have been watching . . . fortunately for you." He gestured towards the Galla dead. "Did you not prosper with her?"

If I said no, I hadn't prospered, and he had a spy at her court to tell him otherwise, or had intercepted my message to Napier, I was done for. If I told him the truth, that the Gallas were taking the field to cut him off, God knew what he would do. I'd seen already how swiftly his mood could change; I daren't risk it. I said there'd been no time even to broach Napier's request, and was subjected to another silent stare.

"No time for talk?" says he. "But time for these –" he gestured again "– to bring you out for death? No, that is not Queen Masteeat's way."

"Not with a fine tall soldier," sniggers Miriam, who seemed to go in no awe of him at all. He paid her no heed.

"So who condemned you? And why?"

I told him the truth of it, since it could do no harm, and he presumably knew that Uliba-Wark had guided me south. "We were separated by your riders at the Silver Smoke; she chose to think I had abandoned her, and these dead men were her hirelings to murder me." I nodded at the clearing. "And there she lies."

"Uliba-Wark? Dead?" Theodore stared, and wheeled abruptly, striding to the group about Uliba's body; they scattered like birds. Miriam followed him in some alarm. "I saw it was a woman, but I did not know her, *negus*, truly . . ."

"It is no matter," says Theodore. He looked down at what remained of Uliba, and shrugged without disgust. "She was a stinging gadfly, a sower of discord, a trouble in the eyes of God and man. She coveted her sister's throne, they say. Behold her now."

"She coveted men, by all accounts," says Miriam, and gave me her jeering grin. "Were you her lover, *ras* of the British?"

I was not about to mention a lady's name, but her question seemed to catch Theodore on the raw somehow, for he stared hard at her, head back, and then at me, and then at her again, and smiled at last, crooking a finger.

"Hither, wanton," says he, and she came to his side. He put an arm about her waist and fondled her chin, and she purred like a kitten and nuzzled him. "Speak not of love to fine tall soldiers," says he. So that explained the licence she enjoyed; one of his concubines, obviously, as well as commanding his killing women. Versatile female. And Theodore of Abyssinia was as jealous as the next man.

And now Damash came rolling back, followed by a groom leading two horses. Behind him the women had finished their revolting chore, and were assembling more or less in ranks, except for Gorilla Jane who was dragging along one of the Galla corpses. Then I saw that it wasn't a corpse, but a living being, bleeding from a dozen wounds. Theodore, still with his arm about Miriam, addressed me.

"*Ras* Flashman, though you come with the power of the English Queen to destroy me, who have wished for nothing but peace between her throne and mine, and laboured by the power of God to that end against the wickedness of evil men, yet I hold no malice in my heart towards you, or your *Dedjaz* Napier, who writes cordially to me and I to him. I take you to be my guest in Magdala, where we shall look into each other's hearts, in love and friendship."

He seemed to expect an answer, so I said, "Much obliged . . . ah, *negus*." He kissed Miriam and toyed with her hand a moment.

"Bring the *ras* to Islamgee," says he, and mounted. Damash was budged into the saddle by the groom, but as they prepared to ride off Gorilla Jane cried that here was the Galla chief still alive, though incomplete, and what should be done with him. At her feet, with her companions crouched over it like vultures, was that dreadful thing, stirring feebly, and I saw it was Goram.

Miriam brightened. "We should question him, *negus*."

"A Galla warrior will tell you nothing," says Theodore. He stood in his stirrups, a hand raised. "The blessing of God upon you brave women. And the blessing also on you, *Ras* Flashman, and His mercy and peace." He wheeled his horse, and as he passed Gorilla Jane and the shattered wreck of Goram, he added: "Throw him on the fire." So they did.

I spent a week as "guest" of the Emperor Theodore, and it was one of the longest of my life. How our prisoners, Cameron and Co., endured it for two solid years is beyond me. There may be nothing worse than being in the hands of a deadly enemy, but finding yourself at the mercy of a lunatic runs it close, for there's no telling what he'll do – load you with chains or send you presents, threaten you with flogging or swear eternal friendship over a glass of *tej*, discuss the causes of the American Civil War or invite you to kill him 'cos life has become a burden – that was Theodore, the maniac who held our lives in his hands, torturing our gracious Queen's consul half to death, and firing twenty-one-gun salutes to celebrate her birthday. Not the worst host I've ever been billeted on, perhaps, but quite the most unpredictable.

There was no way of foreseeing, as they brought me away from that place of slaughter where the Gallas died, that those seven days of horror and hope, of living on the razor's edge, were to see the final act of the astonishing melodrama, part-tragedy, part-farce, known as the Abyssinian War. For me, it was the last mile of that wild journey that had begun a few short months ago in Trieste. I tell you it as it was; it's all true.

It was still pitch dark and drizzling gently when we set out, Miriam and I and a few others mounted, with the rest of those female crocodiles trotting behind. I didn't reckon we'd gone far by sunrise, five miles perhaps, and then we were in a stony desolation of tall cliffs and deep ravines, rounding a mighty eminence of rock on our right hand and following a saddle that connected it to another towering flat-topped height a mile or so ahead, which came into full view as the dawn mist lifted and the sunlight struck it and turned it for a moment into a mountain of gold. I asked where we were.

"Selassie," says Miriam, pointing ahead and then jerking a thumb at the cliff to our right. "Fala."

These were the names I'd heard only yesterday, in Fasil's room at Masteeat's camp . . . yesterday, dear God, it seemed an eternity ago! I pictured that sand-table model and tried to match it to what I was seeing . . . yes, there below us was the road that Theodore had made for his artillery, winding between Fala and Selassie, with folk and carts moving along it, and gangs of what looked like men in chains. As near as I could judge we were coming from the south-west, and if you look at my map you'll see what was about to come into my view as we rounded Fala.

Beyond the saddle, at the foot of Selassie, was a group of tents – or pavilions, rather, for they were larger and set apart from the camp of little bivouacs at the northern end of the long plain that I knew must be Islamgee. And at the far southern end of that plain, less than two miles from where I sat transfixed, was a great tower-ing cylinder of black rock sprouting out of the plain like a column fashioned by some giant sculptor – and the reason I sat transfixed was that I knew what it was before Miriam said the word: "Magdala".

So there it was, the eagle's nest, the stronghold where Mad King Theodore had held a handful of British and German cap-tives for four years, his last outpost where he would be trapped with nowhere to run, for I didn't doubt that Masteeat's regiments would even now be marching to cut him off from that wilderness of peaks in the hazy southern distance. And there, below me on Islamgee, was his army – how many strong? Seven thousand, ten? Was he waiting there to meet Napier in the open, or would he retire into Magdala, pulling up the metaphorical drawbridge – gad, if he did, that rock would be a bastard to take by storm! Or might he even march to meet Napier, who must be close by now, surely . . . And on the thought I turned to gaze north-westwards, straining my eyes across that rock-strewn plain that stretched away across the Arogee plateau directly below us, five miles and more to a

194

distant dark line running across our front, which I knew must be the chasm of the Bechelo. From it the King's Road wound across the undulating land to Arogee and between Fala and Selassie to the very foot of Magdala.

Surveying that broken ground, bordered by hills and gullies, it struck me that Theodore could do a sight worse than choose the third course – advance beyond Arogee to lay ambushes in the rough country bordering his road; better that than being besieged in Magdala or meeting our people on the flat plain of Islamgee where they'd make mincemeat of him in open battle . . .

Miriam gave a cry of excitement and stood in her stirrups, shading her eyes and pointing – and as I followed her finger I felt that same wild thrill of disbelief giving way to joy that I'd felt in the garden of Lucknow when we'd heard, ever so faint on the morning air, the far whisper of the pipes that told us Campbell was coming. For it was there, through that shimmering heat haze and the last wisps of mist, on the lip of the plateau beyond the Bechelo . . . as though to a cue, the last actor was coming on to the stage, with no sound of pipes or rumble of gunfire, heralded only by tiny shining pinpricks of light barely visible in the dusty distance, and I'd ha' given a thousand for a glass just then, for I'd seen 'em too often to be mistaken – lance-points catching the morning sun . . . But whose? Bengali Native Cavalry? Scindees? For instinct told me they must be ours, and now it was confirmed by eyes that were younger and sharper than mine.

"*Farangi*!" cries Miriam, with an added oath. "On Dalanta! The Negus was right – those vermin of Dawunt and Dalanta should have been destroyed! They have lain down before your people! Aiee, they come! See there, they come!"

"How d'ye know they're my people?"

I didn't know, then, that Theodore had fallen out with the tribes on the Dalanta plateau, which lies north of the Bechelo river, slap across Napier's line of march, and that the obliging niggers had cleared the way for us.[42] But I could read the consternation on Miriam's pretty face.

"They can be no one else! We had word when they crossed the

Jedda three days ago; now they are on the lip of the Bechelo, and once across the ravine . . ." She gave a disgusted shrug and spat, and I gazed towards salvation and concluded reluctantly that I daren't try a run for it, not on a miserable Ab screw that was bound to founder within a mile. Besides, all I had to do was wait; Napier was far closer than I'd dared to hope, and even with the Bechelo chasm to cross, which I knew from Fasil's model was three-quarters of a mile deep, he couldn't be more than two days' march away. I absolutely smacked my palm in delight, and Miriam cried out scornfully:

"Ha! You rejoice at their coming? But what of their going, when the Amhara drive them like sheep back to Egypt?"

I knew she didn't believe it, just from her sullen scowl. "If the Amhara are mad enough to try, they'll find those sheep are wolves," I told her. "They'll eat your army of peasants at a bite . . . no, they'll not need to, for their guns will blow your rabble to bits, and the elephants will trample the dead." Unless Theodore has the sense to go to ground on that bloody rock, I might have added, but didn't.

"Elephants!" She shuddered; they're mortal scared of jumbo, you see, being convinced he can't be tamed. She looked thoughtful, and as we rode on I guessed she was wondering how she'd fare in person if Theodore took a hiding. Sure enough, after a moment:

"Suppose your people triumphed . . . what would they do to Habesh?"

"To a pretty lass like you, you mean? I know what I'd do."

"No!" cries she fiercely. "You would protect me!"

"Would I now? In gratitude for wanting me fed into the fire?"

"You were a prisoner then!" She rode closer, and said in a low tone, "Now, if your people triumphed, you could do me good . . . and I would be grateful." Softly, with her knee against mine, if you please.

"My dear, you're a girl after my own heart," says I. "But what if *your* side won, eh? They won't . . . but just suppose . . ."

"Then I would protect you from the wrath of Theodore! As I shall, even now."

"I doubt if he'll be wrathful with me just now," says I. "Not with the British Army on his doorstep."

She stared at me. "You do not know him! Oh, believe me, *ras* of the British, you know him not at all!"

In fact, she was wrong; I did know him, all too well – but I'd forgotten, you see. I thought of him as the well-spoken soldier I'd mistaken for a bodyguard – given to sudden bursts of temper over trifles, if you like, and didn't care two straws about roasting an enemy, but that's African war for you. But I'd not associated that man, who'd seemed to be sane enough, and a reasoning being, with the ghastly tales I'd heard of atrocities, of women and children massacred, of frightful tortures practised on countless victims . . . I'd forgotten Gondar, and that dreadful garden of the crucified. Yet that horror had been the work of the intelligent, earnest man who'd cross-examined me so briskly, and smiled and joked and dallied with the bonny bint riding beside me. It didn't seem possible . . . until we rode down from the Fala saddle to the camp below Selassie. Then it became all too horribly plain.

The first intimation came when we had to halt at the King's Road while a procession of Ab prisoners shuffled by. There were hundreds of them, in the most appalling condition, starved skeletons virtually naked, many of them covered in loathsome sores. Every one of them was chained, some in fetters so heavy they could barely drag them along, others manacled wrist to ankle with chains so short they couldn't stand upright, but must totter along bent double. The stench was fit to choke you, and to complete their misery they were driven along by burly guards wielding *girafs*, the hippo-hide whips which are the Ab equivalent of the Russian *knout*.

"Who in God's name are they?" I asked Miriam. "Rebels?"

"Huh, you'll find no living rebels here!" says she. "They die where they're taken."

"So these are criminals? What the hell have they done?"

Her answer defied belief, but it's what she said, with a shrug, and I was to learn that it was gospel true.

"What have they done? Smiled when the King was in ill humour – or scowled when he was merry. Served him a dish that was not

197

to his taste, or mentioned tape-worm medicine, or spoken well of someone he dislikes, or came in his way when he was drunk." She laughed at my incredulity. "You don't believe me? Indeed, you do not know him!"

"By God, I don't believe you!"

"You will." She surveyed the last of that pitiful coffle as it staggered past. "True, not all have committed those offences; some merely had the misfortune to be related to the offenders. Oh, yes, that is enough, truly."

"But . . . for *smiling*? Tape-worm medicine? And he takes it out on whole families? How long have they been chained, for God's sake?"

"Some, for years. Why he brings them down now from their prison on Magdala, who knows? Perhaps to preach to them. Perhaps to kill them before your army arrives. Perhaps to free them. We shall see."

"He must be bloody mad!" cries I. Well, I'd heard it said often enough, but you don't think what it means until you see the truth of it at point-blank. And here was this lovely lass, riding at ease in the warm sunlight, tits at the high port and talking cool as you please of a monster to rival Caligula. She must have read the stricken question in my eye, for she nodded.

"Yes, he is a dangerous master, as his ministers and generals will tell you." She smiled, chin up. "But those who know him, and his moods, and how to please him, find in him a devout and kind and loving friend. But even they must learn to turn his anger, for it is terrible, and when the fit is on him he is no better than a beast. Is that mad, *Ras* Flashman of the British? Come!"

She led the way across the road to the nearest pavilions, the first of which was the great red royal marquee with carpets spread on the ground about it, guards on the fly, and servants everywhere. Groups of men in red-fringed *shamas* were gathered before the other large pavilions, evidently waiting, and the plain beyond was covered almost to Magdala by a forest of bivouacs and shelters. The army of Abyssinia was at rest, thousands of men loafing and talking and brewing their billies like any other soldiers, save that these were black, and instead of shirt-sleeves and dangling galluses there were white *shamas* and tight leggings, and as well as the piled firearms there were stands of spears and racks of sickle-bladed swords. They looked well, as the Gallas had done, and perhaps as soon as tomorrow they would go out to face the finest army in the world under one of the great captains. And how many of them would come well to bed-time? How many Scindees and King's Own and Dukes and Baluch, for that matter? Fall out, Flashy, thinks I, this ain't your party; lie low, keep quiet, and above all, stay alive.

Easier said than done. There was a stiffening to attention of the groups outside the tents, the servants scurried out of sight, and Miriam suddenly whipped a noose over my head and thrust me out of my saddle crying, "Get down! Be still!" as down the hill came a procession in haste. In front was Theodore, with a *chico* holding a brolly over his head, and in his wake a motley crowd of guards and attendants. I staggered but kept my feet, and was about to protest when Theodore, striding full tilt and shouting abuse at two skinny wretches hurrying alongside him (astrologers, I learned later) caught sight of me, and let out a yell of anger.

"You! You have betrayed me! You lied to me!" He came at me almost at the run, fists clenched and by the grace of God he was carrying nothing more lethal than a telescope, which he flourished in my face. "You swore you had no talk with the Gallas – yet they have marched, in their thousands, and lie now below Sangalat! How came they there? By Masteeat's order! And who prompted her?" He flung out a hand in denunciation. "You! As Christ is my witness, I had nothing in my heart against you! Judas! Judas!" bawls he, and swung up the telescope to brain me.

Two things saved me. One was Miriam's horse; startled by someone raving and capering a yard away, it reared, and since Miriam was holding t'other end of my noose I was jerked violently off my feet and went down half-strangled, but out of harm's way. My other saviour was one of the astrologers who ran in front of Theodore, waving his arms and crying out, possibly a warning that the omens weren't favourable for cracking heads – in which case he was dead right, for Theodore smashed him full on the crown with the telescope, and it was a lethal weapon after all, for it stove him in like an eggshell.

It had happened in seconds. I realised that Miriam, seeing him come down the hill in a towering rage, had sensibly decided that the more captive I looked the better, so she'd noosed me – and in an instant there beside me lay the corpse of the poor prophet with his skull leaking, and Theodore was dashing down the telescope, staring at his victim, and suddenly burying his face in his hands and running howling towards the red pavilion. He seized a spear from one of the guards on the fly, and began to stab the surrounding carpet, cursing something fearful. Then he flung the spear aside, shook his fists at heaven, and darted into the pavilion . . . and the assembled military and civilian worthies stood silent and thoughtful, determined not to look at each other, like a convocation of clergy when the bishop has farted extempore. They knew the unwisdom of noticing, having seen his royal tantrums before.

"Come!" snaps Miriam, and led me quickly in behind one of the nearest tents, where she dismounted and removed the noose. "Sit on the ground, say nothing. All may yet be well. I must see Damash." And off she went, leaving me in some disquiet, sitting obediently and trembling like an aspen, an object of studied lack of interest to the aforementioned worthies; they acted as though I weren't there, which suited admirably: I'd no wish to be noticed, especially by the frothing maniac in the red pavilion. I'd seen his quicksilver change of mood during the night, from mild to angry, and the sight of those wretched prisoners, and Miriam's explanation, had convinced me that he was fairly off his rocker . . . but none of that had prepared me for the homicidal rage of a moment ago. That settled it. He was a murderous maniac – and I was his detested prisoner.

I'll not weary you with my emotions as I sat there in the sun, or my terrors when presently a squad of burly ruffians in leather tunics arrived, bearing manacles, and marched me away from the tents to a little stockade within which stood a small thatched hut with a heavy door. They thrust me in, ignoring my inquiries for Miriam and Damash (I didn't ask for Theodore), chained me, and left me in stuffy half-darkness to meditate on the mutability of human affairs, with a couple of spearmen outside.

Some things were plain enough – Masteeat and Fasil had lost no time, the Galla cordon that Napier had wanted was in place, and Theodore knew it; since he'd been on top of Selassie with a telescope he would also know that Napier was within striking distance, and that the game was up with a vengeance – hence, no doubt, his irritable conduct to your correspondent. And whether he chose to fight, fly, or laager on top of Magdala, the pressing question was what he would do with his European prisoners – cut our throats out of spite and die with harness on his back, or hand us over in reasonably good condition like a sensible chap . . . which he wasn't.

There was no way of even guessing. On the one hand, here I was in chains, which boded no good, but didn't suggest hasty execution, and Miriam had said all might yet be well. And since Theodore had kept our folk captive, often in chains, for years without killing any of 'em bar a couple of Ab servants, it looked odds on that he'd spare our lives . . . but then again, the man was barmy, and there was no telling what he might do now that his back was well and truly to the wall.

To keep my mind from glum speculation, I tried to remember how many times I'd been in chains before. Four or five, perhaps? Proper chains, that is, not the darbies used by the A Division peelers to restrain obstreperous revellers, but your genuine bilboes. There'd been Russia, when Ignatieff had caged me half across Central Asia, and the Gwalior bottle dungeon, and China when the Imps collared me before Pekin, and Afghanistan when that frightful bitch Narreeman was going to qualify me for the Hareem Handicap . . . at which point it struck me that my present situation, while most disturbing, was grace itself compared to these unhappy memories. I could only hope that I'd not be called on to walk in my new fetters, for they were easily the heaviest I'd ever worn, wrist manacles like double horseshoes, ankle irons two inches thick, and all connected by chain that could have lifted an anchor. And Cameron and Co. had had to wear these for months! Well, I'd not have to carry 'em for more than a day or two, one way or the other . . . and on this consoling thought

I fell asleep – something I hadn't done, bar my brief drunken stupor following Masteeat's feast, for more than forty-eight hours.

A dazzling light and commotion at the doorway brought me back to life, trying to start up and failing thanks to the weight of those infernal clanking manacles. The door was open, someone was hanging a lamp from the roof beam and retiring, and as the door crashed shut again I was aware of a swaying figure in the middle of the room, a man whose *shama* had slipped from his shoulders so that he was bare to the waist. He gave a mighty belch and advanced unsteadily towards me, half-tripping over a large basket of bottles and food which the lamplighter had placed on the floor.

"How are you, how are you, my dear friend, my best of friends?" cries this apparition, whooping with laughter. "Thank God I am well! Are you well? Ah, my good friend, my heart rejoices to see you, for the friendship I have entertained for you has not diminished. Be of good cheer, for though you are bound with fetters, as Samson and Zedekiah were bound, even with fetters of brass, yet . . . yet . . ." His voice trailed away, muttering: " . . . and . . . and, who else? Yes, Jehoiakim also was bound, and Manasseh! They were bound, by the power of God! And so was Joseph, who was sold for a servant, whose feet they hurt with fetters, and he was laid in iron." He gave another crazy laugh and almost fell over. "But have no fear, for the hour of your deliverance is at hand!"

My eyes had recovered from the lamp-glare, but I could hardly believe them, for the newcomer was Theodore, King of Abyssinia, and he was staggering drunk.

* * *

Just as Peacock's Mr McQuedy, discussing condiments for fish, could imagine no relish superior to lobster sauce and oyster sauce, so I, on the subject of bizarre conversation, had never thought to meet a crazier discourser than Hung-Hsiu-Chuan, leader of the Taiping Rebellion, who was hopelessly mad, or Mangas Colorado, chief of the Mimbreno Apache, who was hopelessly drunk. I discovered in that hut under Selassie that I'd been quite wrong; King Theodore was both hopelessly mad *and* drunk, and could have given either of

202

them a head start and a beating in the race to Alice's tea party. If you've the patience, and know my earlier papers, you may make comparison with the following record of our chat, from the moment he plumped down, hiccoughing and beaming, in front of me, and spilled out the contents of the basket of food and drink.

I'd had no opportunity to study him at close quarters before, for our first meeting had been by flickering firelight, and at our second his face had been so contorted with rage as to be nigh unrecognisable. Now, with his black skin (for he was blacker than most Abs) shining with sweat, his eyes staring and bloodshot, and his mouth grinning slackly, he wasn't your portrait painter's ideal model; still I could weigh him well enough, and what I saw through the haze of booze and confusion was not an ordinary man.

He had force, no other word for it, a pent-up strength that was as much in the mind as in the body – and the body was impressive enough. He wasn't above middle height, but he had the shoulders and arms of a middleweight wrestler, a chest like a barrel tapering to a slim waist; there wasn't the least lip of flesh above his waistband. Groggy with drink as he was, I guessed he could move like a striking snake if need be; when he poured out cups of *tej* his hands were deft and steady.

But the real power was in the eyes, bright and piercing despite the blood-streaks and the occasional drunken tears; there was no tipsy vacancy about them – and that in a way was the shocking thing, 'cos by rights he should have been goggling like the last man out of the canteen. Drunk, yes, but it didn't *suit* him; you felt he'd no business to be bottled. It was like seeing the Prince Consort or Gladstone taking the width of the pavement singing "One-eyed Riley". And he was a sight handsomer than either of 'em; forget his tendency to slobber and stare and he was a deuced good-looking fellow, fifty or thereabouts with a pepper-and-salt dusting to grizzle his hair, which was braided in tails down the back of his head; his nose was hooked and prominent and his lips were thin when his mouth was shut, which it wasn't at the moment. But his normal expression, when sober, was pleasant and alert. When he went mad, which he was liable to do at any moment, he looked like a fiend out of Hell.

203

So that's the Emperor Theodore, as best I can limn him for you. One last thing before I get to his chat: I've never seen a black face that looked less African: slim, fine-boned, like a dusky Duke of Wellington. Oh, and he had a curious habit, just occasionally, of spitting thoughtfully when he spoke; just a sideways ptt! of the lips, disconcerting until you got used to it.

Theodore [*jovial, passing a cup of* tej]: We shall drink the vintage of the grapes of Ephraim! Ah, my friend, I have been impatient to see you, and to bring you comfort in the prison-house. Even as the Lord looked down from the height of his sanctuary, so I too heard the groaning of the captive. A toast! Name it, my friend!

Flashy [*taken aback*]: Eh? A toast? Me? Ah, well, let's see ... Here's how, your majesty!

T: Let me shake your hand. Ah, your chains; do they fret you painfully?

F [*toadying warily*]: Oh, just a bit ... no trouble, really –

T: Do you know why you are chained?

F [*cautiously*]: Well, I imagine it's because your majesty misunderstood about my ... my dealings with the Gallas – perfectly natural mistake, of course, could have happened to anyone –

T: What are the Gallas to me? You are the one who has misunderstood, my friend, if you think you are chained as a punishment. I chained you as I chained your countrymen, because the British Government thought me cowardly and weak. But now I have released my good friend Mr Rassam, and Lieutenant Prideaux, and I shall release you also, to show I am not afraid. [*Earnestly*] I had to chain you, in order to release you. If you were not chained, how could you be released? [*Laughs heartily and drains cup of* tej.]

F: How indeed!

T: I also chained them because I knew that must bring against me a British army, trained and disciplined, an army such as I have longed to see. [*Sighs*] I only hope God will spare me to see them before I die. [*Drinks again.*]

F: Will your majesty fight them?

T: If it is God's will. My soldiers are nothing compared to your disciplined army, where thousands move in obedience to one. If they come in love and friendship I shall be so moved as to be unable to resist them, but if they come with other intentions I know they will not spare me, so I shall make a great bloodbath and afterwards die. [*Emits the grandfather of all belches, closes eyes, and appears to fall asleep.*]

Relief was flooding through me, and not only because he was behaving like an intoxicated Cheeryble and plying me with liquor; it would be another story in the morning when his majesty awoke with a head like a burst beehive and started playing Ivan the Terrible. But at least he wasn't about to kill me, had spoken of my release, and as good as promised to give in without a fight if Napier came "in love and friendship" – which could be managed, surely. Then again, he'd so many screws loose that you couldn't be certain of anything he said, especially when he was half-seas over. It was of academic interest, but I wondered if his claim that he'd imprisoned our people deliberately to provoke an invasion might not have something in it, unlikely though it seemed . . .

Theodore [*waking with an almighty yell*]: Damocles! By my death, I am Damocles, with a blade poised above my head, suspended by a horsehair! [*Stares up*] Do you not see it, about to fall? Am I not Damocles?

Flashy [*taken by surprise*]: Wasn't he the chap who was tied up so that he couldn't get at his rations . . . or had to roll something up a hill . . . didn't he? A vulture . . . ?

T: The British army is that blade, coming to pierce me, and I know not what to do! What will happen? I am like a pregnant woman; I do not know whether it will be a boy or a girl or an abortion! [*Starts to weep, drinks deeply.*]

F: Your majesty, may I make a suggestion? A moment ago you spoke of love and friendship between yourself and our *Dedjaz* Napier, and I can tell you he'd cry "Amen!" to that with three times three. Well, if you were to send me to him, I could settle things in no time –

T [*suddenly fierce*]: And tell him the disposition of my army, and where my great guns are sited, and my mortar Sevastopol! Ah, my friend, you do not deceive me! That is what you would settle!

[*Swaying drunkenly, yelling with rage.*] Was this a thing planned with Masteeat and the Gallas? Were you put into my hand so that you might spy out the nakedness of the land –?

F [*horrified*]: Good God, no!

T: – and shall I cut off your garments to the middle, even to your buttocks, as the Ammonites did to the servants of King David, thinking them spies? [*Baring his teeth savagely*] Shall I cut off more than your garments . . . and will you then confess?

He was absolutely screaming now, this frenzied drunkard who a moment since had been calling me his dearest friend, and bab-bling of Damocles and pregnant women, and I could only sit pet-rified, unable even to scramble back because of my fetters, while he shook his fists and threw himself to and fro in his fury. He began to bay like a hound, beating his temples, and then buried his face in his hands as he'd done when he killed the soothsayer, wailing bitterly. I daren't say a word, waiting and praying to God he'd come out of it into one of his sane moods. At last he raised his head, filled his *tej* cup, sank the contents at a gulp (Heaven knew how much he had on board, gallons I shouldn't wonder) – and then, as God's my witness, he noticed that my cup was empty and hastened to fill it, with mumbled apologies. His eyes were rolling in his head, and *tej* was dribbling down his chin and on to his naked chest, but he steadied after a moment, regarding me owlishly.

Theodore: Do you know there is an ancient prophecy that a European ruler will meet a ruler of Habesh, and whether they dispute in combat or not, afterwards a monarch will reign in this country who is greater than any before? That prophecy is about to be fulfilled, but will I be that greatest of kings? Is that to be my destiny?

F [*with confidence*]: Not the slightest doubt about it, in my opinion. Who but your majesty, I mean to say –?

T [*doubtfully*]: It may be this woman who sends her soldiers against me.

F: You don't mean the Queen! Good gracious, your majesty, that shot ain't even on the table! I can assure you, Sir Robert Napier is under strict orders to withdraw as soon as the captives have been released –

T: When did the British lion leave its kill untasted? You have eaten half the world, and shall Habesh be spared?

F: Of course it will, honour bright –

T [*gloomy*]: If they spare us it will be because we are not worth the conquest. England laughs at me and derides my poverty. [*Pauses*] Do they despise me because my skin is black?

F: Certainly not! We ain't Yankees! Why, more than half the army that is coming against you is made up of nig— Indian troops, what? Dam' stout fellas, too –

T: But few in number! How lowly they value me, that they send a handful of the mighty British power . . . How many? Twelve thousand came over the sea, but how many now stand above the Bechelo? Ten thousand? No. Five thousand? . . . Two thousand . . .?

The voice was slurred with drink, the thin lips hung slack in the sweating black face, but under half-lowered lids I caught the glint of a watchful eye . . . or thought I did.

F: Can't say, your majesty. Enough, I guess.

T: If Miriam were to ask you, in ways too dreadful to speak of, would you tell her how many is "enough"? No matter. [*Hiccoughs, sinks another quart or so of* tej, *lowers chin on chest, sighs.*] You are my dear friend. I will not permit a hair of your head to be harmed. Let me embrace you. [*Lunges forward from sitting position, flings arms round F's neck, groans and belches, falls asleep.*][43]

As before, there was nothing to be done but sit waiting; you don't wake a mad drunkard even when he's snoring in your ear; nor do you heave him off. I'd ha' been there till morning, no doubt, but someone had been eavesdropping, and when the conversation ceased he decided to take a look, cautiously opening the door and popping his head in, a ferrety little cove with a bright eye and a clever smile. He put a finger to his lips, slipped inside, took a look at majesty comatose, nodded, and tapped him smartly on the shoulder. And damned if Theodore's head didn't come up like a jack-in-the-box, full and all as he was.

207

"It is time to retire, *getow,*"* says the ferret. "You wish to be abroad at dawn, remember. And you will not wish," he added, glancing at me, "to keep your guest from his rest."

"*Man abat?*"† cries Theodore, startled. "Ah, it is you, Samuel! Did I call you?" He closed his eyes, blew out his cheeks, and gave me a huge beam. "Oh, my friend, we have talked long and drunk well, have we not? And indeed it is time to part, if not to sleep. Is my queen awake?"

Samuel hesitated. "The royal lady Tooroo-Wark is on Magdala, *getow*. With your son Alamayo. But Meshisha is here, and may be –"

"I asked for my queen – my new queen!" bawls Theodore, suddenly enraged. "Not my bastards! Summon her, my lady Tamagno, that I may present her to my friend . . . my guest, you say . . . Go!"

Samuel vanished, and Theodore calmed down enough to refill our cups. "Tamagno is to be my queen," says he. "Alamayo, who is my true son and heir, you shall meet tomorrow. I wish to have him educated at a great English school, such as one I have heard of . . . Harrah?"

"Harrow? Certainly not, your majesty. Lair of bestial. Parvenus. Rugby's the place for your lad . . . and Meshisha, did you say?"

"Meshisha is a by-blow, gotten in an evil hour," says he. "A bastard, an idle great fool, but one must employ one's children, the false get as well as the true. Ah, but here is my true queen that shall be! Tamagno, this is my friend, the *Ras* Flashman, who brings us comfort from the army of the white queen Victoria, wherefore we do him honour!" He waved a hand wildly in introduction, and the lady and I appraised each other as she rolled in, with Samuel holding the door obsequiously.

My first thought was why the devil was Theodore even looking at her when he had beauties like Miriam to play with. Madam Tamagno was fat, coarse, and looked what she was: a whore, for while Theodore

* *Geta* means master, *getow* supreme master.
† "*Man abat?*" lit. "Who's your father?" seems to have been an Abyssinian catchphrase used as a facetious greeting, not unlike "What's up?" or "What's cooking?"

might talk of making her a queen, in fact she was only his chief concubine. Unlike most Ab women, she painted, and while they tend to conceal their passionate appetites behind demure appearance, this one wore her lust on her sleeve, or rather in her lecherous expression. Someone, I forget who, described her as the most lascivious-looking female he'd ever seen, and recalling the hungry leer with which she surveyed me, I can't contradict him. She was dressed to match, in the gaudiest silks with a profusion of bangles and necklaces, all tarted up for work, as her first words showed. For when Theodore reached up to fondle her fat paw and slaver it with a drunken kiss, and she'd stripped me in imagination and torn her eyes away, she reproved him playfully for neglecting her while he rioted with foreign prisoners in the cooler. "And I left lonely," she murmurs.

No prisoner but a guest, cries he, and staggered to his feet with his trollop and Samuel assisting. But then he seemed to forget about me altogether, for he embraced her with mawkish endearments, pawing and nuzzling, and I dare say would have set about her on the spot if she hadn't guided him out, bestowing one last wanton smile on me as she went. I was glad to watch her go, for she was seventeen stone of dangerous desire if ever I'd seen it, the sort who don't care about driving a lover crazy by the way she licks her chops over every new fellow she meets. I'd trouble enough just then without a jealous Theodore running amok; he was like a mine primed to explode, and no way to anticipate him.

For consider: in short order he'd tried to brain me, had me loaded with chains only to bring me booze and jollity like a boon companion, quoted Scripture like a Scotch elder, raved at me as a spy and conspirator, threatened me with mutilation, babbled nonsense and burst into tears, tried to pump me for military intelligence, wondered about having me tortured, sworn eternal friendship, collapsed in a drunken stupor, and introduced me to his black gallop.

Eccentric, eh? I just hoped to God that Napier might get here in time.

You've probably never worn chains, and may be interested to know that they can be a sight easier to put on than to take off. The Ab variety consist of massive links between anklets which are secured with soft iron rivets; once hammered shut, they have to be pried open with a wedge, which likewise has to be hammered with a sledge, and damned unnerving it is to have a grinning blackamoor swinging it down full force, jarring the anklet open, and if he misses his aim you'll never set that foot on the ground again. Then they slip a leather rope into the anklet, and half a dozen strong men pull it open wide enough to get your foot clear. It takes half an hour and hurts like sin.

I wore my fetters for less than twenty-four hours. What it was like to wear them for months, and even years, I learned next day, when all the prisoners, not only the Europeans but Ab rebels and the like were brought down from Magdala. After I'd been freed and given a breakfast of bread and *tej* I was seated under guard on a pile of stones near the red royal tent, and watched the captive procession winding its way slowly across the Islamgee plain, through the little hutted villages to the tents of the camp. They were still some way off when there was a commotion behind me, and here comes Theodore down the hill from Selassie, with his astrologers and courtiers and the ferret Samuel. When he saw me his majesty gave a great halloo of greeting and came striding to me with both hands out, clasping mine as though I were a long-lost brother.

"My friend, I see you are well!" cries he. "I too am well, and rejoice to see you at liberty! Did you sleep well? Are you refreshed? Let me tell you what I have seen! Your army is crossing the Bechelo, and we have seen elephants descending into the ravine. What does that mean, *Ras* Flashman?"

I told him it meant big guns, and he rounded on his followers. "You hear? Did I not tell you, but you doubted me? You know nothing! But the hour is coming when you will learn! Go now, assemble the leaders of the regiments, all officers, and the leaders of sections! I shall address them presently. Now, my friend, let us sit – see, your people are coming from the *amba*, and will soon be with us. Let us drink to your meeting!"

For a man who'd been ripe to roll in gutters only a few hours earlier, he was uncommon spry, and in full fig: a cloth-of-gold coat adorned with silks of many colours, and the most extraordinary pants of what looked like tinsel. He was in such cheerful fettle I wondered if he'd been using hasheesh, but from what I learned later he had no indulgences of that kind, no doubt because booze and fornication occupied most of his leisure time. You'd not have thought he was about to be deposed and possibly slain by an invading army, for he was all hospitality, pledging me in *tej* and summoning sundry of his military big-wigs to make them known to me – Hasani, commandant of Magdala, austere and unsmiling; the portly Damash, whom I already knew; Gabrie, the army commander; Engedda, his chief minister, and several others whose names I disremember. Then I must be shown his artillery park below Selassie, and especially his mighty mortar, Sevastopol, an enormous lump of metal weighing seventy tons and mounted on a wagon with drag-chains which it took five hundred men to pull, he told me proudly. Had I ever seen the like? In truth, I hadn't, and said so, admiringly, but thinking privately that no one in his right mind would have built such a piece, for at that size it couldn't be accurate, and what's the use of a gun that takes all day to position? I reckon his German workmen had simply done what he'd bidden them, and kept their thoughts to themselves.

"You cannot conceive the labour of bringing this wonder to my *amba*!" cries he. "You have seen my road, but oh, my friend, if you had witnessed our toil, through rain and storm and mud, across rivers and plains, over mountain and desert, and my faithful people on the point of exhaustion, and myself straining on the ropes as we dragged our great guns onward and ever onward. Never was such a journey – no, not even Napoleon himself could have accomplished it!"

Oh, sing us a song, do, thinks I – but d'ye know, when I think of that park of artillery, big pieces, and that monstrous beast of a mortar, I have to admit that, mad or not, he was one hell of a sapper and gunner. A hundred miles over hellish country, months on the road with his soldiers marching on their chinstraps and out of food and forage, their strength dwindling by the day, and still he'd kept 'em going by fear and will and example, through hostile country, for with Menelek and Gobayzy in arms, and Masteeat's Gallas on the lurk, and Napier on his way, Theodore hadn't a friend to his name on that hellish trek from Debra Tabor.

"We had to plunder as we went," he told me, slapping his great mortar proudly, for all the world like some motorist showing off his new machine. "We were like to starve, and the peasant jackals of the villages, who had kissed my feet in the days of my power, hung on the flanks of our army, stinging like mosquitoes when they dared, and cutting the throats of stragglers. So, when we took prisoners," says he with satisfaction, "we burned them alive. Aye, a long march, and slow . . . Now, tell me, why does *your* army march so slowly, and why have they come by the salt plain?"

I told him that Napier left nothing to chance, and had calculated time and distance and supply to a nicety, and set his pace accordingly; as to his route, across what Theodore called the salt plain, it was the shortest way to Magdala. I weighed every word, you may be sure, for I knew that however amiable he might be just now, the least little thing could turn him into a murderous maniac. I had to force myself to remember that, in the face of his smiles and cheery chat, but 'twasn't easy. Here he was, in his harlequin coat and glittering pants, sitting at ease on a gun carriage, laughing and sipping *tej*, all geniality as he turned the talk to every topic under the sun – the range of our rifles, and our courts martial, and did the Queen ever review her troops, and my opinion of the Prussian needle gun, and the probable cost of his boy's education at an English school, and what difficulties he might face being black and foreign, and was it likely, did I think, that he'd take up with an English girl . . . it was all so pleasant and *normal*, hang it, that I wondered was it possible that this portended a peaceful outcome – in effect, a surrender? I daren't hope; with this demented bugger, there was no knowing.

And as he talked, his army was falling in on the great plain of Islamgee, rank upon rank, spearmen and swordsmen and riflemen and cavalry by the thousand, white-robed fighters with their banners before them, churning up the dust in rolling clouds, through which appeared presently the Magdala prisoners, plodding wearily to the tent-lines.

The Europeans were in the van, and a sorry lot they were, like tramps on the look-out for a hen-roost; if you'd seen 'em at your gate you'd have set the dog on them. There were a dozen or so of them, all strangers to me, of course, but I guessed that the two in red coats must be Prideaux of the Bombay Army and Cameron, the consul whose imprisonment had started the whole row. Prideaux was your Compleat Subaltern, tall, fairish, with moustache and whiskers; Cameron was burly and black-bearded and had a crutch under one arm. They, and one or two of the others, walked in the oddest way, lifting their feet high at every step, as though treading through mud or heather. That, I discovered, is what wearing heavy irons for months on end does to you; they'd been relieved of them only a few days ago.

Leading the group was a chipper little dago with a bristling head of hair and soup-strainer to match, and at his elbow a hulking fellow who was all beard and pouched eyes; they were Rassam and Blanc, and they were the fellows who, with Prideaux, had carried the first request for Cameron's release to Theodore two years ago, and been promptly jailed themselves. Who the others in the group were I don't know, and it don't matter, for these four were the ones singled out by Theodore for introduction to me. He hailed Rassam effusively, with his usual inquiries about health and happiness and had he slept well, and then took them aback by announcing me with a fine flourish. For of course they all knew me, by name and fame, and shook my hand in turn, with varying degrees of enthusiasm, which I found mighty interesting.

Rassam didn't like me – or rather, he didn't like my presence. You see, he'd been the leader of the pack, on account of being in some sort of political job at Aden, and was their spokesman with Theodore, with whom he was very thick. I don't say he toadied (and I'd not blame him if he had, with a creature like Theodore), but he was at pains to be busy, very much the Emperor's confidant, and I guess he feared being cut out by the celebrated Flashy. If that seems odd, well, captivity breeds strange germs in people's minds, rivalries and enmities flourish, and little things wax great. Of course, he was some kind of Levantine Turk or Bedouin *chi-chi*, so you'd not have expected him to behave like the British prisoners.

Prideaux was the youngest, thirty-ish or thereabouts, cool as a trout with an affected lazy look which I guessed concealed a sharp mind and a deal of hard bark; from the way he glanced towards Theodore I knew that captivity hadn't cracked him. Nor had it done anything to Cameron's spirit, although it had played havoc with his body; he'd been racked and flogged even worse than the rest, and was a sick man, but he had that dogged, quiet manner which is generally admired, especially by devout Christians. Not my style, but useful in companions in misfortune. Blanc was a sawbones in the Bombay medical service, grave and tough, and respected by the chief men on the *amba* for his skill in doctoring them and their families.

Rassam, as I say, wasn't glad to see me; Prideaux was, and showed it; Blanc was, but didn't, for demonstration wasn't his style. Cameron was too used up to do more than acknowledge me, and of course all four wondered what my arrival portended, what news did I have of Napier's progress, and what, above all, was Theodore about to do.

That last remained a mystery. He sat the five of us down before his tent, and started gassing about everything under the sun – how his fancy dress was made of French silk, how he had had to rebuke Damash for belittling our army, and then a great harangue about a rifle that someone had stolen from the King's tent several months before and poor Damash had led an expedition to recover it and been cut up by the Gallas. From that he passed on to the Crimea, and the American war, and I noticed that Cameron, Blanc and Prideaux had nothing to say, but Rassam was in like quicksilver, always echoing Theodore, and evidently afraid that I'd put him in the shade, having been in both campaigns. I took no part, until Theodore summoned his little son Alamayo, a bright nipper of six, and I chaffed him about going to Rugby, while Rassam listened with a stuffed smile. But not a word was said about Napier, or Theodore's intentions, and I could feel Prideaux fairly bursting with impatience beside me.

At last Theodore said we might retire to rest in a tent that had been set aside for us, and we withdrew, except for Rassam, who stayed, hinting that he'd be glad of a private word in the King's ear.

"No doubt to pay him a few well-chosen compliments," says Prideaux. "Would you believe he wrote Theodore a letter congratulating him on getting all his artillery to Magdala? He'll be offering to taste his food next."[44]

"Policy," says Blanc, shrugging. "Theodore likes him, and if he takes advantage of it, do we not all benefit?"

"I just wish *he* didn't seem to like *Theodore* quite so much," says Prideaux. "I like to be sure our spokesman is on our side. But that's no matter," he added, turning eagerly on me. "However did they come to take you, sir, and what can you tell us? Is Napier about to attack?"

I'd made up my mind to tell them nothing of my mission to Masteeat, on the principle of least said, soonest mended, and also I was leery of Rassam. So I said I'd been on a long scout and run into an ambush. Napier I believed to be no more than a day's march away, but did Theodore mean to fight him, that was the point? I asked if they had any notion.

"All we know is that he is insane," says Blanc, "and altogether unpredictable. He has received a letter of ultimatum from Sir Robert Napier, and Rassam urges him to write in reply, but it is dangerous even to hint that he would be well advised to sue for peace."

"Theodore'll fight," says Cameron, sounding dog-tired. "He cannot back down now."

"Then God help us all," says Blanc. "But I believe you are right, Consul. Even if he faces certain defeat, he will give battle, out of pride and superstition. Oh, he is ruled by his astrologers, and his lunatic fatalism! You heard him just now, lamenting his lost rifle? He regarded it as a talisman, and is sure that catastrophe will follow if it is not recovered! That is why he is here, at Magdala – nothing but superstition." Seeing my expression, he laughed, and explained.

"Magdala is another talisman; he believes that while he holds it, he cannot fail. Only last week he cried aloud that while he had lost all Abyssinia, Magdala remained, and he would hold it and emerge again as a conqueror. He truly believes it, too."

"He can't believe it!" Automatically I added: "He must be –"

"Mad?" says Prideaux. "You've noticed, sir? Yes, his majesty is a trifle erratic."

"We can thank God for it," says Cameron. "If he didn't think of that rock as a symbol of victory, he would not have determined to hold it . . . and God knows where we would have been taken to by now. At least we're here, where Napier can find us."

They were silent, and I knew they were thinking: "If we survive." At least they were sane enough to do nothing but wait; no wild talk of trying to break out, or blow up the powder magazine which was only a few yards from our tent, by the artillery park. Captivity had taught them patience; that was evident from what they told me of schemes for escape that had been considered and rejected, of plots with the rebels to storm the *amba* in Theodore's absence, and of the hideous consequences of conspiracies gone amiss, with the guilty being mutilated and flung over cliffs, and one girl of sixteen being flogged to death with *girafs*. Small wonder that attempts to suborn their jailers hadn't got far, although in some respects even leading men on the *amba* had been helpful and friendly, despite the risk of arousing Theodore's displeasure.

Thus there had been a continuous correspondence carried on with our politicals in Egypt and Aden, with letters sewn into the clothes of Ab couriers, and supplies of money and comforts coming in for the prisoners. You may read about it at length in the memoirs of Blanc and Rassam, if you've a mind to, and it's the strangest tale

– in a way, my own experience of Theodore mirrors it in minia-
ture. For sometimes they'd been treated as honoured guests, sometimes beaten and tortured; splendidly fed with luxurious dinners of
seven courses, and loaded with chains; well housed and allowed
the freedom to wander, tend their gardens, and promised early
release, then dragged away from one prison to another. There had
simply been no pattern to their strange existence. No wonder, when
Samuel the ferret came to summon us back to the royal presence,
my companions exchanged anxious looks. "Now what?" wonders
Prideaux. "Chains or candy?"

In fact it was to be given an alarming reassurance – reassuring
because it was a promise from Theodore, speaking at his sanest,
that in the event of danger we'd be put in a safe place, along with
his family; alarming because it suggested that battle was imminent.

That was not my only anxiety. Among the great concourse of
priests, generals, courtiers, astrologers, and servants assembled
before the red pavilion to hear his majesty's pronouncements were
a number of his women, with the bloated "Queen" Tamagno to the
fore. She was seated with her attendants close to the King, being
fanned with great ostrich plumes, and once again I was conscious
of being appraised like a prize bullock in the ring. Prideaux muttered beside me.

"Careful o' that one, sir. She's a Haymarket Hussar,* and quite
desperate altogether." From which I gathered that he, too, had taken
the lady's fancy, and avoided her for his own good.

"Haymarket or Grant Road?" says I, and he said 'twas no joke,
Theodore being a real mad miser with his women. "A fellow on
sentry-go at the hareem cadged a cup of *tej* from one of the concubines, and was lashed to a pulp. Best to keep together when the
likes of Madam Tamagno's on the prowl; safety in numbers,
what?"

"Unless she likes to drill by platoons," says I, and he exclaimed
"I say!", at which point Theodore announced that it was time for

---

* Haymarket Hussar: a courtesan of the better class. Grant Road was the prostitutes'
quarter in Bombay.

217

him to address the troops, who'd been waiting patiently in the sun for an hour or more. So we were marshalled by Damash, and trooped obediently in the King's wake through the camp to the plain where the flower of the Habesh military stood at attention in orderly silence, and gazing at the huge array under the silken banners, I found myself praying that Napier would keep to the open ground.

The speech was pure Theodore, a rousing address contradicted at the end. He began by trotting before them on a stallion and then dismounted to climb on a rock, displaying himself in his rainbow attire and delivering a great harangue against the invaders of the country. "Understand," bellows he, "that in a day or two you will be obliged to confront the finest army in the world outside Africa, men far superior to you in strength and in arms, whose very uniforms are bedecked with gold, to say nothing of their treasures, which can only be borne by elephants!" That'll cheer them up, thinks I, but then he went on, flourishing his arms on high.

"Are you ready to fight?" bawls he. "To fight, and enrich yourselves with the spoil of these white slaves! Will you conquer, or will you leave me in the lurch? Think of my great deeds in the past, of my conquests, of great battles in which you have triumphed over my enemies! You have adorned your weapons with *their* weapons, ha-ha! [*Prolonged cheering.*] When these white kaffirs approach you, what will you do? You will wait until they fire on you, and before they can reload, you will fall upon them with your spears! [*Less enthusiastic cheers.*] Your valour will meet with its reward, and you will enrich yourselves with spoils beside which this rich dress that I am wearing will seem but a shabby trifle." [*Sensation, and clashing of spears and swords.*]

Stirring stuff, and I was remarking to Prideaux on the neat way he'd cried up our army and then changed tack by depicting us as lambs to the slaughter, when a beaming old codger at the head of one of the foot regiments stepped forward, brandishing his spear and shouting:

"Oh, only wait, great king, until these foreign asses make their appearance! We'll tear them to pieces, and those who are lucky enough to escape will have a sorry tale to tell in England!"

To which any intelligent leader would have responded with a hearty grin and a flourished fist. So what does Theodore do, eh? Waits for the cheering to die down, and then cries:

"What are you talking about, you old fool? Have you ever seen a British soldier? Do you know what weapons he carries? Why, before you know where you are he'll have given you a bellyful of bullets! These people have cannon, elephants, guns without number! We can't fight them! You think our muskets are any good? If they were, they wouldn't have sold them to us!" And while his army stared in amazed silence, he turned to the priests and generals and courtiers. "It's your fault, you people of Magdala! You should have advised me better!"

D'you know, for a second I thought he was trying a dam' silly joke? But he wasn't. All in a moment his black mood had come on him, and he was telling the truth. Why, heaven only knows. He'd given his troops jingo and ginger, and now he was striding off to his tent with a face like a wet week, leaving 'em stunned and silent with the fight knocked clean out of them. By the way, if you doubt my story, look at Blanc and Rassam.

After his parade, he flung himself aboard a mule and rode up Selassie to spy out Napier's movements. He can't have liked what he saw, for he came down in the foulest of tempers; we were dining in our tent, but we heard him screaming curses, and soon after there was a volley of musketry which seemed to come from the direction of the Fala saddle. A few single shots sounded a moment later, and Rassam told one of the servants to find out what was afoot, but the guards on our tent wouldn't let him pass.

So we waited, wondering, and then word came. Theodore had remembered that a few months before one of his storekeepers had deserted and taken refuge among the Gallas; the recollection had sent him into a frenzy and he had ordered up the storekeeper's wife and infant, who had been in prison since the desertion. They and five other of his Ab prisoners had been taken to the nearest precipice, shot by a firing squad, and their bodies thrown down the cliff. The later single shots had been the finishing off of those who were still alive after the fall.

"Including the child?" says Cameron, and Samuel, who had

brought the news, said yes, including the child. He begged that we should not remonstrate with Theodore, who had embarked on another drinking spree, and was still undetermined what to do about Napier, whose troops were believed to be preparing to cross the Bechelo river next morning.

When Samuel had gone there was a long silence, broken by Prideaux.

"Napier will be here the day after tomorrow."

More silence and then Rassam says: "We must do nothing to excite the King's . . . passions. In the morning I think I shall ask him to communicate with Sir Robert."

Nobody said aye or no to that. Nobody wanted to utter a word that might influence Rassam, who might in turn influence Theodore, perhaps with terrible consequences. It all hung in the balance – Napier's progress, Theodore's madness, sheer blind chance. Blanc muttered something in Latin, and I asked what it was.

"A quotation I recollected from somewhere," says he. "'At the mercy of Tiberius.'"

I'm not good on dates as a rule, but I know
the next day was April the ninth, because Rassam said it aloud as
he made an entry in his journal, and it stays fixed in my memory[45]
as the day on which I was forced to witness one of the foulest
crimes I've ever seen. As you know, I'm no stranger to human
wickedness and cruelty and death; slaughter in battle aside, I've
watched mass scalpings and blowing from guns and the knouting
of a Russian peasant, and I've seen the torture pits of Madagascar
and what was left of the occupants of a New Mexican hacienda
after the Mimbreno Apaches had come to call. But what happened
on the eve of Good Friday at Islamgee was an atrocity apart – I
can't tell why, unless it's because 'twas so unexpected and unreal
and without sense or reason, committed not by a primitive savage
but by a man who only moments before had been earnestly considering Christian ethics and the problems of Church and State.
Blind passion I can understand, and cruelty for its own sake, but
I guess madness is a law unto itself. And yet none of these, not
anger or sadistic bloodlust or lunacy, even, has ever seemed to
me sufficient explanation for what happened on that day at
Islamgee.

Yet it began tamely enough, after a peaceful night in which the
five of us slept undisturbed in our fine silk tent, with the other
European prisoners and the German workmen in lesser tents close
by. No one spoke of last night's murders, and we were at breakfast
when a messenger arrived bearing compliments to Rassam from
the King, which delighted him, and an order for me to present
myself to the royal presence instanter, which didn't. I wasn't

specially happy myself to be singled out, but there was nothing for it, so off I went.

There was great action afoot in the camp, and on the north end of Islamgee where the ground rose to the Fala saddle. A mighty crowd of prisoners had been herded together by the troops; there must have been several hundred, chained and foully dirty, squatting in the dust, and recalling the mob of them I'd seen yesterday I found myself wondering how Magdala had contained them all, for that's where they'd come from; it struck me Theodore must have had half the local population in close tack – rebels, criminals, folk whose faces didn't fit, but now it seemed there was to be a great jail clearance, for the armourers were passing among them with hammers and leather straps, setting them free, and great rusty piles of fetters were in evidence, while their late wearers wandered about looking dazed and lost. Still, I took it as a good sign; perhaps his mad majesty was seeing sense at last.

My hopes were soon shot; he might be wearing his humane socks, but he was pulling on his jackboots over them. Beyond the assembled prisoners the slopes up to the Fala shoulder were crawling with troops, and they were dragging his artillery pieces along a newly made road to the summit on which the morning mist was just beginning to blow away. My heart sank, for I knew the Fala height commanded the Arogee plain which Napier's force was bound to cross, and a well-placed park of artillery could play havoc with our advance if the Ab gunners knew their business.

My messenger and I were mounted, but we had the deuce of a job forcing our way up the crowded slope and along the narrow roadway. It was churned to mud by recent rains, and the carts carrying the guns were up to the axles in the red glue. The great mortar Sevastopol was chained in place on its enormous cart, with hundreds of hauliers straining on its huge hawsers, slithering and ploughing through the muck, and Theodore himself on the cart yelling orders and encouragement. It began to rain, coming down in stair-rods that pitted the mud like buckshot, and the steam came off the sweating gangs in clouds; we were sodden in no time, and our beasts were fairly streaming down their flanks.

222

Theodore waved and roared to me to come on the wagon with him, which I was glad to do, for he had Samuel and a couple of servants holding great brollies overhead. Even so, he was soaked, and presently tore off his shirt and stood bare to the waist, laughing and rubbing the water over his chest and arms as though he were in a bath. He seemed in capital spirits, exulting over the damage that his mortar would do, "for there has never been such a weapon in the world, and how will your soldiers be able to endure it? Even its thunder will terrify the bravest; they will scatter like frightened sheep!"

I said he'd never seen British and Indian soldiers, and they'd not scatter, because they knew that noise never killed anyone. He looked a bit downcast at this, so I asked him, greatly daring, if he'd decided to fight.

"If I must!" cries he. "I do not want war, but who is this woman who sends her soldiers against a king? By what right does she come to steal my country?"

I wasn't going to argue, and he ran on about how he had been insulted, and it was not to be borne; he had written in good will and friendship, as one monarch to another, and had been ignored (which I knew was true), and he'd never have laid a finger on any of our people if Cameron hadn't conspired with his enemies the Egyptians, and he'd have let that pass, even, if only he'd been shown the courtesy due to his rank, but it was plain that the British Government looked down on African kings as petty rulers of no account. So what else could he do, by the power of God, but defy those who had despised and affronted him, even if he died for it?

With him shouting at me through the downpour, getting angrier by the minute, and poor Samuel struggling with his brolly in the wind and beseeching me with his eyes to say something to turn away wrath, I cried that Theodore was absolutely right, he'd been disgracefully put upon, no question, and it was just a shame that so many fine men, Ab and British, should have to die because our Foreign Office had no bloody manners. Even as I said it, I realised that I'd struck a good line, so I expanded on the arrogance, stupidity, and downright laziness of our civil servants, but what could you expect from folk who'd gone to disgusting dens of vice and ignorance like Harrow and Eton, and had he given any further thought to the idea of sending that splendid little lad to Rugby, capital school, been there myself . . .

It may be that the best way to talk to a maniac is to drivel as much as he does, especially if you don't let him get a word in. My balderdash quite disconcerted him, and by good luck the great wagon suddenly lost a wheel, we had to leap clear for our lives, and Sevastopol finished up to its trunnions in mud. It took a couple of hours to right it, and another hour to reach the top of Fala, by which time the rain had cleared, and the sun broke through the sullen clouds – and there, far across the plain of Arogee, was the Dalanta plateau above the Bechelo, black with the tiny figures of men and animals. Hurry, hurry, old Bob, thinks I, you're almost there.

Gabrie, the Ab field-marshal, was in charge of emplacing the guns, and making by far too good a job of it for my liking, while Theodore stood Napoleon-like on the edge of the bluff, arms folded, sombrely regarding the distant deployment of the army that was coming to destroy him. He seemed not at all alarmed, remarking that it would be most gratifying to see how a European general disposed his troops, and was it true that Napier was the best commander of his day? I said he was the best we had, careful and steady but sure, perhaps not as inspired as Wolseley or the American Lee, but safer than either, and less prodigal of his soldiers' lives than Grant.

He nodded. "You think he will destroy me?" says he, and I saw what I hoped was a chance.

"Not if you meet him in love and friendship, *getow*. Those were the words you used to me, if you remember."

"I said if *he* came in love and friendship!" He pointed towards the Bechelo. "Do you see them there? He is the invader, I am the besieged! Would you have me submit to the thieves who come to rob me of my throne, of my country?" He was starting to shout now, striding to and fro, waving his arms and shooting angry glares at me. "That is the counsel of cowards like Damash and Dasta and the fool Samuel! Where is he? Where is Samuel?" He looked around, stamping, but Samuel, luckily for him, wasn't on hand. Theodore stood snarling for a moment, snapped at one of his attendants to give him a *shama*, and once he'd wrapped it round his shoulders he came muttering to me.

"They would surrender, Damash and the others. They hate me, all of them, and would run away if they had the courage. Why do they not kill me, eh? Because they fear me, by death, and dare not strike!" He was starting to froth again, and the mad stare was in his eyes. "Well, they had better kill me, because if they do not I shall kill them all, by the power of God, one at a time!" Suddenly he seized me by the shirt, thrusting his face into mine, raving in a whisper.

"You know I must sleep with loaded pistols under my pillow? They know it, too, and fear to murder me in my bed! They would poison me, but my food and drink are tasted! But I do not fear!" He released his grip, closed his eyes, and began to mumble to himself as though in prayer. Then he looked up at the darkening sky, and his voice was shaking. "If He who is above does not kill me, no one will. If He says I must die, no one can save me!"

It came out in a yell, and I looked round to see what Gabrie and his staff were making of it – but they weren't even looking at him, but busied themselves even more with the teams slewing the cannon into place. They knew he was stark mad, but they were too fearful to do anything about it. And it wasn't just fear; they were in thrall to him, to the sheer power of his will and spirit. I felt it too, as well as my terror of him; he had that force that I'd seen in others, like Brooke of Sarawak and old John Brown; they weren't to be resisted, or reasoned with, just avoided if possible – but I couldn't avoid Theodore.

And then in a moment the morbid fury that had possessed him so suddenly was gone, and he was striding about the gun positions, commending and criticising and even laughing; I saw him slap an Ab gunner on the shoulder and say something that set them in a roar; then he was deep in consultation with one of his Germans, climbing up on to Sevastopol to examine the firing mechanism. He was still chuckling as he came back to me, putting a hand on my shoulder confidential-like.

"They are easy to amuse, are they not? Do you not find it so, with your soldiers? Come, we shall go down and drink a little *tej* together." He seemed content to walk, nodding to the gunners and assuring them that when they were called on to load up and fire, he would be on hand to direct them. They cheered and hammered their hilts on the guns as we went down the hill.

"You heard me speak to them yesterday, my friend, did you not? Did I rouse them on to battle? Did I inspire them? Oh, my good friend, I was fakering,* no more than that. But they believe, because they are simpletons and love me." It didn't seem to occur to him that they might just as easily believe what he'd shouted at the old general, that they were doomed to defeat. "If I say, 'Fight, my children!' they will fight, even if it means death. But are your soldiers any different, *Ras* Flashman? Why do they do it, my friend?"

I told him, because they took the shilling; the sepoys, for their salt. He said it was a great mystery, and waxed philosophical about the minds and motives of fighting men – sane, sensible chat such as you'd hear in a gathering of civilians, if not from soldiers, who ain't interested. But the point is, if you'd seen and heard him then, you'd have said here was this intelligent, good-humoured, perfectly normal man of authority, with not an ounce of harm in him. Quite so.

We came off the Fala saddle just as it began to drizzle, with clouds gathering overhead and the light starting to fade. It was about four in the afternoon, and the armourers who'd been freeing prisoners were packing up their traps and shepherding those who were still chained to some old broken-down stables on the south side of the Islamgee plain, not a furlong from Theodore's tent and ours. They were to be kept there overnight, and freed next day, the last of the six hundred or so whom Miriam and I had seen being brought down from Magdala two days earlier. About two hundred had been freed yesterday, but only half as many today, most of the armourers having been diverted to the work on Fala. Those still chained and sent to the stables were more than two hundred in number.

---

* Bragging. Not in *OED*, but apparently a favourite word of Theodore's.

I'm exact about this so that you can be clear about how things stood on that close, sultry afternoon as I walked with Theodore and his attendants to his pavilion, aware of a slight commotion from the chained prisoners as they were driven towards the stables. I didn't know, of course, that they'd had no food since they'd left Magdala, and only such water as they'd begged from the soldiers' camp nearby. Nor did I know that most of them were "political" prisoners who'd offended, often in the most trivial ways – as Miriam said, by laughing when his majesty was in the dumps, and vice versa.

Impatient at still being in irons with another hungry night ahead of them, they were in no mood to go quietly to the stables, hence the row they were making, but no one paid much heed, least of all Theodore; three o'clock was when he started drinking as a rule, and being an hour late he lost no time in embarking on a splendid spree in his tent, with the *tej* flowing like buttermilk, and myself expected to go bowl for bowl with him. I couldn't; the amount he sank in the first hour would have put me on the floor, and he jeered at me for a weakling and summoned "Queen" Tamagno to join us, vowing that she would show me how to drink.

Which I'm bound to say she did, seating her ponderous bulk beside him and laying into the liquor like a thirsty marine. Theodore applauded and kept her goblet brimmed, kissing and caressing her between his own hearty swigs, murmuring endearments like a lovesick swain, which was sufficiently repellent, but what was truly unnerving was that she never took her eyes off me once. I believe he sensed her interest, for after a while he left off cuddling and told her to leave us, and she heaved up her great jelly of a body in its gaudy silks and went, giving me a last long stare over her fat shoulder. Again, I was damned glad to see her away.

When she'd gone he drank in silence for some time, pretty moody, eyeing me in a most discomforting way, as though on the point of an outburst, but when it came it was the last thing I might have expected. For he heaved a great sigh, supped some more *tej*, and exclaimed:

"My dear friend, do not misjudge me. I truly love you, not you

227

alone but my good friend Mr Rassam, and Mr Prideaux also, although it is difficult to love the Consul Cameron who betrayed me to the Egyptians. But I try." A longish pause in which he stared at the roof of the tent. "I also love the Dr Blanc, who has healed many of my people. But you I love most of all, for you have shown no fear of me." Then I'm a sight better actor than I thought I was, thinks I. "I have behaved ill to you, dear friend, but I had an end to serve." He paused again, looking heavy, and then came the most astonishing declaration I ever heard from this astonishing man.

"I never used to believe I was mad," says he, and the tears were rolling down his cheeks. "People said I was mad, but I did not believe it. But after the way I have behaved to you, raising my hand to strike you, putting you in chains, I believe I am mad." He gave a great retching sigh, wiping his cheeks. "But you will forgive me. As Christians we ought to forgive each other."

I cried amen to that in a hurry, assuring him there was nothing to forgive, he'd behaved like a perfect gentleman, and if all kings played such a straight bat the world would be a better place . . . that was the gist of it, anyway.

"I try to be a good Christian," says he, "although some of the priests doubt my devotion. It is the bane of a monarch's life, in all religions and countries, that his priests are forever at work to gain ascendancy over him. It was so, I have heard, with some of your English kings. My priests, in their insolence, say that I wear three *matabs* – a Christian one, a Muslim one, and a Frankish one! What folly! I told them: 'You pretend that I wish to change my religion, but it is a lie! I would sooner cut my throat!" And on that he stopped, drank, and raised his head to listen.

I'd been aware for a few moments of another sound above the faint murmur of the camp, but only now, when he cocked his head, frowning, did I identify it: a distant chant, one word over and over: "*Abiet! Abiet!*", which means "Lord, master" in Amharic, and with it now came a faraway clashing of chains, and Theodore was exclaiming impatiently and calling out to know what was the matter. Samuel came hurrying to explain that the chained prisoners were pleading for water and bread, and knowing his unpredictable majesty I'd not have been surprised if he'd told Samuel to shut them up p.d.q., or ordered him to serve them a hearty supper.

He did neither. For a moment he sat perfectly still, and then came to his feet without haste, staring from Samuel to me and back again, and then his expression changed, uncannily and quite slowly, from blank to wondering to frowning to growing rage and then to such a glare of demonic malevolence as sent a shudder up my spine. He let out an almighty scream of fury, scrambling over his couch to snatch up his sabre from the table, and swept it from its sheath.

"Swine! Filth! Treacherous vermin! I shall school them, by the power of God!" He lunged at me, seizing my arm, and dragged me after him. "Come! Oh, come and see how I teach them to squeal for food while my faithful soldiers are starving!" It was news to me that they were starving, but I didn't mention that. He was bawling for his guards, hauling me out of the pavilion, hurling Samuel out of his path, and rushing on, brandishing his sword. I'd no choice but to run with him, for his grip was like a vice on my arm, and I'd no wish to resist and have him decapitate me.

"Guards! Guards!" he kept shouting. "Attend me! To the stables!" They came running out of the dusk from the tents, and behind me I heard Rassam's voice demanding to know what was up, and Samuel begging him to go back to his tent and keep his companions under cover. I'd have given a pension to join them, but Theodore urged me on, vowing vengeance on the villains who'd dared to disturb his leisure. There was a squall of rain, I remember, just as we reached the stable buildings near the edge of the Islamgee cliff, and a rumble of thunder overhead.

"Bring them out!" bawls Theodore. "Let us see these pampered animals! Have them out, I say!" He let go my arm at last, yelling at me out of a face that seemed to have lost all human expression; he was like a demented ape, spraying spittle and gibbering at me. "You'll see! You'll see!"

A guard drew the bar from its sockets and flung open the double doors, and a chained woman, bent double, stumbled out into the half-light. Theodore ran forward, shrieking curses, and brought down the sabre in a sickening cut that fell between neck and shoulder and almost severed the arm. The woman fell screaming, blood spurting up in a fountain, and as a second prisoner blundered out Theodore buried the sabre in his skull. It snapped with the force of the blow and the fellow sank dead with the foible embedded in his brow, leaving the bloody truncheon of the sword in Theodore's hand. He glared at it, mouthing incoherently, and raised it to slash his next victim . . . a naked boy of about five who came running out, howling, with his fists screwed into his eyes.

Stricken horrified as I was, I thought, that'll sober him, the beastly lunatic, and indeed he did throw the bloody shard of the sabre away, but he screamed an order at the nearest guard, and the brute seized the child and hurled him wailing over the cliff.

That was how it began, the horror in the twilight at Islamgee, but it got worse. For with that ghastly infanticide, his mad rage seemed to cool, and I thought that ends it, but I was wrong; he continued his hellish extermination of the prisoners with a calm deliberation that was infinitely more terrible than his murderous fury; killing in a frenzy is at least to be understood, but what can you say of one who, in level tones, inquires of a poor devil his name and offence, and on being answered, almost idly condemns him to be flung to his death?

That is what Theodore did to two hundred prisoners in the next two hours. As thus:

"What is your name, and country, and why are you here?"

"Maryahm, great *abiet*, of Magdala! I only laughed with my friend Zaudi, your page –"

"Away with him!"

So Maryahm was flung down two hundred feet, and a moment later Zaudi followed him, condemned because he'd handed Theodore a musket that had misfired.

You may think I am inventing horrors to freeze your blood, but look in Blanc and Rassam and you'll find it's simple truth. He sat on a rock, like the chairman of governors at a prizegiving, mad as a hatter, and as each unfortunate was dragged out there was the same ritual of question, answer, and execution, with musketeers being sent down the cliff to finish off any survivors. Some went begging and screaming, a few flung defiance at him, others went sheeplike, without protest. Two young lads, I remember, were thrown over because their father had taken liberties with one of the royal concubines, but when the man himself was hauled out, Theodore had him unchained and let go. That was the folly of it; no sense, no logic, no reason, and the lousy bastard didn't enjoy it, or even care. He just killed them, and I watched, and marvelled, and found myself hoping that Arnold was right, and that there was a Hell for him.

Blanc says 307 were thrown down, and 91, all rebel chiefs and his deadly enemies, were reserved for slaughter another day. Rassam puts the total of dead at 197, of whom he says only 35 had committed any crime, the rest having broken cups or lost rifles or laughed, like Maryahm, or been the sons of a flirtatious father. I take Rassam's figure as more likely, but I was too stunned to keep count. I don't even know why he stopped; probably because he was bored, or it was getting dark.[46]

He was silent on the way back to his tent, insisting that I join him for a supper which I couldn't bring myself to eat, but sat mute while he gorged with great appetite and drank himself insensible after an almighty prose about his ancestors and how he'd fight to the death and be worthy of them. "You will see my body," says he, slurred and bleary-eyed over his last cup, "and say there is a bad man who has injured me. But you will bury me in Christian ground, because you are a friend." Then he fell off the couch.

Wiseacres assure me he was in the grip of remorse, or tortured conscience. No such thing. He was a drunken sot as well as a monster, and that's all about it.

I left him grunting like a Berkshire hog and made my way through the dark and driving rain to our fine silk tent, and there wasn't a soul within. I demanded of the sentry where they were, and he gave a shifty grin and said they had been moved, by order, to one of the smaller tents. I asked by whose order, and he grinned shiftier yet, and said I might have the place to myself. I was used up and shaking with the hellishness of what I'd seen, so I rolled

231

inside, half-undressed, blew out the lamp and collapsed on my *charpoy*.

And I dreamed, such a beautiful dream, of being in that sunny meadow by the Clyde with Elspeth, and we were talking nonsense to each other, and began to kiss and play, and suddenly she was changing and turning black, and becoming Mrs Popplewell of Harper's Ferry and glorious memory, crying that I was her sho'nuff baby and taking fearful, wonderful liberties, throwing herself astride of me and going like a Derby winner . . . and I was awake in that darkened tent on Islamgee, and 'twasn't Mrs Popplewell but some elephantine succubus, smothering me with mountains of fat, and I knew in a trice that it was "Queen" Tamagno, the randy bitch, who'd bribed the sentry so that she could crawl in and have her wicked will of me, and I was debating in confusion whether to cry "Unhand me!" or let her go her mile, when I heard a distant voice crying aloud, and it wasn't conscience or my better nature but blasted Theodore coming to the surface through an ocean of *tej*, and a ghastly vision smote me of the fate of those who had the bad luck to be related to people who made advances to royal concubines, and I gave one almighty heave and sent unrequited love, all seventeen stone of her, flying from the *charpoy*. She hit the floor with a fearful flopping sound, and before she'd even had time to squawk I was through the fly of the tent like a startled fawn, seizing the sentry by the throat and demanding directions. He gasped and pointed as Theodore's voice was heard again, louder this time, calling for his creature comfort, and I hope she heard him and did her duty like a good little concubine. But by that time I was under canvas, tripping over sleepers in the dark and burrowing under a pile of blankets.

I fell asleep, and in the morning it was as though none of it had happened, not the horror of the murdered prisoners, or my flight from the embraces of that female hippo – unspeakable tragedy followed by terrifying farce. But it did happen, and I dare say the shock of it all would have preoccupied me if great events had not claimed my attention. For April the tenth, Good Friday, was the day the Bughunter uncorked his killing bottle.

232

There are days when you get up and smell death in the air, and that Good Friday was one of them. It was a grey, close morning, with ugly clouds that bore the promise of storm, and waking to the memory of the evening's horrors drove my spirits to the cellar. I told the others what I'd seen, and it struck them silent until one of 'em, I forget who, dropped to his knees and began to intone the Lord's Prayer. They thought it was all up with them, and when Theodore came on the scene in a raging temper, and ordered everyone back to Magdala, except me, Prideaux shook my hand in what he plainly thought was a last farewell. I didn't; my guess was that Theodore was keeping his word to put them in a safe place, and you may be sure I demanded to go with them, but he wouldn't hear of it.

"You are a soldier!" cries he. "You shall be my witness that if blood is shed, it shall not be my wish! I have word that your army is across the Bechelo and advancing against me. Well, we shall see! We shall see!"

Rassam pleaded with him to send a message to Napier, but he vowed that he'd do no such thing. "You want me to write to that man, but I refuse to talk with a man sent by a woman!"

Which was a new one, if you like, but sure enough when a letter arrived from Napier for Rassam, Theodore wouldn't listen to it and swore that if Rassam wrote to Napier that would be an end of their friendship. So off they went to Magdala, but Rassam slipped the letter to me, begging me to persuade Theodore to look at it. He was no fool, Rassam, for he and the others were barely out of sight when Theodore bade me give the note to Samuel, who read it to him. It was a straight courteous request for the release of the prisoners, and for a long minute I hoped against hope as he stood frowning in thought, but then he lifted his head and I saw the mad glare in his eye.

"It is no use! I know what I have to do!" He turned on me. "Did I not spend the night in prayer, and do I not know that the die is cast?" Since he'd spent most of the night getting blind blotto, and thereafter roaring for his whore, I doubted if his decision had been guided by prayer, much; I think the effect of his massacre was still at work in him, but I'm no mind-reader. All that mattered was that the last chance of a peaceful issue had gone, and it behoved all good men to look after Number One, and bolt at the first chance.

It never came. He kept me with him all day, and since he was never without his bodyguards, to say nothing of servants, and his generals coming and going, I could only wait and watch with my hopes diminishing; plainly the grip was coming, and the question was, when he went down to inevitable bloody defeat, would he take his prisoners with him? Fear said yes; common sense said no, what would be the point? But with a madman, who could tell?

There was a terrific thunder-plump at about noon, and then the sky cleared for a while and the heat came off the ground in waves; it was breathless, stifling, and even when the cloud thickened and rain began to fall in big drops, it brought no coolness with it. Five miles away, although I didn't know it, Napier's battalions were fording the muddy Bechelo barefoot, and climbing out of that mighty ravine in sweltering heat, short of water because the river wasn't fit to drink, breasting the long spur that brought them to the Afichu plateau that I'd marked on Fasil's sand-table, and coming near exhausted to the edge of the Arogee plain. That was the main column; the second force came up the King's Road, which I'd warned Napier to avoid – and he almost paid dear for ignoring my advice.

Runners brought word to Theodore of our army's approach, and from early afternoon the Ab army, seven thousand strong, was moving into position from the Islamgee plain to the lower slopes

234

of Fala and Selassie. Theodore himself, with his generals and attendants and your reluctant correspondent, went up the muddy slope to the gun emplacements on the Fala summit, and looking back I had my first proper sight of what Napier would be up against: rank upon rank of robed black spearmen and swordsmen and musketeers swinging along in fine style, disciplined and damned business-like with waving banners and their red-robed commanders, five hundred strong on horseback, marshalling them to perfection. I didn't know what force in guns and infantry Napier might have, but I guessed it wouldn't be above two thousand, and I was right; odds of three to one, but that wouldn't count against British and Indian troops . . . unless something went wrong, which it dam' nearly did.

From the Fala summit we got our first sight of the approaching columns, almost three miles away across the great expanse of rock and scrub, on the far side of Arogee. Theodore was like a kid in a toyshop with his glass, turning to me bright with excitement and bidding me look and tell him who was who and what they were about. It had begun to rain in earnest now, with lightning flashing in the black clouds and a strong wind sweeping across the summit, but the light was good, Theodore's glass was a first-class piece, and when I brought it to bear I almost dropped it in surprise, for the first thing I saw was Napier in person.

There was no mistaking him, for like old Paddy Gough he affected a white coat, and there he was, a tiny figure sitting on his pony on a knoll about two miles away with his staff about him, and not a thing between him and us except some Bombay and Madras Sappers skirmishing ahead of his position. No place for a general to be, and it was with some alarm that I traversed the glass and got an even greater shock, for I could see that the bughunting old duffer was courting catastrophe all unaware – and I wasn't the only one who'd noticed.

His own position, with the first column still some distance behind him, was dangerous enough, but over to the right, coming up the King's Road, was the second column, and it was led by a convoy of mules, barely escorted, with supply train written all over 'em – rations, ammunition, equipment, the whole quartermaster's store of the brigade simply begging for some enterprising plunderer to swoop down on them . . . and here he was, at Theodore's elbow, leaping with excitement at the heaven-sent chance.

He was old Gabrie, the Ab field-marshal, who'd come thundering up from the Fala saddle where he'd been supervising his army's assembly, flinging himself from his horse and bawling:

"See, see, Toowodros, they are in our hands!" He was an old pal of Theodore's, all ceremony forgotten. "Let us go, in God's name! We have them, we have them!"

If Theodore had been as smart a soldier as Gabrie . . . well, we might have had a disaster to rank with Isandhlwana or Maiwand, but he hesitated, thank God, and lost the chance. And since it all happened with such speed, so many different factors together, I'd better take time to explain.

The march up the spur and the Afichu plateau to Arogee had taken longer than expected, thanks to the broiling heat, the steepness of the climb, and the fact that they didn't think they were marching to battle, but merely to sites to pitch camp. Napier wasn't expecting an Ab attack, and got too far forward (in my opinion), and the baggage column had easier going on the King's Road and likewise arrived too quickly in an exposed position. Phayre got the blame, justly or not I can't say. If Theodore had allowed Gabrie to attack at once, the baggage column was done for, and that might have spelled disaster; I say might because Napier was a complete hand when it came to improvising, as he was about to show.

Well, Theodore hesitated to cast the dice, with Gabrie pleading to be let loose. Not long, perhaps, but I reckon long enough, before he cried, "Go, then!" Gabrie was off like a shot, waving his scarf to advance the army, and Theodore yelled to the gunners to fire. The German workmen had been measuring the charges, but the Ab gunners manned the pieces, and the first salvo almost caught Napier himself, a chain-shot landing a few yards behind him. And by then he'd had another nasty start, as the whole crest from Fala to Selassie suddenly came to life with seven thousand Ab infantry rolling down to Arogee like a black-and-white tide, bellowing their war-songs and bidding fair to sweep away the Sappers screening

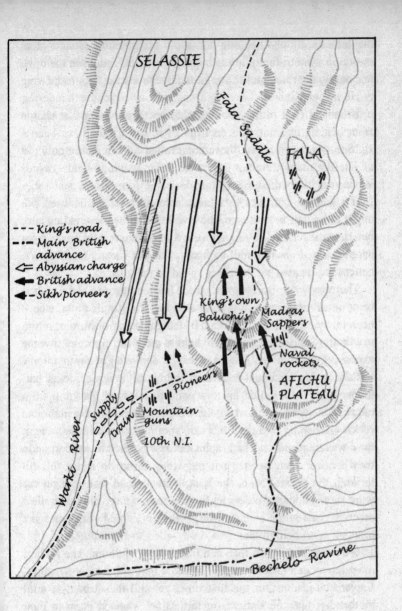

SELASSIE

Fala Saddle

FALA

- - - King's road
- · - · Main British advance
⇦ Abyssian charge
⬅ British advance
◄ Sikh pioneers

King's own
Baluchi's Madras
Sappers

Naval
rockets

AFICHU
PLATEAU

Pioneers

Supply
train

Mountain
guns

10th. N.I.

Warki River

Bechelo Ravine

237

Napier's knoll, who had only muzzle-loading Brown Bess to stem the flood. And to the right the baggage column, caught in the open and barely guarded, must be engulfed by the savage legions bearing down on it.

I thanked God in that moment that I was watching that charge from behind, and not from in front of it, for it must have been a sight to freeze the blood, those great robed figures racing down in a chanting mass almost a mile from wing to wing, sickle-swords and spears flourished, black shields to the fore, braids and robes flying, and out in front old Gabrie, sabre aloft, his brilliant red silk cloak billowing behind him, the five hundred scarlet-clad cavalry chieftains at his back. From above it looked like the discharge from an overturned ant-hill spilling across the plain towards an enemy caught unprepared by the sheer speed of the attack.

That was when Bob Napier earned his peerage. He had a couple of minutes' grace, and in that time he had the King's Own, who'd been hurrying towards the sound of the guns, skirmishing past him to join the Sapper screen, and in behind the khaki figures I saw the dark puggarees of the Baluch. As they deployed, waiting for the onslaught, Napier opened up with the Naval Brigade rocket batteries which he'd called up to a point just behind his knoll. In a moment the white trails of smoke were criss-crossing the plain, the rockets smashing into the Ab ranks, cutting furrows through them; they wavered and checked, appalled at this terrible new weapon they'd never seen before, but then they came on again full tilt through the pouring rain, the King's Own stood fast, and on the word three hundred Sniders let fly in a devastating volley that blew the red-coated horsemen's charge to pieces and staggered the infantry mass behind them.

Why they didn't run then and there, I can't fathom. The rockets must have been terror enough, but now they were meeting rapid-fire breech-loaders for the first time, yet still they came on until the Sniders and the Enfields of the Baluch stopped them in their tracks, and they gave back, firing their double-barrelled muskets as they went and being shot down as they tried to find cover among the rocks and scrub oaks. The King's Own advanced steadily, a mounted officer who I guess was Cameron keeping them in hand; still the Abs retreated and died . . . but they never ran, and I guess my time there must have made me an old Abyssinian hand, for I find myself writing *"Bayete, Habesh!"* on their behalf. There, it's written. In their shoes I'd not ha' stopped running till Magdala.

While this was happening, Theodore was pounding away with his Fala battery, which I realised was unlikely to damage anyone (the chain-shot that almost did for Napier must have been a great fluke), but on the right the baggage of the second brigade was in mortal peril. The right wing of the Ab charge was thundering down on it, the spearmen singing like Welshmen, careless of the shells bursting above them from the guns of the Mountain Train formed up on the King's Road ahead of the baggage. Our guns were flanked by the Punjabi Pioneers, burly Sikhs in brown puggarees and white breeches, and as the Abs came surging up the slope to their position, letting fly their spears, they were met by two shattering volleys – and then the Sikhs were charging them with the bayonet against Ab spears and swords, smashing into their ranks like a steel fist, outnumbered but forcing the robed tribesmen back, and standing by Theodore on Fala I had to clamp my jaws tight to stop myself yelling, for I remembered their fathers and uncles at Sobraon, you see, and within I was crying: *"Khalsa-ji! Sat-sree-akal!"* There's no hand-to-hand fighter in the world better than a Sikh with his bayonet fixed; they scattered the spearmen like chaff and charged on, and I saw the fancy red puggarees of the 10th Native Infantry among them as they pitchforked the enemy into the gullies – those same ravines that I'd marked on Fasil's table as a death-trap if we'd blundered into them.

There were more Abs trying to outflank the baggage convoy, but the Sikhs and Native Infantry shot them down among the rocks, and the few King's Own who acted as baggage guards stood off those who got within striking distance. But this part of the action was too far for me to see, and events on Fala were claiming my attention.

Theodore's half-dozen cannon had been belching away to no good purpose, partly because his Ab gunners were incompetent, partly because the German loaders, I suspect, were making sure that the charges were all wrong. Why chain-shot was being used, I couldn't figure, because it's a naval missile, but that's Theodore's army for you: lions for bravery but bloody eccentric. But even if his gunners had been Royal Artillery they'd have had the deuce of a job, for firing dropping shot from a height is a dam' fine art.

So is building, loading, and firing mortars. Theodore's pet toy, Sevastopol, may have been the biggest piece of ordnance in the history of warfare for all I know, but the German artisans who cast it, never having made a gun before, botched it either accidental or a-purpose, for at its first discharge it blew up with an explosion you could have heard in Poona. I suspect it was deliberate mischief [47] from the fact that there wasn't a squarehead in sight when it was fired, and only the Ab gunners felt the full force of the blast which killed three or four and wounded as many more; it nearly did for Theodore himself, but fortunately for him there was an unwitting guardian angel on hand to save him.

I see it plain even today: the gunners climbing on the mortar housing, the rabble of attendants and staff watching from a respectful distance, the gunners at the other pieces holding their fire, the rain squalls sweeping across the muddy plateau, Theodore on his mule with his umbrella at the high port . . . and I had just turned to take a towel from a servant to wipe the water streaming down my face, when a tremendous rushing thunder seemed to burst out of the ground itself, the very earth shook, and bodies, debris, and gallons of mud were flying everywhere. I wasn't five yards away, but by one of those freaks for which there's no accounting the blast passed me by; I didn't even stagger, and was thus in a position to move nimbly as seventy tons of solid iron, jarred loose from its housing by that colossal explosion, toppled ponderously in my direction.

Which was capital luck for his Abyssinian majesty, thrown by his startled mule and landing slap in my path as I dived for safety. Ask any man who's been hit foursquare by a fleeing Flashy, fourteen stone of terrified bone and muscle, and he'll agree that it's a moving experience; Theodore went flying, brolly and all, and I landed on top of him while the enormous mortar, belching smoke, rocked to a standstill on the very spot where he'd been trying to keep his balance.

His words as we scrambled, mud-soaked, to our feet, were most interesting. "You saved me!" he yelled, and then added: "Why?" Some questions are impossible to answer: "I beg your pardon, I didn't mean to," would have been true but inappropriate, but I suppose I made some sort of noise for he stared at me, looking pretty wild, and then turned to the ruin of his mortar, gave a strange wail and clasped his head in his hands, and sank to his knees in the puddles. Unlike mine, his emotions were not shuddering terror at our escape, nor was he overwhelmed by gratitude. I suppose the fact was that Sevastopol had cost him a deal of labour, dragging it half across Ethiopia, and here he was literally hoist with his own petard. And serve the selfish bastard right.

His grief for his useless lump of iron was quickly cut short as a Congreve rushed past overhead, and another absolutely struck one of the cannon, spraying fire and shrapnel everywhere and mortally wounding the Ab gun-captain. The Naval gunners had found our range, and several more rockets hissed above us, weaving crazily, for they were no more reliable than they'd been years before when I'd fired them at the Ruski powder ships under Fort Raim. One came a sight too close for comfort, though, scudding between the guns and killing a horse. For the first time I saw Theodore scared, and he wasn't a man who frightened easy. He clasped his shield before him and shouted: "What weapons are these? Who can stand against such terrible things?" But it didn't occur to him to leave the summit, although presently he bade the gunners cease fire. "They do not fear my shot!" cries he, and began to weep, pacing about the summit and finally taking station on the forward edge to stare stricken at the final retreat of his army.

For it was as good as over now, a bare hour and a half after he'd started the fight with his first gun. The plain was thick with dead and dying Abs, the defeated remnant scrambling back over the rocky slopes of Fala and Selassie, turning here and there to fire their futile smooth-bores and scream defiance at the King's Own and Baluch advancing without haste, picking their targets and reloading without breaking stride. The sun was dipping behind the watery clouds, and then it broke through as the rain died away, sending its beams across the battlefield, and a splendid rainbow appeared far away beyond the Bechelo. It was damned eerie, that strange golden twilight, with the rocket trails fizzing their uncertain way over the field to explode on the Fala saddle, and the muffled crack of the Mountain Battery's steel guns, the red blink of their discharges more evident as the dusk gathered over Arogee.

Messengers had been galloping up since the onset, mostly just to hurrah at first, but now came the news that old Gabrie had gone down, and presently it became clear that most of those scarlet-clad cavalry chiefs had fallen with him. Theodore threw his *shama* over his head, crying bitterly, and sat down against a gun-carriage. Now he wouldn't look down at the carnage below, or at the wreck of his army stumbling wearily back over the Fala saddle to Islamgee, but at last he dismissed the gun-teams, keeping Samuel and myself and his pages with him. When darkness fell, Ab rescue parties ventured out with torches to find their wounded, whose wails made a dreary chorus in the dark, and Speedy told me later that when our stretcher-bearers, whom Napier had sent out to bring enemy wounded to our field hospital, had encountered Ab searchers in the dark, they'd worked together without a thought. Our medicos patched up quite a few of Theodore's people, which, as Speedy observed, made you realise how downright foolish war can be.

But then, 'twasn't really a war, nor Arogee a proper battle. Like Little Big Horn, it was more of a nasty skirmish, and like Big Horn it had an importance far beyond its size.

On the face of it, there wasn't much for the *Gazette*. No dead on our side, although I believe a couple of our thirty wounded died later, and only seven hundred Abs killed – I say only, you under-stand because when you've seen Pickett's charge and the Sutlej awash with thousands of corpses, Arogee's a fleabite (provided you ain't one of the seven hundred, that is). For our fellows, it had been a day's shooting, but for the Abs it was Waterloo. They'd been shot flat, massacred if you like, by Messrs Snider and Enfield, gallant savages decimated by modern weapons . . . but for once the liberals can't sniff piously over that, for even at close quarters, steel against steel, Ab swords and spears had been no match for Sikh bayonets. For the Abs, it was shameful disaster, and for Theodore it was finis.[48]

For our side, it was something unheard of, a victory without loss at the end of a campaign that had been supposed to end in catastrophe. But Speedy told me there was no joy in our camp, only pity and admiration for a foe who hadn't been good enough, and a perverse irritation that it hadn't been worth all the toil and effort. T. Atkins and J. Sepoy had expected a real battle, an Inkerman or Balaclava, a Mudki or Ferozeshah, against a foe they could touch their hats to. Arogee had been a sell; the Abs had been no opposition at all – oh, they'd tried, and been a mighty disappointment.

That, I can assure you, is what my countrymen felt. Victory had been so easy that they felt cheated. D'you wonder that I shake my head over 'em?[49]

It was well after dark before Theodore could rustle up the will to bestir himself. He sat for a good two hours like a man stunned, not seeming to hear the cries of the wounded below Fala, or that sudden ghastly scream which told us that the jackals and hyenas were at work. At last he summoned Samuel and dictated a letter to Rassam asking him to make his peace with Napier. I can give it exact, for Samuel gave me a copy later, as evidence that he'd done his bit to bring about an armistice. It was a real Theodore effusion:

My dear friend, how have you passed the day? Thank God, I am well. I, being a king, could not allow people to come and fight me without attacking them first. I have done so and my troops have been beaten. I thought your people were women but I find they are men. They fought very bravely. Seeing that I am not able to withstand them, I must ask you to reconcile me to them.

He gave it to a couple of the Germans to take to Magdala, and then we went down to Islamgee, through a torch-lit purgatory of dead who'd been brought up from the battlefield, and wounded being cared for by their comrades. It was raining again, and the guttering

243

flares shone on rows of shrouded corpses, and on lean-tos and tents where the Ab surgeons were at work. Under one long canopy were laid the scarlet-clad bodies of some of the five hundred chiefs who had led the charge and been peppered by the King's Own and Baluch, who'd supposed that one of 'em must be Theodore.

He stood silent a while, looking at them, and then moved slowly along the line, stopping now and then to touch a hand, or lay his own on a forehead, before turning away. Someone called his attention to another body in a tent nearby, and when they drew back the shroud who should it be but Miriam, looking pale and beautiful and very small. It took me aback; I'd forgotten her in the tumult of the last few days, and seeing her lifeless gave me a shock that I find hard to describe. I mean, I bar vicious bitches who are prepared to burn me to death by inches, but she'd been a lovely peach and I'd have dearly liked to explain the Kama Sutra to her by demonstration. So I can't say I was grief-stricken, or even moved, much, just sorry as one is to see a beautiful ornament broken, and irritated by the waste.

Some of her mates were around her, keening what I guess was a death-song, and I asked the ugly little trot I'd christened Gorilla Jane how it had happened. Miriam hadn't been in the battle, but watching with the others from the Fala saddle, and a screaming fire-devil had exploded by her: a rocket. The others had escaped injury, so I guess bonny little Miriam was the only female casualty of Arogee. Well, at least I gave her a moment's thought, which was more than Theodore did; he spared her not so much as a glance as he strode on to his tent. Gratitude of princes, what?

*   *   *

You'd ha' thought, would you not, that it was now all over at last? His army had been thrashed out of sight, he'd confessed with bitter tears that there was no resisting such weapons, and he'd asked Rassam to make peace for him. He changed his mind in the course of the night, which he spent getting raging drunk, and vowing that he'd be damned before he'd sue to Napier, but by dawn he was seeing reason again (for the time being) and I was treated to the sight of Prideaux, in full fig, limping down from Magdala to get his marching orders from the Emperor: he, and one of the German prisoners, a preacher named Flad, were to go with one of Theodore's sons-in-law, a nervous weed named Alamee, to open negotiations with Napier.

His majesty was in his sunniest mood by now, inquiring after Prideaux's health, pressing drink on him, and complimenting him on his appearance – at which I couldn't help smiling approval, for our jaunty subaltern was putting on dog in no uncertain manner. His old red coat was sponged and pressed, his whiskers shone with pomade, his cap was on three hairs, his cane under his arm, and his monocle in his eye. Rule Britannia, thinks I, and stamped my heel in reply to the *barra salaam** he threw me as he and his companions rode down to Napier's head-quarters beyond Arogee. Theodore watched their progress through his glass from the summit of Selassie, and was much gratified when one of his scouts panted up to report that the party had been received with cheering and hats in the air.

If he thought that this natural rejoicing at seeing two of the prisoners free at last was a happy omen, he was brought back to earth when they returned in the afternoon with Napier's reply. By then his mood had changed for the worse, thanks to his chiefs, who came to the Selassie summit en masse to point out that he still had nine-tenths of his army in good fettle, and if they fell on Napier by night, when artillery and rockets would be useless, they could make him sorry he'd ever crossed the Bechelo. Whether Theodore believed this or not, he was looking damned surly by the time Prideaux and Flad and Alamee returned to inform him that Napier's terms amounted to unconditional surrender, with the prisoners freed and Theodore willing to "submit to the Queen of England", with a promise that he'd be given honourable treatment.

Reasonable enough, considering the trouble and expense we'd been at, and the barbarous way he'd behaved, wouldn't you say? But you ain't the descendant of Solomon and Sheba, with notions

* Big salute.

of imperial grandeur, unable even to contemplate submitting your sacred person to the representative of a mere woman who'd added injury to insult by ignoring your letter and then invading your country. Just to show you how far he was from understanding us, his first question was: did honourable treatment mean we'd assist him against his enemies, and would we look after his family – wives, concubines, numerous offspring, etc?

Flad, who interpreted, put this to Prideaux, who said, being an honest English lad from a good home, that we'd do the decent thing, goodness me. Flad was explaining this in diplomatic terms when Alamee, who'd been hopping nervously as Theodore's scowl grew blacker, seized his majesty's arm and drew him out of earshot, chattering twenty to the dozen.

"Talkin' sense into him, I hope," says Prideaux to me. "Is the feller changin' his mind? His army don't look like surrenderin', I must say!" Nor did they, ranged in their silent thousands on the lower slopes of Selassie beneath us, and on Fala across the way. "Never saw so many glowerin' faces! Well, he'd better swallow the terms, 'cos they're the best he'll get – what, after the way he's carried on, keepin' us chained for two years, torturin' poor old Cameron, butcherin' his own folk right and left! The man's a blasted Attila! And if he expects Napier to just say, 'So long, old fellow!' and pack his traps, he's sadly mistaken!"

"He's mad, remember," I told him – and what happened next bore me out, for Theodore began to rage and stamp as Alamee pleaded with him. "Please, Father, there is no hope!" he was crying. "The choice is surrender or death! The English *dedjaz* swears that if a hair of the Europeans' heads is touched, he will tarry here five years if need be to punish the murderers – his words, Father, not mine!"

"Be silent, imbecile!" bawls Theodore, and there and then sat himself down on a rock and dictated a reply to Napier at the top of his voice, while we and his chiefs and minions listened in disbelief. For you never heard such stuff, starting off with a Theodoric rant about the Father, Son, and Holy Ghost, and then a great harangue – *not addressed to Napier*, but to the people of Abyssinia, and how they'd fled before the enemy, and turned their backs on him, and hated him, after the way he'd fed their multitudes, the maidens protected and unprotected, the women made widows at Arogee, and aged parents without children ... amazing babble, while he glared up at the heavens and his admiring court exclaimed in awe.

"He's slipped his cable," mutters Prideaux. "God help us!"

But now Theodore seemed to remember to whom he was writing, for he complained that Napier had prevailed by military discipline, the implication being that it wasn't fair "and my followers who loved me were frightened by one bullet, and fled in spite of my commands. When you defeated them, I was not with the fugitives. Believing myself to be a great lord, I gave you battle, but by reason of the worthlessness of my artillery, all my pains were as nought ..."

You may think I'm exaggerating, that no one could blather such nonsense, but it's there in the Blue Books, and I heard it up yonder on Selassie, how his ungrateful people had taunted him by saying he'd turned Muslim, which wasn't true, and he had intended with God's help to conquer the whole world, and die if he couldn't fulfil his purpose, and he'd hoped after subduing Abyssinia to lead his army against Jerusalem and expel the Turks. And if it had been dark at Arogee he'd have licked us properly. Not since the day of his birth had anyone dared lay a hand on him, and finally, a warrior who had dandled strong men like infants would never submit to be dandled by others.

So there. When he'd done dictating, he had the scribe read it over to him, which gave Prideaux the chance to tell me that Napier sent his compliments and congratulations, the Gallas had the southern approaches sealed, and he'd despatched another agent to Masteeat to see that my good work was continued.

"Sir Robert was quite bowled over at first to hear that you had fallen into Theodore's hands, and Captain Speedy – what a remarkable chap he is! – wondered if you hadn't allowed yourself to be taken on purpose." Prideaux was regarding me with that look of wary respect that my heroic reputation invariably excites in the young. "Sir Robert said why ever should you do any such thing,

247

and Captain Speedy said it might be all for the best, because if it came to a point, you would know what to do. Sir Robert asked what did he mean, but Captain Speedy made no reply." Prideaux coughed and fixed me with an earnest eye. "I tell you this, Sir Harry, because after a moment's reflection Sir Robert told me to give you his order that whatever befell, you were to remain with the Emperor Theodore and use your best judgment." He coughed again. "I'm not sure what he meant, sir, precisely, but I'm sure you do."

I knew all right, as the Gates of Fate clanged to behind me. Whatever befell, I was to use my best judgment to ensure that the Emperor of Abyssinia didn't leave Magdala alive.

Sound political biznai, of course. Theodore could not be allowed to go free and unpunished, the country wouldn't stand for it. On t'other hand, he'd be a most embarrassing prisoner to call to account. Much better for all concerned if he simply left the scene, and who better to shove him off the tail of the cart than good old Flashy, favourite ruffian of the Foreign Office, Palmerston-recommended, practically by Appointment Assassin Extraordinary to Her Majesty, demises discreetly arranged, moderate terms . . . if I were a sensitive man (and not a little flattered to be regarded as the most fatal nemesis since Jack Ketch) I might easily be offended. 'Twasn't the first time; I'd been sicked on to murder poor old John Brown in '59, as you know, but shirked, so the Yankees had to do it themselves, to the disgust of the world, and serve 'em right.

In the meantime, having finished listening to his own letter and nodded approval, Theodore had to endure another bout of impassioned whispering from Alamee, who was terrified that the letter would bring down Napier's wrath on everyone's head. Prideaux explained to me that our people, Speedy especially, had left Alamee in no doubt of what would happen if the war went on, and scared him to death by having Penn show him our guns and rockets; Speedy had also hinted that if Alamee and the other chiefs didn't restrain Theodore, it would be the worse for them. But whatever warnings Alamee was pouring into the royal ear seemed to be having no effect; he was told to hold his tongue, Prideaux and Flad were sped on their way with the letter, and when Prideaux asked for a drink of water before setting off he was told peremptorily that there wasn't time.

I couldn't guess what Napier would make of the lunatic message, but one thing was sure: he daren't take action that might risk the prisoners. There was no knowing what Theodore was liable to do. At the moment of despatching the letter he was ready for a fight, and so were his followers, but within an hour he seemed to be thinking better of it. He called a council of his chiefs, insisting that I and his German artisans attend, and even placed me on a stool beside his seat of state. Then, with his chiefs ranged in a semi-circle before him – a dozen black villains with their spears and swords across their knees, looking daggers at me and the square-heads – he began to shout abuse at them, much in the style of his letter to Napier: they had betrayed him when his back was turned, they were sheep when he wasn't on hand to inspire them, they were a heathen generation whom he had nourished and sheltered in a heathen land, but now he was here to lead and inspire, and out of the evil that he had done, good would surely come. So let them speak: what was to be done?

They were in no doubt. I can see them now, the dark faces with their teeth bared, the clenched fists thumping their knees as one after another voted to kill the prisoners and fight to the death; *Ras* Engedda, the chief minister, even hinted that Theodore had been too soft altogether; the prisoners should be herded into a hut and burned alive if Napier attacked. This was received with acclamation by all but two, Alamee and another, and I feared the worst until I noticed that Theodore was looking sourer with each successive vote for the war party, and all of a sudden he exploded.

"Are you blind that you cannot see the English want only their prisoners? Let them go and we shall have peace, but if they are hurt not one of us will be left alive! You urge me to war and reproach me for weakness, so kill me if you will, but do not revile me!" He was fairly foaming, driving his spear into the carpet again, and they piled out in haste, all but *Ras* Engedda and Alamee and another whom he sent post-haste to bring the prisoners down from Magdala. Then he calmed down, and gave me the sanest, happiest smile.

"Be of good cheer, my best of friends!" says he, and to the Germans: "And you also, good friends and servants who have

250

worked so well for me. Soon you will be with your rescuers."

Which cheered them up no end, and they went out blessing him and tugging their forelocks – and they were no sooner through the fly than he snatched a pistol from his belt, shoved it between his teeth, and squeezed the trigger – and it misfired. But he was a trier, the same Theodore; before I'd time to think "That's your sort, old man!" he'd thumbed back the second hammer, and if Engedda hadn't made a flying dive, the interfering ass, and knocked the piece from his hand, the pavilion canopy would have needed laundering, for this barrel went off splendidly and blew a hole in the tent-pole. After which Theodore groaned, sighed, threw his *shama* over his face, lay down, and went to sleep.

I, out of sheer curiosity, picked up the pistol and took the cap from the barrel that had misfired. It looked sound, so I tapped it smartly with the pistol butt, and it cracked with a puff of smoke. Why it had missed fire, heaven knows; perhaps there's a fate that looks after mad monarchs.

Dr Blanc told me later that when they received the summons to go down to Theodore, they were sure they were going to die. The Abs guarding them were full of woe and weeping, bidding them farewell, and when they came down the track from the Kobet Bar Gate of Magdala and across the Islamgee plain towards the Fala saddle, sure enough there was a firing party waiting for them, and your correspondent having the conniptions as I watched the ragged little party plodding towards us. For when a messenger had come to tell Theodore they were on their way, he had suddenly roused himself, bidden me sharply to accompany him, and strode out on to the Islamgee plain, calling for a file of musketeers.

He stopped on the edge of the precipice, a bare couple of furlongs from the spot where he'd massacred the prisoners (whose corpses, you'll be charmed to know, were still lying in heaps on the rocks below, in our full view) and ordered the musketeers to fall in against the cliff which rose sheer behind us. The road on which we stood was no more than a narrow ledge between the cliff and the drop. Theodore beckoned me to his side, and when the prisoners hove in view round a bend in the road he sent his lad Gabr to tell Rassam to approach alone. At this Engedda, who had stalked after us with a face of thunder, demanded to know what was to do.

"Will you let them go?" bawls he. "Will you fawn on this creature – and you, a king, and he a white cur?" Talk about bearding the lion, but Theodore only waved him away and went to meet Rassam, shaking hands, inquiring warmly after his health, sitting him down on a rock and asking if he wanted to go down to Napier now, or wait till next day, since it would soon be dusk. Rassam said, whatever suited his majesty, and Theodore began to cry, and burst out: "Go now, then, and the peace of God go with you! You and I have always been friends, and I beg you to bear in mind that if ever you cease to befriend me, I shall kill myself!"

If I'd been Rassam, I'd have gone while the going was good, for with Theodore it never stayed good for long, but he was a sparky little ha'porth, glancing back at the others waiting, and then looking a question at Theodore, who cried: "Or I may become a monk!" Rassam asked, what about the others, and Theodore shouted: "You had better go! Yes, go now!" He gestured angrily as Rassam hesitated before turning away. "Go, I say! Begone, in the name of God!"

But Rassam didn't go more than a yard before he stopped, and Theodore snatched a piece from the nearest musketeer and cocked it, Engedda gave a cry of triumph, and I thought, oh, Jesus, this is where it ends, for even if he spares Rassam who's his favourite he means to do for the rest of us including me . . . for he'd turned away from Rassam to face the remaining prisoners, and he was mouthing and weeping and presenting his musket as they began to walk towards us.

There weren't above a dozen of them, and who most of 'em were I can't tell you, for I never inquired, but the one in front saved all their lives, and no doubt mine. He was Henry Blanc, the Bombay medico, bluff, burly, and a bearcat for nerve, for he was sure his time was up, but here he came at a steady stride, head high and beard a-bristle, and "Good day, your majesty!" says he, while Theodore glared tearfully with his finger twitching on the trigger, and that brisk greeting, so unexpected, had him all adrift, and he gave back a pace, lowering his piece, and absolutely asked Blanc

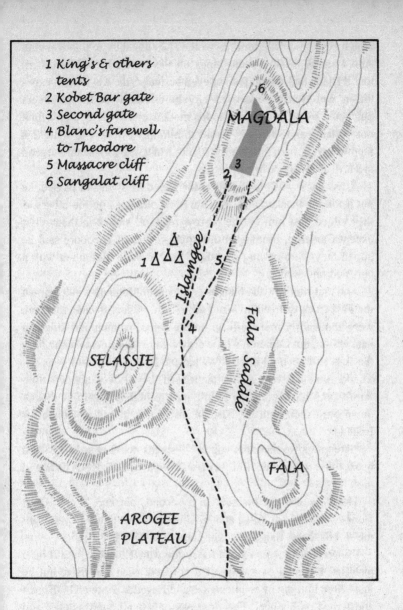

1 King's & others
  tents
2 Kobet Bar gate
3 Second gate
4 Blanc's farewell
  to Theodore
5 Massacre cliff
6 Sangalat cliff

MAGDALA

Islamgee

Fala Saddle

SELASSIE

FALA

AROGEE
PLATEAU

how he did, and bade him farewell as he passed by to join Rassam. And I know, for I've seen things on the knife-edge all too often, that if Blanc had shown fear, or even hesitated, the Abyssinian expedition would have ended in bloody failure with the prisoners butchered by that madman and his musketeers. Well, he didn't funk nor hesitate, and since it's thanks to him that I'm here to write this memoir, well, here's to Henry Blanc, M.D., staff assistant surgeon to H.M. Bombay Army. *Salue!*[50]

After that it was plain sailing, for Theodore's wild fit passed, he put aside his musket, and cried farewell blessings on the others as they edged past him on the narrow road, all smiles in their relief except Cameron, limping on his stick, for when Theodore said he hoped they were parting friends, Cameron bade him adieu with a curt nod and went by.

And that was how the famous prisoners of Magdala walked down the Fala track to freedom – not all of 'em, by any means, for there were about forty more still up on the *amba*, women and kids and hangers-on, but Cameron's little crowd were the principals, the ones the fuss had been all about.[51] When the last of them had gone by, Theodore stood staring after them as if they'd been his departing family, and blow me if he didn't start to blubber again, and sank down on a rock with his head in his hands. It was too much for Engedda.

"Are you a woman, that you cry?" shouts he. "Let us bring them back, those white men, kill them, and run away! Or let us fight and die!"

Theodore was on his feet in a second, blazing. "Fool! Dog! Donkey! Have I not killed enough these past two days? D'you want me to kill these, too, and cover Habesh in blood?"

I'd never seen a man stand toe to toe with Theodore, and if he'd pistolled Engedda on the spot I'd not have been surprised, but he just stared him out of countenance, and Engedda growled in disgust and turned on his heel. Theodore passed a hand over his eyes and gestured after the departing prisoners. "Do you not wish to go with your friends, *Ras* Flashman? It is done now. You are free to go."

Ironic, you'll agree. A few hours earlier, I'd have been up and

254

away with a roundelay . . . but since then Prideaux had brought Napier's orders, and they were not to be disobeyed, not if I was to keep my credit. Well, it was no great matter now; Theodore was crying uncle, the Queen's man was back in the Queen's keeping, and all that remained was the occupation of Magdala by her forces – and the disposal of its ruler, whatever that might entail. I was bound to stay, so I came to attention, regimental as you please.

"Thank'ee, your majesty, but with your permission I'll stay awhile. Perhaps I can be of service to your majesty."

He frowned, bewildered, and then the tears were welling in his eyes again, coursing down the black cheeks as he clasped my hand and regarded me with owlish emotion.

"Oh, my friend, my dear friend in Christ! My soldiers betray me, my people turn against me, my generals revile me . . . and from the ranks of my enemies comes one friend to stand by me!" He wrung my fin like a pump handle. "Ah, you strange British! I did not know you until now! There are no people like you in all the world! None, none, I say!"

"Oh, I don't know about that," says I, but he swore in choked accents that it was so, and sat down on his rock again, howling with sentiment and mopping his face. Then he had a quick pray, saying he had hardened his heart for many years, but now God had softened it, with some assistance from me, and Satan had been at work on him, but was now driven out, and he regretted the discourtesy of his letter to Napier, and must put that right.

"For this is Easter, and we are all Christians and friends," says he. "You are my best friend of all, and I shall open my heart to you and to all your people!"

Which he did next day with a civil note to Napier and a gift of a thousand cattle and several hundred sheep;[52] bent on reconciliation he might be, but he was no fool, knowing that if Napier accepted them, it was tantamount to a truce and might even be regarded as a settlement, since he'd freed the prisoners, which was supposedly all that was required. Crafty old Theodore – but equally crafty old Napier, for he refused the gift, but responded with a decent gesture, sending up the body of old Gabrie, which our stretcher-bearers had collected from the battle-field of Arogee.

Flad brought it back, and Theodore was much moved; because of some misunderstanding by the interpreters, he didn't realise at this time that Napier had rejected his cattle, so he was all gladness and good humour, bidding Flad jovially to go up to Magdala and collect Mrs Flad and the remaining prisoners, "and God give you a happy meeting." So Flad went, and a stranger procession you never saw than that which presently emerged from the Kobet Bar, for where I'd expected about forty Europeans, there was a caravan of more than two hundred folk, mostly black or *chi-chi*, for most were servants, with a few Ab wives and *chicos* of the prisoners. There were more than three hundred beasts laden with baggage, and it looked like the Exodus as they churned up the dust down the winding track from Magdala rock, through the empty market stalls at the foot, and out across the deserted plain of Islamgee. There was hardly an Ab soldier in sight, for they'd struck their camp and withdrawn to Selassie and Fala.

Theodore watched them go by from his pavilion. He'd sent for his queen – the real one, Tooroo-Wark, a lovely slip of a lass – and her son, little Alamayo, and at her request sent a nurse to one of the prisoners' wives, a Mrs Morris, who was about to pup, and indeed did so the next day in the British camp; they called the kid Theodore in appreciation. Mrs Morris had a *palki*; Mrs Flad and the other wives were on mules, and presently they disappeared down the road to Arogee, men, women, beasts, babes in arms, porters, bags and baggage – and that, Theodore seemed to think, was the end of it.

How wrong he was he learned on that sunny Easter Sunday evening, when word came that Napier had turned back his cattle, and it sank in at last that we would settle for nothing less than unconditional surrender, which must mean what he had always dreaded: the delivery of his royal person to a foreign enemy. Perhaps that fear was in his mind when he had his gun-teams drag the artillery from the Fala summit to the far end of the Islamgee plain, either in an effort to convince Napier of his peaceful intent or to prepare a last defence for Magdala. I don't know which, but I know that his high spirits when the prisoners left wore thin as the hours went by, and no good word came from Napier.

"What more can they want? Oh, my friend, have I not done all that they asked? They have beaten my army and broken my power; it must be peace, my friend, tell me it must be peace!"

If he said it once he said it a dozen times, but there was no re-assuring him. In the pavilion lamplight the handsome face was tired and haggard; he'd aged a year in a few days, and I'll swear his hair was even greyer. Strange, there was nothing mad about him now, just a flat sober certainty in his words when Meshisha, his execu-tioner, who'd been in charge of taking the cattle down to our lines, came back after dark to report that they'd been turned back by Speedy; the mention of that name struck Theodore like a blow.

"The *Basha Fallaka*! My enemy, always my enemy! So now, having got what they want, these people will seek to kill me!" He stood, fists clenched, a picture of despair. "There is nothing left for me here. The time has come to find a new home in the place where I was little, long ago. There, by the power of God, I may find peace at last."

* * *

You can always tell when something is coming to an end. You know, by the way events are shaping, that it can't last much longer, but you think there are still a few days or weeks to go . . . and that's the moment when it finishes with a sudden bang that you didn't expect. Come to think of it, that's probably true of life, or so it strikes me at the age of ninety – but I don't expect it to happen before tea. Yet one of these days the muffins will grow cold and the tea-cakes congeal as they summon the lads from belowstairs to cart the old cadaver up to the best bedroom. And if I've a moment before the light fades, I'll be able to cry, "Sold, Starnberg and Ignatieff and Iron Eyes and Gul Shah and Charity Spring and all the rest of you bastards who tried to do for old Flashy, 'cos he's going out on his own, and be damned to you!"

This cheery reflection is brought on by my memories of that

Easter Sunday night, when I knew the curtain must soon come down on Magdala, perhaps in a day or two . . . and 'twas all over, receipted and filed before Monday sunset. It happened so quickly that I can remember only the vital moments; the hours between have faded. (Mind you, a shell splinter in the leg is no help to leisurely observation; we'll come to that presently.)

But I'm clear enough about the almighty row that broke when Theodore summoned his chiefs and told 'em it was time to cut and run, that they must be off before dawn, making for Lake Tana where Napier could never follow them. They shouted him down, swearing they could never assemble their families and goods in such short time, and demanding that he make peace. He cussed them for disloyal cowards and they heaped reproaches on him.

"If you had not released the captives we could have made terms with the *farangis*!" cries one.

"And if they had refused we could have cut the white dogs' throats and made the hearts of their countrymen smart!"

"Aye, at least we could have been revenged! As it is, we have no choice but to make peace!"

"We are your men to the end, but only if you make terms. If you will not, you are alone."

He might have read the end of his rule in the scowls on their black faces, but he still couldn't bring himself to surrender. He told Damash to start dragging guns and mortars from Islamgee up the rocky track to Magdala, and Engedda, the firebrand, thinking this meant a last stand, swore to stand by him, but the rest dispersed in sullen silence, and it was from that moment that the desertions began in earnest. Scores of warriors and their families left their posts on Selassie and Fala, and only a few hundred were prepared to help Damash move the guns, while Theodore struck his camp below Selassie. Then we must all retire across the Islamgee plain in the gathering dark, Flashy aboard a mule with his heart in his boots, for like Engedda I assumed that his fickle majesty had changed his mind yet again, and was determined to fight it out. I was mistaken, but before I come to that I must tell you how the land lay in the closing act of our Abyssinian drama.

From the deserted village market-place at the far end of the Islamgee plain, Magdala rock rose three hundred feet sheer, with only one way up: a narrow track that was really no more than a ledge running steeply up the cliff-face. Near the top it turned sharply to the right towards Magdala's first gate, the Kobet Bar, flanked by a high wall and stockade reinforced by thorn bushes. The gate was massive, with supporting towers and a sloping roof like that of a lych-gate. Fifty yards behind it was a second gate, and beyond that lay the Magdala plateau proper with its little township of houses and churches and the palace, big thatched buildings of typical Ab design.

One thing was plain: given a few decent guns, the Salvation Army could have held Magdala against anyone, Napier included, and if Theodore had got his cannon up to command that narrow track, there would have been no shifting him until his water ran out. But he didn't, thanks be; and once he and I and his immediate following had struggled up past the gun-teams sweating and blaspheming in the dark, and reached the Kobet Bar Gate, he realised their task was hopeless, and there was nothing for it but flight or surrender.

There must have been about twenty of us in the little guard tower flanking the gate, waiting breathless on the word of that haggard figure standing with his head bowed in thought. I remember Engedda grim-faced, and little tubby Damash exhausted after his gun-dragging exertions; Hasani, the Magdala commander, Wald Gabr the valet and gun-bearer, and others whose anxious black faces I can still see in the flickering torchlight but whose names I never knew. At last Theodore lifted his head, and the old barmy light was back in his eyes.

"Warriors who love me, gird yourselves!" cries he, and shook his spear. "Leave everything behind but your arms, and follow me! Hasani, assemble them and those others who remain true at the upper gate! Away!" And as they trooped out, he turned to me. "Dear friend, we part here. You can serve me no longer. I go now beyond your army's vengeance, and you and I will never meet again." He seized my hand in both of his. "Farewell, British soldier! Think kindly of Theodore who is your friend! If you should hear of my death at the hands of my foes, do not grieve. My destiny is my destiny!"

He strode out with a flourish worthy of Macbeth, and I heard him bawling orders to Hasani. I was left, mighty relieved and quite used up, with a couple of Ab artillerymen for company; the rest were lying tuckered out, down the track by their abandoned guns; there was no point in my moving, with Islamgee crawling with confused and disgruntled warriors who mightn't take kindly to a stray *farangi*. Better to wait patiently for Napier to arrive, so I disposed myself for a nap, thanking God I was rid of a royal knave.

I wasn't, of course. He was back at dawn with his fretful followers, several hundred of 'em; they'd tried to break out of Magdala by the back door, which would have meant a terrifying descent of the Sangalat cliffs in pitch darkness, if they'd been mad enough to attempt it. They'd been discouraged by the presence of Gallas who were waiting for them at the foot of the precipice chanting, "Come down, beloved, oh come down!" I must say I liked the Gallas' style.

With his retreat cut off and the greater part of his army milling about down on Islamgee, waiting to surrender, I was sure he must call it a day. But even now he couldn't bear to submit. He told his little band of loyalists that they and any others on the plateau were free to go, and if he was disheartened at the stampede down to Islamgee, he didn't show it. With the few score who remained he made a last futile attempt to bring the guns and mortars up the track, and when that failed he had them piling rocks behind the wings of the Kobet Bar Gate, lifting and carrying himself and shouting encouragement.

It wouldn't have been tactful to stand watching while they laboured away, so I waited until the gate tower was empty, purloined Theodore's telescope which he had left with his baggage, and withdrew along the inside of the wall to a spot where I could take survey of the Islamgee plain. There were a few folk in the market-place at the foot of the track, children playing on the guns which had been left behind by Damash's crew, but farther along the plain there were great multitudes of Abs of every sort, civilian and military, stirring in a confused way but going nowhere – waiting for the invaders to arrive, in fact. They were thick on the slope of

Selassie, a bare mile from my perch, and farther off I could see them on Fala; there must have been a good twenty or thirty thousand of them.

How long I sat watching I'm not sure, but the sun was well up and disappearing behind dark rain clouds when I heard a faint distant sound that had me on my feet and put an abrupt end to the barrier-building at the gate – the whisper of a bugle far off beyond Fala, and now the mass of folk on Islamgee were moving off towards the sound, and streaming down the Selassie slope to the gap leading to Arogee. There was sudden activity at Kobet Bar, men moving down the track to the guns which Damash had been able to get part way up; I saw Theodore ordering them as they tailed on the tackles, trying to haul the heavy pieces up the steep incline but making poor work of it. There was a great murmur from the moving throng on the plain, and then another faraway sound rising above it, stirring and shrill, and I found myself whispering "Oh, oh, the dandy oh!", for I knew it of old, the music of the Sherwood Foresters, and it couldn't be more than a couple of miles away, beyond the Fala saddle, growing louder by the minute, and now the movement of the crowds was becoming a flood, and damned if I wasn't doing a Theodore myself, brushing the tears from my cheeks, and muttering about the young May moon a-beaming love, the glow-worm's lamp a-gleaming love, and even exclaiming aloud, "Good for you, old Bughunter, that's your sort!", for here he was, horse, foot and guns, at the end of the impossible march to the back of beyond which the wiseacres had sworn could never be made.

His army was as he'd said it would be, bone weary and struggling up the last few miles, filthy and sunbaked and rain-sodden and still unsure of what was waiting, for rumour said that Theodore had ten thousand warriors at his back, and as he looked up at the heights of Fala and Selassie on either hand, Napier must have shuddered at the thought of how his force could have been shot to tatters by an enemy with heavy pieces determined to dispute his passage. Now, on the Fala height that might have been our undoing, there were figures moving, and when I steadied the telescope on the parapet, there in the glass circle were the green coats of the Baluch,

261

their Enfields at the trail as they came on in skirmishing order, and behind them the devil's own legion of the 10th Native Infantry, Sikhs and Pathans and Punjabis in all the colours of the rainbow, and along the Fala saddle I could make out the red coats and helmets of the Sappers with their scaling ladders, and khaki-clad riflemen were swarming up the Selassie slopes, but whether Sherwoods or King's Own or Dukes, I couldn't tell.

There was no fighting at all, for the Abs had no thought but total surrender, and thousands of them laid down their arms and trooped on to Arogee while our people were struggling to get the mountain guns on to the Selassie summit, to be turned on Magdala if need be. That ain't liable to happen, thinks I, not with Theodore down to his last few hundred and his guns still stuck halfway up the mountain – and as though in contradiction of that thought, there he was, the lunatic, going hell-for-leather on horseback down the track to the market-place, with a score of riders at his back, Engedda and Hasani among them. A trumpet sounded, and across the Islamgee plain I saw the glitter of sabres where a squadron of bearded sowars were cantering to meet them – Bombay Lights, I'm told, and just the boys to do Theodore's homework for him if he lingered.

He did, though, standing in his stirrups, flourishing his sword and yelling defiance. I was too far away to make out the words, but according to Loch, who commanded the Lights, he was shouting challenges, daring anyone to meet him in single combat, taunting them as women, boasting of his prowess – "Theodore's finest hour", according to some romantic idiot, but it didn't last long, for no one took the least bit of notice of him, and behind the Lights the Dukes were advancing in open order, halting and firing by ranks, and his majesty and friends were obliged to scatter and run. I watched them scrambling back to the Kobet Bar Gate, one of 'em clutching a bloody arm, Theodore last man in, still waving his sword and shouting the odds.

Now was the time to hammer some sense into him at last, so I abandoned my perch and came back to the gate where the members of his sortie were unsaddling and gasping for breath. Theodore was

throwing his reins to Wald Gabr and ordering everyone to the para-
pets; apart from his riders there were perhaps fifty or sixty warriors armed with muskets – and they were preparing to hold their
fortress against three British and two Indian battalions, three detach-
ments of cavalry, four batteries of artillery, plus Sappers and Miners,
the Naval Brigade, and those Sikh Pioneers who had given them
bayonet at Arogee. Sixty against the three and a half thousand that
Napier was about to launch at Magdala.

I didn't know, then, how great the odds were, but it was plain
that he was staking everything on a frontal assault with the pick of
his army; Islamgee was turning into a parade ground for British
infantry, six companies at least of Dukes in the lead with the Royal
Engineers and the Madras Sappers and Miners at their head – the
storming party whose work it would be to mine and blow open the
gate – and behind them the Sherwoods in line, and then the reserve
battalions, and far in the rear I could see the Armstrongs and steel
guns deploying under Selassie, and there were even elephants
coming into view with the mortars.

It wasn't a time for ceremony. Theodore was stripping off his
gaudy harlequin robe, bare to the waist until Wald Gabr threw a
plain coat over his shoulders; I marched up to him and handed him
his glass.

"You must raise a white flag," says I. "There's nothing else for
it. Take a look from the wall."

He took the glass in silence, motioned me to follow him, and
turned to jump nimbly on to the parapet, where his musketeers were
already lining the firing-step. I took post by him as he surveyed
the advance, still distant but inexorable, rank upon khaki rank with
the red Sappers before, the Dukes' Colours flapping in the rainy
gusts, swinging along with rifles sloped and bayonets fixed, and
the Foresters' band breaking from "Young May Moon" into "British
Grenadiers". Theodore lowered the telescope, smiling as he shook
it in time to the music.

"What a sight!" cries he. "It is a pleasure to behold! Ah, my
friend, they do me great honour! I shall make a noble end!"

I kept my head and my temper. "There's no need to make an

end, your majesty! They ain't coming to kill or to conquer! They have what they came for –"

"But it is not enough," says he quietly, and you never saw a calmer, saner man in your life. "They must have me also, for their pride, and for their country's honour. They have had a long march." He put his hand on my shoulder, still smiling, resigned and a little weary. "Come, my friend, there should be no false words between you and me, no twisting of truth, no pretences. They must have me as a prisoner. You know it, and I know it. Is it not so?"

"They'll treat you well . . . honourably. I've known the *Dedjaz* Napier all my life – he's a good man, and you know he respects you as a brave soldier. He'll treat you as a king, not as a prisoner."

I believed it then, but later I wasn't so sure. Even as we were speaking, our cavalry was skirting round to cover the west flank of Magdala, and reining up in horror at the rotten, stinking corpses of the three hundred captives he'd flung from the Islamgee cliff. Aye, that would have taken the shine off his surrender, if he'd made one . . . which he was not about to do, as he made plain in one of the strangest farewells I've ever heard. He shouted to Engedda and some others who were reinforcing the rocky barrier behind the gate, directing them to join the defenders on the parapet, and then turned to me.

"Now, my good friend, my friend of only a short while but no less dear for that, you must go up into the city." He gestured towards the second gate and the thatched buildings on the plateau beyond. "There you will be safe until your people come." I started to protest, but he held up a hand to silence me.

"I will fight. It is all that is left. Afterwards, you may see my body, and perhaps you will say, 'There lies a bad man who has injured me and mine.' Perhaps you will not wish to give me a Christian burial." He paused, frowning at me. "Will you be good to him who has despitefully used you, forgiving him by the power of God?"

I must have said something, heaven knows what, for he went on – and so help me, these were his words, with the enemy at the gate, his pathetic rabble returning fire, and the rain starting to come down in sheets.

"There is a custom which I should wish to be observed, the wrapping of my body in a waxed cloth – my queen will know how it should be prepared. When this has been done, and the body exposed to the sun, the heat causes the cloth to adhere to the flesh, thus forming an impervious shroud which will help to preserve the body. Will you see this done, my friend?"

The only answer in the circumstances would have been a bewildered "yes", if I'd had time to give it, but at that moment one Millward, commanding the mountain guns and rockets at the foot of Selassie, let fly a tremendous and wonderfully accurate barrage; all at once the ground was shaking with shell-bursts, rockets smashed into the wall, and Theodore and I were blown off our feet by the blast of one shell that fell just inside the gateway. Stones and dirt came pattering down on us as we scrambled to our feet, deafened and shaken, the gateway was hidden in a cloud of smoke, and out of it reeled Engedda, chest and shoulder drenched in blood, his mouth wide in a soundless scream. Theodore was running towards him when two more shells exploded within yards of us, throwing up columns of earth and filling the air with the whine of shrapnel. I saw Theodore stagger but run on, and thought, good luck to your majesty, it's your fight, not mine, as I fled for dear life up the twisting rocky gully to the second gate. Common sense told me that Napier wouldn't shell the town with its Ab civilians, and indeed Millward had strict orders to that effect and his gunners dropped their shot all on the main gate and wall – but rockets are another dixie of skilly altogether; they go where they list, and it was one of these that laid me low.

I heard the shrieking hiss and ear-shattering explosion, choking white smoke was all about me, and I felt a tremendous blow on my left calf, not painful but numbing, as though it had been sandbagged. I went down like a shot rabbit, cracking an elbow on the rocks, but heaved myself up in haste as another rocket screamed by and exploded near the second gate. Like a fool, I tried to run, my wounded leg gave way beneath me, and I went head-first into a large rock by the wayside and lost all interest in the proceedings.

They say that from the first cannonade to the final storming of the main gate was three hours, but it might have been three days or three minutes for all I knew. How long I was unconscious I cannot tell, but when I came to, and the first dizzy moments had passed, I was being heaved into a sitting position on a boulder beside the second gate, Theodore was standing a few yards away, a rifle in his hand, his valet Wald Gabr was supporting me with an arm about my shoulders, muttering instructions which I was still too dazed to make out, waves of pain were coursing up my left leg which was wrapped knee to ankle in a bloody cloth which oozed crimson on to my boot, and it penetrated my clouded senses that I'd been wounded. The air was crackling with small-arms fire, thunder was rumbling overhead, the rain was pelting harder than ever, and as Theodore turned from looking down the hill and strode past us without a word, tossing aside his rifle in the second gateway, I looked down the hill myself and saw a sight which I can see still, clear as day, forty years on.

Only a stone's throw below us the Ab musketeers were falling back from the wall, and above the parapet a flag was fluttering in the fierce wind, a little way to the left of the gate. At first I thought it must be some banner of Theodore's, but then there were helmets and khaki tunics either side of it, and now they were tumbling over the wall, and the flag was being flourished from side to side as the fellow carrying it was boosted up bodily by his mates to stand on the top. That was when I saw it was a regimental Colour, and here they came, a regular flood of riflemen, whooping and cheering like billy-o, charging the Ab musketeers who fairly ran before them.[53]

Khaki tunics and white robes were struggling in the gateway, bayonets against spears, and clubbed firearms on both sides; khaki was winning, and as the Abs were driven back some of our fellows were tearing aside the piled stones from the gates, which were thrust wide to admit a crowd of cheering attackers, Sappers and Pioneers and a great mob of Irish of the Dukes. They chased the Abs along the wall, and spears and swords and muskets were being flung aside as their owners threw up their arms in surrender. A few of the hardier spirits were running up the rocky path towards us, turning to fire a last shot at our fellows, and getting a fusilade in return. Shots sang above us and splintered the rocks around us, and Wald Gabr ran from my side, seized Theodore's fallen rifle, and thrust the butt into my left arm-pit.

"*Tenisu, dedjaz, tenisu*! Up, up, for our lives!"

Sound notion, and if you think it's agony to run hobbling with a splinter of steel buried in your calf muscle, you're right, but it's wonderful what you can do when Snider slugs are buzzing about your ears. I knew better than to try to identify myself in the heat of battle; with my improvised crutch going and Wald Gabr holding me up on t'other side I lurched through the gate, screaming at every step, and ahead of us Ab civilians were scattering up the slope, mothers with *chicos*, old folk and striplings, all frantic to escape the murderous struggle behind us.

Ten yards ahead there was a great bale of forage bound with cords, six foot square, and a capital place to go to ground, for my leg was giving out, leaking blood like a tap, my improvised crutch slipped from my grasp, and I lunged at the bale and grabbed it to save myself pitching headlong. I hauled myself round the bale by its cords, so that it was between me and the mischief behind, but lost my hold and fell on all fours, being damned noisy about it, too, for my leg was giving me gyp. Wald Gabr sprawled beside me, and then strong hands seized my arms and hauled me up, yelping, and it was Theodore, gripping me under the shoulders and gently easing me into a sitting position with my back to the bale.

"Be still!" He was breathing hard. "Go, good and faithful

servant!" says he to Wald Gabr. "God prosper you . . . and have you in his keeping!"

The lad hesitated, and Theodore laughed and slapped him on the arm. "Go, I say! Get you to Tigre again! Take a king's thanks . . . and blessing! Fare well, gun-bearer!"

Wald Gabr turned and ran, and Theodore watched him disappear among the huts. Then he looked past the bale towards the second gate, still breathless and rubbing the rain from his face; the plain *shama* over his shoulders was wringing wet and clinging to him. The firing behind had slackened, but there was a distant shouting of orders followed by a ragged cheer. He closed his eyes for a moment and sighed before he spoke, and these were his words, and mine, on that rainy afternoon on Magdala height:

Theodore: I shall never go to Jerusalem now. There will be no Tenth Crusade. [*Draws pistol, offers it butt first.*] Suicide is an abomination in God's sight, a sin not to be forgiven. Oh, friend, will you do a last kindness to your enemy?

Flashy: Don't be a bloody ass! Throw it away, man! They ain't coming to kill you – put up your hands and give in, can't you? It's all up, dammit!

Theodore: You will not? Do I ask too much, then? So be it. Perhaps God, who marks the fall of humble sparrows and proud kings, will forgive even this, in His infinite mercy . . .

Flashy: God don't give a tuppenny dam one way or t'other! Give over, you crazy bastard –

But he was cocking the piece, and now he put the muzzle in his mouth and his thumb on the trigger, and blew the back of his head away. The explosion threw him back, off his feet, but by some freak convulsion of his hand the pistol flew into the air and fell beside my wounded leg. His body twitched for a few seconds and then shrank and was still, head on one side and a bloody puddle spreading beneath it. I could see his face; unmarked, impassive, untroubled, the eyes closed as though in sleep.

D'you know, I wasn't even shocked at the abruptness of it? It seemed fit and proper, somehow, and I thought then what I think still, that it was a thing almost fore-ordained, as though he'd been searching for it all his life. And there it was, and that was all about it; short, sweet, simple, and saved everyone a deal of bother.

I clenched my eyes shut with a spasm of pain, and when I opened them my eye fell on the pistol, and on the silver plate on its stock. I picked it up, and laughed aloud, but not in mirth. The plate was engraved:

Presented

by

VICTORIA

Queen of Great Britain and Ireland

to

THEODORUS

Emperor of Abyssinia

as a slight token of her gratitude

for his kindness to her servant Plowden

1854

Ironic, you'll agree, but now came a clatter of running feet, and into sight on my right came two khaki ruffians, helmets askew, dirty bearded faces alight with devilment. The nearer covered me with his rifle.

"Jayzus, ye're white!" cries he. "Who the hell are ye, den, and what's to laugh at?"

"Put up that piece and come to attention, you rascal!" I've encountered T. Atkins (and P. Murphy) often enough to know how to bring him to heel when the battle-lust is on him. "I'm Colonel Sir Harry Flashman, Seventeenth Lancers! Get me a medical orderly!"

"In de name o' God!" cries Paddy. "An' is it yerself, den, Sorr Harry? Be Christ it is, an' so ye are! 'Tis himself, Mick, de Flash feller – beggin' yer pardon, Sorr Harry –"

"Are yez sure?" says Mick, all suspicion. "He looks like a bloody buddoo to me."

269

"Buddoo? Will ye hear him? Did I not see Ould Slowcoach pin de cross on him at Allahabad – beggin' his pardon an' all, Sir Colin, I should say – but man, Sorr Harry, I doubt ye're woundit –"

"Who's de nigger?" demands Mick, scowling at Theodore's corpse and plainly still doubtful of me.

"The King of Abyssinia," says I. "Let him be – and damn your eyes, get me an orderly and a stretcher!"

"At once, at once!" shouts Paddy. "Run, Mick, an' see to't! Just you bide there, Colonel Sorr Harry, sorr, an' give yer mind peace –"

"There's no Seventeenth Lancers in your man's colyum," says Mick. "An' if there was, whut's he doin' here ahead o' the Colours, even? Tell me dat, Shaughnessy!"

Shaughnessy told him, in Hibernian terms, but I paid him no heed, for more bog-trotters were arriving, with wild hurrahs and halloos, pausing a moment to gape at me, and then at Theodore's body, for now there were Abs on hand tugging at their sleeves and pointing – "Toowodros! Toowodros!"[54] Presently the man Mick returned with an orderly who set to work on my injured calf, making me yell with the fiery bite of raw spirit in the wound, and drawing cries of delight and commiseration from my audience as he held up a gleaming two-inch sliver of shrapnel which he had removed from my quivering flesh.

"Nate as Hogan's knapsack!" they cried. "A darlin' little spike, compliments o' Colonel Penn!" and laughed heartily, urging me to be aisy, Sorr Harry dear, for I must ha' tekken worse at Balaclavy, sure an' I had, is dat not so, eh, Madigan? It was a mercy when a Colour Sergeant came bawling for them to fall in, and they melted away, all but the orderly and Private Pat Shaughnessy, my self-appointed sponsor and protector . . . and suddenly I felt not too poorly at all, for all the throbbing discomfort of my leg, and my aching skull, sitting with my back to the bale in the gentle rain.

I'd been here before . . . wounded and propped up against a gun-wheel at Gwalior ten years since, at the end of the great Mutiny, with the same tired, overwhelming feeling of relief because I knew 'twas all over at last, and here I was none too much the worse, watching content as the Duke of Wellington's Irish fell in, with the markers shouting, and a young chap was planting the Colour to thunderous cheers and helmets flying before all came to attention for "God Save the Queen" followed by "Rule, Britannia", and the orderly was bidding Shaughnessy bring me a stretcher, and a huge figure with a spreading black beard was stooping over me with a roar of greeting, and my hand was being gripped in an enormous paw.

"Good God!" cries Speedy. "Sir Harry!"

"Right enuff y'are, yer honour!" agrees the departing Shaughnessy. "'Tis himself, so it is, an' none other!"

"You're wounded!" cries Speedy. "But you're well, what? Oh, this is famous! It will crown Sir Robert's day! We'd almost given you up after Prideaux said Theodore wouldn't release you!" He pumped my hand, beaming. "And here you are – and what a splendid job you did with the Gallas! Sealed this *amba* tight as a drum – oh, aye, we know how he tried to run for it! But who'd have thought Magdala would fall so fast and easy! Thanks to you, sir! Thanks to you!"

Which was music to the ears, of course . . . and then he glanced round at a cry of "Toowodros! Toowodros!", and there was an Ab eagerly identifying Theodore's body for a couple of officers who had just come up.

Now, what followed meant nothing to me at first, but it did an hour later, after . . . well, the events I'm about to relate. They're no great matter, but they provide an interesting glimpse of human nature, I think, and demonstrate how people will believe what they want to believe, and honourable men will swear to what they think is a damned lie, never realising that it happens to be true. Thus:

Speedy heard the Ab, and stared, shot me a brief wondering glance, and strode across to the corpse. He bent over it and came back exclaiming "Phew!" in astonishment. Then he checked, and I saw he was looking at my left hand which, to my surprise, was resting on Theodore's revolver. Speedy glanced back at the body, then at me with just a hint of knowing in his eyes, and stooped quickly to snatch up the gun and thrust it under his tunic.

"We'll have you under cover in a jiff – out o' the rain!" cries he, and Shaughnessy arriving with the stretcher, he and the orderly bore me into one of the thatched houses nearby. Speedy chivvied them away, Shaughnessy adjuring me to hiv a care, Sorr Harry man, dear, and outside the bands were striking up "Hail the Conquering Hero Comes", almost drowned out by another great roar of cheering. It was Napier, never far behind the infantry as usual, come to take possession of his conquest; Speedy stood chafing in the doorway, and I heard him summon a soldier and order him to stand guard and let no one in or out.

There were a couple of scared-looking Ab women in the house, and Speedy dashed them some dollars, telling them to give me a flask of *tej*, and whatever else I might need. Then he was off, promising to be back presently, and I guess about an hour passed, in which I discovered I could walk with only a little discomfort, and the women brought me some *humbasha*,* and I sat listening to the bands playing and the bustle and shouted orders until I heard Speedy returning – and Napier with him, his voice raised in anger, which wasn't his style at all.

"Have him covered up at once!" he was barking. "Good God, was there ever anything more disgraceful? Have him taken into a house directly and made decent! Has the Queen been informed? Ah, Rassam is seeing to her; very good." I was to learn that his great bate was about Theodore's body lying in the rain, stripped almost naked by chaps seeking souvenirs. Speedy said something I didn't catch, and Napier said: "To be sure, the doctors must examine the body tomorrow and report to a board of inquiry . . . now, where is our Ambassador Extraordinary?"

This as he appeared in the doorway, helmet in hand, with Speedy at his elbow muttering that the less said the better, at all costs the press mustn't get wind –

"Sir Harry!" Napier was gripping my hand, eyes alight in the tired old face. "No, no, sit still, my dear fellow! Not too painful a hurt, I trust? Ah, that is good news!" Then he was echoing Speedy's earlier congratulations, thanking me for "a task well done as only

---

* A large flat loaf of coarse bread.

you could have done it," without which the campaign might have come adrift, and so forth, etc. "It was a body blow when we learned you'd been taken, I can tell you. But we'll hear all about that presently, and your other adventures. For the moment it's enough that you're here!" He beamed, paused a moment, and sat down, fingering his dreary moustache.

"So . . . the work's done, by the mercy of Providence," says he. "And the King is dead. A sad end. But not untimely. How did it happen?"

I told him straight, suicide. He glanced at Speedy, and nodded.

"Suicide," says he. "I see."

Something in his tone made me repeat it. "That's right, sir. He put the piece in his mouth and let fly."

Another thoughtful nod. "Apart from yourself, was any other person present?"

"No, sir. No one."

"Very good." He looked decidedly pleased. "Very good. Dr Blanc will confirm your account when he examines the body tomorrow."

"Johnson'll convene the board of inquiry. They'll make it official," says Speedy. "Suicide, that is."

There followed a brief silence during which I kept a straight face. Suddenly it had become plain that they were under the incredible delusion that I had shot Theodore, but they didn't care to say so in as many words, which was vastly diverting. Of course it was what they'd wanted, and had hinted to me through Prideaux, and Speedy, having seen the pistol in my hand and Theodore stark and stiff, had concluded that I'd done the dirty deed to save H.M.G. the painful embarrassment of having to try and possibly hang the black bugger. ("*But no one must ever know, Sir Robert . . . controversy . . . press gang, scoundrel Stanley . . . questions in the House . . . uproar . . . regicide,* scandalum magnatum . . . *honour of the Army . . .*")

Which explained why, within an hour of the last shot in the war being fired, when the Commander-in-Chief should have been consolidating his victory, with a hundred important military matters awaiting his decision, he was here post-haste to ensure a conspiracy of silence, leave me in no doubt that I'd not suffer for my good

273

deed, and join Speedy in regarding me with that rather awed respect which says more clearly than words, gad, you're a ruthless son-of-a-bitch, thank God.

I might have protested my innocence, but I didn't get the chance.

Napier was addressing me in his gentlest voice, with that old familiar Bughunter smile.

"Harry," he began. So I was "Harry" now, without any formal honorific; well, well. "Harry, you and I have known each other ever so long. Yes, ever since you lobbed that blessed diamond at old Hardinge . . . 'Here, catch!'" He gave a stuffed chuckle. "You should have seen their faces, Speedy! However . . . that's by the way." He became serious. "Since then, I have known no officer who has done more distinguished service, or earned greater fame, than you . . . no, no, it is true." He checked my modest grunts with a raised hand. "Well, what I wish you to know is that whatever services you may have done in the past, none has been more . . . gratefully valued, than those performed in Abyssinia. I refer not only to your mission to the Queen of Galla, so expertly accomplished, but to that . . . that other service which you have done today."

He paused, choosing his words, and when he resumed he didn't look at me directly. "I know it cannot have been easy for you. Perhaps to some of our old comrades, those stern men with their iron sense of duty, men like Havelock and Hope Grant and Hodson (God rest them), it might have seemed nothing out of the way . . . but not, I think, to you. Not to one in whom, I believe, duty has always been tempered with humanity, yes, and chivalry. Not," he concluded, looking me in the eye, "to good-hearted Harry Flashman." He stood up and shook my hand again. "Thank you, old fellow. That said, we'll say no more."

If I sat blinking dumbly it was not in manly embarrassment but in amazement at his remarkable misreading of my nature. All my life people had been taking me at face value, supposing that such a big, bluff daredevilish-looking fellow must be heroic, but here was a new and wondrous misconception. Just because I'd tickled his funnybone years ago by my offhand impudence to Hardinge, and been hail-fellow Flash Harry with the gift of popularity (as

Thomas Hughes observed), I must therefore be "good-hearted" . . . and even humane and chivalrous, God help us, the kind of decent Christian whose conscience would be wrung to ribbons because he'd felt obliged to do away with an inconvenient nigger for the sake of the side.

That was why Napier had been gassing away like a benign vicar, judging me by himself, quite unaware that I've never had the least qualm about kicking the bucket of evil bastards like Theodore – but only when it's suited me. You may note, by the way, that for once my eye-witness report conforms exactly with accepted historic fact. All the world (Napier and Speedy excepted) believes that King Theodore took his own life, and all the world is right.

I messed in Napier's tent that night, with Speedy and Merewether and a couple of staff-wallopers, and Henty and Austin of the *Times* the only correspondents. Henty was eager to know what I'd been up to, but Napier proved to have a nice easy gift of diplomatic deflection, and a frosty look or two from Austin showed Henty what the Thunderer thought of vulgar curiosity.

"We must beware of the others, though," says Speedy later, when he and I were alone with Napier. "Stanley's a damned ferret, and his editor hates us like poison.[55] The less they know of Sir Harry's activities, the better."

I didn't see that it mattered, but Napier agreed with him. "You should not become an object of their attention. Indeed, I think it best that your part in the whole campaign should remain secret. If it were known that you had been our emissary to Queen Masteeat's court, it would be sure to excite the correspondents' interest, and if they were to discover that you were alone with Theodore when he died, it might lead to . . . unwelcome speculation." Speedy was nodding like a mechanical duck. "Fortunately, when Prideaux brought the news that you were in Theodore's hands, I was able to send another agent to Queen Masteeat to carry on the work you had so expertly begun. You will not mind," says he, giving me the Bughunter smile, "if I mention him in my despatches, rather than yourself?[56] For security, you understand. Have no fear, your credit will be whispered in the right ears – and what's a single leaf more or less in a chaplet like yours?"

There was nothing to say to this, and I didn't much care anyway, so I allowed myself to succumb to the Napier charm.

"It means you'll be spared the labour of a written report!" cries he genially. "You can do it verbatim, here and now! Give him a b. and s., Speedy, and one of your cheroots. Now then, Harry, fire away!"

So I told 'em the story pretty much as I've told it to you, omitting only those tender passages with Uliba and Masteeat and that bint at Uliba's *amba* whose name escapes me ... no, Malee, that was it ... and the attempt on my virtue by Theodore's queen-concubine. Nor did I tell them of my plunge down the Silver Smoke. Why? 'Cos they wouldn't have believed it. But the horrors of Yando's aerial cage, and the atrocities of Gondar, and my ordeal at the hands of the kidnappers whom Uliba had ordered to abduct me so that she could do me atrociously to death, and how I'd been rescued by Theodore's fighting women, and Uliba given her passage out – these I narrated in my best laconic Flashy style, and had Speedy's hair standing on end – an alarming sight.

"Impossible! I cannot credit it!" He was horror-stricken. "You say Uliba tried to kill you? Had Galla renegades carry you off so that she could ... could murder you? No, no, Sir Harry ... that cannot be –"

"I'm sorry, Speedy, but it's true." I was deliberately solemn now. "I would not believe it either, had I not seen it. I know you had the highest regard for her – not least for her loyalty. So did I. But I know what she did, and –"

"But why?" bawls he. "Why should she wish you harm?" He was in a great wax, glowering through his beard like an ape in a thicket, suspicion mingling with his shocked disbelief. "It wasn't in her, I tell you! Oh, I know she was a vixen, and cruel as the grave to her enemies, and would have seized her sister's throne – but that was honest ambition! She was true to her salt, and to her friends –"

"A moment, Speedy," says Napier. "You may have touched it –

her designs on the Galla throne. Did she," turning to me, "try to enlist your help in her coup? Because if she did, and was refused, might she not, in resentment –"

He was interrupted by Speedy's furious gobble of protest; plainly Uliba had kindled more than mere professional admiration in his gargantuan bosom, and he simply could not bring himself to believe her capable of murderous betrayal . . . and yet here was the redoubtable Flashman swearing to it, so it must be true. But WHY? Fortunately she was no longer alive to tell how I'd tried to kick her into a watery grave (not that anyone would have believed her; after all, Masteeat hadn't); still, it would be best if some perfectly splendid explanation for her sudden hatred of me could be found; an explanation that would convince Speedy beyond all doubt. Napier's wouldn't wash with him, but I had one that would lay him out cold . . . so I waited until his indignant wattling had subsided, and weighed briskly in.

"'Fraid that won't answer, Sir Robert. Oh, she'd have welcomed our help in usurping her sister's crown, but she never asked me point-blank. Dare say she might have done, but as I told you, Theodore's riders pursued us, we were separated, and when I reached Masteeat's court, Uliba had made her bid and failed and been arrested –"

"With respect, Sir Harry," roars Speedy, showing no respect whatever, "we know that! But it don't answer the question why she should want you dead! Bah, it's madness! I will not believe it!" And then he gave me the cue I'd been waiting for. "What offence could you possibly have given her, to provoke such . . . such malice?"

I sat frowning, tight-lipped, for a long artistic moment, took a sip at my glass, sighed, and said: "The greatest offence in the world."

Napier's brows rose by the merest trifle, but Speedy goggled, bewildered. "What the . . . whatever d'ye mean, Sir Harry?"

I hesitated, drew a deep reluctant breath, and spoke quiet and weary, looking anywhere but at him. "If you must have it, Speedy . . . yes, your protégé Uliba-Wark was a first-class *jancada*, a brave and resolute comrade, as fine a scout and guide as I ever struck . . .

and a vain, proud, passionate, unbridled, promiscuous young savage!" What I could see of his face through the furze was showing utter consternation; he was mouthing "Promiscuous?" dumbly, so I made an impatient noise and spoke quickly.

"Oh, what the devil, she made advances, I rejected 'em, and I dare say you've heard of the fury of a woman scorned! Aye, think of Uliba, a barbarian, a cruel vixen as you've said yourself . . . scorned!" Now I looked him in the eye. "Does that answer you?"

Between ourselves, I ain't sure it would have answered me, but I'm a cynical rotter. To decent folk, the sight of bluff, straight, manly old Flashy (good-hearted, remember), badgered into saying things that shouldn't be said, dammit, traducing a woman's good name, and a dead woman at that . . . well, it's a discomforting sight. The man's so moved, and reluctant, you're bound to respect his emotions. You wouldn't dream of doubting him.

Speedy was making strange noises, and Napier answered for him. "I am sure it does."

"My . . . my dear Sir Harry!" Speedy sounded as though he'd been kicked in the essentials. "I . . . I . . . oh, I am at a loss! I . . . I know not what to say!" He didn't, either, muttering confused. "Uliba . . . so trusted . . . oh, wild, to be sure . . . but depraved? A traitress? And to attempt your life . . . wounded vanity . . ." He made vague gestures. "I can only beg your pardon for . . . oh, I did not doubt your report for a moment, I assure you!" Bloody liar. "But it seemed so impossible . . . I could not take it in . . ."

Here he ran out of words, and drew himself up, beard at the high port, shaking his great head while he clasped my hand, and I meditated on the astonishing ease with which strong men of Victorian vintage could be buffaloed into incoherent embarrassment by the mere mention of feminine frailty. Something to do with public school training, I fancy.

"My dear chap!" I clapped his arm in comradely style; it was like patting an elephant's leg. "I'm sorry, believe me. Truly sorry." Sigh. "I can guess what you feel . . . disappointment, mostly, eh? When someone lets you down . . . Well, best just to have a drink and forget it, what?"

The board of inquiry sat next day and decided that Theodore had shot himself. A reasonable conclusion, given that Blanc testified that there were powder burns in the oral cavity and the back of the head was missing, but since the report didn't mention these details, and the verdict was what Napier and Speedy wanted, I dare say that they continued to believe that mine was the hand that fired the fatal shot.

They buried Theodore next day, in the ramshackle thatched *amba* church, at the request of his sad, pretty little queen, Tooroo-Wark. I loafed along out of interest, not respect. There were only a few on hand: the Queen, the boy Alamayo, a guard of the Duke's Irish (but no saluting volley), and fat little Damash nursing a wound and terrified he'd be hanged for resisting our attack. I reassured him, and he gave a great sniff.

"And now you leave us without a king! We were born in bondage, and must die as slaves. Why do you not stay to govern?"

I told him we didn't want to, and 'twas up to him and his like to govern themselves.

"You mean we must cut each other's throats," grumbles he. "This is Africa." I told him to mind his manners and not interrupt the ancient dodderer of a priest who was gabbling the service. The corpse had been nicely wrapped, by Samuel, I believe; they shovelled it into the shallow grave, and that was the end of the heir to Solomon and Sheba and Prester John.

They like to say he was mad, as though that paid for all, but I saw him sane as well as mad, and a vile, cruel bastard he was, as foul as Caligula or Attila, and got only a tiny part of what he deserved. I remember Gondar, and the slaughter of Islamgee, and if anyone ever deserved a Hell, he did.

Meanwhile, the campaign was done, the captives free, Magdala in immense confusion with thousands of Ab fugitives to be looked after, herded down into the plain, and protected from the surrounding Gallas, who not unreasonably were athirst for a share of the loot of the *amba*. They were disappointed, for the Micks and Sappers and little Holmes of the British Museum got in first, and the Gallas were dispersed by rifle fire, which I thought a mite hard, since their blockade had been so vital to our success. As to the loot, I heard there was a fair amount of precious stuff picked up, but most of it was bought up by the prize-master and sent down to Arogee on the elephants.[57]

For once – and for the only time in my experience of sixty years' soldiering in heaven knows how many campaigns – there was no butcher's bill. We hadn't lost a man in storming Magdala, just seventeen wounded, and with only two dead at Arogee and one careless chap who shot himself accidentally on the march up,[58] I doubt if we had more than half a dozen fatalities in the whole campaign, mortally sick included. If there were nothing else to testify to Napier's genius, that casualty return alone would do, for I never heard of its like in war.[59]

I spent only one night on the Magdala *amba*, for the place was as foul as a midden, and became a positive bedlam when the looters discovered a great cache of *tej* in the royal cellar. Private Shaughnessy and his chums came calling, eager to pay their respects and inquire after my health, Sorr Harry man, dear – it's hell to be popular with the riff-raff. So after seeing Theodore planted, I took a mule down to Napier's head-quarters at Arogee, and found myself a billet with Charlie Fraser, who commanded the staff and was colonel in my old regiment, the 11th Cherrypickers. Not that it was much quieter there, for there were upwards of thirty thousand Abs about the place, warriors as well as civilians who'd fled from Magdala. Among them were the two queens, Tooroo-Wark and Tamagno, and their retinues, and nearly three hundred of Theodore's political prisoners, princes and chiefs, who'd been in the *amba*'s jails. Some of 'em had been in captivity for fifteen or twenty years, and one for more than thirty.

I'd been lucky. The great tyrant had held me for less than a week, and now it was all over, the captains and the queens would shortly be departing,[60] and I could rest content at last with only a mild ache in my calf, and take my ease after dangers and hardships nobly borne, resigned to endure the discomfort of a ride to the coast, followed by a tranquil voyage home at H.M.G.'s expense. You've come through again, old lad, thinks I; no public credit, perhaps, but Napier's right, you ain't short in that line. Half a million in silver through your hands, and not a penny of it to bless yourself with, but what o' that? Elspeth and I had enough between us . . . and the mere thought of her name brought the glorious realisation that in a few short weeks I'd be reunited with all that glorious milk-white goodness that had been lying fallow (I hoped, but with her you never could tell) while I'd been wasting myself on Mexican trollops and suety frauleins and black barbarians. I could close my eyes and see her, taste her red lips, inhale the perfume of her blonde curls . . . oh, the blazes with gallivanting about the world, I was for home for good this time, and the sooner Napier broke camp and marched north, the better.

At that, he stayed not upon the order of his going. With Theodore dead, Abyssinia was without a ruler, and while Napier was adamant that the succession was no business of ours, he felt bound to settle the possession of Magdala itself, and ensure the safety of its inhabitants – that, he insisted, was a matter of national honour. But Magdala was the first horn of his dilemma: it lay in Galla territory, but Theodore had captured and held it for ten years as a bulwark against Muslim encroachment on Christian Abyssinia, and Napier didn't want to change that. So it was decided to offer the *amba* to Gobayzy of Lasta, the closest available Christian monarch. From all I'd heard, he was a sorry muffin, but it was no concern of mine, although I'd have given the place to Masteeat, for old gallops' sake. She had the same notion, as did Warkite, her elder sister and rival for the supreme monarchy of all the Galla tribes; with Uliba now singing in the choir invisible they were the only claimants to the throne, and sure enough, within two days of the fall of Magdala, up they rolled to Arogee to state their cases.

Warkite was first to arrive, a plain, querulous creature but not quite the witch-like crone I'd been led to expect. Her handicap was that while Masteeat had a son who'd make a king some day, Warkite's boy had been murdered by Theodore, and though she had a grandson, he was reputed illegitimate. She'd been consorting with Menelek, King of Shoa, the despised "fat boy" who had once laid siege to Magdala but lost his nerve and turned tail when it was at his mercy. Now, she made a poor impression on Napier, lamenting her misfortunes, railing against Masteeat, and looking less regal by the minute.

Napier asked Speedy and me aside what we thought. I said that if it came to a war Masteeat would eat her alive, having the men, the brains, and the will. Speedy agreed, adding that Masteeat had turned up trumps against Theodore, and should be recognised Queen of Galla, whoever had Magdala.

So that was Warkite for the workhouse. When Napier asked if she couldn't be reconciled with her sister, she let out a great screeching laugh and cried that if they made peace today, Masteeat would betray her tomorrow. Word came just then that Masteeat was expected hourly, and Warkite was off like a rising grouse, never to be seen again.

I confess I was looking forward to my Lion Queen's arrival, and she came in style, with an entourage of warriors and servants, sashaying along under a great brolly borne by minions, her imposing bulk magnificent in silks of every colour, festooned with jewellery, a turban with an aigret swathing her braids, and bearing a silver-mounted sceptre. The whole staff were on hand to gape at her, and she acknowledged them with a beaming smile and queenly inclinations, head high and hand extended in regal fashion as Napier came to greet her. She was overwhelming, and for a moment I thought he'd kiss her hand, but he checked in time and gave her a stiff bow, hat in hand.

He was about to present his staff when she gave a great whoop of "*Basha Fallaka*!" at the sight of Speedy, while I was favoured with a sleepy smile but no sign at all of recognition; since the last time we'd met had been at the gallop on the floor of her dining-room, I thought her demeanour was in quite the best taste, friendly but entirely decorous. To the others she was all dignified affability, being still sober. Napier clearly was impressed, and as Speedy remarked to me: "There's our Queen of all Galla, what?"

They gave her dinner, and she entranced and appalled the company by laying into the goods like a starving python; as Stanley reported: "She ate like a *gourmande*, disposing of what came before her without regard to the horrified looks ... pudding before beef, blancmange with potatoes ... emitting labial smacks like pistol cracks." She also drank like a fish, shouting with laughter, more boisterous and vulgar with every draught ... and no one, even Napier, seemed to mind a bit. It may have been her exotic novelty, or her undoubted sexual attraction, or simply the good nature that shone out of her, but I think there was also a recognition that despite her gross manners she was altogether too formidable to be over-looked.[61]

Speedy and I were the only ones present who could talk to her directly without an interpreter, and when she'd spoken with him a few minutes alone over the coffee, she beckoned me to take his place beside her. Watching her across the table during the meal, I'd been bound to wonder what she knew of the fate of Uliba-Wark, if anything, and if she might refer to it; now, she did, but in a most roundabout way, and to this day I can only guess how she came to learn what befell on that ghastly night. Perhaps some Galla escaped the massacre; I can only repeat what she said after I had filled her cup with *tej*, and she had gulped it down, wiped her lips with the tail of her turban, and smiled her fat-cheeked saucy smile.

"The *Basha Fallaka* says I am to have my fifty thousand dollars. Your *Dedjaz* Napier – what a fine and courtly man he is! – has pledged his word. But", she pouted and took another swig, "he does not say whether I am to have Magdala." She looked a question.

"If my word goes for anything, you will. But you know it's been offered to Gobayzy."

She giggled maliciously. "Gobayzy will shudder away like a

283

frightened bride! What, accept an *amba* surrounded by my warriors? He'd sweat his fat carcase to a shadow at the mere thought. No, he will refuse, beyond doubt."

"Then Magdala's yours, lion lady. There is no one else."

She nodded, sipped and wiped again, and sat for a moment. Then she spoke quietly: "Uliba-Wark is at peace now. My little Uliba, who loved and hated me. Perhaps she loved and hated you also. I do not know and I do not ask." She took another sip and set down her cup. "You were there when she died. No, do not tell me of it. Some things are better not known. Enough that she is at peace."

That was all she said to me, and I saw her only once more, on the following day outside her splendid silk pavilion, when Gobayzy sent word that he was honoured by the offer of Magdala, but on the whole he'd rather not. So the *amba* was hers, says Napier, but she must understand that he was bound to destroy its defences and burn all its buildings, to mark the disapproval (that was the word he used, so help me) of its late ruler's conduct in daring to imprison and maltreat British citizens. She assured him that fire could only purify the place, and departed with her retinue, borne in a *palki* and smiling graciously on the troops who cheered her away.

The same afternoon Magdala was set on fire. The King's Own had it cleared of its last inhabitants by four o'clock, the Sappers and Miners had laid their charges, and presently in a series of thunderous explosions the gates and defences were blown up, the last of the cannon destroyed, and the whole ramshackle town with its thatched palaces and prisons and houses put to the torch. It went up in a series of fiery jets which the wind levelled in a great rushing of flame which, as Stanley says, turned the whole top of the *amba* with its three thousand buildings into a huge lake of fire. The whole army watched, and I heard a fellow say that Hell must look like that, but he was wrong; the Summer Palace burning, that was Hell, wonderful beauty smashed and consumed in a mighty holocaust; Magdala was a vermin-ridden pest-hole which its dwellers had been only too glad to leave.

Indeed, they couldn't get far enough away from it, and it was a swarming multitude tens of thousands strong, men, women, *chicos*, beasts and all their paraphernalia, that set off from Arogee that same day, down the defile to the Bechelo; that was Napier's other great concern, to see them safe beyond the reach of the Galla marauders who'd been denied the plunder of Magdala and were itching to make up for it at the expense of the fugitives. Our troops rode herd on them the whole way, but Napier would run no risks, and had cavalry patrols escort them for another twenty miles beyond the river.

The next day, the eighteenth, the army set off north, with the Sherwood Foresters leading the way, their band thumping out "When Johnny Comes Marching Home Again" and "Brighton Camp", and behind them the Native Infantry sepoys swinging along followed by the jingling troopers, the Scindees and lancers and Dragoon Guards, and behind them the guns and the matlows of the Naval Brigade, and last of all the 33rd, the Irish hooligans of the Duke of Wellington's, the long khaki column winding down the defile, dirty, bedraggled, tired, and happy, catching the drift of the music on the air and joining in:

> I seek no more the fine and gay,
> They serve but to remind me,
> How swift the hours did pass away
> With the girl I left behind me

Napier sat his horse by the track, with Speedy and Charlie Fraser and Merewether and myself, watching them go by, and how they roared and cheered and waved their helmets at the sight of him, the old Bughunter who'd taken them there against all the odds and now was taking them back again. He smiled and nodded and raised his hat to them, looking ever so old and weary but content, turning in his saddle to gaze back at those three massive peaks where he'd wrought his military miracle – Selassie and Fala gilded in the morning sun, and beyond them Magdala like a huge smouldering volcano, the plume of black smoke towering up into the cloudless sky.

"Going home now, gentlemen," says he, and Merewether said something about a great feat of arms, and how the country would acclaim the army and its leader. Napier said he guessed the Queen and the people would be pleased, and H.M.G. also, no doubt, "but you may be sure it will not be all unalloyed satisfaction. It never is."

Speedy wasn't having that. "Why, Sir Robert, who can complain except a few miserable croakers – no doubt the same Jeremiahs who swore the campaign was doomed in the first place – and now they'll carp about the cost? As though such a thing was to be fought on the cheap with a scratch army and fleet! They've had it at bargain rates!'

"I doubt if the Treasury will agree with you," laughs Napier, in high spirits. "No, I was thinking rather of the wiseacres in the clubs and newspapers who will find fault with us for doing no more than we were sent to do: rescue our countrymen. I dare say there will be voices raised in the House demanding to know why we have left a savage country in confusion and civil war –"

"Which is how it was for centuries before we came!" cries Charlie. "And the Ethiopian can't change his skin, can he? He'll go murdering whether we're here or not!"

"The Chief's right, though," says Merewether. "There's bound to be an outcry because we're not leaving a garrison to pacify the tribes and police the country – oh, and distribute tracts to folk who were Christian before we were! As though Abyssinia were a country to be pacified and ruled with fewer than ten divisions and a great civil power!"

"Which would call for an expenditure of many millions, far more than we have spent – and with no hope of return." Napier was smiling as he said it, but I wondered if some hint of censure had already reached him from home. They'd given him a free hand, and he hadn't stinted.

"And if we were to occupy the confounded place, Mr Gladstone would never forgive us!" says Merewether. "What, enlarge the empire, bring indigenous peoples to subjection, and exploit them for our profit! Rather not!"

There was general laughter at this, and Napier said with his quiet smile that we must resign ourselves to being regarded as callously irresponsible or rapaciously greedy. "Brutal indifference or selfish imperialism; those are the choices. As an old Scotch maidservant of my acquaintance used to say: 'Ye canna dae right for daein' wrang!'"[62]

More laughter, and Charlie said, well, thank goodness at least no one could complain that there had been dreadful slaughter of helpless aborigines by the weapons of civilisation. "'Twasn't our fault jolly old Theodore kicked the bucket!" he added. Merewether said thank goodness for that, and I could feel the uneasy silence of Napier and Speedy. No doubt it was out of consideration for me that Napier checked his mount until I was alongside, and then says cheerily: "You're very silent, Harry. Have you no philosophic reflections on the campaign? No views on what should or should not be done now that it's over?"

I glanced back at the smoke rising from Magdala like some huge genie escaping from his bottle, and then at the long dusty column of horse, foot, and guns swinging down the defile. And I thought of that hellish beautiful land and its hellish beautiful people, of Yando's cage and the horrors of Gondar, of bandit treasure aswarm with scorpions, of the terrifying thunder of descent into a watery maelstrom, of a raving lunatic slaughtering helpless captives, of fighting women drunk on massacre, of a graceful she-devil aglow with love and ice-cold in hate ... and was finally aware of the gently smiling old soldier waiting for an answer as we rode in sunlight down from Arogee.

"My views, sir? Can't think I have many ... oh, I don't know, though. Wouldn't mind suggesting to Her Majesty's ministers that next time they get a letter from a touchy barbarian despot, it might save 'em a deal of trouble and expense if they sent him a civil reply by return of post ..."

[*On which characteristically caustic note
the twelfth packet of the Flashman Papers
comes to an end.*]

APPENDIX I:

The Road to Magdala

Perhaps because it was so unusual, perhaps because it was such a triumph, the Abyssinian War has attracted an embarrassment of authors, who have covered every aspect of the campaign. Holland and Hozier's official report is the main source work, dealing with everything from the overall narrative of operations to the rates of pay of native water-carriers; Blanc and Rassam have described the experiences of the prisoners, and the march has been covered in detail by Stanley, Henty, C. R. Markham's *History of the Abyssinian Expedition*, 1869, A. F. Shepherd's *The Campaign in Abyssinia*, 1868, and others. But for those who would like good shorter works by later historians, they cannot do better than Frederick Myatt's *The March to Magdala*, 1970, and Moorehead's *The Blue Nile*, which in its portrait of the river and its history includes an account of Napier's march. The *Diary* of William Simpson of the *Illustrated London News* has been previously mentioned, and one cannot omit the week by week coverage which that paper gave to the campaign, with excellent illustrations.

Finally, whoever wishes to understand events which led up to the war, and the history of the country in which it was fought, will find Frank R. Cana's essay in the Eleventh Edition of the *Encyclopedia Britannica*, 1910, most helpful, while Percy Arnold's *Prelude to Magdala*, 1991, is invaluable as a detailed and authoritative work on the diplomatic preliminaries to the war.

APPENDIX II:

Theodore and Napier

It is curious that although Flashman's involvement in the war was peripheral, he probably knew Theodore, the man in the eye of the storm, better than anyone except perhaps Rassam and Speedy. He is also the foremost authority for those remarkable sister-queens, Masteeat and the mysterious Uliba-Wark, and for the conduct of the Galla part of the campaign. No one saw the Abyssinian side of the crisis as closely as Flashman.

Trying to make sense of the Emperor is really a waste of time. He is beyond the reach of psychiatrists and psychologists, and even if he were not it is doubtful if they could understand let alone explain him. Flashman does not try, and one can say only that his portrait of Theodore, drawn at close range if on brief acquaintance, tallies closely with those which have come to us from Blanc, Rassam, and other contemporary authorities. Almost all the thoughts and ideas, and even the very words, which Flashman attributes to him, are to be found elsewhere, in the reports of other witnesses, and in Theodore's own letters. His massively split personality, his wild swings of mood, his periods of rational, even light-hearted conversation contrasted with his ungovernable rages, his benevolent impulses, his evident urge to self-destruction, his drunkenness, his restless energy, his undoubted abilities, and his truly devilish wickedness – all these things which Flashman describes are echoes of what others saw in this strange, gifted, proud, and all too horrible man.

For when all's said, when his undoubted virtues have been admitted, his courage, his generosity, his patriotism, his educated intelligence, his devotion to his faith, his military prowess and personal attractions ("the best shot, the best spearman, the best runner, the best horseman in Abyssinia"), and when allowance has been made for the difficulties he faced in trying to rule an ungovernable country, the provocations to a haughty spirit inflicted by British bad manners, the crippling loss of his adored wife and best friends, and the intoxicating effect of absolute power – after all this, there is no escape from the conclusion that Theodore of Abyssinia was a monster to rank with the worst in history.

His atrocities, his slaughters and tortures and mass executions, his deliberate sadistic orgies carried out in cold blood as well as hot, are well attested, and leave one with the same dumfounded horror produced by the first pictures of Belsen, the same disbelief that human beings can do such things, and inevitably one falls back on the word applied to the Hitlers and Stalins and Ivans and Attilas: madness.

It is a useless term, of course. Whether Theodore was clinically certifiable or not is beside the point; he was mad in any usual sense of the word. The difficulty, for the layman at any rate, is that he was also undoubtedly sane, at least occasionally. His early life, if stained with the ruthlessness and cruelty which later became obsessive, was in other ways a model of enlightened rule. He tried to abolish slavery and reform taxation, but given the anarchy prevailing in the country, and the difficulty of controlling his defeated rivals, his efforts to drag the country out of its medieval state were bound to fail. His ambitions, his vision of himself as a crusader of destiny who would rebuild the Abyssinian empire and extend it to Jerusalem, proved to be his undoing, and he made a mistake which was to prove his ruin by making war on the Wollo Gallas in an attempt to convert them to Christianity. He won Magdala, and by his murderous cruelty created the mortal enemy who would help Napier to bring him down.

His reputation has been so appalling that it has caused a kind of reaction, and he has had, if not apologists, at least compassionate writers trying to understand him. Alan Moorehead, for example, writes of the accepted view that he was a mad dog let loose, but adds that while this was true in many ways, the appalling reputation does not fit him absolutely. "A touch of nobility intervenes." Describing Theodore as an elemental figure defying destiny, he goes on to say that "if one can overlook his brutalities for a moment, one can see that he was an utterly displaced person, a Caliban with power but none to guide him; he had no place." Unfortunately the brutalities cannot be overlooked, and any attempt to make sense of Theodore can only end in the simple banal conclusion that there was real evil in the heart of him, and that the best thing he did in his life was to end it.

Flashman's précis of his early years, and of the causes and course of his quarrel with Britain, are accurate so far as they go, and for those who seek more detail, or are interested in Theodore as a case for the consulting room couch, the works cited in the Notes will be of interest.

* * *

ROBERT CORNELIS NAPIER (1810–1890) was born in Ceylon into one of the great military families. He entered Addiscombe, the East India Company College, when he was 14, was commissioned into the Royal Engineers, and in half a century of soldiering built a reputation second to none in the Victorian army. He and Flashman had served together in the First Sikh War, the Indian Mutiny, and the China War of 1860, and Flashman is hardly exaggerating when he credits his friend with "half the canals and most of the roads" in Northern India. For Napier's engineering was quite as distinguished as his fighting record; he was a friend of Brunel and Stephenson, and when he was forced to take three years' leave after a serious illness when he was only 20, he spent much of it studying railway and canal building. He was a fine landscape and portrait painter, and at the age of 78 was still taking lessons in colour mixing. He was also a geologist and student of fossils, and a Fellow of the

Royal Society, which may be why Flashman christened him the Bughunter.

Napier's service record is too long and varied to set down in detail, but Flashman has given a succinct and fair sketch of a life which was all the more remarkable for Napier's struggle with ill-health resulting from wounds and hardship. Few general officers before or since have seen more close-quarter action, which was one reason why he was so well regarded by his soldiers, British and Indian; another was the close interest he took in their welfare out of the line as well as in it; he encouraged physical fitness and rec-reation, presented prizes for shooting, and as Commander-in-Chief in India instituted a weekly holiday every Thursday, which came to be known as St Napier's Day.

Indeed, he seems to have been an unusually nice man, pleasant, courteous, and modest to a fault. Flashman, who seldom has much good to say of his commanders, not only admired him but liked him, too, and remembers, as everyone seems to have done, the gentle voice and sudden brilliant smile.

He and his army received a hero's welcome home from Abyssinia, and he was created Baron Napier of Magdala. A more unusual honour, perhaps, was the double eulogy he received from both Disraeli and Gladstone, the latter concluding his tribute by speaking of gratitude, admiration, respect, and regard – "I would almost say with affection for the man."

On retirement he became Governor of Gibraltar, a field-marshal, and Constable of the Tower. He received a state funeral, the most impressive since Wellington's, and is buried in St Paul's Cathedral. His statue stands in Waterloo Place, London. (H. D. Napier, *Field-Marshal Lord Napier of Magdala,* 1927; H. M. Vibart, *Addiscombe: Its Heroes and Men of Note,* 1894.)

APPENDIX III:

Abyssinian Names

In the Explanatory Note mention was made of Flashman's wild inconsistency in spelling Abyssinian names. He was not alone. When the Abyssinian campaign began, virtually no proper names of places or people were known outside the country, and everyone writing about it seems simply to have pleased himself; thus we hear of Theodore's Queen as Tooroo-Wark, Teriwark, Teru-Wark, Terunsheh, Terunish, and even Terenachie; his second "queen-concubine", whom Flashman calls Tamagno, is also Yetemagnu and Itamanya; his valet Wald Gabr is also Welder Gabre. The same is true of place-names, so I have simply chosen the spellings which Flashman uses most often. Rather more serious are the discrepancies in maps of the period, and here again I have used Flashman's own crude sketch, which differs no more from the rest than they do from each other. It seems right and proper that the word "Abyssinia" means "confusion", or so I am told.

NOTES

1. It is not entirely clear why the Maria Theresa dollar was so popular. Speedicut suggests that its silver was of unusual purity, but Samuel Baker, the hunter and explorer, noted that the effigy of the Empress "with a very low dress and a profusion of bust, is, I believe, the charm that suits the Arab taste." (*The Nile Tributaries of Abyssinia*, 1867). [p. 3]

2. "Dickey", meaning shaky or uncertain, has a currency of centuries, but "in Dickie's meadow", meaning in serious trouble is, or was, a North Cumbrian expression, and it has been suggested (fancifully, no doubt) that since Richard III was in his younger days Warden of the West March with his head-quarters in Carlisle, where he is commemorated in one of the city's principal streets, Rickergate, the proverbial "meadow" may have been Bosworth Field. [p. 3]

3. The mystery of Flashman's service in the French Foreign Legion remains unsolved. It may have been after the U.S. Civil War, before his enlistment with Maximilian, or at some earlier date in North Africa, as references elsewhere in the Papers suggest. This is the first time desertion is mentioned, but without time and place. One thing is clear: he must have made his peace with the French authorities before 1877, the year in which he was awarded the Legion of Honour. [p. 4]

4. Flashman is recalling another service to the Austrian royal family, when he foiled a plot by Hungarian nationalists to assassinate the Emperor Franz-Josef at his hunting lodge in Bad Ischl in 1883. He was rewarded with the Order of Maria Theresa and a waltz with the Empress Elisabeth. (See *Flashman and the Tiger.*) [p. 5]

5. No doubt Flashman's Mexican papers will have more to say of this remarkable and rather mysterious adventuress. All that we know of her origins is that she was probably American and had been a circus bareback rider before she met and married Prince Felix Salm-Salm, a German soldier of fortune, when he was serving in the U.S. Civil War. After the war the Salms' taste for excitement took them to Mexico, where Felix became Maximilian's chief a.d.c. and Flashman's colleague. The three were involved in efforts to rescue the Emperor before his execution, and Princess Agnes has left some account of these in her *Ten Years of my Life* (1868), the frontispiece of which shows a handsome, striking lady of obvious intelligence and determination. Aside from these facts, and what Flashman writes of her, the only other detail that

we have is that she owned a pet dog, Jimmy, who was her constant companion. (See *Flashman and the Tiger*, and *Maximilian's Lieutenant, A Personal History of the Mexican Campaign, 1864–7* by Ernst Pitner, tr. and edited by Gordon Etherington-Smith, 1993.) [p. 6]

6. Details of the Emperor Maximilian's last voyage may be found in newspapers of the day, and there is an excellent account in the *Illustrated London News*. Needless to say, Flashman has the ceremonial off pat, even to the curious triple coffin and the waterfront procession. [p. 9]

7. There must have been 250 of these boxes, each containing 2000 dollars, according to the cash account of the Treasury Officer to the expedition. [p. 12]

8. A Bootneck or Leatherneck is a Royal Marine, supposedly so-called from the leather tab securing the uniform collar in the nineteenth century, or possibly from the leather neck-stock. Leatherneck was adopted as a nickname for the U.S. Marines early in the twentieth century. Royal Marines were also known as Jollies, which according to Eric Partridge was once the nickname of the London Trained Bands. [p. 12]

9. Work on the Suez Canal, the brainchild of the French diplomat Ferdinand de Lesseps, began in 1859, and the waterway was opened to navigation in 1869. It had cost almost £30 million, and in 1875 Disraeli acquired 176,602 shares for £4 million, giving Britain a 44% holding. The canal was indeed built by what amounted to slavery, the forced labour (*corvee*) of the Egyptian peasants being enforced by the rawhide whip of the overseers (*courbash*). (John Marlowe, *The Making of the Suez Canal*, 1964.) [p. 16]

10. In fact, Flashman's consignment of dollars was a modest part of Napier's "war-chest", about one-ninth. The financial accounts of the expedition show a total of 4,530,000 dollars paid in numerous instalments up to May 14, 1868, which the accountants estimated as equivalent to £969,343.15.0, but these were only the shipments of silver; the total cost of the expedition was far higher. Disraeli, the Chancellor, originally asked the House of Commons for £2 million, with a further £1.5 million in the following year if the campaign was protracted; eventually the total cost was close to £9 million, a vast sum which appalled Parliament. In fairness to Disraeli, it was impossible to tell what such an expedition into unknown territory would cost; on the other hand, there was tremendous waste, partly because Napier was given carte blanche and gave no thought to economy. (See "Supply of Treasure and Financial Arrangements" in volume 1 of the official history, *Record of the Expedition to Abyssinia* by Major T. J. Holland and Captain H. M. Hozier, 1870; *Prelude to Magdala* by Percy Arnold, 1991.) [p. 16]

11. This version of the Red Sea crossing by the Children of Israel is also to be found in *Harper's Hand-book for Travellers in Europe and the East*, 1871 edition, a guide for American tourists compiled by W. Pembroke Fetridge. [p. 16]

12. Seedeboy, sidiboy, Anglo-Indian slang for an African, usually a labourer (see Kipling, *The Lost Legion*, "We've starved on a Seedeboy's pay"). Eric Partridge points out, in his *Dictionary of Slang and Unconventional English*, the irony that the word derives from *sidi*, a lord. [p. 20]

13. Flashman's memory is playing him false. He may well have seen, in late January, 1868, the cartoon of Theodore, as well as *Punch*'s complaint about the cost of the expedition, since these appeared in early December, 1867, but the suggestion of exhibiting the Emperor in a cage is from *Punch* of May, 1868, when the campaign was over. [p. 21]

14. Flashman's experience of Abyssinia was brief, barely more than two months in which he saw comparatively little of the country and its people. What he did see he reported with his usual accuracy, and his descriptions of costume and racial characteristics are borne out by contemporary artists. His enthusiasm for the beauty of the people, especially the women of Galla, is shared by other travellers. Most early descriptions of the country dwell at length on its churches, and religious customs and artefacts, some of which are strange to European Christians, but while Flashman has little interest in these, his notice of curiosities is reliable. The *Illustrated London News* drawings are invaluable, as is J. C. Hotten's *Abyssinia and Its People*, 1868, an anthology drawn from every traveller of note up to that time, including the first British Consul, Plowden, King Theodore's friend and adviser. [p. 24]

15. James Bruce (1730–94) was indeed something of an eccentric, a scholar, traveller, businessman, linguist, antiquary, and the first of a distinguished line of Scottish explorers in Africa. Born in Stirlingshire and educated at Harrow, he was a splendid athlete and horseman, six feet four inches tall, red-haired, reckless, combative, and "swayed to an undue degree by self-esteem and the thirst for fame". In the course of an adventurous life Bruce was British Consul at Algiers, a perilous post when the Barbary pirates were still active, survived shipwreck by swimming ashore at Benghazi, explored Abyssinia and reached the source of the Blue Nile, won the confidence of the royal family (and the admiration of a beautiful princess) by using his amateur medical skill to treat smallpox and the plague, and astonished the warriors by showing them how to break wild horses and by his marksmanship. "His intrepid bearing and his great physical strength and agility fitted him," says his biographer, "to overawe a barbarous people."

His own countrymen were less easily impressed, and his account of his adventures was disbelieved by the educated (and caused some scandal) although it sold well in book form. Bruce's overbearing style and touchiness were no help, and Fanny Burney noted that "his grand air, gigantic height, and forbidding brow awed everybody into silence." He retired to Scotland in dudgeon, and died when, hurrying to show a lady to her carriage, he tripped and fell downstairs, landing head first, and never regained consciousness. Since his death virtually everything that he related about Abyssinia has been proved to be true. (James Bruce, *Travels to Discover the Source of the Nile in the Years 1768–73;* Dictionary of National Biography; Margery Perham and J. Simmons, *African Discovery*, 1942) [p. 24]

16. The Prince of Wales, later Edward VII, married Princess Alexandra of Denmark on March 10, 1863. Other matters which may have commanded the Foreign Office's attention about this time were the Greek Assembly's election of Prince Alfred, Queen Victoria's second son, as King of Greece

(an honour which was declined); the division of Poland into provinces by Russia; Maori risings in New Zealand, and the advance of French troops on Mexico City which led to the installation of Maximilian as emperor. [p. 25]

17. Public pessimism was such that Holland and Hozier devoted space to it in their official report. Letters to editors "drew ghastly pictures of the malaria of the coast and the insalubrity of the country. At one time the expedition was to die of thirst, at one time to be destroyed by hippopotami. Every beast antagonistic to the life of man was . . . to be found in the jungles or the swamps. Animals were to perish by flies, men by worms. The return of the expedition was regarded as chimerical, the massacre of the prisoners as certain." The report also noted the "merciless" rise in insurance companies' rates for officers volunteering, "who were regarded as rushing blindfold into suicide." But competition for places was fierce, and newspapers were besieged by would-be special correspondents. [p. 27]

18. The 33rd Foot were the Duke of Wellington's Regiment, also known as the West Yorkshires, but consisting largely of Irishmen, and notoriously ill-disciplined. But they were to be, with the 4th Foot (King's Own), and the 45th (Sherwood Foresters), the vanguard of Napier's force. [p. 30]

19. George Alfred ("G.A.") Henty (1832–1902) shares with R. M. Ballantyne the leading place among writers for boys. He was born in Trumpington, educated at Westminster and Cambridge, and volunteered for hospital service in the Crimean War. This led to his appointment as organiser of the Italian hospitals in the 1859 war with Austria, but after a brief interval in which he worked as a mine manager in Wales and Sardinia, he returned to his first love, military journalism, and for ten years followed the drum with Garibaldi in the Tyrol, Napier in Abyssinia, Wolseley in Ashanti, the Russians at Khiva, and the Turks in the Serbian war of 1876. He covered the winter campaign in the Franco-Prussian war, was in Paris during the Commune, and in Spain with the guerrillas in the Carlist rebellion. Most of his work was for the *Standard*, but eventually the strain of campaigning told on his health and he devoted himself to more sedentary writing.

Henty's boys' stories were hugely popular, and in them he covered a vast range, mostly of military and naval campaigns, skilfully blending juvenile derring-do with well-researched background. As a typical Victorian, imbued with patriotic pride and holding by straight and sturdy old-fashioned values, he is well out of step with modern fashionable thought, but even today his books, antique in style and outlook though they are, can be of great value to the student of history. He was a good writer with a fine descriptive gift, and can give a more vivid and convincing picture of a period and its people than most academic historians; as an example I would cite his *In Times of Peril*, in which he brought day-to-day experience of the Indian Mutiny to life for his young readers – and not a few older ones. The late John Paul Getty owned a complete set of Henty, and was said to read them over and over again.

Henty's memoir of the Abyssinian War, *The March to Magdala*, was published in 1868. [p. 30]

20. This implied criticism does less than justice to Brigadier-General (later Sir) William Merewether, who was one of the stars of the expedition. An experienced frontier fighter in India, where he served in the Scinde Horse (Flashman's "Scindees") he was also a shrewd and decisive political officer, and was agent at Aden when the Abyssinian crisis arose. It was as a result of his urgings that a reply to Theodore's letter was eventually sent, and he kept in constant touch with the prisoners. He carried out the first reconnaissance and chose Zoola as the beachhead, and as political officer was in charge of intelligence for the expedition. [p. 34]

21. There is little to add to Flashman's description and assessment of Captain Charles Speedy except to note that he was in fact six feet six inches in height and broad in proportion. A splendid picture of him in full Abyssinian costume is held by the Army Museums Ogilby Trust; he is indeed an overpowering sight. [p. 35]

22. This suggests that a much greater quantity of silver was carried up to Napier with Flashman's party than the contents of a single strong-box. Half a dozen riders would hardly be needed to carry 2000 dollars, large coins though they were. [p. 36]

23. The flogging of the driver caused understandable indignation, but whether the Rev. Johann Krapf was responsible is unclear. He was an old Abyssinian "hand" with a great affection for the country, and it was for his long experience of Africa that he was enrolled in the expedition. He was apparently the first explorer to report snow in Africa, on Mount Kilimanjaro. [p. 43]

24. The popular fame of Sir Henry Morton Stanley (1841–1904) rests on his memorable greeting to Dr Livingstone, and to a lesser extent on his African exploration, but he was also a first-class reporter, and his despatches from the campaigns which he covered for the *New York Herald* put him in the first rank of war correspondents. Born John Rowlands in Denbigh, Wales, he ran away from a workhouse, sailed to America as a cabin boy, and was adopted by a New Orleans merchant named Stanley. He served on both sides in the U.S. Civil War, and then became a journalist, covering the Abyssinian War, the Ashanti War, and the opening of the Suez Canal; his explorations included his finding Livingstone and leading an expedition to relieve Emin Pasha, who was "Chinese" Gordon's governor of the Equatorial province of Sudan. Whether Emin or Livingstone needed or wanted to be found is a point still debated. Stanley settled back in Britain, was knighted, and was Unionist M.P. for Lambeth, 1895–1900. His account of the Abyssinian campaign, in *Coomassie and Magdala* (1874), is racy, colourful, packed with good detail, and essential for any study of the expedition.

    Captain Speedy's anxiety is a tribute to Stanley's reporting skill, but it is not clear why he refers to him as "the Chicago wallah" when Stanley was working for a New York paper. [p. 47]

25. George Broadfoot and Lord Elgin, Flashman's political chiefs in the Punjab and China respectively. [p. 58]

26. Napier was married twice. His first wife, by whom he had three sons and three daughters, died in 1849, and he married his second wife, Mary Cecilia

Scott, in 1861, when he was 50 and she was 18. According to Alan Moorehead, "She appears to have run his household in Bombay – and it was an entertaining household where good dinners were served and French was spoken – with something of her husband's air of quiet authority." They had six sons and three daughters. (Moorehead, *The Blue Nile,* 1962.) [p. 58]

27. Speedy here is referring to the Blue Nile, which flows from Lake Tana south-eastwards before looping west and north-west to join the White Nile at Khartoum in the Sudan. James Bruce reached the source of the Blue Nile in 1770 and supposed he had reached the source of the main Nile river, but this (the White Nile) was not conclusively identified until 1860–2 when John Hanning Speke and James Grant traced its course from Lake Victoria, which Speke had discovered some years before. Grant served as a political officer on Napier's Abyssinian expedition. (See also Note to p. 131.) [p. 61]

28. Several members of the expedition mention the lady in the tower as a mysterious figure, but there is much disagreement about her and the whereabouts of her captive husband. To one writer she is a "princess" whose husband is held by Kussai of Tigre; Stanley and another name the captor as King Theodore himself; Holland and Hozier's official account agrees with Flashman that the persecutor is Gobayzy of Lasta. She is also variously described as "high-born and disconsolate", "inconsolable", and pining away her life "in incessant grief and pinching poverty"; there is general agreement about her vow of seclusion in her tower. Only Flashman gives her a name and personal description, and since he knew her intimately and none of the others seems even to have seen her, readers may be inclined to accept his account as authoritative. (Henty, Stanley, Holland and Hozier, and William Simpson, *Diary of a Journey to Abyssinia, 1868.* Simpson was a journalist and artist with the *Illustrated London News* whose diary has been edited and annotated by Richard Pankhurst, 2002.) [p. 63]

29. Flashman does not exaggerate. Mr St John is an enthusiast whose observations are to be found in Hotten's *Abyssinia and Its People* (see Note to p. 24). [p. 78]

30. Readers of the Flashman Papers do not need to be told that his one real talent (aside from his boasted expertise with horses and women) was for languages. He was a brilliant linguist and an unusually quick study, often mastering a language in weeks; he was being modest in telling Napier that he could "scratch by" in a dozen but was fluent in only six, and it is not surprising that he quickly acquired enough Amharic for simple conversation. It has been the Abyssinian language since the late Middle Ages, when it replaced Ge'ez, the tongue of those Semitic people who crossed from Arabia to Ethiopia long ago. Ge'ez means literally "the free" and was applied to the people also; it is still used for liturgical purposes. An expert on Ethiopian languages, E. Ullendorf, says that Amharic bears the same kind of relationship to Ge'ez as French does to Latin. (See E. Ullendorf, *Exploration and Study of Abyssinia,* 1945.) [p. 102]

31. "Palmer's Vesuvians", a patent match which burned with a sputtering flame, a favourite with cigar smokers. [p. 109]

32. The atrocities described by Uliba-Wark are all well attested; indeed they are only part of the catalogue of horrors to be found in the histories written by two of the prisoners held by Theodore: *Narrative of the British Mission to Theodore of Ethiopia* by Hormuzd Rassam, 2 vols, 1869, and *A Narrative of the Captivity in Abyssinia*, 1868, by Dr Henry Blanc. These are two of the most essential works on the Abyssinian War, and between them give a graphic and detailed picture not only of the privations of their imprisonment, and of the plotting and politicking which took place between them and their captors, but are invaluable for their portraits of Theodore himself. They will be referred to frequently in these Notes. [p. 111]

33. Flashman is almost certainly referring to the First Sikh War of 1845–6 and the China War of 1860, which he has described in *Flashman and the Mountain of Light* and *Flashman and the Dragon*. [p. 111]

34. The yellow scorpions of the genus *Buthus* are found in north-east Africa and the Sahara. Baby scorpions climb on the mother's back after birth and remain there until they are big enough to fend for themselves. [p. 120]

35. Richard Burton and John Hanning Speke attempted to find the source of the Nile in 1857–9, but Burton fell ill and Speke reached the source on Lake Victoria alone. Burton queried his findings, and after Speke and Grant in 1868 confirmed Speke's original discovery (see Note to p. 61) Burton renewed the controversy. He and Speke were due to debate the question before the British Association on September 15, 1864, but on that same morning Speke was accidentally killed while partridge-shooting. [p. 131]

36. Flashman's cavalier attitude to dates is a vexation, but this passage gives some indication of his movements in the mid-1860s. The reference to Chancellorsville places him in the United States in May 1863, and we know he was at Gettysburg two months later, and in Washington when Lincoln was shot (April 1865). It is just possible, but highly unlikely, that his service (to both sides) in the U.S. Civil War was interrupted by a return to England in late 1863 or 1864. When he arrived in Mexico is uncertain, but his mention of Queretaro places him in the country between February and May of 1867, since that was the period in which Maximilian based himself at that royalist stronghold, where he was captured by the Juaristas. It seems plain, then, that between April 1865 and February 1867 Flashman returned to England at least once, and probably twice, since he speaks of "intervals" in the plural.

   One would be inclined to commiserate with Elspeth if it were not clear from the Papers that, while they were deeply attached to each other, she bore his frequent absences with equanimity. [p. 135]

37. It is not surprising that Flashman expected to be disbelieved, since in his day no one had survived such a plunge down a waterfall. Not until October, 2003, when an enterprising American deliberately allowed himself to be borne over the Canadian section of Niagara Falls, and lived, did anyone make such a descent. The Canadian Fall is estimated at 158 ft; the Tisisat Fall which Flashman survived is approximately 150 ft. Tisisat is one of the most glorious sights in Africa, the Blue Nile bordered by beautiful green banks and flowing smoothly past little jungly islands and rocks before it plunges over

the lip. "It is an extraordinary thing that they should be so little known," writes Alan Moorehead, "for they are, by some way, the grandest spectacle that either the Blue or the White Nile has to offer." The Victoria Falls are considerably higher, and are known as "the smoke that thunders". Tisisat, "the silver smoke", was discovered by two Portuguese missionaries, Paez and Lobo, in the early seventeenth century. (Moorehead, *The Blue Nile*.) [p. 144]

38. We cannot tell where this camp was, and must assume from Flashman's account that it was less than a day's ride from Tisisat, probably in the direction of Magdala. Queen Masteeat was evidently on the move at this time, and a week or so later we know from Holland and Hozier that she was at a place called Lugot, not given on the maps but said to be only five miles from Magdala. [p. 147]

39. Lucien Maxwell (1818–75), frontiersman and landowner, was one of a party of mountain men, led by Kit Carson, who rescued Flashman from Apaches in 1850 (see *Flashman and the Redskins*); he later became proprietor of one of the largest private estates ever known, the Maxwell Land Grant. The trick which he taught Flashman of proffering a pistol-butt in apparent surrender to an opponent and suddenly rolling it into the palm to cover him, was known to gunfighters as the road-agent's spin; the border shift consisted simply of tossing a pistol from one hand to the other. The Las Vegas referred to is not the Nevada gambling resort, but an earlier settlement in New Mexico. [p. 147]

40. Flashman was not exaggerating. His account of an Abyssinian orgy is almost identical to that of James Bruce a century earlier, the chief difference being that at the feast Bruce attended in Gondar, the steaks were cut from a living cow indoors in the presence of the guests, the beast's bellowing being the summons to table. Both sexes were present, and Bruce describes how, after the banquet, "Love lights all its fires, and everything is permitted with absolute freedom. There is no coyness, no delays, no need of . . . retirement to gratify their wishes . . . they sacrifice both to Bacchus and to Venus. The two men nearest the vacuum a pair have made on the bench by leaving their seats, hold their upper garment like a screen before the two . . . and if we may judge by sound, they seem to think it as great a shame to make love in silence as to eat. Replaced in their seats again, the company drink the happy couple's health, and their example is followed . . . as each couple is disposed. All this passes without remark or scandal, not a licentious word is uttered, nor the most distant joke upon the transaction." [p. 176]

41. Theodore used guerrilla raiding parties during his march from Debra Tabor, and after his arrival in Magdala, and prominent among them were his "Amazons". Dr Blanc writes: "He had formed the strongest and hardiest of the women of his camp into a plundering band; he was much pleased with their bravery, and one of them having killed a petty chief . . . he was so delighted that he gave her a title of rank and presented her with one of his own pistols." This description seems to fit Flashman's "Diana", with her silver shield and pistol. [p. 189]

42. The "falling out" had taken place when Theodore's troops plundered the

villagers of the Dalanta plateau, who had previously helped him as road-makers and porters on his march from Debra Tabor to Magdala. Furious at his betrayal, they gave their assistance to Napier's advance. It is estimated that Theodore destroyed no fewer than 47 villages around Magdala, massacring 7000 people and pressing men into his service. According to Blanc, he was concluding a final raid in person at the time of Napier's arrival at the Bechelo river (April 6–7); this must have been the raid, which was partly a foray for supplies as well as a scouting operation against the Gallas, which resulted in Flashman's rescue and capture. (See Note to p. 221, which confirms the date.) [p. 195]

43. If Theodore's conversational flights seem outlandish, they are nevertheless authentic. He obviously had a habit of repeating himself, and giving free rein to his paranoia, during his drinking bouts, and his curious comparison of himself to an expectant mother, his allusions to the sword of Damocles, and the Scriptures, and making a great bloodbath, are all to be found in Blanc and Rassam. His attitude towards Britain was a mixture of genuine admiration (he seems to have been truly excited at the prospect of seeing her army in action, even against himself) and deep resentment, for which he can hardly be blamed, at her apparent contempt for him; he seems to have suspected that he was despised for being primitive and black. [p. 207]

44. Hormuzd Rassam, an Iraqi Christian born in Mosul, was considered an odd choice as envoy to Theodore by his contemporaries, and by historians since. He had worked with the archaeologist Sir Henry Layard in what was then Mesopotamia, studied at Oxford, became a British citizen, and was assistant to Merewether at Aden when he was sent to Abyssinia to try to persuade Theodore to release the prisoners. The general opinion of him seems to have been that he was altogether too submissive in his dealings with the Emperor; "too soft, too compliant, too yielding," says Moorehead; Stanley was not favourably impressed, and there were many who thought a tough senior soldier would have been a better choice. Maybe; in Rassam's defence it has to be pointed out that while he may have been deferential, and caused Theodore to treat him more as a courtier than an envoy, it worked; a tougher and more outspoken ambassador might well have provoked the Emperor into much harsher measures against the prisoners.

Prideaux and Blanc had been in Rassam's mission and were taken prisoner with him; the other captives apart from Cameron were German and other European missionaries, with their wives and servants, and the German artisans already in Theodore's employ were prisoners in all but name. The total of Europeans held prisoner has been put at 60, of whom only Cameron and Rassam can be said to have had diplomatic status. [p. 215]

45. For once Flashman gives an exact date, and we can deduce his movements for the previous week at least. He must have arrived at Queen Masteeat's camp on April 6, been kidnapped the same night and rescued by Theodore's women, arrived in Theodore's camp at Islamgee on April 7 and spent the night in chains, and met Rassam and the other prisoners on April 8.

Before April 6 we can only estimate that he spent about a week with the fisher-folk who nursed him through his fever, so he probably went over the Tisisat Falls near the end of March. Working back, we place him at the Zaze monastery about March 24, which does not accord with his statement that it was then a week before Palm Sunday, which in that year fell on April 5. Plainly this was just a mistake on his part; for Flashman, an error of four days more or less is nothing, and we can only be grateful that he deigned to make a note of April 9 when it arrived. Since he was with Napier on February 25, his journey with Uliba-Wark must have taken about four weeks. [p. 221]

46. Of the many atrocities committed by Theodore, the massacre of prisoners at Islamgee is by far the best documented. The principal witness is his valet and gun-bearer, Wald Gabr, who in a statement taken by Speedy testified that he himself had shot three of the victims on the Emperor's orders. His account bears Flashman out entirely; indeed he is if anything more horrific, for he says that the first victim, the bound woman, was actually *cut in two* by Theodore, who then shot two more women before ordering the other prisoners to be thrown over the cliff alive, those who survived the fall being shot. Blanc and Rassam both describe the cold-blooded examination of the prisoners remaining after Theodore's first drunken rage had subsided, each person being asked for name, country, and crime, many of which were utterly trivial; the great majority were then flung over the cliff. Blanc and Rassam differ on the numbers killed; Wald Gabr says simply: "No one counted the victims, we were all afraid." (Blanc, Rassam, Wald Gabr's statement to Speedy, in Holland and Hozier.) [p. 231]

47. Reading between the lines of Blanc's memoir, one is inclined to agree with Flashman that Theodore's German artisans may have sabotaged his great mortar. In describing the Emperor's raid on the island of Metraha, where he burned most of the population alive, Blanc mentions that some fugitives took to their canoes, but when Theodore ordered his Europeans to fire on them with small cannon, "they complied, but to Theodore's great disappointment, failed to hit any of the fugitives." In his next paragraph Blanc writes of the artisans' failure to cast Sevastopol at their first attempt, and their eventual success only after Theodore himself had (with some technical skill, it must be said) redesigned the smelting process. Taking these two incidents together, it seems that the Germans were by no means eager to make a success of casting or operating Theodore's ordnance; the artillery of which they had the loading on Fala was singularly ineffective, and the bursting of Sevastopol was a huge blow to Theodore's morale; he had hoped it would have a shattering effect on his enemies. Estimates of its weight vary, one saying only five tons, others seventy. Rassam's book has a fine illustration showing the enormous bell-like contraption being dragged uphill by hordes of workers, and it is said to be still lying half-buried in the ground at Magdala today. [p. 240]

48. The battle of Arogee is well described in Holland and Hozier, and by Stanley and Henty. The latter wrote a separate account in greater detail for *Battles of the Nineteenth Century*, vol. 1, 1890, and there is an admirable essay on the battle, D. G. Chandler's "The Expedition to Abyssinia, 1867–8", which

is to be found in *Victorian Military Campaigns*, edited by Brian Bond. Flashman's version is sound, but he adds nothing to the one point of controversy, the exposure of the army's baggage to attack, which Theodore fortunately delayed. Henty was in no doubt that if Napier had been facing a European enemy, disaster must have followed; as it was, Napier was quick to retrieve the position. What seems to have happened is that Colonel Phayre, the Quartermaster-General, had reported the defile from which the baggage was emerging to be safe and guarded, when it was not; it has also been suggested that Napier himself had miscalculated the speed of his own advance, and that the baggage got ahead of him. Holland and Hozier tactfully glide over the incident. [p. 243]

49. The feeling in Napier's army is reflected in Henty, who pays tribute to the bravery of the Abyssinians, emphasising that they retreated, but did not fly, and that not a spear or a gun was thrown away. He writes of "a slaughter, hardly a fight, between disciplined well-armed men and scattered parties of savages scarcely armed at all." The firearms of the Abyssinians were certainly inferior to the Sniders and Enfields, but Henty is not quite fair to the Sikh Pioneers who enjoyed no advantage of weaponry against the enemy spear and swordsmen, were outnumbered, and still won a decisive victory with their bayonets, as Flashman, a veteran of the Sikh War, notes with satisfaction. For the rest, his account of the battle is well corroborated on the British side, and by those who were with Theodore. [p. 243]

50. When Blanc came face to face with Theodore, "I was quite prepared for the worst, and, at that moment, had no doubt in my mind that our last hour had come." Theodore reached for the musket of the nearest soldier, "looked at me for a second or two, dropped his hand, and in a low sad voice asked me how I was, and bade me good-bye." This accords with Flashman, but Blanc is modest about outfacing the Emperor, saying that it was mere accident that he was first to approach Theodore, who had no animosity towards him; "the result would have been quite different had his anger been roused by the sight of those he hated." [p. 254]

51. There is an interesting group photograph of the principal prisoners taken after their release. It includes Cameron wearing his cap and holding a crutch; Dr Blanc, burly and serious; Rassam quite brisk and dapper; Prideaux lounging on the ground, arms folded and looking both languid and jaundiced; and the two missionaries, the Rev. Stern whose alleged criticism of Theodore helped to start the crisis, and the Rev. Rosenthal with Mrs Rosenthal and their baby. Blanc and Prideaux are wearing their shackles. (Army Museums Ogilby Trust.) [p. 254]

52. This was a letter of apology for what Flashman calls Theodore's "lunatic message" of the previous day. Both are quoted in full in Holland and Hozier, and there can be no better evidence of Theodore's violent swings of mood. They are truly extraordinary productions, and Napier can have been in no doubt that he was dealing with a highly unstable and dangerous man. It may be significant of how Theodore saw himself that the first letter, an astonishing rant, is headed from "Kasa, whose trust is in Christ, thus speaks",

while the apology, much more moderate in tone and accompanied by the gift of cattle, comes from "the King of Kings Theodorus". Kasa was his name before he assumed the title of Emperor, the name of his humble beginnings. Flashman's account of Theodore's behaviour at this time, his relations with his own leading men, his diplomatic exchanges with Napier, and his inability to decide whether to fight or surrender, are confirmed in Rassam and Blanc, and by his valet Wald Gabr (see Note to p. 270). [p. 255]

53. What Flashman was seeing was the first breaching of Magdala's defences. The attack had proceeded as he describes, with the British advancing en masse across Islamgee and the artillery barrage covering the troops as they climbed up the narrow track leading to the Kobet Bar Gate. Some were wounded by the fire of Theodore's defenders, but the Sappers reached the gate, only to discover that the powder charges needed to blow it in had been forgotten. The Duke of Wellington's 33rd had come up, and a party of them ran along the wall to a point where Private Bergin and Drummer Magner forced a way through the thorn hedge and scaled the wall. Ensign Wynter was boosted on to the wall carrying the 33rd's Regimental Colour, and waved it to signal that the wall had been carried. This was the last time the Colour of the 33rd was carried into action. (See Chandler.)

There is general agreement with Flashman's view that if Magdala had been properly defended with artillery, the British attack – and indeed the war – might have ended very differently. Whether Theodore's gunners would have been capable of mounting such a defence is another matter; they had made poor work of it on Fala at the battle of Arogee, and one concludes that, for all his military talents, Theodore was not a master of the art of gunnery. [p. 266]

54. The best corroboration for Flashman's account of Theodore's suicide, and indeed for his description of the Emperor's movements and behaviour in the week they were together, is Theodore's valet and gun-bearer, Wald Gabr. In a statement made to Speedy, the valet recounted his service with Theodore over a period of five years; he was obviously deeply devoted to his master, but made no attempt to gloss over his atrocities, and indeed confessed his share in them (see Note to p. 255). He describes Theodore's attempted suicide, his release of the prisoners, his hopes of a peaceful settlement, his attempt to escape from Magdala, his galloping on the plain and challenging the British cavalry, and the bombardment and storming of the *amba*. Finally, he tells how Theodore released him from his allegiance and then shot himself, precisely as Flashman says, before the arrival of the first British troops. Stanley, in one of his more colourful passages, gives a romanticised account of the two Irishmen of the 33rd who were the first soldiers on the scene. Wald Gabr's statement is quoted in full by Holland and Hozier.

Stanley has a slightly purple description of the body, which he viewed soon after Theodore's death: "His eyes, now fading, gave evidence yet of . . . piercing power . . . the lower lip seemed adapted to express scorn." The features showed "great firmness and obstinacy mingled with ferocity", but

Stanley admits he may have been influenced by Theodore's shocking reputation. Compare the *Times'* description of "bloated sensual indulgence about the face, by no means heroic or kingly", but "the forehead intellectual and the mouth singularly determined and cruel." It was also noted that "a strange smile lingered about the lips". [p. 270]

55. It is not clear whether Speedy is referring to James Gordon Bennett, founder and publisher of the *New York Herald*, or his son and namesake who succeeded him in control of the paper in 1867, the year in which H. M. Stanley was sent to cover the Abyssinian War. Bennett junior later sent Stanley to the Ashanti War of 1873–4, and, most memorably, in search of Dr Livingstone. If either of the Bennetts was an Anglophobe, it evidently did not influence Stanley's reporting, which is not only meticulous in its detail but eminently fair. [p. 275]

56. This explains why Flashman is not mentioned in Napier's reports, or in Holland and Hozier, and the credit is given to Mir Akbar Ali, a subject of the Nizam of Hyderabad, who was attached to the expedition because, as a Muslim who had made the pilgrimage to Mecca, it was thought he would make an ideal envoy to Queen Masteeat and the Gallas. Plainly Flashman's advent on the scene caused Napier to change his mind and send him in Mir Akbar's place, as a far more experienced intelligence agent whose military seniority would also impress the Galla queen and her generals; it was, as Napier said, a task tailor-made for Flashman's supposed talents. Since he was to travel in native disguise, he was given the name of Khasim Tamwar, and in inventing a background and history for him, Napier simply used that of Mir Akbar Ali. Then, when Flashman was captured by Theodore, Mir Akbar was despatched at the last minute to complete the work of organising the Galla encirclement of Magdala.

In his report to Napier, Mir Akbar claims sole credit for persuading the Gallas, so there is a considerable discrepancy between his version and Flashman's, and readers must decide for themselves which to accept. There is no doubt that Mir Akbar did valuable work in the last days of the campaign, for which he was paid at the far from generous rate of £25 a month, roughly the same as the expedition's lower-grade interpreters. (See Holland and Hozier.) [p. 275]

57. Looting at Magdala was on a small scale compared to the orgies of plunder and destruction which Flashman witnessed in the Mutiny and in China. There was plenty of glitter among the stuff strewn on the ground, according to Stanley, but much of it was of little value, and he noted that some of the prisoners (he does not name any) were foremost among the looters. But some treasures there were: gold, silver, silk, furs and skins, carpets, weapons, and quantities of manuscript. Mr Holmes of the British Museum was "in his glory" when the precious things were auctioned off, his only rival in the bidding being Flashman's friend Fraser, who had the wealth of the 11th Hussars' mess. The auction realised £5000, the proceeds being divided among the non-commissioned troops who had crossed the Bechelo; each man received about four dollars. The elephants which carried it away, and

which had played such a vital part in the campaign, carrying guns and mortars, were 39 in number; five had died on the march. [p. 280]

58. This casual reference to the death of Colonel Robert Alexander Dunn, V.C., suggests that Flashman can only have heard of it at vague second-hand without knowing who was involved. Dunn was from his old regiment, the 11th Hussars, and had taken part in the Charge of the Light Brigade at Balaclava, where he won the only V.C. awarded in that action, for saving the lives of a troop sergeant-major and a trooper. He was C.O. of the notorious 33rd Regiment, the Duke of Wellington's, and died on January 25, 1868, in a shooting accident. [p. 280]

59. Flashman does not mention Abyssinian casualties in the brief battle for Magdala. More than 60 died in the fighting for the first gate, with about twice as many wounded. Even with the 700 dead and 1400 wounded at Arogee, the total of casualties in the campaign is unusually low for a nineteenth-century war. [p. 280]

60. Queen Tooroo-Wark ("pure gold") died of consumption a month later on the journey north, and was buried by Coptic priests, the King's Own providing a guard of honour and music. She was only 18. She had not been happy with Theodore, and is said to have conspired against him, but something like a reconciliation seems to have taken place in the last days of the war. In accordance with Theodore's wishes their son Alamayo went to England with Napier, and was educated at Rugby. He died when he was 19, and is buried at Windsor. [p. 281]

61. "Fat, fair, and forty" was how Stanley described Queen Masteeat, possibly misquoting Speedy, and from his account it is obvious that he liked her for much the same reasons as Flashman: she was handsome, gaudy, jolly, given to "hearty, boisterous guffaws", and had a gargantuan appetite. For the rest, we have only Flashman's description of her court and conduct; that in spite of her self-indulgence she was a shrewd and formidable personality we may judge from the fact that Napier had no hesitation in preferring her to Warkite and assigning Magdala to her. As to Flashman's description of her pet lions, it is interesting that King Theodore had a similar menagerie; a picture in *L'Annee Illustre*, 1868, reproduced in *Prelude to Magdala* shows him surrounded by them. [p. 283]

62. Britain's intervention had done little to change the pattern of civil war and near-anarchy prevailing before 1867, and this continued after the British withdrawal. Kussai, King of Tigre, whose neutrality had been of considerable help, was rewarded with gifts of ordnance, small arms, and supplies, which helped him establish himself in the north of the country; he aspired to overall monarchy, and for twenty years fought rivals and foreign invaders, defeating Gobayzy and repelling Egyptians, Italians and Dervishes. He was killed in battle against the Dervishes in 1889, and succeeded by the despised Menelek; the "fat boy" achieved supreme power and inflicted a crushing defeat on Italian invaders at Adowa in 1896. This was not forgotten, and Abyssinia was briefly conquered by Mussolini's forces before the Second World War, which effectively destroyed Italy's empire.

The brief exchanges among Napier's staff have echoes which continue to be heard today. Should Britain have stayed, and pacified the country, assuming the white man's burden? There are those who think so; one writer accuses Napier of dodging the issue, and holds that Britain's leaving Abyssinia did not become her as well as her manner of entering it. This seems rather hard, when it is remembered that Britain had no wish to invade Abyssinia, and did so only on gross provocation. Looking back, it is difficult to see why the pacification of a country to which Britain owed nothing should have been thought (to paraphrase Bismarck) worth the bones of a single British soldier or Indian sepoy. Of one thing we can be sure: if Britain had stayed, revisionist historians would certainly have condemned it as another act of selfish imperialism. [p. 287]

ABYSSINIA

N
W ← → E
S

0   20   40   60   80

Statute miles

Axum

Idaga
Takazy
Micara

Simien Mountains

Sokar •

• Gondar
• Azez

LASTA

Gorgora

Kerissa

Lake Tana

BEGEMDER

Adeena •

• Debra Tabor

Kourata

Zage

Baheerdar

Tisisat Falls

METCHA

Blue Nile

38°